MVFOL

DOES MY BODY OFFEND YOU?

MAYRA CUEVAS AND
MARIE MARQUARDT

Alfred A. Knopf

New York

THIS IS A BORZOI BOOK PUBLISHED BY ALFRED A. KNOPF

Visit us on the Web! GetUnderlined.com

Educators and librarians, for a variety of teaching tools, visit us at RHTeachersLibrarians.com

Library of Congress Cataloging-in-Publication Data is available upon request.
ISBN 978-0-593-42585-5 (trade) — ISBN 978-0-593-42586-2 (lib. bdg.) — ISBN 978-0-593-42587-9 (ebook) — ISBN 978-0-593-48768-6 (intl. pbk.)

The text of this book is set in 11.25-point Baskerville MT Pro.

Printed in the United States of America
April 2022
10 9 8 7 6 5 4 3 2 1
First Edition

Mayra:

Para Mami, con todo el amor.

Gracias por esta vida preciosa.

Marie:

For my daughters, Mary Elizabeth,

Pixley, and Annie, with all my love.

Thank you for making each day of this life precious.

Thank you for getting in trouble. Good trouble.

—John Lewis

What you're about to read is a fictionalized story inspired by a number of real events. Versions of this story have happened to many people throughout the country. Maybe something like this happened to your classmate. Your sister. Your best friend. Or even you.

26 Days After Hurricane María

Orange Park, Florida

PART ONE

My silences had not protected me. Your silence will not protect you. But for every real word spoken, for every attempt I had ever made to speak those truths for which I am still seeking, I had made contact with other women while we examined the words to fit a world in which we all believed, bridging our differences.

—Audre Lorde, "The Transformation of Silence into Language and Action"

MALENA

I'm not a superstitious person, but my abuela Milagros says catastrophes come in threes. I'm starting to believe she's onto something.

First came this beast of a hurricane called María, which caused our Island more devastation than we can mentally process. Mami and I are now stranded in the swampland that is Florida—our second stroke of bad luck. (The only upside is I get to hang out with my cousins every day, instead of just once or twice a year.)

And now, because irony is Lady Fortuna's weapon of choice, thanks to those very cousins, my mala suerte trifecta may be complete.

How do I avert this third disaster looming over me before it wrecks what's left of my life?

I reach for the medal of La Virgencita hanging around my neck, which Abuela says protects me from the mal de ojo. A cold chill runs down my spine as I step back from the full-length mirror attached to my bedroom door. I don't know which sight is more pitiful, my reflection or the mishmash of secondhand furnishings around me—mostly donations from a local church drive for María evacuees.

This is bad. The skin on my back has gone from brown to angry red. The color of a Caribbean lobster that's just been pulled from a pot of scalding water. It turns out bathing suits make for terrible landscaping apparel.

Yesterday, after my cousin Soraida back-talked Tía Lorna one too many times, *we*—because Tía Lorna sees me as an accessory to my cousin's shenanigans—were forced to clean and mow their backyard. All afternoon, I pruned bushes while the sun literally licked my back.

My cousin Carlos went shirtless too, but somehow he managed to get a great tan. It's so annoying that guys don't have to worry about their boobs hanging out. Or about how to fall asleep if you can't lie on your back.

I bet Carlos slept like a baby last night.

Not me. I barely slept at all. Lying on my stomach was pure torture, thanks to the two mountains that have recently risen from my chest. No one told me that *double D* really stands for "doble dolor"—double the pain.

Where did these things come from, anyway? Besides Soraida, I don't know many other fifteen-year-olds that have to shop for "big-bust bras." My abuela says the Rosario women were all blessed with the precious "gift" of "tetas grandes"—a clear sign of our female strength, she reassures me.

"Wear them proudly," she loves to say.

But this morning, they feel more like an enormous inconvenience than a gift.

Mami knocks on my bedroom door and peers in.

"You ready, nena? I can't be late. They're short-staffed at the ER," she says in Spanish.

It's a small comfort that at home we only speak in our mother tongue—Puerto Rican Spanish.

Mami opens the door a little wider. Her scrubs are covered in palm trees and flamingos standing on one leg. They're what my cousin Soraida mocks as "Florida chic." Mami says the kids at the pediatric ER where she works love them. The cute pink birds apparently help ease her patients. I wish they would do the same for me.

"There's no way I can wear this." I drop the bra dangling from my fingers onto the bed. "It stings." I turn so she can get a better view of my back.

Mami walks in and sits on my bed. She pulls a penlight from a pocket in her top and aims it at my skin, inspecting at close range.

"You have first-degree burns," she says in her no-nonsense medical voice. "Did the ointment we spread on last night not help?" She picks up the white tube on my nightstand and reads the label. "I'll bring you something stronger from the hospital."

Then, switching to her other no-nonsense voice, that of the Puerto Rican mother, she adds, "I told you to wear sunscreen."

"I couldn't find it." I jerk away, trying to hold back the wave of irritation that washes over me.

For four years, Tía Lorna has harped on and on about the virtues of life in Florida. "People really know how to live here," she likes to say. "The government gets things done. The people are not a bunch of vagos and sinvergüenzas. There's plenty of money for anyone willing to work hard." Tía could sell the American Dream to the gringoest of gringos.

I never thought my parents would fall for Tía's Disneyfied depictions, but that was *Before* María—before a Category 4 hurricane uprooted our lives and replanted us 1,200 miles away from home. *After* María, they bought the dream, hook, line, and sinker.

The weekend of Abuela Milagros's seventieth birthday, Mami and I flew to Jacksonville to celebrate, vaguely aware that another hurricane was barreling toward the Island. Papi was supposed to come with us, but he works as a local supervisor for the Federal Emergency Management Agency. It had only been ten days since Hurricane Irma skirted Puerto Rico, blasting the northeast coast with hundred-mile-per-hour winds. He had to stay behind to deal with Irma's wreckage.

"There's a prayer chain going around the world, mija," Abuela said as we ate too-sweet birthday cake, watching María's deadly approach from Tía Lorna's living room. "See how Irma went away? Same thing is going to happen with María. Nothing to worry about. The prayers will keep the Islita safe."

They didn't.

The prayers decidedly Did. Not. Work.

God just flat-out ignored us.

María wrecked the Island beyond recognition. And with it, she destroyed my life. A life filled with friends I'd known since birth, a school where fitting in was easy and my teachers told me I was a "natural leader," and a home with two loving parents. A life that I didn't fully appreciate until it was gone.

We arrived in Jacksonville with one carry-on suitcase each. Mine was packed with a couple of cute dresses, my favorite strappy sandals, and a bathing suit, basically everything I needed for a birthday weekend.

Tía Lorna arranged a collection for us at her church, and now, as a result, we have two single beds, a couch, a coffee table, pots and pans, tableware, and a brand-new fondue set. We're still considering what to melt first: cheese or chocolate. Tough decision.

Through the church's connections, Mami landed a job as a

physician assistant at a local hospital's pediatric emergency room. Tía was quick to point out that she's making more money here in Florida for the same work that she was doing back home. "Money isn't everything," I tried to argue. But given our current state, everyone ignored me.

I enrolled in the same high school as my cousins. And Papi is still in Puerto Rico. God only knows when we'll all be together again. No use praying for any miracles, I guess.

"I can't go to school like this," I protest, waving my hands in front of my bare chest in an exaggerated gesture.

"They're just breasts, Malena. Everyone has them." Mami rummages through the few items hanging in my closet. There's not much to pick from. In hindsight, I did an awful packing job, even for a five-day trip.

"All of my stuff is dirty," I remind her. Which is how I ended up wearing my one-piece bathing suit with the scooped back to rake grass clippings. Our new apartment doesn't have a washer-and-dryer hookup—because, as we learned, this costs extra—so I'll have to wait until next Saturday, our allotted laundry day at Tía Lorna's. Our dirty laundry has literally become a source of family drama. The solution: alternating weekends so that we don't get in the way of Carlitos's pristine baseball uniforms.

"You can wear one of my shirts," Mami says, heading to her room. She returns with a flowery tunic that's far too big for me.

"Can't I just stay here?" I plead. "We still have a bunch of the church donations to unpack. I'm pretty sure I saw an ice cream maker somewhere." I'm grateful for the kindness of all those strangers, but it's funny, the things people think you will need to rebuild your life. "I can sort everything while you're at work. Maybe make some homemade ice cream?"

"I don't want you missing any more school." She takes the

tunic off the hanger and tugs on a loose thread. "You can't afford to fall behind."

"I'm doing fine," I mumble.

"Lorna thinks that if you keep up your GPA and get more involved—"

I cut her off. "Tía Lorna has an opinion about everything."

"I think she's right about this. Between your grades and extra-curriculars, you may be eligible for a full scholarship when you graduate. The next three years will go by fast, and the colleges here are expensive. It's not like Puerto Rico."

What is she talking about?

I look away, too overwhelmed by the same argument we've had every other day since we got the apartment. To me, our re-location is temporary. A Band-Aid to get us through the rebuild-ing efforts back home. Once our condo in San Juan is fixed and power and running water are restored, we'll go back to the same contented existence we had before. An existence that included lazy afternoons on the beach at Ocean Park, those tropical fruit paletas you can only get in Old San Juan, and Sunday-night fam-ily dinners at El Mesón de Pepe. If I close my eyes, I can almost taste the savory sauce in the mofongo de mariscos.

They say that the coquí frogs native to Puerto Rico can't sur-vive outside the Island. I'm starting to understand why. Every pore of my body longs for home.

That's what I'm begging La Virgencita for every night.

My old life, just as it used to be.

Sure, I've dismissed any concept of an all-powerful, wish-granting God. But, strangely, I'm becoming the same sort of candle-lighting, rosary-praying, kneeling Catholic as my abuela and her mantilla-wearing friends. Talking to La Virgencita is dif-ferent. For some reason, I still believe she cares.

"Raise your arms," Mami says.

"It hurts," I complain.

She gently slips the tunic over my head so that it doesn't come into contact with my raw skin. "See? That's not so bad. You can't see anything."

I turn left and right in front of the mirror, assessing my chest. The last thing I want is to become That Puerto Rican Who Doesn't Wear a Bra. That would be so much worse than the person they already see: That Puerto Rican Who Lost Everything to María.

I'll take Poor María Malena over Braless Boricua.

———

Miraculously, I manage to move through the morning unnoticed. I've been keeping my math and chemistry books continuously pressed against my chest as I make my way between classrooms.

By fifth period, I'm relieved to be halfway done with the day. I take my seat in Ms. Baptiste's class, waiting for my cousin Soraida to walk in. When she does, she drops a granola bar and a banana onto my desk.

"I didn't see you at lunch. Were you hiding your tetas in the library?" she asks with a smirk.

Find a Puerto Rican slang dictionary and look up the word *candela*, and next to it you'll find a picture of Soraida. She's loud-mouthed, brash, and unapologetic, and she completely lacks a filter. Her long mane of curly brown hair and big expressive brown eyes only add to the effect. On most days she's a royal pain in the ass, but I love her anyway.

"I like hanging out in the library," I tell her. "I miss my books."

"You're such a nerd, prima."

It's true. I love learning new things, especially in this class.

Originally, I signed up for video production because Soraida was in it, but I'm completely geeking out on cameras, composition, lighting, and storytelling.

And I adore the teacher, Ms. Baptiste. She's always dressed in bold colors, with flashy gold earrings and a wrist full of bracelets. It's oddly reassuring to be in her presence. Not only is she from Trinidad and Tobago, which practically makes us Caribbean neighbors, but she also shows some cool documentaries. Last week, we watched a short film titled *He Named Me Malala,* about a Pakistani teen who was shot in the face for speaking out to defend girls' right to education. She was even awarded the Nobel Peace Prize—at seventeen!

Watching that documentary, I was in awe. In the film, Malala said remaining silent is like giving up, and we have to raise our voices to speak the truth. To quote a reggaeton song, that girl's got babilla.

Ms. Baptiste calls it "owning your narrative."

How can a girl who's been through such a horrible experience turn her life into a message so powerful that it's changing the world? I have no idea.

As for me, I'm just trying to stay quiet, keep my head down, and survive. At Sagrado Corazón, I was a *doer.* Here, I'm a spectator. Mostly binge-watching the documentaries Ms. Baptiste tells us about in class. Which makes me both a coward and a total nerd. I guess Soraida is right.

"Have you talked to your dad?" Soraida asks, turning to face my desk.

"For, like, a second last night. He's running operations in the mountains."

"Wait, how long is he staying there?" she asks, her eyes wide.

I shrug, trying to avoid the pity in her eyes. "As long as he's needed."

"How did he call you from way up there?" she asks.

"He borrowed a satellite phone from someone."

"Doña Lucrecia, that vieja down the street, keeps going on and on about how her son calls her every day using a satellite phone." Soraida pauses, clears her throat, and adjusts her voice so it's high-pitched and nasal, like Doña Lucrecia's. "Yo no entiendo. Why doesn't everyone have one of those phones?" She curls her lips and pinches her nose as if something smells rotten around us. Her Doña Lucrecia impressions always make me snicker.

"She's such a come mierda, that vieja," she adds, her face falling back to normal. "Her son's house didn't have any damage. Of course it didn't! The guy lives in freaking Montehiedra. Those mansions up on that hill are like fortresses."

I let her ramble until she runs out of steam and possibly even forgets what we are talking about. I don't want to think about Papi right now with a classroom full of strangers around me. Missing him hurts too much.

Ms. Baptiste calls for our attention, and I do my best to focus on class. It's proven to be a good distraction from my island troubles. A few times a week she guides us through a meditation session. She says it can help us deal with stress and clear our minds. At first I thought it was a little woo-woo, sitting there in silence for ten minutes, watching our thoughts. But over time it's become a release. For those ten minutes, the heaviness in my chest lifts, evaporating like fog at sunrise over the mountains of Cayey.

We've all just closed our eyes, and Ms. Baptiste is telling us to center our breath, when someone knocks on the door. Ms. Baptiste answers and all eyes fly open to see who it is.

"Miss Rosario," Ms. Baptiste says after the woman at the door has left. Soraida and I exchange a glance.

Technically, my name is Malena Malavé Rosario, Malavé being my father's last name and Rosario my mother's. Back home, everyone uses both names—I mean, Mami lent me her body for nine months; carrying her name is the least I can do.

But when Mami registered me at Orange Grove, the admissions lady wrongly assumed that Malavé was my middle name, and I ended up as Malena Rosario on all their forms. They still haven't fixed it.

"Malena Rosario," Ms. Baptiste says, remembering there are two Rosarios in her classroom. The school, however, didn't mess up Soraida's name. She shows up as Soraida María Ramírez Rosario on all the forms, to the confusion of every non-Latinx teacher.

"Dr. Hardaway, the assistant principal, needs to speak with you," she says, handing me a big orange plastic disk that looks like a flattened Frisbee.

I can't figure out why she's handing me this Frisbee until I read the words HALL PASS written in bold black letters.

"Am I in trouble?"

Ms. Baptiste exhales, her shoulders drooping slightly. She leads me into the hallway and gives my chest an apologetic glance. Suddenly my whole body feels exposed—like I'm standing completely naked. I actually shiver. I should've brought one of my books to cover myself.

"You're excused from my class, Malena. Don't worry about today's assignment. Okay?" Her voice is kind, but I catch a tinge of concern in her eyes.

"Her office is at the end of the hall." Ms. Baptiste points down the long narrow corridor, tainted sickness green by the ceiling's fluorescent lights.

I walk toward Dr. Hardaway's office, wishing I were meeting with Sister María de Lourdes instead. When my old principal invited me to her office, it was usually to congratulate me on some killer school event I'd organized or to share a big idea for our next student-council meeting. I have a sinking feeling this is not that kind of meeting.

When I arrive at Dr. Hardaway's office, the school secretary seems to know exactly who I am, even though I don't remember meeting her. I can't help thinking it has something to do with my María evacuee status. *Poor María Malena.*

I take a seat and wait, temporarily absorbed by a goldfish swimming in circles inside a too-small glass bowl. I'm tempted to set it free. Fish belong in the sea.

"Miss Rosario, Dr. Hardaway will see you now," she says.

This is not the only time I've been in Dr. Hardaway's office. My first visit was a few days after María, when it became clear there was no home for us to go back to.

We didn't have any transcripts from my old school, so Mami and I had to meet with the school counselor to sort out my classes. The counselor, Mr. Cruz, is a Chicano hippie who insisted we "hablar en español," even though we assured him we were both fully bilingual. He thought it would be a good idea to place me in English as a Second Language until I had enough time to "adapt."

"You can take off some of the pressure," he said in his peculiarly slow-paced, airy voice. The whole time, his hands were doing this slow-dance sway in front of him. "Sometimes we are the river, sometimes we are the waterfall, and sometimes we are the brook."

I stared at him, both pissed and confused. What the heck did flowing water have to do with me enrolling in English Lit?

Mami earnestly explained that I had always attended a private bilingual school and that it was unacceptable to place me in an ESL class. Once the word *unacceptable* comes out of Mami's mouth, there's no turning back. She eventually gets her way. Every. Single. Time.

So we asked for a meeting with the school principal, Mr. Davis, and were promptly told that Mr. Davis didn't handle student placement. We had to meet with one—there are four total!—of the assistant principals, Dr. Hardaway, for any questions about my schedule. Technically, Dr. Hardaway is the "disciplinary AP," but she also moonlights as the testing and placement coordinator. It seems like every AP has three or four jobs. So what exactly does Mr. Davis do? Who knows. I've barely even laid eyes on the man. All I know is that, apparently, it takes multiple people at this school to do the job of one nun at Sagrado Corazón.

Mami and I met with Dr. Hardaway and argued my case. As a result, she asked the English teacher to test my language skills. I've never been prouder to nail an exam in my life.

"Miss Rosario, please have a seat," Dr. Hardaway says, a polite smile on her lips.

Today, her flaming red hair is loose around her shoulders, calling all attention to her most striking feature. I try not to stare.

My eyes quickly dart about the room, as if I'm seeing it for the first time.

I take in the floor-to-ceiling shelves packed with books and magazines. A vase overflows with eucalyptus branches, the source of a minty-pine odor. It strikes me how orderly and clean everything is. Not a pencil out of place.

I settle into one of the leather chairs in front of her desk, mindful to keep my skin away from the backrest. Every time my back comes into contact with a hard surface, a sting of pain spreads like tiny electric pinpricks.

Dr. Hardaway studies the open folder in front of her. My name is printed on the tab. One hand absentmindedly dips a tea bag in and out of a mug.

"Is it Rosario or Malavé?" she asks, eyes on the documents.

"Malavé Rosario."

"Oh yes. I remember now. We need to get that fixed." She scribbles something on a yellow sticky note and adds it to my file. Then she turns her full attention back on me.

"I'm sorry to interrupt Ms. Baptiste's class, but it has come to my attention that you came to school without a bra. Is that correct?"

Following this statement-question, two things immediately happen: (1) I'm left speechless. (2) I forget all my English.

¿Que dijo? ¿Brasier? ¿Quiere saber si tengo puesto un brasier?

My brain is having a conversation with itself in Spanish and desperately trying to sort out why this middle-aged white lady wants to know if I'm wearing a bra.

I nod, unable to utter even a one-syllable response.

Dr. Hardaway sighs. Then she gives me the same pitiful smile I got from all my teachers when they found out I was a María evacuee.

Pobrecita María Malena.

"Miss Rosario," she begins, but I interrupt her.

"Malavé Rosario," I remind her again, my voice strained.

"Miss Malavé," she says with an apologetic nod, still not getting it right. "I want you to feel comfortable here." She rests both arms on her desk and leans forward. "Consider this office a safe space."

Safe? I'm feeling about as safe as I did watching a thick mass of storm clouds inhale my home. It didn't matter that my body wasn't on the Island; the winds and the rain swallowed my heart whole—like Dorothy and the tornado in *The Wizard of Oz*.

My arms instinctively cross over my chest, pressing against my breasts as if they need to be protected from this woman.

"I was told a teacher was uncomfortable with your attire," she says.

I feel my face go as bright red as the skin on my back. A teacher? A blurry shuffle of faces plays across my mind. I didn't see anyone look uncomfortable. Did I not notice? I think I would've noticed.

I sink deeper into my chair. The leather groans under my thighs, sounding as strained as I feel.

"Ms.—" she starts to say, then seems to change her mind. "It doesn't matter who it was." She sits up, squaring her shoulders. Her eyes scan a note attached to the folder with a paper clip. "One of your teachers expressed concern this might be disruptive, and it's our job to protect you from any unwanted attention." She pauses, and I can see that she's expecting me to say something. But I can't come up with a coherent response. My brain is a jumble of panicked thoughts—in two languages!

Ms.? A female teacher sent me here? Language aside, I'm having an impossible time understanding why another woman would think my *tetas* are a problem. Doesn't she also have a pair?

Maybe hers aren't as big—and inconvenient—as mine.

"Now, let's see here. . . ." She turns back to the papers in the file. "We want to set you up for success. I know you just moved here. And back home at the . . ." She reads from a registration form she's holding between her fingers. "At the Sah-grah-doe Coh-rah-zion?"

"Sagrado Corazón," I say meekly, reaching for the medal of La Virgencita around my neck. My current state of incredulity has reduced my voice to a murmur.

"Right." She sets the form back in place and closes the folder. "Their dress code may have been a little more relaxed, is my guess."

I almost laugh out loud. Sister María de Lourdes would have smacked this woman's hand with a wooden ruler. The dress code at Orange Grove is a joke compared to the Catholic school run by nuns I attended in San Juan. White cotton shirts with our school's insignia embroidered on the sleeve were mandatory, along with blue tartan jumpers hemmed just under the knee. Our shoes had to be black oxfords, worn with white tube socks that covered our calves. I never thought for one moment that I would miss those stifling uniforms.

But here I am.

"I burned my back," I explain, painfully aware of how the anxiety of this conversation is making my accent more pronounced. "If I put on a bra, my skin will come off. My mom is a physician assistant, and she said I have first-degree burns." I try hard to keep my voice even. I refuse to be the Loud Latina making a scene at the assistant principal's office.

"That may very well be the case, but I can't have you going back out there until this is resolved," she says, gesturing to my chest. "Your nipples are clearly visible through that shirt."

By now all the blood has rushed to my face and neck. I can feel the throbbing of my veins in my temples. My shoulders fold inward, trying to create a hollow space between my chest and the shirt, where I can hide my too-big breasts. Anything to make this woman stop gawking at me like my body somehow offends her.

"I think I have an idea," she says, picking up the receiver on her desk phone. She pushes a few buttons and waits for someone to pick up on the other end. "Nurse Hopkins? I'm sending Miss Malena Malavé"—she glances in my direction and smiles—"Rosario your way. Can you please give her a couple of pantyliners to cover her nipples? She didn't wear a bra to school today."

At this exact moment, I want the tile floor to crack open and devour me, body and soul. *Please, if there's a higher power listening, let it be so.*

"Uh-huh," she says, nodding into the receiver at something I can't hear. "She will need to hold them in place with a little tape. Otherwise they'll fall off. Make sure you can't see anything. She's on her way now. . . ." She scribbles something on a notepad and then hangs up.

My head is spinning in a vortex of shame and anger. Why couldn't Mami just let me stay home? Why are my freaking breasts so big? And why is this woman asking me to put pantyliners—of all things!—over my nipples? How much more humiliating can this situation possibly get?

"Excellent," she exclaims, in a tone that makes me cringe. "That'll take care of it." She's smiling as if this idea of hers is something to be proud of. Then she hands me another orange Frisbee—a hall pass to the nurse's office. "I've used that trick myself a few times. I saw it on a beauty blog once and it's come in handy." She chuckles to herself and offers me some candy from a jar on her desk. I take a Jolly Rancher, afraid to refuse her.

She takes a Hershey's Kiss for herself. "I have a sweet tooth," she says almost apologetically. "But all in moderation." She breaks apart the foil wrapper and pops the chocolate into her mouth. "It's like my yoga teacher always says, 'We must find balance on and off the mat.'"

I can't get out of that office fast enough.

On my way to the nurse's office, I call Mami from my cell phone.

"Malena? Is everything okay?" She sounds winded, and I can hear sirens in the background.

"I just got called into Dr. Hardaway's office for not wearing a bra," I say, fighting back the tears welling in my eyes. "They want me to tape on pantyliners!"

"Room 6A," Mami calls out to someone speaking loudly nearby. Maybe a doctor or nurse? "I have to go, Malena. I have a toddler coming in from a car wreck. No car seat. Can you believe it? Just do whatever they tell you. We'll talk later. Te amo, nena."

I'm about to say that I love her too, but the call drops before I have the chance. I know she's busy saving lives, but it hurts that she's not here with me. I may not be getting wheeled into the ER, but I need her too.

I fold my arms over my chest and brave the long walk to the nurse's office, praying to La Virgencita that no one will see me.

I can't believe this is who I've become—a girl called out of class to be punished. A girl who wants to be invisible.

CHAPTER TWO

RUBY

Because it's Monday and Mondays inevitably suck, I'm sitting in Ms. Markowitz's history class, stressing. I've just started my period, and I'm ninety percent positive I don't have a tampon. I lean down to slowly unzip my backpack, trying not to make too much noise, since she's showing a film. I rifle around for a while, checking all the pockets. Nothing but pencil stubs, old gum wrappers, and a broken THIS IS WHAT A FEMINIST LOOKS LIKE button that I used to wear all the time, way back when I lived in Seattle. *Who knew I still had that thing?*

I pick up the button to inspect it and feel a sharp pinprick against my thumb. *Ouch.* A small drop of blood is forming.

I should have known that looking back into my past would hurt. Life was easier in Seattle. Was it better? I'm not sure. But definitely simpler.

I lean forward to whisper to Nessa. "Hey, do you have a tampon?"

She shakes her head. "Uh-uh. Jo and I switched to Goddess Cups."

Why does it come as no surprise to me that Jo and Nessa use Goddess Cups?

Nessa and Jo are basically attached at the hip. They've been dating *forever,* and they are so deeply connected that my best friend, Topher, and I joke that they're starting to look alike. If we didn't love them both so much, we'd probably massively resent their unattainably perfect romance.

"Ick." I fake shudder. "Tried the Goddess Cup once. Never again."

Nessa shrugs. "Your body, your choice." She turns to look at me. "But you know you're slowly poisoning yourself, right?"

Ms. Markowitz stands up. "Ruby? Nessa? Is there an issue?"

"Sort of?" I reply, unsure whether this constitutes an "issue." Clearly, though, it's nearing emergency status. "I need to go to the nurse."

"Are you sick, Ruby?" Ms. Markowitz asks.

"No need to worry," I assure her. "I just started my period and I don't have a tampon."

Predictably, half the class snickers and a couple of girls slump down in their seats.

"You know," Topher calls out from the back of the room, "if the administration would provide free tampons in bathrooms, Ruby wouldn't need to interrupt class."

This is why I love you, Topher.

Topher Pérez is a force of nature. I'll never forget how he swooped in to save me at approximately 4:13 p.m. on the afternoon of my tenth day at Orange Grove High.

"If I may, Ms. Markowitz," Topher continues, "toilet paper is seen as an essential, right? The administration doesn't expect us all to carry around our own rolls."

"That's enough, Topher," Ms. Markowitz announces, in a voice that reveals both her frustration with Topher's frequent proclamations and her guarded respect for his insights. "Come get a hall pass, Ruby."

Topher always vows it was *me* who saved *him*. But we both know the truth.

When Topher and I met last fall, I was the awkward new girl, starting my junior year as far across the country from home as geographically possible, and a universe away from my old high school.

My nana needed heart surgery, and Mom and Dad wanted to care for her during her long recovery. So, at the end of my sophomore year, they both took early retirement and we packed up and left everything behind—our friends, our home, our schools and neighborhood, my favorite teahouse with the mismatched sofas and weird open-mic nights. I spent an entire summer at my nana's side, obsessing alternately over her recovery and my pending "fresh start" at Orange Grove High School.

Nana recovered beautifully, but my fresh start was a disaster.

The first ten days at Orange Grove were utterly brutal. Everyone knew everyone, and I knew no one. My first attempt at making friends was a disaster. And no one else appeared to have issues navigating the labyrinth of hallways, the enormous rows of lockers, the military-like precision of the daily schedule.

I didn't exactly *need* a "fresh start." My life in Seattle was good, but everything about it had been routine, expected. I'm the baby in the family. My big sister, Olive, is seven years older than me. She forged the path: what schools we would go to, what activities we'd do, even our fashion sense. I adored Olive. But even more, I wanted to be like her. When Olive cut her bangs, I cut my bangs. When Olive found a new indie band to love, it immediately became my favorite. And any issues that Olive cared about—from saving baby seals to combating gentrification in Seattle's Central District—those issues became my burning passions too.

By the middle of tenth grade, though, Olive had finished college and moved all the way across the country, and the whole thing was starting to wear on me—still living in the enormous shadow of my perfect older sister. With Olive in Atlanta and rarely in touch, I began to wonder: Did I even like the way I looked with bangs? Was indie music too . . . depressing? How much did I really care about baby seals? (I mean, I care about them in the conservation sense, but are they *the* cause that drags me out of bed on Saturday morning for a protest?)

So, on that rainy spring afternoon, when my parents both came home from work early, sat me down at the kitchen bar, and announced the move to Florida, all three of us found ourselves shocked by my reaction.

"Sounds like fun," I said, my voice laced with enthusiasm. Far from being stressed or angry, I was genuinely excited.

Sure, I would miss the teahouse, my favorite bookshops, and a handful of the neighborhood kids I'd grown up with. But those friendships had long before drifted, when we'd all graduated from our liberal, high-achieving neighborhood school and had to decide what to do next. They'd moved on together, to an enormous regional middle school. I'd followed my sister to a tiny hippie private school on the other side of town, where the middle and high schools combined were smaller than my fifth-grade class.

I didn't mind how small it was, and the transition felt easy. But listening to my parents explain the plan, I realized that I was practically desperate for something unexpected, something new. I couldn't wait to find out who I would be without Olive ahead of me, deciding everything for both of us.

Who was I, in those first days at Orange Grove? Those heady days of independence that I had so eagerly anticipated? I was a pathetic loner, anonymous, confused by the enormous building and all its rules and regulations, and homesick for Seattle.

To my shock and horror, I even found myself wishing I'd walk into a classroom and have the teacher greet me with some version of "Hello, Ruby! So good to have a McAlister girl in my class. What's that fabulous sister of yours up to these days?"

I'd thought I wanted to be anonymous, to build a life at Orange Grove on my own terms. But it felt impossible to get my bearings. My old school encouraged us to roam freely across campus, eschewed desks as too constraining, loved for students to lounge on sofas or perch on beanbags as we discussed politics and current events. People here were into other stuff—stuff I honestly didn't know much about. Like sports and dances, mascots and school pride.

So, on my tenth day at Orange Grove, after an epic morning pep talk from my dad, I forced myself to wander awkwardly through the annual clubs-and-activities fair (another thing my old school didn't have) on a desperate search for kindred spirits. Pep talks, I should note, are my dad's superpower.

I shuffled through rows and rows of tables, clusters of students who already seemed deeply connected: thespians and debaters, Christians and robotics pros. I didn't have any hobbies, I wasn't particularly religious, and I definitely couldn't act or build robots. I just wanted to be a part of something—anything!

I saw Marvin Wells, a supersmart guy from my English class, standing next to a Black Student Union poster. Since I'm white, I knew BSU wouldn't be the club for me. Still, I sensed that Marvin and I could be friends, so I started to head toward his table. By the time I got there, he was surrounded by a bunch of people

I didn't know. I totally lost my nerve and passed right by them, staring at my feet. So I walked on, searching, hoping, practically praying for a feminist club, something like the Girl Up chapter that Olive had started at my old high school—the first in Washington State. Did they even have Girl Up in Florida?

I was about to abandon my club search when I saw Topher, perched alone on top of a table in wingtips and a kick-ass vintage vest, his loose curls bobbing along to a beat that only he heard. Unlike me, Topher seemed incredibly cool, utterly unflappable, and perfectly comfortable being on his own.

"Well, hello there," he said. "You look like a woman who knows a thing or two about current events."

He gestured toward a clipboard and I awkwardly scrawled my name and email address below only two others: Jo Richards and Nessa Van Horne. Then I flashed a goofy grin and hurried out of the gym, not saying a word.

Afterward, when I pulled out of the parking lot, I noticed Topher sitting under an awning at the public bus stop, the afternoon sun beating down on him. An hour later, after I finished picking up some groceries and prescriptions for Nana, he was still there, sweating in the Florida heat while still managing to appear entirely cool and collected.

I gathered all the courage I could muster, pulled up to the bus stop, and rolled down my window. As the air-conditioning blasted toward him, I called out. "Hey, it's Ruby . . . from the club fair?" I said hesitantly. "Need a ride?"

"An angel cometh down from the heavens!" he sang, dramatically gesturing with his arms and chin lifted to the sky. "My most fervent prayers to the universe have been answered!"

I laughed out loud and he threw open the passenger door to climb in.

"Haul ass," he said, tapping on the digital clock on my dash. "We've got seventeen minutes to get to the corner of Park and Stiles. I'm gonna get fired if I'm late to work *again*."

We sped across town to the Raceway gas station, where I now know he spends almost every weekday evening behind the counter, popping Skittles and casually working his way through the complicated equations of AP Calculus. On that crosstown sprint, talking and laughing as if we had known each other for years, we began a friendship that I'm certain will last for at least one lifetime, if not several.

I turn toward the back row and give him a grateful nod as I get up to approach Ms. Markowitz's desk. I can't resist whispering, "Think about it, Ms. Markowitz. If all men needed tampons, I can guarantee every public-school restroom in the country would keep them stocked."

That makes her smile. "You've got a point there, Ruby," she whispers back. "Maybe you and Topher should take it up with the administration."

"Maybe we will," I say.

I grasp the orange hall pass disk and walk away, suddenly feeling a spark, an energy—that little thrill of purpose and direction. Maybe it's finally my time to do something new and exciting, something that matters.

———

Heading toward the nurse's office, I decide I'll stop by Mr. Cruz's office later, to talk about the tampon thing.

I adore Mr. Cruz. He's the sponsor of our Current Events Club—a Southwestern hippie who was somehow transplanted to North Florida. As a fellow Florida transplant, I feel a deep connection with him. Plus, he makes us great tea. I mean, the man is seriously into tea. But he's also the guidance counselor, and he does tend to lean a bit too far in on the words of wisdom.

Every Thursday afternoon, at the end of our club meetings, Mr. Cruz makes us repeat together this little nugget of truth from John F. Kennedy: "Efforts and courage are not enough without purpose and direction."

The man's got a point. Our little crew could use some purpose and direction. At least he doesn't force us to meditate like Ms. Baptiste did. She's pretty cool too. Her film studies class was my favorite elective of all time, despite the forced meditation sessions. Ten minutes alone with my addled brain is about nine minutes and fifty-five seconds longer than I can handle.

Nurse Hopkins, though. She is decidedly not cool. She and I don't get along particularly well—not since she accused Topher of truancy last spring, when he missed a few days of school because his grandma was sick and his mom had to work. She made him procure a note from his grandma's doctor *and* his mom's boss. The whole thing was so humiliating for him. And it was excruciating to watch—knowing there wasn't a damn thing I could do to help.

After that whole debacle, I took to calling her Nurse Ratched—not to her face, of course. I'm not quite so brazenly disrespectful.

When I get to her office, the nurse has the DO NOT DISTURB sign hanging on the doorknob, and she's with a girl I've never seen before, talking intently. I lean against the wall and watch through the window, trying to get a sense of how long I'll need to wait. The situation is getting dire.

The girl's hair is pulled into a high ponytail and she's wearing a flowery tunic that looks like something from my grandmother's closet. Sure, Nana has great taste, but still. The tunic seems off, somehow. It doesn't fit with her cute jeans and strappy sandals.

Then the strangest series of events begins to unfold. Doris, the school secretary, nudges past me, hissing, "You'll need to wait here, young lady," as she enters the nurse's office and closes the door in my face. I watch through the glass pane as the girl stands perfectly still in the center of the room, eyes downcast and shoulders slumped, while Doris and Nurse Ratched pace around her. And, to make things especially super weird, they're both looking intently at the girl's boobs.

Honest to God. The nurse is staring right at this poor girl's tits, her hand gently cupping the edge of her chin, as if she's deep in concentration. Doris stands beside her, reading glasses pushed down on her nose, her eyes squinting and her stout neck thrust slightly forward. They exchange words I can't hear, while the girl seems frozen in place. The only difference between this girl and a living statue is the slight quiver of her bottom lip and the rush of heat turning her skin red, from her neck all the way to her cheeks.

Some seriously baffling shit is going on in there. Nurse Ratched begins making strange gestures around her own boobs, pressing them in with her hands while simultaneously pushing them up slightly. Doris nods and smiles in agreement, as if whatever the nurse is saying constitutes some sort of brilliant revelation.

What is happening?

The girl seems significantly less impressed. She slumps even deeper and crosses her arms over her boobs, in the classic *please stop staring at my chest* posture—the one every girl has learned to perfect by the age of fourteen. Even me, and I'm totally flat-chested.

Nurse Ratched drops into her office chair and opens the middle drawer. Then she pulls out a roll of surgical tape, like the kind

Nana uses to cover stitches with gauze whenever she's had another big mole removed (occupational hazard of being a lifelong volunteer on the sea-turtle patrol).

She thrusts the tape toward the girl, who takes it in one hand and inspects it, her face twisting into a grimace. The girl briefly turns in my direction and I catch a glimpse of her face. She's young, with a pretty, heart-shaped face, big shy eyes, and perfect eyebrows that haven't yet submitted to wax or tweezers. I don't think she's wearing any makeup at all, but she's blushing over an enviably clear complexion. Maybe she's a freshman. Maybe that's why I've never seen her before.

Doris turns to approach the door, and I jump back and press my body against the wall, hoping she won't notice that I've been peering through the glass. She throws the door open and announces, "The nurse will see you now," as she totters past me on kitten heels.

"Can I help you with something, Ruby?" Nurse Ratched asks in a tone that makes it clear she has no interest in helping anyone with anything.

"Just need tampons," I say, heading toward the back corner, where she stashes them in a wicker basket. I've been through this drill before.

The girl is already there, digging through the boldly marked MENSTRUAL PRODUCTS basket. I stand back and watch as she pulls out two thin pantyliners wrapped in pink plastic.

She glances at me and our eyes meet. Her expression is stunned—bewilderment mixed with sheer horror. It's as if she's just been told her plane's about to go down. My own gaze narrows and my eyebrows arch into what can only be described as a classic *What the fuck?* expression. I know she gets it. She shakes her head and looks down at the basket and the two pantyliners she is grasping in her hands. She passes me the basket, catching my gaze once more, and then she rushes past me, her eyes spilling over with tears. I watch her leave, and she's clutching her chest even tighter than before.

After she's gone, I can't shake that look in her eyes. It makes my heart a little sore. Why didn't I say something? Ask her what in the world just happened in here? Offer to help her somehow?

I'm both pissed and annoyed that—again!—I have to witness Nurse Ratched being her odious self with a student. And again there's nothing I can do.

I reach into the MENSTRUAL PRODUCTS basket, searching for super-absorbency tampons while my mind works to piece together the meaning of the incredibly messed-up events that just unfolded.

"Hurry up," Nurse Ratched commands, interrupting my thoughts, her voice abrasive, as always.

"Going as fast as I can," I reply, trying my very hardest (and likely failing) to keep the irritation from my voice.

"And don't take more than you need," she barks, as if she's discovered my sinister plan to hoard the school's tampons.

"Just two," I say, holding the tampons up to demonstrate my compliance.

I flash a big fake grin and then head through the door, straight toward the nearest bathroom stall.

I'm in there pulling myself back together when I hear a sniffle, and then a stifled sob. I glance down to see that the stall beside me is occupied. Jeans and cute strappy sandals. It's that girl.

Rip of plastic, crumple of paper backing, thud of metal trash receptacle opening and closing, another quiet sob.

Maybe she bled through her jeans. It's happened to me before, and yeah, it sucks. But why not a pad or tampons? What's with the pantyliners? Plus, the big-ass tunic she's wearing would cover any stains. If not, there's always the old sweater-tied-around-the-waist trick. I bet Topher would have one she can borrow. He's all about the sweaters, no matter how extreme the Florida heat.

I stand up and look through the gap between the stalls, ready to render aid. But what I see is not at all what I expect: The girl's shirt is pulled up around her neck. She's not wearing a bra, and she's trying to strap a freaking pantyliner over her nipple with tape.

Is Nurse Ratched forcing this girl to cover her nipples? With pantyliners, of all things? She really is a heartless tyrant.

I knock twice on the wall separating us.

"It's me," I say. "From the nurse's office."

She drops her tunic fast, covering her boobs, and stares at me like I'm nuts. I guess she's got legitimate evidence. I am looking at her tits through the gap in the bathroom stall.

"I heard you crying and . . . are you okay?"

"I'm fine," she says. But she's not fine, not anywhere near it.

"Hey," I whisper. "You know you don't have to do that."

"Excuse me?" The girl's voice is so quiet and timid that I barely hear.

"You don't have to cover your nipples with those things. I mean, really! That's just . . . wrong!"

"But the nurse . . . the dress code." Her voice is so tentative, so worried. It makes me want to bust through the stall and give her a hug.

That would be beyond weird, though. I don't even know her.

"Whatever Nurse Ratch—I mean, Nurse *Hopkins* told you isn't true," I try to assure her. "Nowhere in the dress code does it say girls have to wear a bra."

Silence.

"Seriously, I've read the thing cover to cover. Several times."

It's true. After Nana finally came home from the hospital that summer, she and I would sit for hours on the back porch. I chatted and entertained her with stories of the flakiest teachers at my old school. When the back-to-school email came from Orange Grove, I was intrigued by the dress code they attached—I'd never had one before.

At my old school, there were plenty of "covenants" and "shared responsibilities" but very few rules. So I had good reason to sit with Nana, side by side in our rockers, and obsess about the back-to-school materials.

In my schoolmarm voice, I read the dress code aloud to Nana, several times. We laughed together at the most weird and absurd items in that strange list of do's and don'ts. ("Yoga pants and leggings shall only be worn beneath a skirt or shorts of appropriate length.") So I know for certain that the dress code says not a word about bras. I would have remembered. I would have had too much fun reading that part with Nana, considering that she and I share in common the genetic trait of completely flat chests.

I hear the door to her stall open. I head out toward the sinks.

She's staring into the mirror. I see an unopened pantyliner and a roll of surgical tape on the counter in front of her. My mind still struggles to process the whole thing. Who would come up with the idea of putting pantyliners over her tits? With tape!

"I can't make them stay on," she says. "Do you think maybe if I take my hair down . . ."

She reaches back and pulls out her ponytail holder. It's sweet, with a little heart charm dangling from it, like something an eight-year-old would wear. She puts it on the counter by the roll of tape and then separates her extremely long, super-silky hair into two parts. She pulls the hair forward so that it covers her boobs.

"Perfect," I say, trying to sound very convincing.

"The assistant principal said I *had* to cover myself with these or else I'd be sent home." She shows me the already-opened pantyliner she's still holding. "You don't think I'll get sent home? I'm new here; I can't get in trouble."

Watching her, I remember all the angst and confusion of my first days at this school, how desperate I was to have someone explain all the strange rules and customs—the hall passes and bells, the lockers and PE uniforms, the complicated online systems for checking and submitting homework assignments. Maybe she's never had a dress code either.

Remembering how lost and alone I felt, I want to help this girl. I want her to feel like someone has her back.

"How could you?" I ask. "No one's gonna notice."

"She said that I was making a teacher uncomfortable. . . ."

"If some pervy teacher has issues with what you're wearing, or not wearing"—I gesture toward her grandma tunic—"that's his problem, not yours."

"Actually, it was a woman."

I throw up my arms in exasperation. "Oh my God," I exclaim. "That's so typical—women policing other women's bodies."

She looks down at her shirt. "This is my mom's cover-up. It's not like I'm trying to look sexy or anything."

"And what if you were?" I ask, my tone defiant. "It shouldn't matter. What you wear shouldn't give anyone permission to disrespect you." I stand taller, trying to project confidence.

"I'm so embarrassed that people could see my . . . you know."

"That's bullcrap. Honestly, I can't see anything under that thing."

"Really? You sure no one will notice?" She smooths over her hair, then fluffs it a little at the ends and turns slowly from side to side, appraising herself.

"With your hair down like that? I'm one hundred percent absolutely positive." I'm trying to sound perfectly confident, hoping that my assurances will help her worry a bit less.

We're both staring into the mirror, and I'm feeling only mildly awkward since I'm carefully observing her boobs. Again.

"Okay, thanks." She turns to look at me. "I'm Malena, by the way."

"Ruby," I say, facing her. "Mondays always suck, don't they?"

She lets out a half-suppressed laugh and then nods. "Yes, always."

The bell rings and I flinch. Malena waves timidly and rushes out the door so fast that she leaves her hair tie on the counter. I scoop it up and put it in my pocket, pressing the heart charm between my thumb and forefinger, vowing that I'll find her later in the day to give it back.

It's the least I can do. I know what it's like to be the new girl.

CHAPTER THREE

MALENA

As I'm walking back to Ms. Baptiste's studio to get my stuff, a question coils around my insides, like a snake squeezing out every bit of air in my lungs: What if this had happened back home in Puerto Rico? What would I have done? I think I know the answer. I would've told the assistant principal, the nurse, *and* the secretary—in Spanish—exactly where they could put their pantyliners, and I would've called Papi to come get me.

But here, the rock-hard anxiety lodged in the pit of my stomach has made me incapable of standing up for myself. Most of the time, I feel inadequate and insecure. I've never been this way before.

In San Juan I went to the same school since kindergarten. The place was practically embedded into my DNA. I never had to think too hard about how to fit in—I just did.

Remembering the confidence of that girl, I want to scream at myself, *Snap out of it, Malena! Get it together!* But it's like screaming into the eye of María. The wind is too loud for anyone to hear my voice, even me.

I stand in front of the classroom door and arrange my hair

one last time before going in. I realize I left my hair tie in the bathroom. *Darn.* Another thing in my new life that will have to be replaced.

I consider going back to get it, but I don't want to run into that girl in the bathroom again. Sure, she was nice and, unlike me, she seemed to know her way around, but she also came across as a little . . . pushy? Tía Lorna says it's because the Americanos are always trying to save the world—even if no one asked them to.

Though I am thankful she kept me from taping on those pantyliners. And I'm glad I'm not the only one who thinks the administration at this school is out of their freaking minds. I mean, what kind of person thinks covering your nipples with menstrual products and tape is an "excellent" idea?

And what's so wrong with my nipples anyway? Everyone has them. I don't see guys having to walk around with pantyliners taped to their chests.

I take a deep, long breath, trying to calm myself before I walk into Ms. Baptiste's studio. I will not fall apart in a classroom full of strangers.

Around me, everyone is taking their time heading to the next class. They are too busy sharing the awesome storyboards they created while I was wasting away my morning.

"Look at this," Soraida says, turning her board in my direction. She's drawn herself driving a red Porsche convertible down a malecón, surf and palm trees in the background. Her loose hair floats wild in the wind, like a sexy Latin Medusa. A group of hot guys stands on the sidewalk, some gawking, others waving. It's part music video, part hair commercial.

"Are they ogling you or the car?" I ask sarcastically. Soraida loves being the center of attention, and I love giving her crap for it. She takes it all in stride.

Right now, I need our easy banter to help me move past what just happened.

"Me, of course!" Soraida bends over the board to shade in a strand of brown hair. "I think it could be the opening scene of a romantic comedy. A beautiful, rich girl from a well-to-do family falls for a handsome but poor guy from the wrong side of the tracks. Like Cinderella, but in reverse."

I chuckle. "I like it. It would be nice if, in the end, he still cooked and cleaned the house."

Soraida makes a note on the back of the board. "Great idea." She writes, *Cooks and cleans in his underwear.* I laugh out loud.

"It would be nice for a change if the *men* did something useful around the house," she says. I catch an edge of resentment in her tone. In Tía Lorna's house, it's up to the women to do all the housework, while the men plant themselves in front of the TV and kick up their feet after a long day's work. Or, in the case of my cousin Carlos, after baseball practice.

Everyone is constantly doting on Carlos, even at school. He's Orange Grove's king of baseball and overall Mr. Popularity. I love Carlos, but sometimes I wish he'd tone it down. It's gotta be tough living in his shadow. It makes me glad I'm an only child.

"Papi cooks and cleans," I remind her. "He even does the laundry."

"That's because Tía Camila is not gonna put up with that machista crap."

Yeah, she's right. My parents support each other with everything. They say it's because their friendship always comes first. I believe them.

I peruse Soraida's drawings, admiring the different camera angles and the neat descriptions written next to each box. I can't believe I missed all this because of a stupid bra—or lack thereof.

"This was so much fun." She slides a set of colored pencils back into their box. "There may be a film career in my future. Where did you go, anyway?"

My stomach churns at the absolute humiliation of having had to parade my tetas for the nurse and the secretary. I push the thought away, too mortified to deal with it.

"I'll tell you later." My mind keeps replaying the conversations with the assistant principal and the nurse, thinking of all the things I could've said and done differently. And that foul look on the secretary's face, like she was smelling milk gone chunky—the memory makes me want to gag.

I pack up my bag and put away the unused materials on my desk.

Ms. Baptiste tries to make her voice heard over the raucous chaos of moving chairs and voices as everyone gets ready to leave. "Remember, your final projects are due the week after Thanksgiving. I want enough time to watch your projects in class before the end of the semester."

"I don't even know what I'm doing yet," Soraida says. "Do you think she'll give me an extension?"

"Doubt it." Like Soraida, I have no idea what my final project will be. The guidelines are pretty simple: produce a five-minute documentary about a topic that is relevant to your life. We can only use original material.

I overheard one of the girls in class say she's traveling to Alabama to interview her grandmother, who was one of the first Black mathematicians for NASA. That's really impressive.

"Do you think I can bribe Ms. Baptiste with Abuela's flan? You know, in exchange for an extension?" Soraida quips.

"It's worth a try. I would do anything for even a tiny slice." Abuela makes the best flan—perfectly creamy with just the right amount of caramel on top.

"Me too," Soraida asserts wistfully.

I wait until the studio empties to approach Ms. Baptiste. I know she said not to worry about today's assignment, but I want her to know that her class is important to me.

"Ms. Baptiste?" I ask.

"Are you okay, Malena?" Her full attention turns from a book on her desk to me. Ms. Baptiste has big, expressive eyes that welcome hard conversations. She would've made a great therapist.

I look down at my notes, unable to meet her gaze. If I do, I may start crying. She is the only person at this school—other than Soraida and Carlos—who feels a little like family.

"Can I make up the assignment?" Two large textbooks are pressed tightly against my chest like a shield. They'll remain attached to my body for the rest of the day.

"I'm sorry you missed the exercise. I think you would've enjoyed it." She passes me a handout with the class instructions. "There are some links to online videos you may find helpful. And you can email me if you have any questions."

"Thanks," I say, taking the handout. "I've actually watched all the documentaries you suggested. I really liked *Joshua: Teenager vs. Superpower.*"

Ms. Baptiste's face lights up. "That is one of my favorites."

"It's hard to believe he's a year younger than me." The documentary, which I watched with Mami, chronicles the life of a fourteen-year-old human rights activist in Hong Kong. Another teenager changing the world.

"It makes you wonder what is possible, no?" She smiles, eyes crinkling around the edges. "If you'd like, I can recommend a few more."

"Yeah, I would love that."

I shift my weight from foot to foot, lingering by her desk longer than would be considered normal. I'm not ready to step into the hallway just yet. What if that teacher who complained is out there? What if she says something? What will I do then? In the hallway, there's nowhere to hide. My heart rate triples. Can a person pass out from embarrassment? Right now I'm convinced that the answer is yes.

"Is everything okay, Malena? You look a little flushed."

The kindness on her face all but does me in. I nod, swallowing the knot forming in the back of my throat. For a flash of a second, my mind wonders whether Ms. Baptiste might have been the one to turn me in.

No, it couldn't possibly have been her.

Could it?

"If something is bothering you, you can tell me. I like to think of my classroom as a safe space."

Another safe space? What exactly is Orange Grove's definition of those words?

Suddenly, I'm overcome with anger. Coming to Ms. Baptiste's class has always been my favorite part of the day. Will I always think of this humiliation, every time I come through the door?

"It's a shame you had to miss class." She shakes her head, clearly exasperated. Her hand swats the air in the direction of the hallway. "A real shame," she tsk-tsks, her Trinbagonian accent more pronounced than usual.

A wave of relief washes over me. It wasn't her.

"I missed your insights in class today," she adds in a softer tone. "You always enrich our discussions."

Before I can say anything, the school secretary appears at the door. Her thick cat-eye glasses hang from her neck as she barges into the classroom.

"I've been looking all over for you." She points at me with a long pale finger. "Dr. Hardaway asked me to give you this." She hands me a thin, spiral-bound booklet with ORANGE GROVE HIGH SCHOOL DRESS CODE written in large bold letters on the front cover. REFLECT YOUR RESPECT appears directly underneath in smaller type.

Reflect your respect? What does that even mean?

"Take it home and read it. The illustrated guide has a lot of examples. I tell all the girls to keep this by their dresser at all times. This is your dressing bible." She chuckles to herself, but I don't react. Neither does Ms. Baptiste, who just clears her throat and looks down at her desk uncomfortably.

"If you have questions, Dr. Hardaway said you should make an appointment with Mr. Cruz," she adds. "He speaks perfect Spanish and can translate anything you don't understand."

I stare at her blankly. First of all, I would rather die than discuss the importance of bras with Mr. Cruz en español. Second, have I not been communicating in English this whole time? If this woman took two seconds to review all the admission forms Mami filled out, she would know that I'm fluent in two languages and proficient in another. Sagrado Corazón also offered French.

"I'll read it tonight." I take a side step, edging closer to the door. The hallway doesn't seem that scary compared to this conversation. "I have to get to precalc."

"Oh, you're on the accelerated track? Mr. Tambor's class?"

The not-so-subtle tone of disbelief in her question tests the limits of my patience.

I nod politely and force a smile, but what I really want to do is call her out. She doesn't even know me. Why is she making assumptions about my math skills? Or my language abilities?

I don't want this woman to peg me as a contestona, but I can't help myself as I say, "Math *is* the universal language."

Ms. Baptiste snorts.

Suddenly, it's the secretary who seems ill at ease. Her spine straightens and her lips purse, deepening the wrinkles around her mouth.

I'm glad she feels uncomfortable. *Welcome to the club, lady.*

I'm tired of people here questioning my intelligence because of my accent. Or thinking that they know a thing or two about my life and my education in Puerto Rico. They don't know squat. They see images of devastation in the news and they think that's the whole story. To them, all 3.6 million people living on the Island are poor, homeless, and desperate.

I'm not used to having to defend my identity. Or being labeled as a "minority," or, even worse, "marginalized," because of it. I'm still trying to grasp the full meaning of those words.

Our new next-door neighbor seemed genuinely surprised to learn that all the Puerto Ricans moving to Florida since the hurricane are U.S. citizens.

I was stunned by her ignorance.

In hindsight, I should've told our neighbor that El Yunque, located on the northeast part of the Island, is the only rainforest in the U.S. National Forest System. That Flamenco Beach in Culebra is one of the top beaches anywhere. And that the Arecibo Observatory has one of the largest radio telescopes in the whole world. It actually monitors asteroids in space to ensure they don't come too close to Earth. So the next time her sorry ass doesn't get hit by an asteroid from space, she can thank the Puerto Rican scientists for keeping watch.

"You'll need to sign the last page." The secretary gestures to the booklet in my hand. "Dr. Hardaway wants written acknowledgment that you agree to follow the rules. This way, we can avoid another incident."

She passes me a blue-ink pen. But I don't immediately reach for it.

I realize, as she stares at me expectantly, that it is physically impossible for me to simultaneously grip the pen, leaf through the booklet, sign the stupid acknowledgment, and hold my books in front of my chest. I would need to sprout a third arm—and even then, I'm sure that would somehow constitute a dress-code violation.

Nipples and third arms shall be concealed at all times.

I set the books on Ms. Baptiste's desk and reach for the pen. I leaf through the booklet and bend down to sign. When the secretary gasps as if I just flushed her goldfish down the drain, I notice, way too late, that the loose neck of the tunic has provided a glimpse of my exposed breasts—and of course she was staring.

What is wrong with these people?

"Miss Rosario, you'll have to follow me to Dr. Hardaway's office," she says.

I silently plead with Ms. Baptiste to intervene.

"Doris, she already missed my class," Ms. Baptiste argues. "Can she go during her study period?"

"Dr. Hardaway was very specific. And she will not be happy with *this*." Her eyes again fall over my breasts, making her face flinch as if she were staring at a car accident on the side of the highway—and apparently I'm the only casualty.

"I can't miss precalc," I insist, annoyed at how small and vulnerable my voice sounds. "We have an exam this week."

"Young lady, you should've thought about that when you got dressed this morning."

At this point, I want to scream and stomp my feet, cry and protest, loud enough that the entire student body of Orange Grove High can hear me, loud enough for my friends sitting under the ceiba tree in the courtyard of Sagrado Corazón to hear me.

But even if they could hear me, no one would care. Sagrado Corazón is being used as a shelter, so I probably wouldn't recognize anyone under the ceiba, and my friends are too busy trying to rebuild their own lives to care about the bra drama in mine. They'd probably even think it was funny—except it's not.

God, what possessed me to take advice from a stranger inside a bathroom stall, of all places?

I should've just taped on those pantyliners, even if they made me massively uncomfortable. My own private pain would've been better than this public humiliation.

"It's okay, Malena," Ms. Baptiste reassures me. "I'll talk to Mr. Tambor."

I nod, unable to utter a thanks without bursting into tears.

I follow Doris, the secretary, to Dr. Hardaway's office—for the second time today.

Along the way, Mami's words from this morning ring inside my head: *They're just breasts, Malena. Everyone has them.*

I can't wait to tell her how wrong she was. If I've learned anything from my high school education today, it is that my breasts are not *just* breasts. If they were, then why would all these women be hell-bent on turning them against me?

After the last bell, I find Soraida and Carlos waiting for me in the parking lot. Carlos has already changed for baseball practice and is halfway lost inside the back of his SUV, organizing his equipment.

I learned during my first week at Orange Grove that Carlos is a minor celebrity around here. He's already been scouted by a professional team but is still trying to decide if he wants to go to college first. He got a couple of offers for a full ride. Everyone expects he'll eventually end up in the major leagues—he's that good.

I guess Tía Lorna's gamble paid off after all. Carlos and his baseball prowess are the reason they moved to Florida in the first place. Add better baseball coaches to Tía's Why Florida Is the Best Place to Live! list. When Carlos turned fourteen, his coach in Puerto Rico told the family he might have MLB potential. That summer, they sold their house in Puerto Rico and relocated with Abuela Milagros to a four-bedroom house in Orange Park, a suburb of Jacksonville, so Carlos could train under some big-name coach. And where, according to my tía, you can raise a "familia decente, far away from the drug dealers and bandidos that live in Miami."

They dragged Soraida kicking and screaming. She didn't want to leave the Island just so that her brother could play ball.

At school, it's super embarrassing to walk next to him between classes or in the parking lot. Girls are constantly hurling themselves at him, like he's already landed a multimillion-dollar contract with the Yankees. It's pathetic.

A ball falls from the back of the SUV, and I catch it before it hits the pavement. The tape holding the pantyliners pulls at the soft skin around my nipples as I bend down. My back hurts. My chest hurts. Every limb in my body feels sore and strained from the tension of this god-awful day.

"Is it okay if I drop you off at our house? I don't have time to make two stops. I have a meeting with my coach before practice," Carlos says.

"I can't leave," I say.

"Why?" He drops a glove inside a black canvas bag and zips it shut.

"I got detention."

"You what?" Carlos's irritated tone is loud enough to get Soraida's attention. She's been sitting in the front seat with her feet propped on the dash, listening to Maluma on the radio.

"What's going on?" Soraida asks, kneeling on the front seat and leaning over the center console.

"Malena got detention," Carlos calls out over the music. Then he turns to me. "What did you do?"

"Nothing," I snap defensively. I toss him the ball I've been holding, and he catches it with his right hand. I'm always surprised by his lightning-fast reflexes.

"You must've done something." His hands rest on his hips in an accusatory stance, rendered ridiculous by the white tights he wears.

I exhale hard, resting against the open tailgate.

"Remember how I didn't have any clean clothes yesterday and I had to wear that bathing suit? Well, my back got sunburned and I can't wear a bra."

Carlos's eyes immediately fall to my chest.

"Seriously?" I spit. "Gross."

"Sorry," he mutters, looking away, embarrassed. The tips of his ears go red. "It was a reflex."

Soraida maneuvers her body into the back seat and leans over it, trying to get a better view of my chest.

"You can't see anything." She's holding her hand over her eyes to block out the glare of the afternoon sun.

"Yeah, that's because they made me tape on two huge panty-liners," I say, exasperated. For a half second I consider pulling up my shirt so they can see the damage for themselves. "I have surgical tape literally all over my chest, the kind Mami uses in the ER. You can close wounds with it. And apparently it also makes for a poor girl's boob lift," I add sarcastically, remembering the little "joke" the nurse and the secretary shared at my expense. To them, this was all oh-so-very clever.

Carlos winces. "Man, that's gonna hurt coming off."

"No shit, Sherlock," Soraida hisses.

"Why did they give you detention, though?" Carlos asks.

"When they told me to put them on the first time, this girl in the bathroom said I didn't have to." She was convincing, that girl—one of those people who's not afraid to fight for what's right.

Even when I had to raise my voice to be heard in student-council meetings at Sagrado Corazón, I always worried I'd come across as too *opinionated*—and maybe, heaven forbid, too *aggressive*. Or, as a teacher once put it, too smart for my own good.

"And you listened to her?" Carlos asks. His forehead wrinkles in a way that makes him look much older than seventeen. "Who was this girl?"

"Hell if I know!" I don't even try to control the indignation I've been suppressing all day. Now, around my family, I'm free to let it all loose.

"Well, do you remember what she looked like?" he asks.

"Carlitos knows allllllll the girrrrls," Soraida teases.

"Shut up, Soraida!" Carlos barks.

"She was tall, skinny, white, short hair, pretty face." I rack my brain, trying to recall an identifying feature.

"That's like half the girls in the school," Carlos says.

"Allllllll the girrrrls." Soraida giggles at her own joke, but this time Carlos ignores her.

"She told me there was nothing about bras in the dress code," I continue. "And the tape is pulling at my skin. I have no idea how I'm taking these things off when I get home."

"Soap and water," Soraida offers. "Or just rip 'em right off."

"The skin will come off!" I shrink away, incredulous at her suggestion.

"Did you call Tía Camila?" Carlos asks.

"Mami was busy," I explain. *Busy saving lives.*

He scratches the back of his head with his free hand, staring off into the half-empty parking lot.

"That sucks. How long will detention take?" he asks.

"An hour after school, every day this week." I sit, slouching against the open tailgate, giving in to the exhaustion of the day. "At least I can do my homework."

"How are you gonna get home?" he asks.

I shrug. "I don't know," I say, trying to keep my voice from breaking. Walking home is not an option in Orange Park. We only live a mile from Orange Grove High, which wouldn't be terrible if there were any sidewalks. Plus, attempting to cross the big stretch of highway between school and our apartment definitely would land me in the hospital—or worse.

"Jesus, Malena. Why couldn't you just put on the—the—you know—" he stammers, turning a hundred different shades of red. What is it with guys and menstrual products?

"They're called pantyliners, you jackass!" Soraida snaps. "And they're meant for your vagina, not your tits."

I gesture at Soraida with my open palm. "Precisely."

"Whatever. This is so stupid," Carlos says.

I clench my jaw, all too aware of how stupid this all is. And equally pissed at Carlos's impatience with my situation. I would love to see him be forced to tape pantyliners over his nipples. But we all know guy nipples—though useless—are not offensive.

"I'll try Mami again." The urge to cry swells inside me, but I blink it away. "Maybe she can pick me up after work."

And just as I think this day cannot possibly get any worse, I see the girl from the bathroom, jogging in our direction, calling out my name.

CHAPTER FOUR

RUBY

I'm already standing next to the SUV, Malena's hair tie dangling from my forefinger, when I notice that she's not alone. A girl about her age is kneeling in the back seat, talking to Malena through the open liftgate, and there's a guy with them that I don't recognize. He's wearing baseball pants and gripping a ball in one hand. Granted, I don't know much about sports, but I'm pretty sure it's not baseball season at Orange Grove. Maybe he plays for another team?

Whatever. Not important. I'm here to check on Malena.

"Thanks," she says, taking the hair tie from me. She shoves it into the pocket of her jeans.

"You left it in the bathroom," I tell her. "I just wanted to—"

The sporty guy steps next to Malena. He's squeezing the baseball so hard that the veins in his forearm pop out.

Trying to ignore his intense negative energy, I focus on Malena. "I wanted to be sure you got it back, and, you know, check in to see how the rest of your day went."

She presses her lips together. "Fine," she mumbles.

The girl in the back seat climbs through to the cargo space and calls out, "Until her mom finds out she got detention."

"Seriously?" My voice goes high. "Detention? For not wearing a bra?"

Malena slumps forward and crosses her arms over her chest. "Sort of," she says quietly.

"Malena." The baseball guy finally speaks, his voice deep and even. "Tell her what happened."

Malena cuts him a sideways glance. "It's fine . . . it's not a big deal."

The girl in the cargo space leans so far out that I'm worried she might fall. "She got in trouble for not doing what the nurse said!" The girl sounds almost excited, like she's sharing juicy gossip. "She got called back to the assistant principal."

"Wait—" I look at Malena. "You mean for not strapping pantyliners to your nipples?" Even as I hear the words come out of my mouth, I'm still shocked by the absurdity of the whole situation.

Malena shrugs.

"Oh my God! That's so . . ." I stop the choice cussword from spilling out of my mouth. "So messed up!"

I vowed to stop swearing last weekend. Even though there's ample evidence that cursing is a sign of emotional intelligence, I'm giving it up. Profanity distracts the listener from reasonable, measured discourse. At least that's what Nana convinced me of in a two-hour debate we had over our morning coffee. And she's kind of a badass.

"Or maybe," the guy with the baseball says in the same low, calm voice, "maybe it's messed up that a random stranger decided she should convince my cousin to disobey the nurse *and* the assistant principal."

Heat rises in my chest, and I feel my cheeks go red. "Wait," I say. "You're blaming *me* for this mess?"

"Did you tell her not to obey the nurse?" he asks, his voice still infuriatingly low and calm.

"I mean, yeah, but—"

"But what?" he asks. "You didn't think detention was a big deal?"

I stumble, trying to form a response. He's starting to freak me out with that voice.

"It didn't cross your mind that this might be an issue?"

I start to feel prickly, hot around the neck. My eyebrows arch and my hands go to my hips. I have a bit of what you might call a quick temper. I've been trying really hard to control the temper (and the language), unless I have a really good reason.

I think Mr. Sporty Balls is about to give me a good reason.

"You want to throw around advice, but you don't want to take responsibility for the outcome," the guy says, his voice calm, as if he's offering directions to the library, or explaining to my nana how to install an app.

"What *outcome?*" I snarl.

He shakes his head slowly from side to side. "Clueless," he grumbles under his breath.

Nana would not like where my mind is headed. I want to hurl some choice expletives at this guy, but I manage to hold my tongue.

"Malena doesn't have a ride home from detention," Soraida jumps in. "And Carlos needs to hit the road. He's late for practice."

"Okay," I say, struggling to keep my voice steady. "That sucks. But maybe she could rideshare or something? Or I can give her a ride."

"See what I mean?" Carlos says, looking at Malena but pointing a finger at me. "This girl is clueless."

This girl is clueless? No, this girl is pissed.

"Asshole."

Carlos winces and steps back. His eyebrows arch and his face twists into . . . surprise? I thought I said it in my head, but based on his reaction, I guess I called him an asshole out loud. It's a little hard to believe no one has ever called this guy an ass, but he's reacting like I've just knocked the wind out of him or something.

He hasn't seen anything yet.

I step forward so that my face is close to his. The heat swelling in my chest makes me feel taller. "First," I announce, rising onto my toes, "you know it was totally effed up what that nurse wanted her to do."

The f-bombs are about to fly . . .

"Second, there's nowhere in that entire bullshit dress code that says girls have to wear a freaking bra to school."

. . . and I'm off.

"I thought maybe Malena should stand up for herself, not just blindly obey rules that don't exist." My arms wave wildly around. It's like they have separated from my body and taken on a life of their own. "I *assumed* there wouldn't be consequences because she didn't do anything *wrong!*"

He leans back and shakes his head slowly from side to side, a smile forming on his lips. "That's right, White Girl. You didn't think about the consequences." He's standing perfectly still, voice calm and even, but his big, broad chest is somehow getting even bigger. "Stay away from my cousin. She'll get by just fine without your help."

"¡Carlos!" Malena cries out. "¡Ya! Por favor. No quiero más problemas."

She grabs his arm and drags him toward the driver's-side door.

I watch Malena practically shove this Carlos guy into the car, still talking sternly with him in Spanish.

I don't know what she's saying, but I hope she's cussing him out.

⸺

By the time I get back to my car, Topher's waiting for me.

"Mr. Cruz said Mercury is in retrograde or something," he says as soon as I open the door. "Maybe he's right. Maybe even the stars are aligned against me."

Turns out that he had a sucky afternoon too.

His mom and grandma didn't show up for their college-counseling meeting. (Yeah, Mr. Cruz is also the college counselor—all in a day's work at Florida's underfunded public schools.) If Topher's mom doesn't step up and deal with his FAFSA forms, Topher's big college dreams are going nowhere. Unfortunately, it doesn't appear that his family gives a crap about his college dreams, or much of anything else. I hate to sound so judgmental, but Topher is such an extraordinary human, and it just doesn't seem fair that the universe placed him with those two.

After the botched meeting, Topher sent me, Nessa, and Jo an SOS:

> IN DESPERATE NEED OF THRIFTING
> THERAPY.

Topher cares deeply about his look, and he's one of the most skilled thrifters I know, but he cares even more about getting into college. More specifically, he wants to go to a college far from North Florida and far, far away from his dysfunctional family.

This goal motivates him to trek all the way across town on the city bus each day to get to Orange Grove, the only school around that offers an IB diploma. Or, as Topher likes to call it, in his mock highbrow accent, "the International Baccalaureate Diploma Programme—for the gifted and those who aspire to be gifted."

Jo, Nessa, and I are aspirational at best, though we did manage somehow to land ourselves on the IB track. They're smart, but both Jo and Nessa are way more interested in making art than in making good grades. As for me, when I came to Florida, I had no idea what IB even was. Olive told me that getting an IB diploma would help me get into college, and I followed my big sister's advice.

So much for forging my own path, huh?

It's not easy, when Olive is so enormously knowledgeable, so incredibly competent, so very far ahead of me. Basically, Olive is *always* right. Following Olive's suggestions is way easier than pushing back, even if it does make me feel deflated and a little pathetic. It's strange how I've started to feel confident and strong in almost every other relationship, but with Olive, I'm always the baby.

Topher and I climb into my car in silence. Of course it feels like a furnace, so I fumble quickly to roll down the windows and blast the air. And I wonder, for the thousandth time, who decided that the state of Florida was actually inhabitable by humans, and how anyone possibly survived here before the invention of air-conditioning.

I notice Topher watching me closely. "Okay, Roobs, spill. What happened?"

"What do you mean?" I ask, fiddling with the air vents.

I feel like I just got hit by a train—or a misdirected baseball bat. I was just trying to help Malena. She seemed so . . . defeated.

I keep running through the whole parking-lot scene in my head, trying again and again to figure out how my simple attempt to return a hair tie turned into a massive blowup. I need to stop thinking about it. About *him*.

Ugh. He is such an asshole. I'll admit that Carlos is easy on the eyes, but once he opens his mouth, it's all over.

"You've got that look on your face. The grimace. Something's off."

"What grimace?" I ask, forcing a plastic smile. "I just can't believe we're going to buy you a sweater when it's literally ten thousand degrees outside."

His phone dings, and he glances down at it. "Nessa texted. They're gonna meet us there."

"Perfect," I say, queuing up the girl-power playlist Topher made for my seventeenth birthday. "Let's go find you some vintage wool."

———

Usually, perusing Fans & Stoves Vintage Mart has a calming effect. The smell of mold and dust starts to soothe me before I'm even inside. I love all the stalls shoved in next to each other. Antique armoires that have been impeccably restored are bumped right up against stained lace tablecloths, chintzy knickknacks, and stacks and stacks of old records.

Today, though, I can't seem to sink into the chaos of it all.

Our thrifting adventure started out with great promise. We found Topher not one but two awesome sweaters: a boxy, bold-striped crewneck and a trim cashmere V-neck that brings out the deep brown of his eyes. *Real* cashmere for eight bucks!

With time still on our hands, I suggested we go on a hunt for

Nana's birthday gift. She turns seventy-eight tomorrow, and I'm desperate to find her a turtle.

For twenty years, Nana has volunteered with her local turtle patrol, cruising down the beach every Sunday morning on a four-wheeler, searching for sea-turtle nests. She's passionate and committed—it's like Nana's version of church. I hope I still have even a fraction of her zeal when I'm in my seventies.

Who am I kidding? I wish I had it now.

After her surgery, Nana had to take a break, but she's been working hard to build her strength enough to climb back on that four-wheeler. So I figured a great birthday gift would be something turtle-related. I just didn't realize how freaking impossible it would be to find a little ceramic doodad shaped like a turtle in this place. I know it's a small thing in the grand scheme of life, but this stupid lack of turtles is about to push me over the edge.

"Any chance your nana's into owls?" Jo calls out from the stall across the hallway. "This vendor has, like, hundreds of them."

I shake my head.

"But just look at this precious face!" Jo holds up a white ceramic owl that looks to be straight out of the 1950s. "How can you resist those eyes?"

"Awww, the little owl has your eyes, Topher!" Nessa coos.

Topher grabs the owl from Jo and inspects it. "Well, yeah," he says. "But he'll need some smooth brown feathers if he wants to be as beautiful as me."

Topher's mom is a white Southerner, and his dad was Afro-Dominican. He died when Topher was three. That's about all we know. He doesn't remember much about his father, but—being his relentlessly optimistic self—Topher always goes on and on about how his dad must have been "one handsome dude."

Having met Topher's mom, I have to agree. She's not particularly attractive, and Topher is beautiful, inside and out. His radiance must come from somewhere.

"Would your nana be into a French country maiden?" Jo asks, holding another antique figurine in her hands.

Topher takes the figurine and inspects it. "This one looks like you two," he says, gesturing toward Jo and Nessa. "Milky skin, rosy-pink cheeks. Y'all got any French in you?"

"I told my dad I want to study art in France next year," Nessa says. "He actually belly-laughed and then announced, for the hundredth time, that the only place I'm going next year is Tallahassee, to study business at Florida State." She plasters a scowl on her face and mimics his deep voice: " 'Art won't pay the bills, Nessa!' "

"We all know Ruby here is the only one of us with any chance for a gap year," Topher says.

"You're so lucky," Nessa tells me. "I'd kill for a gap year."

It's true. My parents have been bombarding me with links to all sorts of precollege enrichment programs: work with orphans in Brazil, support victims of sexual violence in Thailand, learn sustainable farming in Costa Rica.

They're all about the gap year, and Olive, too. After college, Olive moved to Atlanta, which means she's only about six hours away from us by car. When she came to visit for Labor Day weekend, Olive actually told me, "Not everyone matures into their purpose as quickly as I did. You really do have unrealized potential. A gap year would help."

Classic Olive. These days, my sister's so-called compliments always leave me feeling inadequate. When I was little, I thought Olive was utterly incapable of mistakes. I wouldn't dare question her. I saw each bit of advice as a precious gift, a sign that I—the baby sister—was actually worthy of Olive's attention. In the past couple of years, though, I've started to wonder: Has she always been so domineering and judgmental?

Olive has her whole life planned out to the minute, and she's executing the plan with exact precision: (1) Enroll in a *U.S. News & World Report* top-ten university. (2) Lead no fewer than three social-activist organizations at said university. (3) Graduate with a dual degree in politics and education, with highest honors. (4) Do Teach for America. (5) Change the world.

Olive has steadily progressed to step five, while I'm still bumbling around, trying to figure out what my step one will be. All I have is an overwhelming array of options that I know I should feel outrageously grateful for.

"Yeah, I guess I'm lucky that way," I say unconvincingly.

Jo takes the French country maiden back from Topher and shoves it in front of my face. "Who really needs a turtle when you could bring this lovely lady home?" she asks, batting her eyelashes in mock flirtation. "Demure face, gently tilted head, bosom slightly heaving over her apron. She simply calls out, 'Take me in the meadow!' "

That's all it takes for my annoyance to flash into anger. "Give me that thing," I demand.

Jo hands me the porcelain figure. I turn it in my hands and inspect it. It appears that 1950s replicas of eighteenth-century French country maidens have a less strict dress code than the girls at Orange Grove High.

"Absurd," I hear myself whisper.

Topher shows up behind me and peers over my shoulder. "I think she looks kinda sweet."

"Oh," I spit out. "You mean you're not so distracted by her French country cleavage that you can't keep track of your sheep?"

Topher, hearing the rising anger in my voice, touches my shoulder gently. "All right, Roobs. Release the porcelain doll before your arms start flailing and something gets broken—how much is that thing?" He reaches around to grab the figurine.

"Are you okay, Ruby?" Nessa asks. "Remember, we talked about this. Let's aim to keep our emotions even."

By *this*, of course, she means my out-of-control temper.

"Are you sure this is about turtles?" Topher asks.

I sigh heavily, releasing all the air from my lungs. Topher gingerly removes the French maiden from my hands and places her between a puppy and a stork. I tell them about Malena, the whole scene with the nurse and the secretary carefully inspecting her chest, and what happened in the bathroom stall.

"I followed her into the bathroom and tried to help her out," I explain.

"You followed her into the bathroom?" Jo asks. "That's a little creepy."

"Well, no." I'm getting flustered. "I didn't exactly follow her. I went in there too. And she was crying. I felt so sorry for the poor girl. She was really upset. I just wanted to help!"

"So, let me guess," Topher says. "You told her the dress code is ludicrous and there's no way she should do what Nurse Ratched said."

"Wait," Nessa breaks in. "Who's Nurse Ratched? I thought the nurse's name was Hopkins or Jenkins or something."

"Seriously, Nessa?" I reply, incredulous. "*One Flew over the Cuckoo's Nest*? The most iconic battle-ax nurse of all time?"

Topher waves his arms in the air and claps twice to get our attention. "Can we focus here, ladies?"

"Yeah, I told her it was ludicrous," I say. "Then she wisely tossed the stupid pantyliners and got in trouble. Detention."

"That's so strange," Nessa muses. "Pantyliners on your boobs. I mean, I guess it would work, but—"

"Oh, it's a thing. There's a ton of beauty-hack videos about it. In one, I saw this girl use pantyliners and duct tape to cover her boobs," says Jo, shuddering at the thought. "That must've hurt like a mother coming off."

"It's one thing to subject yourself to that willingly, but it's totally obscene that a school employee would force someone to do it!" I interject.

"True, that," Jo says.

"After last period, I went to check on her," I continue, "and her obnoxious cousin, Mr. Sporty Balls, got all mad at me and accused me of butting in."

"Well," Topher says pointedly, "you did sort of butt in."

"Okay, yeah. But she didn't break any rules. I'm positive about this. Did I really deserve for this guy in baseball pants to go off on me and call me Little Miss Privileged White Girl?"

"He actually said that?" Nessa asks.

"Not exactly. He did call me White Girl, though, and said I don't know anything about 'consequences.'"

"Dude's got a point," Topher says, shaking his head. "*All* y'all are privileged white girls."

"Okay, sure," I admit, "you have every right to say that, Topher." Nessa and Jo nod in agreement. "But Mr. Carlos Sporty Balls?" I spit out. "He doesn't know a thing about me! I've never even met the guy!"

"Wait, was this guy in a baseball uniform named Carlos?" Jo asks, suddenly excited and bouncing on her heels.

"Yeah, and Malena and the other girl were all stressed out because he had to go to practice, like he's the king of the universe or something." I feel my face go hot with the recollection.

"Oh my God, Ruby!" Jo's grinning from ear to ear, like I just told her I won the lottery. "You got in a screaming match with Carlos Rosario!"

"Well, technically *he* wasn't screaming—"

"Carlos Rosario, God of Baseball!" Jo exclaims, practically bursting with enthusiasm.

"Uh-oh," Topher mutters. "Here she goes."

Jo is utterly and completely obsessed with baseball. In the opinion of Nessa, Topher, and myself, this is just plain weird. I'm still trying to figure out Jo's baffling shift of tone when she starts rattling off stats, as she tends to do.

"Carlos Rosario had a 1.50 ERA and a 9–0 record last season. His pitch speed is ninety-four. I think it's the best in the state, maybe the entire Southeast." She's still bouncing up and down; her eyes are all wide and bright. "He'll probably get signed right out of high school. He's *that* good."

"Figures," I mumble. "I wonder which comes first: the random baseball skills or the misogyny?"

"It's true," Nessa chimes in. "A lot of those pro baseball players are *players*."

"Whatever," I say. "Let's drop this conversation and find a damn turtle. I gotta get home. It's my night to make dinner."

Topher, Nessa, and Jo set off on the mission, and I'm left sorting through a box of chipped porcelain figurines, trying to avoid obsessing about the asshole baseball player and what he said.

Am I clueless about consequences? Would *I* be punished at Orange Grove for going without a bra? And if not, why not?

There's only one way to find out.

CHAPTER FIVE

MALENA

Mami had to work late again, so Tío Wiliberto picks me up from my first day of detention after he closes the auto shop where he works as a master mechanic on luxury cars. I had to sit by myself for two hours at a McDonald's across the street from the school. At first the women behind the counter kept eyeing me for not having ordered any food. Tía Lorna doesn't like it when we ruin our appetite by snacking before dinner. Finally, I broke down and got a small fries and a Coke. What else was I supposed to do?

Tío and I ride in silence for a while. His hands and forearms are covered in dark grease stains and his clothes reek of gas and exhaust fumes. He's not as easy to talk to as Papi, but I love that he's a humble man not inclined to bouts of idle conversation. It's a peaceful drive. And right now, I *need* some peace.

My phone beeps and I get a text from Mami, saying she'll meet me at Tía Lorna's in time for dinner.

I used to complain about her erratic schedule at the hospital in San Juan, but at least she wasn't working twelve-hour shifts. Now she usually leaves for work before I'm up, and by the time she's through fighting downtown traffic in the evenings, there's not much Mami left to go around. Life in Florida has proven much more exhausting than Tía Lorna predicted.

I miss the slow pace of our days back home. The ocean breeze weaving through the large rooms of our condo, infusing the house with the smell of salt water and sunshine. Papi and me cooking dinner while Mami was at work. Laughing about this or that. Conjuring up spontaneous adventures.

Like the time he decided that he would teach me how to fly a chiringa. He packed us Cuban sandwiches and "invested" in a massive bird-shaped kite in vibrant shades of purple, orange, and yellow, with multiple streamer tails fluttering behind.

We drove to Old San Juan and parked by the big green at the entrance of El Morro, the colonial Spanish fort built to protect the capital city. It was a breezy afternoon, and the longer summer days ensured we had plenty of sunshine left.

Papi taught me how to pull at the line to get just the right amount of tension, to steer left and right, in big round circles and infinity loops. I watched him drop elevation until the kite almost hit the ground and, at the last moment, snap the line to make it soar again.

I let the image of that chiringa take flight again as I sit quietly inside the cab of Tío Wiliberto's pickup. My forehead leans against the partially opened window, and I listen to an old salsa by Héctor Lavoe playing on the radio, one of Papi's favorites. My head naturally bobs to the steady rhythm of the clave, which pulses through the speakers like a strand of musical DNA.

Tío Wiliberto removes a worn pack of cigarettes from under his seat, keeping one hand on the steering wheel. He brings the pack to his mouth and clenches a single cigarette between his teeth. Then he pushes a lighter button next to the radio and waits for the coils to heat up. His thumbs tap the steering wheel to the beat of the music. When we stop at a red light, he cups his hands around his mouth to light the cigarette.

"Don't tell your tía," he says, blowing smoke out the driver's-side window.

Like she doesn't already know, I want to say. But it's not my place to interfere, so I keep my mouth shut.

"I spoke to Alberto today," he says, referring to Papi. "He's been up in the mountains—Utuado, Adjuntas, Jayuya . . . all destroyed." He takes a long puff of his cigarette and lets the smoke out slowly. "Pérdida total. Makes a grown man wanna cry."

I gaze at his greasy right hand wrapped over the steering wheel, the now-familiar tightness of loss and grief deep in my chest.

"They're saying the death toll could be in the thousands . . . no one knows."

He takes a long drag on his cigarette, then slowly exhales a cloud of smoke out his open window. I want to ask him who "they" are. FEMA? The government? The news? The social-media groups that people on the mainland are using to track down their loved ones? I desperately want to know what else Papi said, but after another long puff, Tío tosses the unfinished cigarette out the window and turns up the music. His knuckles are taut over the steering wheel. His lips purse. He's done talking. We both stare straight ahead, and drive the rest of the way in a heavy silence.

To help ease the hopelessness, our whole family has volunteered at several ¡Puerto Rico Se Levanta! donation drives held at Tía Lorna's church. I've found the kindness of strangers impossible to measure—proof that there really is more good than evil in the world.

Along with dozens of other volunteers, we've packed shipping containers with water, baby supplies, medicines, and tons of other basic necessities. I feel useful doing something with my hands, actually helping. But with an ocean between Florida and the Island, our help just won't get there fast enough. Shipping aid is a frustrating, maddeningly slow process.

When we reach Tío's house, he pulls into the driveway and puts the truck into park.

"Hay que resignarse, mija," he says, turning to look at me.

I nod in understanding.

Resignación.

I've lost count of how many times I've heard that word in the last six weeks. It's one of those Spanish words with so much hidden meaning, impossible to fully translate into another language. Some people say it means "to accept"—as in "we have to accept that which we cannot change." Something about the word makes me want to scream at anyone who speaks it. Because it's a word that hides the truth: all our frustration, unresolved pain, and anxiety. *Resignación* is not a peaceful word. It's shallow and disingenuous—like giving up.

Inside the house, Tío Wiliberto grabs a Medalla beer from the fridge and takes the plate of food Tía Lorna has left out for him. "Too many women," he grumbles, disappearing into the rec room with its massive flat-screen TV. He promptly closes the door behind him.

Tía Lorna, Abuela Milagros, and Soraida are gathered around the dining table making pasteles, the savory masa bundles that everyone here confuses with Mexican tamales. It's annoying— they're not even made from the same ingredients. We usually eat them around the holidays, and with Thanksgiving and Christmas coming soon, Abuela Milagros has been roping us into her hourslong pastel-making marathons.

In Puerto Rico, pasteles are a culinary art form, and Abuela Milagros is considered a master craftswoman. Her masa has the perfect balance of yautía and green plantains, and a little extra mashed pumpkin that she calls her "secret ingredient."

I take in the singsongy sounds of Spanish conversation around the table and wrap them around me like a cozy handmade blanket.

I kiss Tía Lorna on the cheek and ask for la bendición. Then I kiss Abuela and she blesses me with a prayer to La Virgencita.

"Camila called. She's on her way," Tía Lorna says. "Are you hungry? You didn't eat any of that greasy fast food, did you?"

"No," I lie, not wanting to get into one of Tía's "fast food will kill you" arguments. "I'll eat with Mami," I add. I don't want her to eat alone after a long day at the hospital.

I take a seat at the table next to Soraida, who's mashing a green plantain against the sharp edges of a stainless-steel grater.

"Your turn," she says, passing me the grater and a whole plantain. "I'll end up with arthritis at the pace these two have me working." She stands, pushing out her chair. It scratches against the tile floor, making a sharp, piercing sound.

"Soraida, por favor. Be more careful, nena," Tía Lorna scolds. "You're gonna mess up the floors."

As is customary, Soraida rolls her eyes when Tía looks away. It's bratty and childish, but something about Tía Lorna's nagging makes Soraida and me regress a whole ten years.

"I'm getting a soda. You want one?" Soraida asks me.

"Sure," I say, pressing down on my first plantain. The trick, I've learned over dozens of pasteladas—that's what we call these pastel-making gatherings—is to keep a steady pace and a light wrist. Too much pressure and by the fiftieth plantain my arm will be cramping from the pain.

Soraida returns with two drinks and takes her seat next to mine. She leans in and whispers, "How did it go?"

I shoot her a warning look. Anything you say at a pastelada— even if whispered—is meant for public consumption. She knows that. Everyone knows that.

"Soraida says you got detention," Tía Lorna jumps in. She's been softening the plantain leaves over an electric hot plate, or amortiguando, as we say.

My eyes cut to Soraida, accusing her of being a chismosa.

She must get the message because her tone turns defensive. "They wanted to know why you didn't come home with us. Did you take them off? The pantyliners?"

"I just got here. When would I have had time?" I snap, losing my grip on the grater and almost peeling the skin off my knuckle.

"It's that mala suerte," Abuela proclaims, as if she's warding off some mal de ojo at the table. "You need a bath in salt water, mija. Cleanse all that bad luck."

Usually I ignore Abuela's "cures," but a saltwater bath doesn't sound like a bad idea. Maybe it will help remove all the surgical tape covering my chest.

"Do you need help ripping everything off?" Soraida offers.

"No!" I spit, pushing down on a plantain too hard. "I'll deal with it when I get home. Alone."

"I don't know why Camila let you go to school like that," Abuela Milagros says in Spanish. "You're a señorita and señoritas need to wear brassieres. Camila should know better."

"You can't be walking around like *that* and think boys won't notice," Tía Lorna says, her voice all holier-than-thou. "It's like you're sending a message."

"What message?" I ask, indignant.

"That you're as loose as your boobs," Soraida points out sarcastically, shooting her mother daggers.

Tía Lorna tsk-tsks. "I'm just glad I don't have to worry about these things with Carlitos. Boys are so much easier."

Even I'm tempted to roll my eyes at this one. "I've already missed too much school," I say. "Plus, they're just breasts—everyone has them. I don't get what the big deal is. Why am I responsible for what pervy boys do or think?"

There's a long silence as Abuela folds in the ingredients for the masa and Tía cuts the parchment paper to wrap the bundles.

"Maybe it's because your tetas are so big," Soraida says, perfectly illustrating how the filter between her thoughts and her speech is missing.

"Whose fault is that?" I counter, irritated. "I didn't get to pick the size."

Soraida turns to Abuela Milagros and chuckles. "The culprit sits at this table."

"You should be proud you got such nice breasts," Abuela says, in the same way other families speak proudly of the color of their eyes or the complexion of their skin. "Women have operations and pay thousands of dollars to get breasts like these. And you both got them for free."

As much as I want to remain upset, I can't help but laugh. We all do.

"Soraida, stop sitting on your hands and get to work." Tía Lorna passes her a ball of cooking twine and a pair of scissors. "Cut the twine. We're almost ready to assemble."

"I don't understand why we can't order these," Soraida whines. "Doña Lucrecia sells a dozen for twenty-five bucks. That's a steal, if you ask me."

Abuela Milagros scoffs. "That vieja doesn't know the first thing about pasteles," she says, indignant. "She doesn't even make her own achiote, and I heard she *buys* her sofrito—that green glob they sell in jars at the supermarket."

Mami comes in through the kitchen door with a loud "Alllllloooo!"—her Spanglish version of *hello*. She goes around the table spreading kisses until her lips finally land on my forehead. Her hands feel so soft and tender around my face, they make my eyes water with tears.

"What happened with the assistant principal, mija?" She caresses the back of my head, and I lean into her hand. Earlier I sent her a long text explaining why I got detention until Thursday. Mercifully, Orange Grove has detention-free Fridays. Instead, our "punishment" is to attend pep rallies for the football team, the Raptors—legendary for having the longest losing streak in North Florida.

Before I can answer, Tía Lorna inserts herself. "Camila, you can't let her go to school like that. What will those people think? That she's some chusma from a caserío?"

I want to tell Tía Lorna to stop making generalizations about people who live in government housing. It's not like our family was raised in the mansions in Guaynabo City. But for Mami's sake, I hold my tongue.

Mami glances at my chest, and I can tell she's second-guessing this morning's decision.

"Maybe I should've let you stay home," she says, sounding as defeated as I've ever heard her. "I'm sorry, nena."

"But, Mami," I say, pulling the *Orange Grove High School Dress Code* out of my backpack, "there's nothing here about wearing a bra. I read it during detention."

Mami glances briefly at the booklet and then sets it aside, just as Tía Lorna brings us two platefuls of arroz con habichuelas and fricasé de pollo.

"Gracias," Mami and I say at the same time.

The familiar flavors of Tía's chicken stew and Abuela's habichuelas guisadas are a balm to my very soul. For the first time today, I actually feel like I'm in a so-called safe space.

When we finish, I take our plates to the kitchen to rinse them. By the time I return to the dining room, Mami is wearing an apron and has joined the pastel assembly line.

I watch her delicate hands pick a piece of parchment paper and lay it flat on the table. She proceeds to paint the parchment with a very thin smear of annatto oil. Her brushstrokes are so light and steady it's like she's working on a masterpiece.

She lays a banana leaf on top of the parchment and then repeats the annatto application. When she's finished, she passes the pastel wrapper to Abuela so she can spread the masa on top.

"Can Wiliberto pick up Malena for the next three days?" Mami asks, reaching for a new banana leaf from the stack in front of her. "I had to take a couple of extra shifts again this week."

"I told you, Dr. Gonzales could get you a job working nine to five in his clinic," Tía Lorna says. "And you'd make a lot more money. Finally pay off those student loans that are weighing you down."

Abuela passes a banana leaf full of masa to Tía Lorna, who then spoons the pork pieces into a straight line down the middle. Everyone loves Abuela's pasteles because you always get a little pork with every bite. Abuela makes sure of it.

"Lorna, it needs more pork on the ends," Abuela demands—case in point.

"I love my job," Mami tells Tía Lorna. "I don't want to spend all day in a plastic surgeon's office giving Botox and liposuction to rich ladies all day. That's not for me. I like the ER. And I love taking care of kids. It's meaningful work."

"Love won't pay the bills, Camila," Tía Lorna says, giving Mami a pitiful look. "Have you heard anything from the condo insurance company? Did your claim go through?"

"Nothing yet," Mami says, absently running a hand over a banana leaf on the table.

A long silence descends on the room. No one wants to acknowledge how precarious our financial situation is at the moment.

After a couple of pasteles are neatly tied at my end of the table, Tía Lorna clears her throat and says, "Well, if you ask me, Malena can't be home alone all afternoon." No one asked for her opinion, but clearly that's never been a deterrent. "Girls at this age need supervision. You're not on the Island anymore, Camila. Here, things are different. The girls are all sueltas and sinvergüenzas. They want to be like those loose white girls who just do whatever they want. No self-respect. And their mothers let them."

I glance at Soraida, just to see her roll her eyes again. And she does! I stifle a laugh.

"I trust Malena," Mami says, half smiling in my direction. I return the smile. "She wouldn't do anything to jeopardize her future."

"¡Las piernas cruzaditas! You hear me?" Abuela Milagros locks her fingers in the universal sign of crossed legs. Soraida and I exchange a knowing glance, trying hard to suppress a fit of laughter. Here comes the virginity talk. "If boys think you're a suelta, they won't respect you. They'll use you for just one thing, then drop you like a tissue after they blow their nose," Abuela argues.

Soraida leans in and whispers in my ear, "Their noses will be the last thing they want blown." I let out a snort of laughter, hitting Soraida hard in the arm. She roars uncontrollably.

"Don't be a fresca, Soraida!" Tía Lorna scolds. But it only makes us laugh even harder. Now we're in full-on head-thrown-back, stomach-holding hysterics. It feels so good to laugh.

After a minute or two, Soraida and I manage to get enough of a grip to continue with our pastelada duties.

Tía Lorna passes the pastel to Soraida, who then folds the parchment and banana leaf to form a neat little bundle. My job at the end of the line is to tie the bundle together with a string, looping it once across the long way and twice across the short way.

Abuela Milagros leaves her station to check on my technique and make sure the string is tight, so none of the masa will seep out while the pasteles are boiling. She inserts a finger between the string and the parchment, then tugs. When the tension holds, she says, "Bien hecho," patting my shoulder and giving me her most approving smile.

"I doubt Wilie can pick her up again this week," Tía Lorna tells Mami. "He had to close the garage early to get her today. His boss wasn't happy." She shoots me a shaming look across the table, as if I didn't feel guilty enough already.

"What about Carlitos?" Mami asks.

Soraida and I exchange a knowing glance. Tía will never go for that.

"I don't think so," Tía Lorna is quick to say. "Practice is all the way on the other side of town. After that, he needs to come straight home, eat his dinner, take a shower, and do his homework.

Bendito, that poor boy works so hard. I can't keep making things more difficult for him."

Mami bites her lower lip, and I can tell she's holding back. We both love Carlos, but we don't think the sun rises and sets on his Boricua ass.

"Can you wait at the McDonald's again, until your tío or I get off work?" Mami asks.

I nod.

"And no eating until you get home," Tía adds, "you hear?"

"Wait, didn't that girl offer to give you a ride home?" Soraida says.

"What girl?" Mami asks.

Soraida opens her mouth to say God knows what, but before she can speak, I kick her under the table. If Tía Lorna finds out I got detention because I followed the advice of a white girl, I'll never hear the end of it.

"It's no one," I say dismissively. Then, with a voice that reeks of resignación, I add, "I'll wait at McDonald's. It's fine, really."

The moment the words leave my mouth, I hate myself for saying them. None of this is fine.

CHAPTER SIX

RUBY

I'm up before dawn to make Nana's birthday breakfast. I mix in the blueberries and pour batter onto the griddle, doing my best to create a cute heart-shaped form. I watch through the window as the sun rises over the river, remembering all those summer mornings when Nana woke up early to make pancakes for me and Olive. She managed all sorts of designs: hearts, smiley faces, and the first letters of our names.

Back then, I never imagined I'd live full-time in Nana's house—it was the sprawling, old, enchanted mansion where my summer days unfolded slowly, lazy like the river. It was so different from my home in Seattle, all angles and clean lines, modern furniture and walls of windows.

Now I sleep every night in the canopy bed that was my summer nest. I study physics in the same window seat where I once curled up to read the entire Baby-Sitters Club series.

With Mom and Dad away, the house is so quiet that I hear the creak of the floorboards when Nana begins to stir. I check the pancakes and reshape one with the spatula, until it at least vaguely resembles a heart. Then I flip it onto a plate where I've already sliced a wedge of cantaloupe and artfully arranged a couple of strawberries with a thin coating of powdered sugar. I balance a glass of orange juice on the plate and head upstairs to Nana's bedroom.

When I get to her room, she's already out on her balcony. I often find her here in the mornings when I come upstairs to say goodbye before school. I set the plate on a table and pull the phone from my pocket to video-call with Dad. He answers, sitting cuddled up with Mom on the deck of a rented bungalow on some island in Indonesia. Each of them is holding a glass of something fruity, and both are quite literally glowing with happiness.

Once Nana got well and I survived my first year at Orange Grove, my parents set off on an extended second honeymoon. Mom and Dad have always been open about how much they love each other, but if their cheesy behavior on our calls is any indication, all the public nuzzling and kissing has really amped up since they left for their trip.

"We're ready to sing," Mom calls out as Dad elaborately clears his throat.

"Is Olive calling in?" I ask.

"She had to get to school early today to run a meeting," Mom replies.

"Someone from the Atlanta mayor's office is coming in to learn about a new program she set up at the school," Dad gushes, beaming ear to ear. "So she'll call Nana this afternoon."

Olive moved to Atlanta right after college to do Teach for America in an underserved middle school. When the program ended, she switched to a different school in the area—one with even lower test scores, even more issues. I'm pretty sure she's running the place by now.

"Cool. Let's sing!" I say, hoping to avoid a long discussion of Olive's countless successes while Nana's pancakes get cold.

I light the candle stuck inside the brass turtle-shaped candle-holder that I (finally!) found at Fans & Stoves, and I use my hip to push open the French doors leading out to the balcony.

Nana is standing at the railing, looking across the river.

"Happy birthday to you!" All three of us sing at the top of our lungs, painfully out of tune. Nana turns to face us and smiles broadly as I make my way toward her. She pulls in a deep breath of air and blows out the candle with ease. It's hard to believe that just a year ago, Nana was incapacitated, out of breath from sitting up in bed.

And now here she is, preparing to climb back on a four-wheeler and ride along the shoreline for hours, marking off turtle nests with heavy stakes. In the heat of summer, she'll be on her hands and knees, digging deep craters, releasing trapped hatchlings from the wet sand.

Nana takes my phone and holds it at a distance. My parents ask Nana if I'm "behaving," and then all three of them laugh, as if this is an absurd question. Dad cracks some joke about how challenging it is to raise a teenager, and Nana replies that she's fairly certain I'm the one "raising" her.

"Indeed," I break in, "which is why we need to say goodbye. I have to feed her breakfast and clean the kitchen before seven-thirty, or else I'll be late for school."

"Yes, ma'am." Dad salutes from across the screen. "The captain has spoken!"

Mom plops down onto his lap and blows a kiss toward me and Nana. "We love you, Ruby, even when you're super bossy!"

"We don't use that word anymore, Mom," I say. "It's the other b-word."

"That's right, Ruby," Dad calls out. "You're not bossy. You're a leader—a woman in charge. Don't you let anyone forget it!"

Dad says stuff like that a lot these days. His enthusiasm is sweet, but I also find it sort of exhausting. Mom, though. She eats it right up. She wraps her arms around Dad's waist and nuzzles her chin on his shoulder.

"I love you," I say, my voice lilting with fake cheerfulness. "Even when you're super disgusting."

I wave goodbye and hang up, then shove the phone in my back pocket while Nana eases into a chair beside her breakfast tray. "So," I ask, "how does it feel to be seventy-eight?"

She dumps syrup over her pancake, enough to make both it and the strawberries swim.

"As sweet as maple syrup," she announces, running her finger across the plate and sticking it in her mouth.

"Hey," I ask, "do you notice anything different about my outfit today?"

She grimaces and looks me over, head to toe. "The cutoff shorts definitely are not different." She shakes her head slowly. "You wear those ratty old things at least twice a week."

"On top?" I ask.

She pops a piece of cantaloupe into her mouth and chews slowly, inspecting my T-shirt. "You're wearing your favorite shirt again, so . . ."

She's got a point. I do love this shirt. It's black, fitted but not too fitted, and it has *Product of Women's Rights* written in cursive across the chest. I got it at the civil-rights museum when I went to visit Olive in Atlanta over the summer.

"Am I missing something?" Nana asks.

I stick out my chest a little and smooth down my shirt. "Well, actually, *I'm* missing something."

Nana squints. "Go and get my glasses from the bedside table, sweetheart. That should help."

I can't help but laugh. "Oh my God, Nana. I'm not wearing a bra. Do you really need your glasses to see that?"

She joins in the laughter. "Oh, sweetie. I'm gonna need my magnifying glass for that!"

Nana's got a point. I have been blessed with a seriously flat chest—like, ironing-board flat. Since I got it from her, she's always quick to remind me how convenient this is: *No lower back problems for us! And you'll never get saggy.* She's also fond of reminding me: *So many of my friends have had to pay for surgery to make theirs smaller. Think of all the pain and money these little girls save us!*

"And *why* have you decided to forgo the bra?" she asks when her laughter finally subsides.

"It's a long story," I tell her, gathering up her empty plate and utensils to take to the kitchen, "and I want you to hear every sordid detail." I head toward the stairs through the French doors. "I'll tell you the whole thing at dinner, okay?"

"Ohhh, I love sordid details," Nana exclaims. "Can't wait for dinner."

In truth, Nana's genes are serving us both well. She looks to be about twenty years younger than most of her peers—even after the surgery. I have the long, lean body of a runner, despite the fact that I quit running entirely when we moved to Florida. (It's way too hot.)

Today, though, I'm wishing my little grapes would stick out a bit more. *Should I put on a tighter shirt?* But that would defeat the point.

Oh, pluck it. I'm just gonna stick with *Product of Women's Rights.*

———

I guess after this morning's conversation with Nana, I should have known it would come to this. It's the end of sixth period, and my braless chest has gone entirely unnoticed all day. I've had to take matters into my own hands.

I'm standing in front of Nurse Ratched, smoothing my hands over my shirt.

"See?" I ask her. "Do you see what I'm *not* wearing?"

Nurse Ratched sighs and leans back in her desk chair. "Ruby, is this really necessary?"

I thrust my chest out and shimmy my shoulders, which elicits little from my tiny boobs and nothing from Nurse Ratched, except another deep sigh.

"Honestly, Ruby, I'm having a hard time seeing what you're getting at."

I guess I should have gone with a different shirt after all.

"Do you need to bring Doris in?" I ask, pulling my shirt tight across my body. "Maybe have her take a closer look?"

"That's enough!" she exclaims, clearly exasperated. "What exactly are you trying to prove?"

"It's really more of an experiment than a proof," I say, making sure that my shoulders are held high. "My hypothesis is that the dress code does not, in fact, uniformly penalize people because of the clothing they choose to wear or not wear—"

"Get to the point, Ruby," Nurse Ratched interrupts, shuffling through papers on her desk. "Coach Simpson is sending over a freshman with a twisted ankle."

"My point is that I should get detention too, even though my boobs don't jiggle. Right?"

She braces her hands on her desk and stands.

"I'm too busy for this nonsense," she snaps. "It's time for you to leave my office."

"Wait!" I say. "You're really not gonna give me detention? I'm not wearing a bra!"

"You want detention?" Nurse Ratched calls out, clearly annoyed as hell with me. "I'll give you detention!"

She picks up her phone and sternly points me toward the door.

Looks like, fourteen months into my Orange Grove Experience, I've finally earned my way into that quintessential high school rite of passage, the one my old high school didn't even have, the one in pretty much every movie or TV show, the one where *all* the magic happens.

I'm heading to detention! I can't wait to tell Nana.

CHAPTER SEVEN

MALENA

I'm sitting in detention. Me. Malena Malavé Rosario, straight-A honor student, never-gets-in-trouble Malena, sitting in detention— for a second day.

God, how did I get here?

And what's worse, unlike yesterday, I have no idea when I'm getting home. For the next three afternoons, I'm supposed to wait at the McDonald's across the street until Mami or Tío Wiliberto can pick me up, but neither has responded to my text to confirm who is coming today. It could be ten p.m. for all I know!

I wonder what time McDonald's closes. Even more pathetic would be having to wait on the curb.

I sigh over the book I'm reading, *Sister Outsider* by Audre Lorde. Ms. Baptiste said we should read it as a companion to a documentary about the author's life. Ironically, it contains an essay about finding your voice in the silence. The words on the page are heartfelt and poetic, meant to inspire. They feel miles away from my reality.

Ms. Baptiste asked us to write a paper connecting our favorite essay in the book to the documentary, but I'm having a hard time coming up with any good ideas.

I'm deep in my own thoughts when someone taps me on the shoulder.

I turn to find "that troublemaker white girl" (as Carlos calls her) pulling up a chair to sit next to me. Unfortunately, the library tables are shared. Why can't they just stick with individual desks?

Last night, Soraida, Carlos, and I sat in their backyard after dinner enjoying the last of Abuela's flan. Carlos went on a rant about how I couldn't trust "these well-meaning Americanas." He wouldn't drop it. He even went and found Ruby on social media, just so that he could prove his point—that she's an entitled brat. He seemed genuinely disappointed that all her recent posts were about how much she loves and admires her abuela, who apparently she's taking care of. It was kinda sweet, but Carlos wasn't buying.

"Hey, remember me? It's Ruby," she says in a low but eager voice.

I stare at her, puzzled. What is she doing in detention?

"I got detention too," she whispers. "I'm not wearing a bra. See?" Her lips press into a smile, as if this is *our* secret to share. I glance at her chest. The poor girl has a body like a surfboard. Abuela Milagros would call her a "flaca con pecho de plancha."

"What are you reading?" she asks, leaning toward me.

I show her the cover.

"Nice! Audre Lorde." An even broader smile takes over her face. "God, I love that book. My nana gave me a copy when I was like twelve."

My eyes cut to Mr. Ringelstein, the hundred-year-old librarian overseeing detention, but he's too busy sorting through yellowed catalog cards (which no one uses anymore) to notice.

"We're not allowed to talk," I mutter, turning back to the book and the essay I've yet to start working on. Maybe she'll get the message and leave me alone.

"Don't worry about him. Mr. Ringelstein doesn't care what we do in his library as long as we're not being super loud," Ruby assures me. "Listen, I'm sorry you got in trouble. But honestly, I think this is bigger than us."

"'Us'?" I ask, giving her a sideways glance and wondering where this conversation is going. *When did this become an "us" situation?*

"That's why I'm here," she says. "I came to school without a bra, paraded my chest in front of Nurse Ratched—"

"Who?"

"God, hasn't anyone seen that movie?" she says, hands flying in the air. "It's a classic."

I stare back, perplexed. Is she aware of how batty she comes across?

"Forget it. It doesn't matter," she says.

I look back at Mr. Ringelstein's desk, anxious that we're going to get caught. I don't need extra days in detention thanks to this girl. Clearly, she doesn't have a Tía Lorna in her life. I'll never hear the end of it if my sentence gets extended into next week. Not to mention the pick-up-schedule family drama that would ensue.

Mr. Ringelstein disappears behind a row of bookshelves, and I exhale the lump of breath I've been holding.

"My point is that Nurse Hopkins didn't even notice," she says, pressing her T-shirt against her chest for effect—like I said, a plancha. "So I insisted that she equally apply the dress code. And presto! Here I am."

It takes me a few moments to grasp what she's saying, mostly because it doesn't add up.

"Wait, you *asked* for detention?" My head tilts to the side in utter disbelief.

"I know it sounds bonkers," she says.

I nod. "Yes. Yes, it does."

Maybe Carlos is right about this girl.

"But hear me out." She pulls the *Orange Grove High School Dress Code* out of her backpack. "There's nothing here about not wearing a bra. So what they did to you is not only arbitrary, but it's totally unfair. Case in point: my boobs. It turns out they are not detention-worthy. I practically had to beg to get here." She points at her chest with both hands.

"Ruby . . ." I say her name tentatively. So far, listening to this girl has been nothing but problematic for me and inconvenient for my family. "I just want to finish my essay and figure out how I'm getting home. I already have enough to worry about."

Ruby sighs, her face falling in disappointment. "I just don't understand how you can let them do this to you. This . . . injustice." She leans in closer. "Didn't you feel humiliated? You must have felt something? Right? I mean, I know I would."

Her eyes bore into mine and I'm forced to look away. My stomach clenches, bending my body slightly into itself. Even my throat tightens, dry and rough as sandpaper. My arms slowly wrap each other at the elbows, level with my chest, forming a protective barrier of my own flesh.

How did you feel, Malena?

I keep my eyes set on the open book in front of me. The words swim on the page until they're impossible to read.

All this time, I've been waiting for someone to ask. Anyone.

Not even Mami really knows how I felt when the nurse ordered me to stand still so she could take stock of my breasts, and when I saw that look of revulsion on the secretary's face.

For as long as I live, I'll never forget the overpowering smell of bleach in that room, and the click-clack of the secretary's kitten heels against the white tile floor.

How did I feel?

Those wandering eyes . . . up and down my body. The dirty, interrogating stares, accusing me of having the wrong kind of body—forcing themselves on me. Implying that I'm indecent, vulgar, and shameless when they don't even know me. Thrusting *their* interpretation of this absurd dress code on me and giving me no say in the matter.

Until Ruby asked the question, I hadn't let myself acknowledge it.

How did I feel?

Violated.

A word I keep stuffing down, because what can be gained from speaking it aloud? It fills me with dread and self-doubt every time I think about it. Is it too strong a word? I don't know. All I know is that even though no one physically touched me, I've never felt like a victim in my own body—until now.

I wipe a rogue tear with the back of my hand and clear my throat.

"Malena, are you okay?" Ruby asks, gently touching my forearm with her hand.

"I'm fine," I assure her, rummaging inside my bag for my water bottle. When I find it, I twist the cap off and take a long swig, blinking away the onslaught of tears.

Don't cry, Malena. Maldita sea, don't cry.

I exhale, slowly releasing every bit of air inside my lungs.

"There's nothing we can do," I say. "My mom tried calling the AP, Dr. Hardaway, this morning. She said I should've stayed home." I scoff. "It's funny, because Mom didn't want me to miss school over something so stupid."

"It *is* stupid," Ruby says.

"But at the end of the day, they make all the rules and we have to follow. That's just the way it is. We don't have a say."

"I don't think that's true," Ruby says with a confidence I find myself envying.

I don't tell her that it feels easier to give up, even if I know what they did is not right. I am fighting so hard already, just to sort out the basics of this new life. Speaking up against the school's oppressive rules feels like an impossible task.

Even if I wanted to tell Dr. Hardaway and Nurse Hopkins how wrong they both are, I wouldn't know how. I'm not Malala from Pakistan or Joshua from Hong Kong. I'm Malena from Puerto Rico, and I've never protested anything in my life!

At Sagrado Corazón, I was student-council vice president and school-newspaper photographer. I was in theater club and played on the volleyball team. Sure, in religion class my hand shot up every time Hermana Dolores instructed us to "believe on faith." But that's different. Hermana Dolores paid attention to my probing questions. She made me feel heard, even when my classmates accused me of being an atheist.

Before María, I could speak up if I needed to—in a really loud voice. The kind of loud only found on an island painted in bright colors and set to the sound of tropical music. An island-girl kind of loud.

But here, that kind of loud feels out of place. I don't know how to be Puerto Rican me around all these people—white,

Black, Asian, even the Latinx kids who grew up in the States. They all seem to have life on the mainland figured out. Most of them walk down the halls brimming with confidence and purpose. Meanwhile, I can't seem to shake off this deep sense of . . . *otherness*. It's depressing.

"It took me an hour to take off all the tape," I confess, wincing at the memory of standing in front of my bathroom mirror, struggling to remove the evidence that yesterday ever happened.

"It's total bullsh—" Ruby throws her hand over her mouth. "Sorry, I'm trying not to cuss. I made this promise to my nana . . . ," she says, her hands taking up all the space between us. "But I digress. What I'm trying to say is this: Why do you get punished because your boobs are bigger than mine? What kind of dress code is that?" Red splotches appear around her neck as her voice grows dangerously loud. I glance up to see if Mr. Ringelstein has noticed, but he seems oblivious. "It's . . . it's . . . unconstitutional, if you ask me! They're not respecting our rights as women and as human beings."

While I wish she would pipe down a little, I find myself agreeing with everything she's saying, and I nod vigorously. *But how could I change things?*

At my old school, the most consequential change I spearheaded was moving our end-of-year dance from the gym to the ballroom of El San Juan Hotel. We had to raise the extra money, but it was a no-brainer. Everyone loved the new venue.

"You're right, I guess. But there's nothing I can do about it," I say, annoyed at the defeatist tone in my own voice. "I can't get into any more trouble. Dr. Hardaway said next time I'll get sent home. My mom will freak out." And my tía? I don't even want to imagine her response.

"Okay, let's think this through. . . ." Ruby's eyes get lost in the bookshelves behind me. They narrow slightly as a *hmm* leaves her mouth. "What about . . ." Her eyes turn into thin slits, as if she's trying to read something at a far distance. "I have an idea," she blurts. "A friend in Seattle—that's where I'm from, by the way—she runs a Girl Up Club. I used to be a proud member."

"I don't know what that is," I say, closing the book in front of me. It's obvious I'm not getting any work done.

"It's a girls' empowerment group. It's even backed by the United Nations," Ruby explains. "They don't have a chapter here. When I asked about it, Dr. Hardaway said I could join Teen Leaders of America, but it's not the same. I joined the Current Events Club instead—also not the same, but whatever."

She takes out her cell phone and searches for something I can't see. "Through Girl Up, I met this totally kick-ass girl, Lucinda."

Ruby pulls up a photo on Lucinda's profile. She's got ebony skin and wild purple hair, dark eyeliner, and big gold hoops hanging from her earlobes. She's wearing a black T-shirt that says FIGHT LIKE A GIRL in bold white letters.

"She seems really cool," I say.

"She is. Her mom is this big-time civil-rights lawyer in Seattle. Anyway, she ran the club at Eastlake, a massive public school. And she organized a huge campaign to change their dress code. Her mom helped her with the legal stuff."

Ruby offers me her phone and I scroll through Lucinda's photo feed. In one picture she's marching for human rights, in another for LGBTQ equality. Someone's captured her speaking through a megaphone while waving an electric-pink poster with *Bitches get shit done!* written across it.

I bet if Lucinda was in my situation, she'd know exactly what to do.

"I was at that march," Ruby says, pointing at a picture on the screen. "It was incredible."

I've never been to a march, so I don't say anything as I pass the phone back to her.

"I think she had to talk to the school board and stuff. I don't remember all the details. I'll reach out to her and ask what their strategy was."

"Maybe she can ask her mom?" I try to tamp down the apprehension bubbling up inside me. "We're just getting information, right? We're not doing anything yet. I need to think about this some more."

Ruby stops typing and looks at me.

"I want to see what our options are," she assures me. "Then we can talk about it and make a decision. You don't have to do anything you're not comfortable with."

"Okay." My lips turn into a reluctant smile. It hits me then how much I miss having friends at school. I love my cousins, but family can be so judgy sometimes.

"Can I see it? Your back, I mean."

I don't know why I agree to show her, but within seconds, I find myself hiding between two tall bookshelves in the back of the library and lifting the back of my shirt.

"Ouch," she says, wincing. "That looks super painful!"

"You have no idea," I say. "My mom had to engineer an undershirt bra for me."

"Okay if I take a picture?" she asks, phone in hand. "Lucinda always says, 'One picture is all it takes to make a point.' I want her to see this."

A voice inside my head—high-pitched like Tía Lorna's—warns me to stop this nonsense. Only trouble can come from going against the system. A system that is completely new to me.

I stare down at my shirt and my breasts. Do I want to make a point?

Do I want some kind of justice for what happened? For *every-thing* that's happened?

Maybe I'm tired of the resignacíon everyone says I should rely on. Maybe I don't want to resign myself to a life that feels so out of my control. Maybe I'm tired of others always calling the shots. Damn, even forces of nature have more control over my life than I do.

A fear, raw and primal, creeps up from the hollow of my stomach into my chest, ripping open my heart. If I don't do something, I will be lost forever. I will become a speck of dust floating in the universe, blown here and there by the winds of the next storm, never quite finding my life After María. Never again having a voice.

"Okay," I say, pulling my shirt higher—as high as it will go. I turn my head, looking back toward Ruby as she takes the picture.

"Now a selfie. I want Lucinda to meet you." Ruby stands next to me, and I stare at the phone stretched out at the end of her arm.

"You're not posting these online, right?" I ask, watching her thumbs fly across the phone screen.

"I'm just sending them to Lucinda. I want her to see how absurd it is that they made you put a bra over that. . . . Seattle's so dreary all the time, people forget what a sunburn looks like."

"Yeah, you should try lying out on a beach in Puerto Rico. Then you'll really know what a sunburn is," I say, and Ruby laughs.

"Give me your number," she tells me. "I'll text you when I hear back from her and we can talk some more."

We exchange numbers and walk back to the table.

My phone vibrates with an incoming text. It's Mami, saying she'll have to stay an extra hour at work, meaning I'll have to sit at McDonald's for three hours, give or take, depending on traffic. I groan in frustration. This will be my fate for the rest of the week.

"What's wrong?" Ruby asks.

"Nothing," I say, shoving my phone inside my bag.

"Is it something I can help with?" She leans in closer.

Part of me thinks she's already "helped" enough. I mean, her "helping" is the reason I'm stranded after school every day this week. But another part of me is wondering if she was serious when she offered to give me a ride. Or was she just feeling guilty at the time?

"My mom has to work late," I say.

"Oh," she exclaims, "I can take you home. It's the least I can do."

"Really? Are you sure?" I don't even try to moderate the excitement in my tone.

She nods, smiling.

I smile too, pulling the phone from my bag to text Mami that I got a ride. I add an *I'll explain tonight* in anticipation of the twenty questions I know are coming.

She just sends me a thumbs-up. She must be really busy.

"I still feel bad for what happened. Even if it wasn't my fault . . . or yours, for that matter," Ruby says.

I shrug. "It was a no-win situation."

"Tell that to your cousin," she says, shaking her head.

"Soraida? She thinks it's my own fault for having big boobs." I scoff. "Never mind that we're both the same size."

"No, I mean Mr. Sporty Balls."

I can't help but laugh. "Carlos?"

"Yeah, him. God, I don't know how you put up with him. He is so . . . so . . . insufferable!"

"Wow. I've never heard anyone call him that." I relish the sour expression on her face. It's oddly refreshing coming from a girl at this school. Knowing that she's not swooning over Carlos—like everyone else—makes me respect her a little more.

"The way he was standing there, squeezing that ball. Who does he think he is?"

I shrug. "He can be a little intense, but he means well."

"A little intense?" Ruby huffs. "He must be impossible to live with."

I'm trying to decide whether to come to Carlos's defense when Mr. Ringelstein leaves his desk and starts turning off the lights in the back of the library.

"Time to go," Ruby says, swinging her backpack over her shoulder. "Hey, let's stop for ice cream. I know this fabulous place nearby. As my nana always says, 'You can't buy happiness, but you can buy ice cream.'"

"Words to live by," I say in mock solemnity. "I can't stay out too late, though. I have to write an essay." I grab my own bag and hold it to my side. My skin is still too raw to carry it against my back.

"Do you want to bounce some ideas off of me? I've read that book like a hundred times."

"That would be awesome."

I feel relief wash over me, and it's not just because I get to avoid McDonald's. I am truly excited to share ice cream and talk books with someone. Soraida is more into smut novels, the kind she has to hide under her mattress so Tía Lorna won't find them. She let me borrow one called *The Highlander Love Curse*. I cringed when reading about the main characters doing it on top of a horse, and in an open field where anyone could see! There is no way Soraida and I are talking about *her* books.

"I'm dying to know how Lucinda reacts to those pictures," Ruby says, glancing down at her phone as we leave the library. "I hope she texts me back while we're hanging out."

It dawns on me then what I've done. Did I really just allow this girl to send half-naked photos of me to a complete stranger on the other side of the country?

What was I thinking?

As we walk out together, I tell myself that it was only one text. To one person. No big deal.

CHAPTER EIGHT

RUBY

My notifications are blowing up.

I roll out of bed, trying to remember what I posted yesterday that could have gotten this much attention. All I can remember is a goofy thrift-shop selfie modeling fedoras with Topher and a couple of reposts. I mean, the selfie was cute and all, but . . .

1,345 notifications.

Holy crap.

Plopping down on my purple shag rug, I start scrolling through. The first thing I see is that selfie I took of Malena and me, posted next to the photo of Malena's sunburned back.

What the living hell?

I scroll up, trying to find the original post.

Lucinda.

Insult to injury? Hurricane Maria evacuee @malenamalavePR has 1st degree burns & gets in trouble for not wearing bra to @OrangeGroveFLHigh. Her friend @rubyroobs goes w/o bra & nobody says a word. #dresscoded #dontdistracttheboys #brownbodiesrepresent

It went up at eight-thirty last night, West Coast time, eleven-thirty my time. I was already deep in dreamland.

Her post has a bunch of replies from random people:

> Fight the power @rubyroobs!

> #DressCodes are obsolete

> Stop shaming girls! #femalebodiesarebeautiful

I'm watching the reactions roll in. I've never seen anything like it. Well, there was that one time when Nick Jonas posted a pic of his abs and he broke the internet. But I've never seen this reaction for a mere mortal. Yeah, I'm into Nick Jonas. He's been with me since I discovered *Camp Rock* at the tender age of eight, and I just can't seem to let him go. (I guess that should have been an early indicator that Olive's indie music wasn't for me.) Since Topher, Jo, and Nessa are total music snobs, I mostly keep my deep and abiding love for everything Nick Jonas to myself.

This may not be as big as Nick's perfect abs, but still, there are so many replies and reposts that I don't even know where to start. I stare at the phone, watching the numbers grow exponentially.

Lucinda's a genius.

I decide to hit DMs first, since there's a reasonable—not totally overwhelming—number of them. The first is from Lucinda, sent around midnight.

> I just jump-started your Orange Grove revolution.
> You can thank me later! Let's talk strategy tomorrow.
> #Girlpower

Then I come across one that leaves me breathless.

> Hi, Ruby. I'm Calista Jameson from Wired for Women.
> I'm very interested in this story. Can we talk?

Oh my freaking God! Calista freaking Jameson! Her short film about the Women's March was an instant classic! The F-Word, her *Wired for Women* column, gets like a million hits. That woman tells it like it is.

And she just followed me. Me! Jo and Nessa are gonna freak out. They are obsessed with her.

I start my reply to Calista.

Hi! How are you? I type. That sounds so stupid. What am I, a second grader? I delete the message and try to start over.

Oh crappity crap! What do I say? How do I respond to a living, breathing feminist icon?

I jump to my feet and begin pacing across the carpet. Then it comes to me: I need to tell Malena. I promised I wouldn't do anything without consulting her first. I promised I wouldn't post the pictures.

Oh my God, she's gonna kill me.

Maybe she knows who Calista Jameson is. Is Calista famous in Puerto Rico? If she is, Malena can't possibly be mad. She'll be freaking out like me! Maybe we can talk to her together. Ooohh, maybe even a video call!

My mind races through all the possibilities, until it flashes back to Malena's face after I asked to take the photo. She seemed so timid, so reluctant, when I told her we needed to make a plan. It's probably her family—that obnoxious baseball cousin and the overenthusiastic girl.

I text Malena.

> Need to talk. Urgent. I'll be in senior lot in 20.

No response.

I head to the closet and pull on my favorite flowery sundress. No bra, of course.

Still no response from Malena.

I throw on some sandals and head out the door.

And then I remember—I haven't even brushed my teeth.

I need to find some chill. How am I going to lead the revolution when I can't even remember basic personal hygiene?

—

The moment Mr. Sporty Balls pulls into the lot in that huge SUV, I run to meet Malena. I catch her eye in the window, but she looks away, like she wants nothing to do with me.

Okay, so this is not exactly how I expected Malena to react.

We had so much fun last night, diving into our melting triple-scoop waffle cones, making fun of the seventies soundtrack that was piped into MaggieMoo's. When "Da Ya Think I'm Sexy?" got going, we started lip-synching the singer's weird raspy voice, wriggling our hips in the plastic booth. By the end of the song, we were laughing so hard that mint chocolate chip almost spewed out of my nose.

It was the most fun I've had in a long while.

And now, twelve hours later, she can't even look at me. What happened?

"Hey, I tried texting you," I say as she gets out of the car. "Did you see your feed?"

Malena looks directly at me and nods her head slowly. "You promised. You said you wouldn't post those pictures."

Her face is puffy, and her eyes are ringed with red.

"Why would you do that?" she asks quietly.

"I didn't—"

I struggle to subdue all the excitement and adrenaline coursing through my body. It takes me a second to form a reply.

"I didn't know till this morning. Lucinda just did it. She didn't ask me," I try to assure her. "Please don't be mad. She thought she was helping."

Carlos and Soraida get out of the car and come to stand on either side of Malena. Soraida's reaction is hard to read. But I can sense Carlos's glare on my skin. It's like he's sending searing laser-beam *stay away from my cousin* signals through his eyes.

I will myself to ignore the strange burning sensations on my skin—to stay focused on Malena.

"Why would she do that?" Malena asks, her voice defeated.

She has a point. Lucinda never asked her permission, and I guess I could have been more clear that the picture was for her eyes only. I shouldn't be surprised, really. I've known Lucinda for a few years, and this is simply how she gets things done. It's a bold move, yes. But her bold moves make change happen. I'm on the verge of explaining all of this to Malena when Carlos interrupts the conversation.

"What, exactly, makes you think you have the right to post half-naked pictures of my cousin for the world to see?" Carlos steps forward to loom over me, his face six inches from mine.

I stumble back, wishing I weren't intimidated by him. But even though his voice carries the same infuriating calm it had during our last parking-lot rendezvous, I can tell he's super pissed. More pissed, even, than last time.

"I didn't post anything," I respond, defensive. "My friend Lucinda did it. And you should be *happy* for Malena—a famous reporter wants to tell her story." I thrust my hand to my hip, trying hard to stay in control. "She's going to get the justice she deserves."

"Justice?" Carlos looks over to Malena, whose face is buried in her phone. "Do you hear this girl, Malena?"

Malena doesn't respond. She seems intent on reading whatever has popped up on her screen.

"She messaged you, too, Malena. Did you see it? Calista Jameson?"

"I totally saw it," Soraida busts in. "That lady has, like, a half million followers." Soraida turns to look at Carlos. Her voice is high and excited. She seems almost as ecstatic as I felt ten minutes ago. At least somebody gets it.

"Malena got a thousand new followers overnight," Soraida exclaims. "She's gonna be, like, famous!"

"I think you mean *infamous*," Carlos grumbles.

Who knew Mr. Sporty Balls had such refined vocabulary?

"No." I shake my head. "You're completely wrong. We're getting all kinds of support. Everyone's one hundred percent behind us."

"Is that so?" Carlos asks, his voice all patronizing and haughty.

"Yes, that *is* so," I say, trying to match his tone. "Have you even read the messages?"

I scroll through my feed.

"'You go, girl! Fight the power! Take down Orange Grove High and its BS dress code!'" I keep reading, trying to make Carlos understand how amazing all of this is.

I look up from my phone. Carlos watches me, eyebrows arched. He appears unimpressed.

"I mean," I continue, "there are a couple of stupid ones. Like:

'Rubyroobs frees the boobs'—ha! Someone made a hashtag: RoobsFreesTheBoobs."

Soraida guffaws. Malena stares at her feet. And Carlos? He just keeps staring at me, stone-faced.

I forge ahead, hoping that if I bring some humor into the situation, it might help dissipate the mounting tension. "It's clever, that hashtag. I've got to admit it. Oh, and then there's *this* lovely one," I say sarcastically. "'Hey, rubyroobs, where are *your* boobs?'" I look up and grin. Because what else am I supposed to do?

"Well, that's just adorable, Ruby," Carlos says.

Condescending asshole.

"Now, why don't you let Malena read a few from her feed?"

Malena looks up, like a deer in headlights. "What?" she asks, stunned. We all turn to look at her.

"Go on," Carlos urges her. "Read her some of your messages."

"I can't even . . . ," she whispers, letting her phone drop to her side. Her eyes fill with tears.

Oh my God, I think she's about to cry. What is going on?

"Carlos, you need to back off," Soraida hisses. "Not cool."

"Just give me the phone, Malena." Carlos reaches out, his palm open.

Malena steps back, shoulders hunched and eyes downcast.

This is all incredibly confusing. If Calista messaged Malena, too, and if Malena's notifications are also blowing up, why isn't she excited?

Soraida and I both watch in silence as Carlos steps toward Malena.

"Please," he says, his voice—remarkably—shifting into an almost gentle tone. He touches her shoulder softly and waits for her response.

Malena looks at his hand on her shoulder and then up to his face, her eyes expectant. "Are you sure?" she asks.

He nods and squeezes her shoulder.

"It's okay," he says. "It'll be okay. I promise."

I study them, surprised to feel a wave of tenderness pass through me. Carlos may be an ass, but he and Malena care about each other. There's no denying that.

Malena looks over to Soraida and she nods encouragingly.

I'm still trying to work out my complicated reaction when Malena hands Carlos the phone. He waits, holding the phone while she climbs into the back seat of his SUV. Soraida slides in next to her. Malena pulls her knees into her chest, making herself smaller, and Soraida wraps her arms around her.

I step forward to try comforting her, even though I'm not sure what's causing her distress, but Carlos stops me.

"Let's go." He nods toward the back of the SUV. His voice is less stony, more human.

When we've rounded the corner and are out of Malena's sight, he thrusts the phone into my hand. "Just read, okay?"

I take Malena's phone and start to read.

> You can distract this boy any day,
> @malenamalavePR—DM me!

"Oh my God," I gasp at the phone. "She's fifteen, you disgusting perv."

He lets out a sigh, but he doesn't respond. I keep scrolling.

> If you don't wanna get #dresscoded
> @malenamalavePR, go back to your own country!!!

> One more reason not to let immoral refugees
> in! Go home, @malenamalavePR #valuesvoter
> #americanvalues

"Go back to your own country? They're sick *and* stupid!"

"Yeah," Carlos whispers, his voice defeated. "You need to keep reading."

> Thank you @OrangeGroveFLHigh for maintaining
> high moral standards. Keep up the good work!!!!!!
> Keep out the bad influences!!!!! #traditionalvalues

> @OrangeGroveFLHigh should expel both of them!
> #Adiosamigos #sendthemhome #buildthewall

"Build the freaking wall?" I exclaim, not looking up from Malena's phone. "Where, exactly? In the Atlantic Ocean or the Caribbean? And why would anybody build a wall to block one part of the U.S. from another?"

I look up at Carlos. He's leaning against the SUV, lips pursed. He clears his throat. "There's more."

His words aren't accusing anymore. Instead, he sounds genuinely worried.

I look back at the phone and take in two more:

> Take it ALL off @malenamalavePR

> TURN AROUND @malenamalavePR—We wanna
> see that sexy #brownbody

"Enough," I say. I don't think I meant to say it out loud. My head is spinning and my gut contracts. I'm gonna be sick. It's not *enough*. It's too much. And it's my fault Malena's being barraged with all of this horrible stuff.

I suck in a long, deep breath and exhale slowly. "Who *are* these sick bastards?"

Carlos shrugs and shakes his head. "I don't know, Ruby. And, honestly, I'm not gonna waste my energy on them and their nonsense." His jaw clenches tight. "But I'll tell you this. I don't want those predators and white supremacists anywhere near my cousin."

"I'm sorry," I whisper. "I'm really sorry this is happening. I promise I didn't mean for her picture to be posted. We just reached out to get Lucinda's advice. We were just wanting . . ."

I let myself look directly at him. My gaze finds his, and his eyes aren't shooting laser beams of anger anymore. Not at all. They're dark and sad, almost vulnerable.

Carlos watches me. "Wanting what?"

I feel my heart start to sputter and my tear ducts tingle.

Oh my God. I'm going to cry. He's staring right at me and I'm going to cry. This is *not* about me. This is *not* the moment for tears!

So I turn away from his surprising eyes, and I launch full-force into one of my nervous rants.

"Wanting what? I don't know, Carlos. But definitely not this!" I say, pointing wildly toward Malena's phone. My head falls into my hand as I hold the phone in my outstretched arm. "I mean, it's not my fault that misogynist, racist, and massively uninformed dumbasses troll the internet." I'm shaking the phone, as if the uninformed dumbasses are actually inside it, and if I shake it hard enough, maybe they'll fall out and run away to hide—like the cowards that they are.

Carlos raises his palms in front of me, urging me to calm

down. I think he's worried I might accidentally hurl the phone across the parking lot.

"But, yeah," I sigh, letting the hand holding Malena's phone drop to my side. "I'll admit it's kinda my fault that this post exists."

"Yes," Carlos replies. "It is." His eyes fall shut and he lets out a long breath. Then he looks right at me, shaking his head slowly from side to side. "And I have no freaking clue why," he says, still shaking his head, "but Malena seems to think you know what you're doing. She won't deal with this situation until she talks to you." He awkwardly clears his throat. "So here's the simple fact: I wanna tell you to get the hell out of all our lives, but I'm gonna have to ask for your help instead."

I nod. I think there was a huge insult in his comment, but also, honestly, this feels like progress.

"I mean," he continues, pursing his lips, "just to get past this situation, and then you can get the hell out of our lives."

So, maybe not as much progress as I hoped for. But I can work with this. I'm totally fine with Carlos and me being out of each other's lives—forever!—but Malena? Maybe if I can help her figure out a way through this, we can get back to where we were last night—back to becoming friends.

"Right," I say, nodding once. "Let's fix this."

"How are you gonna fix it, Ruby?" he asks, incredulous. His eyes find mine again. Gaze steady and strong. But his brow furrows and his lips press together.

I feel myself shrug, and then immediately get mad at myself for making such a defeated gesture. Malena trusted me. Carlos wants my help. I need to step up. But really, how do you fix something like this?

"We have to talk to Malena."

Carlos nods in agreement, and we walk around to the back

seat of the SUV. He opens Malena's door. We stand side by side watching as Soraida comforts Malena, cooing soft words in Spanish and brushing her fingers through her hair. Carlos grabs the phone from me, then reaches down to take Malena's hand.

"We're gonna figure this out," he says.

I feel like an intruder, an outsider. I'm cutting into a family moment. But then Malena looks up at me, expectant.

What am I supposed to say?

"We can delete your account," Carlos says quietly to Malena. "We'll end it—right here and now."

"Are you nuts?" Soraida snaps, gesturing toward Malena's phone. "She's probably picked up two dozen new followers in the last three minutes. This could be big. Malena could *be* someone."

"Malena," Carlos says softly, "you don't need to put yourself through this. You don't need to put Tía Camila through this—or Tío Alberto. Just end it."

He looks at me again, those big worried eyes boring right into my soul.

"Right, Ruby?" he asks.

I find myself in the very unusual position of not knowing what's right, not sure which one of her cousins Malena should listen to. Soraida wants Malena to grab on to this moment and use it to amplify her voice. Carlos doesn't want her to get any more hurt than she already has been. And as much as I've wanted to dismiss him as a paternalistic bastard, it's so clear that he cares about her. Honestly, I sort of see his point.

I want Malena to fight back.

I want her to *want* to fight back.

But I also want her to feel safe.

Malena deserves to feel safe.

So I lean in and ask her, "What do *you* want to do, Malena?"

CHAPTER NINE

MALENA

It took me all day to form the words: "No me puedo quedar callada." Now, as I stand in our apartment's kitchen, my decision comes out clear and firm for Mami to digest. I can't stay silent.

This primal fear is tearing me apart from the inside: if I don't find my voice now, it will be lost forever.

It's like Ms. Baptiste always says: "Story is power. If you don't own your narrative, someone else gets to frame it to suit their agenda." I get that now. If anything, those online trolls gave me a real-life example.

I want to choose how to tell my own story. I want to hold that power.

Sure, those nasty social-media messages knocked the wind out of me. But I can't give those people—especially ignorant asshats who don't even know Puerto Rico is part of the United States—any power over me. I refuse to be a speck of dust they blow away with their hate-filled words.

"I have to do *something*," I say, pleading for Mami to understand.

Mami and I stand shoulder to shoulder, preparing dinner in our tiny kitchen.

I have to step aside so Mami can open the fridge. She pulls out a container of precooked onions and dumps them over a pan of chicken breasts. The marinated meat sizzles, filling the kitchen with the delicious smell of mojo and caramelized onions.

We've spent the last hour going over every detail of my day—minus the nasty posts. I don't want her to worry. I told her about Ruby, Lucinda, and Calista Jameson. How Ruby and I responded to Calista's message, but since we're both minors, she can't speak to us without the consent of a parent or guardian.

Ruby said it was my decision, but if I want to talk to Calista, she and her grandmother are all in. I bet her abuela thinks landing an interview with a top reporter is pretty awesome. Mami, though, is a different story.

"Mami, por favor," I implore. "You have to admit that what Dr. Hardaway and the nurse did is not right. I felt so . . . so . . ." I can't even say it.

Mami turns to look at me, waiting for me to finish my thought. I bite my lower lip, unable to form the one word I know captures exactly what I want to say.

Violated.

When it's clear I can't say it aloud, Mami reaches for my shoulder and gives it a squeeze.

"I get it, nena, but talking to a reporter just seems so extreme. Maybe I can try meeting with Dr. Hardaway in person."

"How is that going to be any different than your phone conversation? She made you feel like an irresponsible parent, which is total crap."

Mami called Dr. Hardaway the morning after the panty-liners. In the same controlled tone she sometimes uses with her injured patients, she told Dr. Hardaway that her daughter was not a troublemaker and did not deserve four days of detention. Dr. Hardaway just referred her to the same stupid dress-code booklet they gave me and followed up with an email outlining how parents should become more involved in the school. I read the email over Mami's shoulder. Whoever wrote it had no notion of working parents.

A heavy, tired silence stifles all the air in the kitchen. Our eyes meet and I can see a full range of conflicting emotions on her face. I think she wants to protect me but doesn't know how. I can't really fault her for that when we are still trying to sort out everyday things like paying bills, buying new furniture, getting cable, and finding a good laundromat, while also adjusting to the "American" way of life, with all its rules and regulations.

The concept of time is a perfect example. Our internal clock is still ruled by island time. On the Island, things happen when they happen—when the time is right. There's a slow, organic rhythm to life that must be respected.

Here, everyone expects us not to *waste* time. Or to be *on time* for everything. We learned this the hard way during our second week in Orange Park. Mami and I arrived fifteen minutes late for a haircut appointment, and the front-desk lady—a middle-aged woman with bright lilac hair—made us reschedule. When Mami asked if she could just cancel, the woman threatened to charge us the full price of the appointment, which Mami had reserved using her credit card.

I mean, how was this our fault? Mami took a wrong turn and we ended up on the interstate at the height of rush hour. Did this woman expect us to part traffic like Moses in the Red Sea? I don't get it.

It only made me long for home, for Gladys Beauty Salón,

where there are no set appointments and a haircut is a day-long affair of special conditioning treatments, trashy magazines, cafecitos, and the shiniest straight blowout anywhere on the Island.

After that fiasco, Mami vowed to find Orange Park's version of Gladys Beauty Salón. I hope she succeeds.

I watch Mami inhale deeply, her shoulders rising as the air fills every tiny vacuole in her lungs. She's still in her scrubs, but she's undone the bun she normally wears to the hospital. Her curls fall in waves around her soft, round face. Mami always looks prettier with her hair down—younger, even.

"I really, really want to do this, Mami," I say for the twelfth time. "I think it's important. I want to talk to the reporter."

Mami reaches for a spoon to taste the tomato sauce in a pot of garbanzo beans. "Pass me the salt and get a little cilantro, too," she says.

I reach inside a top cabinet to find the saltshaker. Then I walk outside to pick leaves off the cilantro plant we're growing in a potted herb garden. Our apartment doesn't have a balcony— another thing we couldn't afford in Florida—so the stoop by our front door is the only sunny option. Such a sad substitute for our beautiful rooftop garden back home, where Mami and I grew all kinds of herbs, exotic orchids, fragrant dama de noche, and vibrant amapolas. But with Papi working in the mountains, and no one to care for our place—not to mention the lack of running water—I'm sure our plants are all dead.

Back in the kitchen, Mami has traded the stove for her laptop. Her browser displays the *Wired for Women* website and Calista Jameson's column.

"Ruby told me she's a really famous feminist writer," I say. "Thousands of people read her posts every month."

Mami doesn't respond. Instead, she scrolls down the page, clicking on random articles, speed-reading the contents.

When the chicken begins to hiss, she closes the laptop and moves back to the stove. Mami's chicken breasts are always seared to perfection, browned just enough to hold in every ounce of natural juice.

"What if the school retaliates?" she asks, grabbing a piece of chicken with a pair of tongs and resting it on a plate. "I don't want your record tarnished over this. A suspension doesn't look good on a college application."

"What about my First Amendment rights? Freedom of speech," I'm quick to say, remembering something Lucinda said during our call earlier today.

After I'd had the morning to process the disgusting posts, Ruby and I met for lunch and called Lucinda. Lucinda apologized and explained that she'd misunderstood Ruby's message. She'd thought we wanted her to *do* something. So she did. She also told me I could report and block all the creeps on social media and set my accounts to private.

Soraida scrubbed my feed clean so I wouldn't have to reread the posts. She also convinced me that it was better to keep it public, in case any more reporters wanted to talk to us.

"The First Amendment?" Mami raises an eyebrow, slightly amused.

"We checked with Ms. Brown, Lucinda's mom. She's a civil-rights lawyer. She said that schools use dress codes to shame girls and unfairly target minorities." I peer at my phone, reading the notes I took during our phone conversation. I knew that if I wanted a shot at convincing Mami to let me do this interview, I'd have to present an airtight case.

"Lucinda got in trouble a couple of years ago because her

baggy shirt slipped off her shoulder during chemistry class. A male teacher pulled her out of class because he felt uncomfortable and the principal sent her home. She and her mom fought to change the dress code and they won. They've done this before. Successfully."

Mami doesn't look impressed. She takes the lid off a pot full of white rice and dips in a serving spoon to turn the cooked grains from the bottom up. "The rice is ready" is all she says.

I keep pushing, undeterred. I'm not letting this go. I *can't* let this go.

A few days after María, when she told me we were staying in Florida, I was too overwhelmed to fight. I remember scrolling through a feed on my phone as Mami and I waited for our order at the Chick-fil-A drive-through. The photos of people, young and old, standing by flattened homes and torn buildings didn't feel real. When we finally got our chicken sandwiches, I felt guilty, holding a hot meal in my hands. It was all too much to take in at once.

If there's one thing I've learned from María, it's that life isn't fair. There's injustice everywhere. Just look at all the people back home who worked themselves to the bone their whole lives, saved money, and made sacrifices, only to have their homes ripped apart by a storm. And, to top it off, have the U.S. government treat us like we are second-class citizens. Like we asked for it, because people couldn't afford to reinforce their roofs, or buy a cistern or a generator.

How does that saying go? When God closes a door, he opens a window? Well, the door was blown shut by María. And I couldn't argue with Mami for wanting to stay here. In a way, our move to Florida was a long time coming, after Tía Lorna resettled half our family here.

Now it's like Ruby just opened a window for me. One that I didn't even know existed. And I'm going to hurl myself through it before it slams shut too. Otherwise I'll risk being trapped forever.

"We're not the first students this has happened to, Mami." I try to sound confident, even though that's not how I feel. "Ruby and I checked. It's happening all over the country. And girls are fighting back."

"I don't know, Malena." She shakes her head, ultra-focused on the rice. "We're so new here. I wouldn't even know how to help you. And I'm already so busy with work, and your dad is not here. . . . This is something we would normally discuss as a family."

"Papi would understand," I say quietly. *I know he would.*

"This all sounds like more than we can handle right now."

"Weren't you telling me to get more involved?" I argue. "That we need to make a new life here?"

"Yeah, but I was thinking more along the lines of the science club, not taking on the school administration." She moves away from the stove and pulls out two dinner plates and silverware.

"Calista is waiting on an answer, Ma. She wants to talk to us tonight."

Mami brings her thumb and index finger to her temples and presses as if she's trying to squeeze out a headache.

For a moment, I hate myself for giving her one more thing to worry about.

"I should've let you stay home that morning," Mami says with that air of resignación we can't seem to stop breathing. "We could've avoided all this."

We need some fresh air or we'll suffocate to death in a dark room. No doors. No windows.

"Lucinda's mom said you were right in sending me to school," I say. "And that the assistant principal was wrong to call me a distraction." I look down at my phone and read, " 'That mentality only deflects the conversation about what is mutually respectful behavior between boys and girls. It perpetuates the belief that girls' bodies are dangerous, and that harassment is inevitable. It puts the burden on the victim.' " I take a breath, proud of myself for getting through that whole spiel.

Mami releases the grip on her head and stares back at me, trying to suppress a smile. I know then that I've won her over.

"Okay . . . ," she finally says. "But I'm concerned that, once we go down this road, there's no turning back. You understand that, right?"

"Yes, I understand," I say. "But I want to do this. I want them to know that this is not right."

"All right," she says more intently. "We'll do the interview."

———

Ruby and her grandma arrive exactly an hour later.

Her abuela is nothing like I expected. She's wearing a flowy linen dress and gladiator sandals. A chunky turquoise necklace dangles from her neck. Her hair is the brightest shade of white I've ever seen—shocking white. Mami holds out her hand, but Ruby's abuela wraps her in a tight hug instead.

"I'm Ruby's grandmother, Joan," she says, pulling back and smiling.

She turns to me, and I say, "Hello, Mrs. McAlister."

"Oh, sweetheart"—she smiles big—"you call me Joan too."

Abuela Joan, I decide to call her. I don't want to sound disrespectful. We just don't call old people by their first name, and *Doña Joan* seems a little too stiff.

"I've heard so much about you, Malena," Abuela Joan says. "I'm so sorry for what your family has been through."

Mami utters a quiet thank-you. I'm not sure either of us knows whether she's referring to the hurricane or my bra fiasco. I guess we've been through a lot.

"Please sit," Mami says, gesturing to the lonely couch in our living room. "Can I offer you some sangría? Have you had dinner?"

"Sangría!" Abuela Joan exclaims. "What a treat! I'd love some. Ruby and I already had dinner—she made me a lovely salad, didn't you, Ruby?"

"I make a mean Caesar," Ruby says.

She's lingering in the middle of the living room, and I'm trying to imagine how she sees our new "home." There's not even enough furniture for all four of us to sit. I feel like I have to apologize or something. I wish they could've seen our beach condo in San Juan before the storm. On Sundays, the whole extended family would gather on our rooftop to toast the sunset and eat Papi's sancocho. It'll be a while before the cleanup crews clear out the sand and debris from the flooding.

I've already set up my laptop on the coffee table so that Mami and Abuela Joan can sit next to each other on the couch while Ruby and I sit at their feet on the floor. I had to think hard about the problem of nowhere to sit here in "the Lakeside Estates— where you can afford to dwell well!"

"Malena," Ruby says, "can you show me your room?"

"There's not much to see."

She cranes her head with eyes wide open and says, "You wanted to show me the, um, the view from the window? Remember?"

The view?

We traded our view of the Atlantic for an artificial lake with a fountain in the middle. At first I couldn't figure out why there was water spewing from the middle of the lake, but when the fountain broke for a couple of days, it all became clear. The fountain is not for decoration. It's to keep the water circulating, so that it won't turn to green, really gross-smelling, scum-covered sludge.

I shoot a puzzled glance her way and she looks back at me with an urgent expression in her eyes. And then I get it. She wants to talk.

"Oh yeah," I say sarcastically. "The fabulous lakeside view. Let's go check it out."

Mami eyes us suspiciously as I lead Ruby toward the hallway. But she's too busy entertaining Abuela Joan to ask any questions.

We head to my room and close the door behind us.

"How are you?" she asks, standing by the door.

I shrug. Tired. Anxious. Excited. All of the above? It's hard to discern.

"I've been so worried." She sighs. "All those horrible trolls and the disgusting stupid things they said to you. It's hard to let all that go, you know?"

Ruby sits on my bed, waiting for an answer that doesn't come. Her eyes land on a framed photo on my nightstand. It's Carlos, Soraida, and me cruising on the net of a catamaran at sunset. It was the best day.

Ruby reaches for the photo with one hand. "When was this?"

"In April," I say, trying to tamp down my longing for the Malena in that photo: confident, carefree, happy. "Soraida and I didn't want a traditional quinceañera, so instead we all went on a cruise to celebrate."

"I've never been on a cruise," Ruby says.

"We had a blast," I say, recalling the nights we spent wandering around the ship, free to do whatever we wanted while our parents were at the club, the theater, or the casino. "We stayed up late every night, then gorged on pizza and ice cream at midnight. And we stopped at a different island every day."

"Wow. Sounds amazing," Ruby says, returning the photo to my nightstand. After a beat she asks, "So, is Mr. Sporty Balls pissed at me?"

"Carlos? Why would he be pissed?"

Her mouth twists into a grimace. "Because you decided not to shut down your accounts? He thinks this is all my fault. I mean, in a way it is. I know I've apologized like a thousand times today, but I'm really sorry. I feel guilty as hell."

"I know," I say. "And Carlos knows too. He's not as much of an asshole as you think."

"I don't think he's an ass . . . ," she says apologetically.

"Um, you called him one?" I chuckle. Carlos's reaction was priceless. I'm pretty sure no one had ever called him that before.

"Fine, maybe he's not an ass, but I still think he's paternalistic. And a misogynist. And probably a total player. Right?"

She looks at me like she's waiting for me to divulge secrets about my cousin's love life. Not gonna happen.

After she realizes I'm avoiding her question, she says, "Anyway, it doesn't matter what he thinks. All that matters is what you want."

Ruby glances over my shoulder, and I don't have to turn around to know what's caught her attention.

"Is that a neon sign?" she asks.

"Yup. Hot lips." I plug it into the wall socket so she can take in the full neon-pink explosion. "It was in one of the church donation boxes we got after we moved here. It came with all these

Baby-Sitters Club books." I show her the box lying half open on my bedroom floor. "I tried reading one, but I think they're meant for little girls. I miss having my own books."

"I may or may not have read the whole series when I was nine." She kneels on the carpet and starts to rummage through the old paperbacks, reading the spines. "Oh, *Logan Likes Mary Anne!*—that was a good one. And *Boy-Crazy Stacey*! Damn, I haven't seen these in forever."

"Do you want them? I was gonna give them away."

"No, sadly, I've let them go." There's a feeling of nostalgia in her voice. "I was a bit pissed when Stacey moved away. It was a total bummer."

I eye her, confused. *Who's Stacey?*

Ruby folds the flaps of the box and stands. "Do you have a library card yet?"

"Not yet. I think there's a library a few blocks from here."

"We could go tonight, after the interview. I'm pretty sure they close at nine. We can get you a card, pick up some books, and then ice cream? I still regret not getting that Extreme Banana Triple Scoop Brownie Sundae. It was your first time at Maggie-Moo's. I didn't want to overwhelm you."

"You should know I could dive into an ice cream pool any day of the week. I think we should split the Sundae Scream!"

"Wait, which one was that?"

"The one with nine ice cream scoops, confetti cake, fudge, whipped cream, wafer sticks, a doughnut, *and* a cherry on top!" The thought of plowing through this monstrosity of a dessert makes us both laugh out loud.

"Let's do it." Ruby claps her hands together, looking like a kid who's just been given a gift. "But I'm warning you, I'll be climbing the walls on that much sugar. And I get super chatty. You might have to put up with me talking about nineteenth-century feminist novels."

I laugh even harder. "That is super specific."

"I've read every Jane Austen novel ever written. And—full disclosure—I have a thing for all three of the Brontë sisters. Not in a sexual way or anything. I just think they're goddesses."

"I know he's not a feminist goddess, but my dad loves Charles Dickens. *Great Expectations* is his favorite. I prefer *A Christmas Carol.*"

"Bah, humbug," Ruby exclaims, scrunching her face, hunching her shoulders, and making a Scrooge-like voice. She looks super silly. "I love that book!"

Right now my smile could put out the sun. Ice cream and books sounds amazing. Ice cream and books sounds a little like my old life.

We hear Mami calling from the living room, reminding us that it's almost time for the interview.

"I'm so freaking excited!" Ruby says as we walk to the living room, where Mami and Abuela Joan are drinking the leftover sangría Tía Lorna brought over on Sunday.

Mami must have just asked Abuela Joan a question, because she's shaking her head no.

"I've never read *Wired for Women*," Abuela Joan says. "I'm not much for online journalism—I still get the Sunday *Times* delivered the old-fashioned way." She turns to put her hand on Ruby's arm. "But Ruby loves it, and these girls are old enough to make their own choices—"

"It's almost time," Ruby interrupts, sitting on the floor in front of my laptop.

I open the video-call application on my computer and wait for it to ring.

My palms are super sweaty, and my heart is drumming so fast

inside my chest that I'm wondering how I'll be able to form a full sentence, much less a coherent response to any of Calista's questions. I take in a deep, slow breath. Now is not the time to come across like I just learned English. I hate how my accent makes me sound when I'm anxious—like I have no idea what I'm talking about.

"I can't believe this is happening," Ruby says next to me, practically bouncing with excitement. She pulls me into a side hug and I'm so nervous I can barely breathe.

Right then, Calista Jameson's call pops up on my screen. I press the answer button and her face greets us from behind thick-rimmed red glasses.

"Hello, ladies," she exclaims, leaning into the camera. "Are you ready to start a revolution?"

CHAPTER TEN

RUBY

It's just another Friday morning.

End-of-the-week, start-of-the-weekend Friday.

I didn't expect this morning to be so utterly and completely normal.

Calista's article went live yesterday afternoon, almost fifteen hours ago. I can't help but feel a little disappointed, watching the hallway drone with the usual Friday activity. Groups stand clustered around cell phones, some laughing and jostling. The quiet students and the ones who haven't yet found their tribe maneuver around them, books clutched tight in front of their chests. Some wear earbuds or stare down at their screens, trying to appear oblivious to the early-morning chaos.

Has anyone else at this school even read the article? Does anyone even care?

I'm not seeing my own little tribe. Topher, Jo, and Nessa must be running late. I want so much to find Malena, to huddle together around our screens and watch the reactions come in, but I'm also a little scared. What if it's bad, like last time? What if it's my fault she decided to press on with this whole thing? What if I'm pushing her too hard?

Or, worse, what if Carlos is right and this is all a terrible idea?

To be fair, Mr. Sporty Balls is not exactly the world's leading authority on feminist activism.

So I try to set the worries aside and I go to my locker, still reeling, because Calista Jameson's interview with us—beautifully titled "I AM NOT A DISTRACTION": FLORIDA STUDENT FORCED TO COVER NIPPLES WITH PANTYLINERS, THEN SENT TO DETENTION— has tens of thousands of shares already. I'm trying not to think about all the random strangers studying the photo of Malena, staring back at the camera lens, stony-faced, the skin on her back exposed. I'm trying not to think of all those people glancing farther down the page to read my words—the pull quotes that stand out in boldface type, and all the other statements buried deep in Calista's story.

I'm also trying not to think about the absurd response that our superintendent, Dr. Gordon Saunders, gave Calista:

"Both students were in violation of the dress code. Their behavior was disruptive to the learning environment. School administrators acted to protect the students and assist them in remedying the issue." When Calista pushed him on whether it was appropriate to make Malena cover herself with pantyliners, Dr. Saunders gave this incredibly pathetic answer: "We are investigating the situation and working to ensure that the dress code is applied fairly and uniformly."

When I think about the "remedy" of Malena subjecting her body to the scrutiny of Doris and Nurse Ratched, and then about all those roving eyes on Calista's article, I start to hyperventilate. I haven't decided whether this fast breathing is from anxiety or excitement—there's a fine line between them.

I push through the crowds and am starting to open my locker when I hear a deep voice call out from across the hall: "Roobs frees the boobs!" I turn around to see Chad Colby and his meat-head lacrosse-player friends gawking and laughing.

Maybe I was wrong. Maybe it's not a typical Friday after all.

"Well done," I say to Chad. "I wasn't sure that you knew how to rhyme." *Or read.*

"Nah, man, he didn't come up with it," the stocky kid standing beside him says, twirling his lacrosse stick. "It's all over social. Like, everywhere."

Chad steps forward and holds out his right hand, as if he wants to shake mine. "We just want to say thank you, Ruby, for the wonderful public service you're doing for all of us."

I reach my hand out and offer Chad a super-firm handshake. "It's my pleasure," I say, looking him directly in the eyes. "You haven't seen anything yet."

As soon as the words slip from my mouth, I sense that I've walked into a land mine. I know exactly where asshole Chad's mind is heading.

"We all look forward to seeing much, much more," he says, turning to face the pack of guys standing around him. "Right, boys?"

They all laugh, the stocky kid throws his lacrosse stick to Chad, who catches it and makes some stupid move in the air, and then they lumber off like a pack of apes following the alpha male.

"Let me know if there's a petition I can sign," Chad says, turning back toward me. "Happy to support the cause!"

"Jackass," I mutter under my breath.

Before I even turn back to my locker, Nessa appears out of nowhere. She grabs my hand and tugs.

"Come see, Roobs!" she says, dragging me across the hall and to the interior courtyard, where Jo and Topher stand surrounded by a bunch of people. They're all looking in the same direction.

"Check it out." Topher points me toward the concrete-block wall.

It's a chalk drawing—a huge one. The shape of a woman's body swirls in a background of rainbow colors, and written in cursive across the top is a question: *Does my body offend you?* It's gorgeous, a work of art. I know Jo and Nessa did it; I've seen enough of their stuff to recognize the style, and Jo's flowing script is unmistakable. I look to the bottom right corner for their signature, but they haven't signed it.

Smart women.

All around us, people are gathering. I watch as a cluster of freshman girls crouch down to pose for a selfie, the woman's shape rising above their heads.

I'm scanning the crowd, trying to find Malena, when Ms. Markowitz slips in next to me and surveys the mural. I glance at her face. Her eyes are wide, and a slight smile pulls at the corner of her mouth.

"What a lovely image," she says, so softly that only Topher and I can hear. "If only the artists had used paint instead of chalk." She turns toward me and winks. "I would have pitched in to cover the costs."

She starts to walk away before I can even react. I'm left with my mouth hanging open.

"Did she just say that?" Topher asks me.

I shrug as a junior on the yearbook staff slides between us, heads toward the mural with a camera, and focuses the huge lens on it.

I follow his lead and pull out my phone to take a picture. I post it to social and tag Calista.

Word must be spreading, because people start streaming out of the cafeteria.

I whisper to Topher, "How did they do it without anyone seeing?"

"No idea," Topher replies. "You know these two women and all their mysterious secrets."

Nessa, leaning in to give Jo a soft kiss on the collarbone, murmurs quietly, "I don't know what you're talking about."

"Nessa and I are open books," Jo adds, brushing her hand lightly against Nessa's jaw.

A flash of envy hits me, and I wonder whether I'll ever share the comfortable intimacy that they have with each other. I watch Jo lean in for a slow kiss.

"Best to keep this particular book closed for a while," Topher says, ignoring their intensely public display of affection. He instead stares across the courtyard toward a set of glass doors, through which Dr. Hardaway, the disciplinary AP, is striding out. Mr. Johnson, the world's grouchiest custodian, walks with her, maneuvering his mop and bucket ahead of them.

"Incoming!" Jo calls out under her breath, pulling away from Nessa's embrace.

Dr. Hardaway stops at my side, glances once at the work of art, and then locks her gaze on me, her face inscrutable.

"Please come with me, Ruby," she says, turning on her heels and striding back across the courtyard toward her office.

"You got this, Roobs," Topher whispers, giving me a stiff pat on the back as I head out behind Dr. Hardaway. "You're a woman warrior. Don't forget it."

I bite hard on my lip, trying to ignore the sound of my racing heart. I turn to look back at the mural just as an ornery Mr. Johnson lifts his mop head and begins to wipe the art away. I hope Malena got to see it. It doesn't really matter, though. He can erase the wall, but he can't get rid of all the photos floating on social media.

Dr. Hardaway continues to barrel ahead of me through the hallway. She doesn't turn back. She doesn't slow down. She doesn't utter a word. She simply marches on, expecting me to follow, and leads me into her office.

"Please take a seat," she says, gesturing toward a black leather chair.

She eases into her desk chair and stares for a few moments at the computer. Then she adjusts the monitor so that I can see it. Calista's article fills the screen.

"Is this really the sort of attention we want to bring to Orange Grove?" she asks, her voice eerily calm. "'Schools shouldn't be in the business of sexualizing girls' bodies'?" She looks up from behind the screen. "'Girls shouldn't be seen as distractions for boys'?"

She's pulling out some of my best quotes, if I do say so myself. I'm not sure what sort of response she's looking for, but it's abundantly clear that we're not here for her to congratulate me.

"I believe you may have misconstrued the administration's actions, Ruby." She shakes her head slowly. "Our intention was to protect a new student from unwanted negative attention."

Dr. Hardaway removes her glasses and rests them on her desk. "No one should have to lose everything, leave behind everything that she knows." She picks up her glasses, examines them, and then places them carefully at the edge of her desk blotter. "The scars of trauma run very deep, Ruby," she says, not looking at me. "Deeper than the eye can see."

"That's sort of the point, Dr. Hardaway," I begin, tentative. "I mean, with all due respect, Malena's bralessness pretty much went unnoticed until you and Nurse Hopkins decided it was a problem."

"Nurse Hopkins and I were making our best effort to protect a vulnerable young woman," she says.

"Vulnerable how?" I ask, trying hard to keep skepticism out of my voice.

"A teacher expressed concern. And you know how teenage boys can be. We wanted to avoid an uncomfortable situation."

"Which boys? Shouldn't you be talking to them instead?"

Her eyebrows arch so high they're about to hit her hairline.

"If anyone had said or done anything inappropriate, they'd have been punished too."

"So you *are* punishing her. *Not* protecting her. I just want to make sure I understand." Am I pushing too hard? A flash of worry burns through me, but I forge ahead. "Plus, I've read the dress code, like, a hundred times now. I don't mean to belabor the point, Dr. Hardaway, but it never mentions bras."

"Be that as it may," Dr. Hardaway says, putting on her glasses to look down at the old-fashioned calendar on her desk, "it's implied."

"Oh," I scoff, feeling my cheeks begin to burn with anger. "So now girls need to be mind readers to understand how to get dressed in the morning?" I hear the frustration rising in my voice, feel my temper heading into dangerous territory. "And whose minds, exactly, should we read? The teachers policing girls' bodies? Our pervy classmates? Or maybe Nurse Ratch—"

I catch myself just in time. Dr. Hardaway would not be thrilled about the nickname, and I'm already on very thin ice.

"I'm sorry," I say, pausing to take in a deep breath. "That was probably—"

"I understand your frustration," she replies, sighing deeply, as if in sympathy. "We may need to build more clarity into the code, Ruby. But it's too late for any changes during this academic year."

"Are you sure it's too late?" I ask, working hard to soften my tone. "What if we petition the school board?"

"It's not going to happen, Ruby." She glances down at her calendar, words neatly written inside each box. "Any change would need to be introduced to the school board during their November meeting—in just over three weeks."

"Three weeks is a long time," I blurt out.

"You have no idea what goes into policy changes at the district level," she says, her tone patronizing. "You'd need a petition signed by ten percent of the student body, faculty backing, a full proposal—all submitted to the board at least fourteen days in advance of the meeting." She looks again at her calendar, while I try to push the anger and frustration back down. "That's only ten days from now. Impossible."

"Nothing's impossible," I retort.

"If you go out there demanding a change to the dress code, you'll get students worked up about something that's never going to happen—not this year, at least." She leans into her desk and stares hard at me. "You need to let it go, Ruby. Do you understand me?"

I nod slowly and release my lip from the grip of my teeth. Suddenly my anger has shifted into something else, something like anticipation.

"Yes," I respond, my voice firm and confident.

And it's true. I do understand. If we want to change the dress code, we need to start the revolution *now*. There's no time to waste.

"Can I go?" I ask, standing up. I'm anxious to get out the door and put a plan into motion. I can feel the energy welling up inside me. I can almost taste the passion, the drive. Oh, how I love this flavor!

"I also want to be sure you're considering your own future," she says, urging me to sit back down. "Disciplinary action will not look good on your record when you apply for college, and it's my understanding that you haven't submitted early applications or completed your common app yet, so this is an important consideration."

"I think maybe that depends on *which* college, and on what kind of disciplinary action," I respond, slumping back into my seat. Why does the conversation always have to turn to college? To the future? When all I want is to grasp onto the *now*? "Plus, I'm planning to take a gap year," I say, hoping this might end the college talk.

Her head cocks to the side. "A gap year? Interesting. What exactly are your plans for the year?"

"I haven't decided yet." I shift in my seat, increasingly uncomfortable with the direction we are heading. I'm having trouble making sense of Dr. Hardaway's sudden interest in my future. And all this talk of my plans brings up the churning in my gut, the deep discomfort with my absolute and utter lack of post–high school goals. "I don't think I'm ready for college," I admit. "Or maybe college isn't ready for me," I add, trying hard to sound more confident than I feel.

"You're absolutely ready for college," she announces.

Why are we talking about this? Why does she even care? Maybe she needs me to go to college to boost Orange Grove's statistics or something. I've heard that's a thing.

"You should keep your options open."

I glance anxiously around the room, my stomach lurching. "I should probably get to class," I tell Dr. Hardaway, my crossed legs bouncing nervously. "I have a lit quiz."

"I'll give you a pass." She leans down, opens a desk drawer, and pulls out a pass. "American Lit?"

I nod curtly, hoping finally to bring our conversation to a close.

"I miss teaching that course," she says, her voice wistful. "What are you reading?"

"The Awakening," I answer, getting to my feet.

"Wonderful book," she says. "I wrote my doctoral thesis on it."

Well, that's a surprise.

Dr. Hardaway stands to hand me a hall pass. I reach for the big orange disk. Before she lets go, she looks off into the distance and says, " 'But whatever came, she had resolved never again to belong to another than herself.' "

It's my favorite line from the book. I'm left there stunned, trying to wrap my head around the fact that Dr. Penny Hardaway and I share this (share anything!) in common.

"I hope the quiz goes well," she says, gesturing toward the door and sending me, dazed and confused, out of her office.

As soon as Dr. Hardaway shuts her door, I will myself to burst the bubbling anxieties about my future and dive into the here and now. I pull out my phone and send a group text to Malena, Topher, Nessa, and Jo.

> Let's make this happen, people! If we want to change the dress code, we need to get a petition going NOW. Meeting at my house Sunday. 10 a.m. sharp. Spread the word. We need all the help we can get!

I wish we could start bright and early tomorrow. (No time like the present, right?) But I promised to drive Nana to the beach for her turtle-patrol meeting. They're training new volunteers to get ready for the season, and Nana's the veteran expert.

Knowing everyone's in class, I don't expect a response. I shove my phone into my backpack and make my way down the hall, deep in thoughts of irony—the irony that this school is making us read *The Awakening*, a landmark work of early feminism, at the same time that its administrators are trying to shut down women's rights and shame us for our bodies.

I can't wait to show Dr. Hardaway how wrong she is. Three weeks? Entire regimes have been toppled in three weeks. It's plenty of time to wake up this school.

Since first period started five minutes ago, the halls are empty. So I'm a little flustered when I see Carlos sauntering toward me, notably without a hall pass. He's walking with a girl. She's gorgeous—big brown eyes, bronze cheeks, a soft Afro wrapped in a red headband. She's wearing a bright yellow sundress that flares at the hip, leather sandals, and teardrop earrings.

"Hey," he says. "What's up?"

The girl stops beside him and cuts me a sideways glance.

I gesture toward him with my enormous orange disk. "Just late to a lit quiz."

"Yeah, I gotta run, too," the girl says, throwing a harsh glare in my direction. "Calculus. You coming, Carlos?"

"I'll catch up," he says.

The girl waves a dismissive hand and turns to leave. Is she jealous of me? Clearly, she doesn't have any reason to be.

I look him up and down as she walks away. "Where's your hall pass, mister?"

"Oh, uh." He shrugs casually. "I was in the training room; they don't really make me . . . I mean, I do a lot of training and the school's pretty chill with it."

"So let me get this straight," I say. "All I have to do to avoid the humiliation of carting around this filthy piece of plastic is learn how to throw a ball?"

He laughs nervously. "You have to throw a ball really fast." His ears go pink. It's kind of entertaining how uncomfortable Carlos is with the special treatment he's getting.

"And what about your girlfriend?" I ask, gesturing toward the girl in the yellow dress, who has just turned back to throw me another death glare. "What's her excuse for not carrying a hall pass?"

"Chloe? She's not my girlfriend," he is quick to respond. "She's my baseball manager. The girl is a force of nature." He nods in her direction. "And maybe a little overprotective of me. But trust me, I'm not her type."

"So you're not into confident women?" I ask.

"I didn't say she's not *my* type," he snaps back. "But I mean . . . Chloe's like my boss. We're not—"

"Into each other." I finish his thought. "Even though you *do* like confident women."

"Something like that," he says, shifting on his feet, the tips of his ears still glowing pink. "So, do you play a sport?" he blurts out, clearly trying to redirect the conversation away from his not-girlfriend and his taste in women.

"Hmm," I say. "I guess we'd need to define *play*. I have abysmally bad hand-eye coordination, so sports with balls tend to be life-threatening. But I used to run cross-country back in Seattle."

"Why not anymore?"

"I'm not much of a joiner."

"More of an instigator, huh?" His eyebrows arch.

I have to admit, that's a good one. It makes me smile.

"Speaking of which," I say, "I just came from the assistant principal's office."

"Which one?" he asks.

Another thing I can't get used to about this school. All the APs are women, which is great. I'm all about women in leadership. But as far as I can tell, these female "assistants" do the work, while the principal—who only shows his face at pep rallies and school assemblies—gets all the credit. *Go figure.*

And the assistant principal every student wants desperately to avoid? That would be the menacingly named "disciplinary AP"—the very AP I just had a cozy chat with.

"Hardaway," I respond.

"Why does that not surprise me?" He grins, and I feel a little tingle down my spine.

What is happening here? I ignore the strange sensation and press on.

"Wanna hear what she said to me? About Malena?"

"I'm guessing you're about to let loose whether I want to hear it or not." He gestures with his hand for me to proceed.

"The oh-so-wise Dr. Hardaway believes they were all trying to protect her, that she was vulnerable and innocent—'poor, poor, disadvantaged Malena.' Can you believe that crud?"

"Yeah," he says. "Protect her by punishing her. That's bullshit."

"Exactly what I said!" I feel my face getting flushed. "I mean, how can a bunch of *women* be so dag-blam *paternalistic?*"

His brows knit together, and he examines my face.

"Why do you talk so weird?" he finally asks.

"Trying to stop cussing," I respond.

"Huh," he says, nodding, still thinking hard. "Interesting."

"It's a deal I made with my nana—not important."

He watches me, concentrating entirely on my face. "Your nana?"

"My grandmother. I live with her."

"And she gets mad when you cuss?"

I laugh. I can't help it. The thought of Nana getting *mad* because of the way I express myself—it's absurd.

"No," I say. "She's not really the getting-mad type."

He tilts his head down, still examining me. "That's cool."

We stand in the hallway, and I feel a warm glow wash over me. It's like for the first time, Carlos is really looking at me, trying to see me, to understand me.

I think maybe I want to understand him, too. Or maybe I already sort of do. Damn, this boy is surprising.

"I better get to class," he says.

"Yeah, I've got a quiz," I say.

But neither one of us moves. It strikes me that in all of our heated and pissed-off interactions, we've never actually been alone together.

It's very disconcerting.

"And thanks, by the way," he says. "Malena told me that you tried to get her to shut down her accounts."

"I tried," I say. "But she has her reasons."

"Her choice, I guess."

What is it with this guy? I just can't pin him down.

"Okay, then." He starts to walk past me, but then turns back.

"Hey, sorry I was such an ass the other day in the parking lot," he says, squinting a little.

"Which time?" I ask.

He chuckles. "Both, I guess? But you sort of deserved it. Both times."

"Oh my gosh!" I exclaim. "Is this your way of saying maybe I don't need to get the hell out of your lives?"

"Hmm"—he bites his lip—"verdict's still out on that one. I'll get back to you."

"I'll be waiting breathlessly for your response," I say, hoping the sarcasm comes through.

I am being sarcastic, right? I'll be honest, seeing him tug on his lip like that actually *has* made me a little breathless.

"And just so you know," he says, "I still think talking to that reporter lady was a huge mistake."

"Wait, did you read Calista's article?"

"Gotta go," he calls out. "As a wise woman once said, 'Girls shouldn't be seen as distractions for boys.'"

He turns away and starts jogging down the hall.

"You *did* read it!" I call out.

He looks back and shrugs big, raising both arms above his shoulders, hands turned up to the sky, eyebrows arched high, and a broad grin across his face.

I wonder, watching him smile: Did Carlos just call me a wise woman? Or a distraction?

And then I start freaking out because I'm not sure which one I prefer.

CHAPTER ELEVEN

MALENA

According to Soraida, Calista Jameson's article is a "game changer." I'm no longer Poor María Malena, Hurricane Victim.

"You're like a Juana de Arco raising the sword of justice against the evils of the school administration," she says, raising a pencil in the air triumphantly. And probably wishing she had a fire-spewing sword and a white horse to sit on.

Me, I'm just praying I don't get burned at the stake.

We're standing by my locker while I grab a few books before I have to meet Ruby in the parking lot for a "linner date"—a great excuse to skip today's pep rally.

"Do you know where she's taking you?" Soraida asks.

"It's a surprise." I grin, excited.

"Ugh. Meanwhile, I'll be stuck with the fam, eating La Llorona."

"Eating what?"

"It's Mami's version of lasagna! Jesus, how is it possible you've gone this long without being forced to eat it? She uses yellow cheese, picadillo, canned tomato sauce—the one you normally use in guisados—and canned vegetables. Why? I don't know. Why can't she just make pastelillo instead?"

"I'm sure it'll be good," I say, thankful that I won't have to eat it. It sounds terrible.

"No. It will not. Why do you think I call it La Llorona?"

I laugh into my closed fist. Only Soraida would compare Tía's cooking with the horrifying image of a wailing ghost mother who is desperately searching for her kids.

"Stop! It's not funny. It's gross," she blurts out, trying to keep a straight face but cracking up. "Just the sight makes you wanna cry!"

By now I'm laughing so hard, I'm actually wiping tears from the sides of my eyes.

"You're so lucky," she says after we've both stopped laughing enough to catch our breath. "My mom never would've let me do that interview."

Soraida swipes at the screen of her phone. She's been glued to that thing all day, providing minute-by-minute commentary on the world's reaction to Calista's article.

"Not that lucky. Mami freaked out when she read about the messages on social media. She made me turn my accounts to private."

This morning, I walked into the kitchen as Mami was reading Calista's article and drinking her coffee. I watched in real time as the expression on her face contorted from pride to disgust to fear. On the call with Mami and Abuela Joan, Calista had asked how we felt, in general, about the posts. But in the article she quoted some of the vilest ones, word for word. Needless to say, Mami was not happy.

"I'm not sure I want you involved in this mess," she said in that stern Puerto Rican–mother voice that leaves no room for debate.

I opened my mouth, ready with a counterargument, but the hurt in her eyes stopped me. I walked away, angry that the online trolls had somehow gotten to us. They had managed to infiltrate our new home with their hatred.

How am I going to change Mami's mind? Again. I don't know.

"That sucks. I thought Tía Camila would be cool with everything. Mami went on a rant this morning over how she thinks Tía has been too *lenient* with you," Soraida says, making air quotes around *lenient*.

I shake my head. Mami is so not cool with this.

"Did Tía Lorna read the article?" I ask.

"Of course she did. She was all like, 'Decent señoritas from good families follow the rules and keep their heads down.' She said nothing good could come from being a desobediente and that you were going to be branded a troublemaker and never get into a good college and probably end up knocked up at seventeen."

My eyes widen in shock. "She *said* that?"

"Well, not the getting-knocked-up part, but I'm sure she probably thought about it."

"Unless I conceive through the blessing of the Holy Spirit, no one is getting knocked up. Juana de Arco died a virgin, remember?"

"The Virgin Warrior," Soraida says wistfully. She read Joan of Arc's Wikipedia page during lunch period and now she thinks herself an expert. "Wait, is Tía Camila letting you go to Ruby's on Sunday?"

"She thinks we're gonna be working on a school project. I mean, I didn't exactly lie; she just kind of assumed . . ."

Soraida guffaws.

"What's so funny?" I ask, amused. Her laughter sounds like a chorus of tropical birds. It's one of her best features.

"Nothing. It's just that you're such a goody-goody, prima. Mami always used to say, 'Why can't you be more like your cousin Malena?'" She laughs and slaps her thigh. "She's not saying that anymore! I'm glad you finally grew a pair."

"Thanks? I guess."

We turn to leave but stop mid-stride when a group of girls I've never met crowds the space around my locker. One of them holds her phone screen in front of my face. I don't have to read it to know Calista's article is displayed. I've lost count of how many times this has happened today.

"This is so cool," the girl says.

"Thanks." I smile politely. "I'm Malena."

"Yeah, we know." The girl's face is beaming. "You're like La Poderosa!"

We laugh at the Spanish honorary title—the Powerful One— mostly because it sounds like the name of a badass Lucha Libre wrestler.

"I'm Beatriz, and this is Nadia and Xiomara," she says.

"Xiomara got sent to detention back in August for wearing yoga pants," Nadia says. "Apparently her Colombian butt was too big to wear to school."

Xiomara turns around and slaps her butt cheeks with both hands. "Made in Colombia!" she jeers, and we all laugh. "There's just no way to hide allll of this."

"Same here," Nadia says, gesturing to her fuller figure. "A teacher said my T-shirt was too snug. Apparently there's something in the dress code that says all tops must be the appropriate size. That's what they call it. What a joke! If I changed into a freaking muumuu, they would still send me to detention—for clothes that are too loose."

Beatriz takes Nadia's hand in hers. It's a sweet, reassuring gesture.

"I mean, I'm fat and proud," Nadia says, sending her shoulders back and her chin high. "I'm perfectly comfortable with the way my T-shirts fit. They show all my curves. It's sexy. But this place is all about body-shaming, if you ask me."

"Preach!" Xiomara exclaims.

"What are you and Ruby gonna do next?" Beatriz asks.

"We're planning a protest," Soraida exclaims. "We're organizing a huge protest."

I cut my eyes to Soraida. "Nothing's set yet," I say, but no one seems to hear me.

"Oh my God! *Yes!* Count us in," Nadia is quick to say. "I'm so sick of this place and its stupid rules."

"It's absurd," Xiomara says. "I have a 4.0 GPA, but all they care about is how my butt looks in a pair of long black pants. You couldn't even see anything!"

"I don't hear anyone calling those tiny track shorts guys wear a distraction!" Nadia argues. "Somehow if you have team spirit, it gives you a free pass."

"I was a Miss Colombian Teen finalist last summer," Xiomara says, tilting her head and flipping her long dark hair over her shoulder. "But I don't think that gives anyone a free pass around here."

"No, it doesn't." Beatriz rolls her eyes at Xiomara. Then she turns to me and says, "Whatever you decide, keep us posted."

"Do you guys want to come to Ruby's on Sunday?" I offer, anxious to show Ruby that I, too, can rally people for the cause. And maybe this is a chance to make some friends who aren't also my blood relatives. "We're meeting to sort out a strategy."

"You really can't afford to lose any momentum with these things," Soraida adds in her all-things-expert voice.

"We'd love to join, if that's okay." Beatriz pulls out her phone, swiping to the contacts page.

We all swap phone numbers. Then I text them Ruby's address.

"Sunday at ten," I say.

"We'll be there," Beatriz says.

"We can march down the halls banging on pots and pans. Stage a good old-fashioned cacerolazo," Nadia says, hitting my locker for effect. "That should get their attention. Right?"

"She's from Venezuela," Beatriz explains. We all nod in understanding. "That's how they roll."

"Pots and pans?" Soraida asks, a note of condescension in her voice. "We're not trying to overthrow a dictatorship."

"But we are! I think a cacerolazo would be perfect! Get the women out of the kitchen. Use the pots and pans against the system," Nadia argues, undeterred.

Soraida's phone dings with a text. She reads the screen and says, "Carlos is waiting. I have to go."

We give each other friendly goodbye hugs and even a kiss on the cheek, the way we do back home. It's nice to have that in my life again.

Before they turn to leave, Nadia pumps both fists in the air and shouts, "¡Que viva la revolución!"

I watch them walk toward the exit—confident in their own skin. These are the bodies we were born into. The bodies given to us by our mamis and our abuelas. What is so wrong with these bodies?

"God, you're like a local celebrity now," Soraida gushes, checking her phone for new updates. "Even cooler than Carlos."

"I don't know about that."

"You need to let me manage your social-media accounts. I can be like your publicist . . . or your agent! We can turn you into an influencer. You can get all kinds of free stuff!" She has that wild look in her eyes that always gets us in trouble. "Look, all the Jacksonville TV stations have reached out for interviews, and some national newspapers, too. This is insane." Then she giggles to herself.

"What?"

"Someone is using the hashtag NippleRiot." She looks up from her phone and grins. "That would look killer on a T-shirt."

"NippleRiot," I murmur to myself. Our rebellion has a name.

"We could make a T-shirt with pantyliners over the nipples." She examines her chest, pressing her T-shirt down against her boobs. "Write #NippleRiot super huge underneath, and then maybe something catchy on the back, like 'Are my tetas too distracting for school?'"

I think back to how I felt standing alone in that bathroom stall, my shirt pulled up, trying to cover myself with menstrual products. I want to hurl the question at Dr. Hardaway. At Doris the secretary. At Nurse Hopkins. And at every other woman who's ever made me feel like there's something wrong with me because of the shape of my body. They should know better.

"It's perfect," I reply.

Soraida and I start walking toward the parking lot, but we're intercepted by Mr. Cruz, who is jogging down the hallway in his Birkenstocks, calling my name. I'm confused by the echo of tiny bells ringing with his every step. Where is that sound coming from?

"What the . . . ," Soraida mutters. "You're on your own, prima. I gotta go. See ya Sunday."

She turns and rushes away. By the time Mr. Cruz reaches me, he's huffing. Today he's wearing some kind of beaded necklace with a talisman of feathers and bells—the source of the ringing.

"I'm glad I caught you before you left," he says, catching his breath.

"Is everything all right?" I ask, suddenly afraid he's bearing bad news from home.

"Dr. Hardaway told me about your new friend, Ruby," he says, absently rubbing the feathers of his talisman.

I exhale, relieved this has nothing to do with Papi.

"I know Ruby well," he says. "She's a great girl. But she sometimes doesn't think things through as well as she ought to." He stares hard into my eyes. "Do you get my drift?"

His drift?

"I see great potential in you, Malena." He smiles encouragingly. "You should know that if there's a suspension on your record, even from the tenth grade, you'll have to report it in your college applications. Doesn't look good."

My shoulders fall a little at this bit of information. "Okay," I say, appreciative of his concern for my future. I know he means well.

"I'm all about asserting your rights, but something like a protest could have a big impact down the line." He closes his eyes, and his face softens. It's sort of like he's meditating right here in the hall. "From the tiniest acorns grow the tallest oaks," he says, eyes still closed. Then he opens his eyes, expectant. "Do you understand what I'm trying to express?"

I nod, wondering instead what kind of trees grow from rebellious seeds.

"You and Ruby have made your point. Now it's time to integrate into the community here at Orange Grove and focus on your academic success." He smiles and rubs his talisman again. "What do you think? Maybe you could even join our Current Events Club. We'll need a new president next year."

My phone dings with a text from Ruby, letting me know where she's parked.

"I'm sorry, Mr. Cruz," I say. "I really have to go. My ride is waiting."

"Just promise you'll think about what I said, okay?"

"Okay," I say, hoping to appease him. I wave goodbye and walk away. It's hard to think about the future when I can barely keep a grip on the present.

He's right about one thing, though. If we're gonna protest, I need to get around the suspension thing. There is no way in hell I'm gonna convince Mami to let me protest if she finds out I'm facing suspension. We need a plan, a good one. And fast.

———

I find Ruby sitting inside her tiny black car talking to someone I can't see and looking miserable. I open the passenger door and slide into the seat, holding my backpack on my lap. A woman's voice is booming through the speakers.

"Malena just got here. I gotta go," Ruby says, mouthing a silent *I'm sorry.*

"Oh, hi, Malena! It's so good to finally meet you," the voice says.

"It's my sister, Olive," Ruby explains.

"Hi, yes, it's great to meet you, too." I had no idea Ruby had a sister. She's never brought her up before.

"How are you liking life in Orange Park?" Olive asks. "Is your family feeling settled? Ruby mentioned you had to relocate because of María. There's actually a student in my class—Alejandro Quiñones from Bayamón. His family also had to relocate." I'm impressed by her perfect Spanish pronunciation.

I nod, then remember she can't see me. "Oh, okay."

"There's like three million people on the Island, Olive. I don't think Malena knows Alejandro from Adam."

Olive sighs on the other end.

"Anyway, we gotta go," Ruby says.

"Call me tomorrow—we'll talk about the protest. I have some ideas," Olive says.

"Mm-hmm," Ruby responds, gripping the steering wheel a little tighter.

"Have fun, girls," Olive chirps before Ruby hangs up. I don't have time to say thanks or goodbye.

Ruby takes a deep breath, her head falling back. "Sorry about that."

"Your sister seems really nice," I say, looking for a place to store my backpack. Ruby didn't waste any time. She used her lunch hour to go buy poster boards and art supplies for Sunday's meeting. I set my bag by my feet, then click on my seat belt before we drive onto the main road.

"I hope you're hungry," Ruby says, shifting to a more cheerful tone.

"Starving." My stomach growls as if to confirm my statement. "See?"

"The hungrier the better. I can't wait to show you this place!"

We stop at a red light and she shuffles through her phone's music player.

"Oh, I've been meaning to ask you, how'd that essay turn out?" she asks, scrolling through playlists and selecting a song.

"Awesome. I got a ninety-six."

"Bring it in!" She high-fives me as a sugary-sweet pop song that I normally associate with preteens starts to play. "Are you okay with Nick Jonas?" she asks.

I shrug. "He's too pop for my taste."

"Hey, hey, there's nothing wrong with pop, missy," she says in mock defense. "What are you into?"

"Spanish sounds. Rock, Latin trap, reggaeton. Ozuna, Pony Bravo, Maluma . . ."

"Do you have any music on your phone?" she asks.

I scroll through my playlists and land on a track by Bad Bunny and Karol G, my favorite female reggaeton artist.

Ruby links my phone's Bluetooth to her car's audio system and in no time we're both swaying to the multilingual beats of "Ahora Me Llama."

"He's from Puerto Rico and she's Colombian," I explain, raising the volume so she can get the full Latin trap effect with its slow rhythms and sultry vocals.

A couple of minutes into the song, Ruby asks, "What is she saying?"

"I own my life, and no one can tell me what to do," I translate.

"I love it," Ruby calls out over the music. The entire car is vibrating with the bass of the synthesizer. For a second, I forget I'm in the streets of Orange Park. This music takes me back to the beachside roads of Isla Verde on a sunny weekend.

Ruby tries to sing along, but her Spanish, unlike her sister's, is honest-to-God awful. She's just making stuff up, but it's hilarious. We're both belly-laughing. And the harder I laugh, the louder she tries to sing in what can only be described as the *worst* Carpool Karaoke of all time.

"You sound like a strangled cat," I say between fits of giggles.

I'm relieved when we pull into a parking lot, because Ruby is practically bent over the steering wheel, she's laughing so hard. I have no idea how she's managed to get us here.

"This is it!" Ruby says, pointing to a building with a painting of a lighthouse on a side wall. A green awning has the words *El Faro* painted in white cursive.

"Have you been here before?" Ruby asks, suddenly self-conscious. "I was so caught up in surprising you, it didn't occur to me that maybe you and your family come here every Sunday or something." She brings her hand to her forehead. "God, I'm such a doof."

"No, I haven't," I say, vaguely remembering Tía Lorna talking about a Puerto Rican restaurant with the same name. Once we're inside, the scene before me needs no explanation. The smell of roasted pork and fried plantains evokes some kind of culinary heaven. My mouth salivates in anticipation.

The right side of the wall-mounted menu is dedicated only to cuchifritos: morcillas, papas rellenas, chicharrones. They have a pastry cabinet too, with guava pastelillos and huge pieces of budín. There's a line of people at the counter grabbing cafés con leche and big rolls of pan sobao. They must double as a bakery. The sounds of Spanish conversation mix with the delicious smell of fried foods, desserts, and espresso. My heart swells with so much joy, I think I might cry.

"Welcome to El Faro, the best Puerto Rican restaurant in all of North Florida," Ruby says proudly.

"How did you find this place? It's—it's—" I stammer, trying to come up with the right word, knowing there's not a big enough word for what this place really is. "It's . . . amazing."

"I did an extensive search," she says, beaming. "I remember

when I first left Seattle—all the things I really missed. Good tea, mostly. And bookstores—I mean, the ones that aren't big boxes." She shrugs. "Anyway, I figured you must really miss Puerto Rico."

"I love it. Thank you, Ruby." I wrap her in a tight hug and she hugs me back.

"I wanted you to feel at home," she whispers. "But here. At home, here."

"It's perfect."

We pull away and it's like I'm seeing Ruby for the first time. I've always known that she's passionate to the nth degree, but I now realize how much she actually cares.

I grab two menus from the counter and Ruby finds an empty table for two. The tables are covered in vinyl fabric with a pattern of bright flowers. The walls are lined with photos of turquoise beaches, hammocks hanging from palm trees, and coconut carts—all screaming two words: *isla tropical.*

I slide into a mahogany chair and pass a menu to Ruby, who is reading an illustrated dessert menu she found propped inside the condiment caddy.

"This tres leches thing looks spectacular. Can we share?" she asks.

"I'm pretty sure you're gonna want your own. Trust me."

Meanwhile, I'm devouring the Spanish descriptions on the menu. Chuletas can-can, arroz con gandules, plátanos maduros— it's delightful.

"Can you order for me?" Ruby asks. "My Spanish sucks. I never understood the gender thing, all the *o*'s and *a*'s. I mean, really." She picks up her fork. "How do you know whether a fork is masculine or feminine?"

"Masculine. But a spoon is feminine," I say, picking up my spoon. "Who has any idea why." I drop my spoon and go back to scanning the menu. "And there can be a hundred students in a room, ninety-nine of them girls and only one guy, and you have to address everyone by the default masculine—*compañeros* instead of *compañeras*. Makes no sense."

Ruby leans over the table and winks as she says, "Maybe the default should be the feminine."

"There's an idea," I say.

Our waitress arrives and I order several dishes to share—ham croquetas, seafood empanadillas, an asopao con tostones, and a platter of lechón asado with arroz con gandules. I add an extra order of sweet plantains, just because I can.

"This is the best surprise ever," I say after the waitress leaves.

"I aim to please. Plus, we needed to properly celebrate Calista's interview. You killed it!"

"Thanks," I say, absently rearranging the condiments on the caddy. "But there's so much I don't know. I've been reading about things like slut-shaming and internalized misogyny. And then this TED talk blew my mind. A girl who got sent home for wearing a tank top said the dress code is just a form of victim blaming. She said . . ." I close my eyes, straining to remember the exact words. "How did she put it?" I look around the restaurant until it comes to me. "She said that first we're dehumanized and then objectified. I've never thought about it that way. It's so true."

A smile takes over Ruby's face as she reaches for my hand across the table. "I'm so freaking proud of you."

I grasp her hand and squeeze, thinking about how easy it feels, sharing my insecurities with Ruby. It's weird how some people feel so comfortable and familiar even though you've just met. It's like we've known each other for years instead of days. Surprising, considering how different our lives are.

"I feel like I'm catching up to what everyone else knows,"

I continue, grateful for the chance to get this off my chest. "All these new terms can get so confusing. I don't even know if I'm using them correctly most of the time."

"Malena, what you've already accomplished is just unbelievable to me," she replies. "I mean, when I was your age, anything I knew about *anything* was because of my sister."

Pride swells in my chest. I've been working so hard, and it's good to hear someone acknowledge it.

"It must be nice to have an older sister," I say. "Someone you can rely on."

Ruby winces, and I know I've touched a nerve.

"Her Spanish is really good," I offer, trying to work out what's made Ruby suddenly upset.

"She's good at a lot of things," Ruby says with a sigh. Her shoulders drop and her eyes fall on the table.

"Are you okay?" I ask, realizing my comment about Spanish may have made things worse.

She meets my gaze. "Yeah, sorry. Things have gotten a little complicated with my sister. It's just that . . . it's hard to explain." Ruby shakes her head and I nod, giving her space to speak. "We used to be so close, but these days she makes me feel like a fumbling loser half the time. Okay, maybe more than half. I know she's wonderful and super accomplished, and I know she loves me, but I wish she would just back off and let me figure things out on my own. You know?"

I get it. My cousins and tíos can be a little stifling sometimes.

"Olive—my parents, too—they're all waiting around for me to become this superhuman person, watching my every move." Ruby looks out the window, her eyes lost somewhere in the parking lot. "Sometimes it's too much. Do you ever feel overwhelmed like that?"

"Are you kidding? Like all the time." I shrug, smiling with my lips closed. "For what it's worth, I think you're kicking ass and taking names."

"Well, that makes one of you." She shakes her head. "I'm pretty sure Olive thinks I'm just messing around, waiting for *her* to kick my ass into gear."

We both laugh. Hearing Ruby's voice, hesitant and a little vulnerable, I wonder: Is this what it would be like to have a sister? Would I be able to share with her all the things I can't seem to tell anyone else? And would she do the same with me?

I'm trying to think of something helpful, to reassure Ruby. Trying to imagine what a good sister would say. But then the food arrives, and we throw ourselves wholeheartedly into the mini buffet between us.

CHAPTER TWELVE

RUBY

"Are you following all of this, Ruby?"

"Mm-hmm," I mumble.

It's a legitimate question. Olive and I have been on the phone for an hour, and I think I've squeezed in about twelve words between all of her advice. It's a lot to absorb. She has managed somehow to simultaneously convey helpful information and make me feel like the world's biggest dumbass. Olive really has become a master of the sandwich compliment: *They've chosen you to lead the charge? I guess Orange Grove doesn't have many activists. I'm so proud of you. I'm sure you'll do great. Just be sure not to get too worked up, you know?*

There *was* a compliment sandwiched in there somewhere, right?

She's moved through a list of detailed suggestions and is now in the pep-talk segment of the call. I'm hoping this means we're wrapping up.

"I know you're excited, swept up in the moment—all the media attention and likes. But you have to stay focused on the big picture."

"Right," I reply. "Stay focused."

I started the call perched at my desk with pen and notebook

in hand, ready to dutifully take notes. Now I'm slumped cross-legged on the purple shag rug in my room, fiddling with the frayed corner that was chewed up by Zoë, my sister's yellow Lab. Olive rescued her from imminent death last spring, which we all thought was heroic, until the two of them arrived at Nana's for Labor Day weekend and Zoë tore through four pairs of shoes and my shag rug.

"This is an opportunity, Ruby," Olive exclaims. "Your chance to make a real contribution."

I glance up at the phone, on speaker, next to my abandoned notes. That's when I notice Nana, standing quietly in the doorway with a stack of fresh towels. I wonder how long she's been listening.

"I'll just leave them here," she whispers, gesturing toward my bed. I nod silently, wishing she would jump in to interrupt my entirely one-sided "conversation" with Olive.

"Think of this as your legacy work—the lasting impact you'll make at Orange Grove," Olive coaxes. "This has the potential to spark a movement. It could be like your version of the Girl Up Club work I did in Washington."

Nana sets the towels down but doesn't leave the room.

"Maybe," I say, returning my focus to the frayed rug.

"Not *maybe*, Ruby. Yes!" She pauses, waiting for my unforthcoming response. "Okay, gotta go pick up Mom and Dad at the airport. The award ceremony with the mayor is Monday night."

I still can't believe my parents cut their second honeymoon short to watch Olive get a trophy. Now, instead of exploring the famous temples of Cambodia, they'll spend the last few weeks of their vacation hanging around hipster coffeehouses in Olive's neighborhood. Their choice, I guess.

"Send pictures, and tell Dad to film your acceptance speech,"

I say, trying hard to bring the appropriate amount of animation to my voice. "It's awesome that they are recognizing your hard work."

It *is* awesome, and I want nothing more than to feel only pride and excitement for her. But it's more complicated than that. It has been for a long while.

"Thanks, Ruby," she says, her voice suddenly shaky. "Yeah, I'll try to remember. . . ." Her voice trails off. It's disorienting, hearing my sister sound anything less than one hundred percent confident.

"Is something wrong, Olive?" I ask.

A beat of silence passes between us. "Just nerves, I guess," she replies. "A lot of people will be there."

"You'll do great," I tell her. She always does.

"Who knows? Maybe you'll be next!" Her voice strains toward optimism.

"Who knows," I reply softly. "Girls do rule the world." My own words sound deflated, almost defeated.

"You mean *women,* Ruby. *Women* rule the world."

"Right," I reply, tittering. "Women."

"Okay, call or text me if you need more advice. I'm always here for you, little sis. You know that, right?"

"Absolutely," I say.

And with that, blessedly, she hangs up the phone.

I release a deep sigh and look up to see Nana sitting on the edge of my bed. She studies the expression on my face and then pats the bed, signaling for me to come sit beside her.

"Everything okay?" she asks gently as I sit down next to her.

She rests her warm hand on my shoulder, and suddenly I'm overcome with emotion. I look away, back to that tear in my favorite childhood rug.

"It can be a little much, can't it?" Nana asks. "Your parents? Olive? All their big plans and expectations?"

I shrug and bite my lip. I'm surprised to feel tears forming in my eyes. Nana leans forward to fold me into a hug.

I nod and let my cheek rest on her bony shoulder. She smells like baby powder, narcissus, and coconut milk, and simply taking in her scent helps calm my jangling nerves.

"You just be yourself, Ruby," she whispers. "That's always enough."

———

I've decided to go ahead and take Nana's advice to heart, which is why I find myself—four hours later—begging Topher to come to a concert with me.

I invited Malena, but she had plans with her mom, who doesn't get much time off. Malena also didn't seem super enthusiastic about going to see Nick Jonas.

She wasn't the only one. Jo and Nessa both responded to my invitation text with the anticipated disdain:

> Not a chance in hell I'm wasting money on
> that vapid pop shit

That one was from Jo. Nessa's response was somewhat more muted:

> OMG Alien Abduction! Ruby's body has been
> inhabited by a teeny-bopping pop fan!!!

But I know good ol' Topher will come through. When he doesn't respond to my text immediately, I call him.

"Hey, you're coming to a concert with me tonight," I say as soon as he picks up.

"No can do, Roobs. My lab partner and I are working on a report."

"You're a senior with a perfect GPA and a 1590 on your SAT," I exclaim. "You can relax a little."

"Gotta get this done by Tuesday—"

"Perfect!" I interrupt. "You've got two full days before Tuesday."

"But—"

"Invite your lab partner," I say, not giving him time to form a response. "I'll get three tickets."

"Damn, you're pushy," he says. "What show is this, anyway?"

"Nick Jonas," I reply, trying to keep my voice steady.

"No, Roobs, for real. Who's playing?"

"For real, Nick Jonas. He's an incredible performer. You'll love him."

He scoffs. "I highly doubt that."

"Pleeeeeeaaaaaaaase?" I beg shamelessly.

I don't know why I've suddenly become so obsessed with this plan. I guess I keep thinking about what Nana told me—about how being myself is enough. Sure, it may be a little embarrassing that I remain enamored with my middle-school boy-band crush. But he's awesome and talented, his songs make me smile, and I adore watching him perform. That's *me*, like it or not.

Plus, I think Topher and I both could use some good old-fashioned fun.

Topher sighs dramatically. "Give me a sec."

I hear him explain to his lab partner, and then I hear a high-pitched squeal.

Yes! Another Jonas Brothers fan.

He gets back on the phone. "She wants to know how you scored the tickets."

"Okay," I say. "So, I haven't quite managed that, but don't worry. I'll take care of it. Meet me downtown in an hour."

"Chloe over here is having an aneurysm, so she's clearly in. And I'm down, if you're paying."

Good ol' Topher.

An hour later I'm standing a block from the venue, holding three scalped tickets to the Nick Jonas concert and giddily jumping around.

Topher heads toward me with the girl who must be his lab partner. As she gets closer, I realize that I know her—she's Carlos's friend, the one who manages the baseball team, the one who threw me several death glares in the hall yesterday.

I'm racking my brain to remember her name when she blurts out, "Oh my God, Ruby, you're the best! This show sold out in, like, five minutes!"

I guess she doesn't hate me after all. Preteen heartthrob Nick Jonas works his magic again!

We head into the theater. Our seats kinda suck, but it *so* doesn't matter. As soon as Nick comes out onstage, the crowd erupts. Chloe and I burst onto our feet. The two of us spend the whole show bouncing up and down on our chairs in the nosebleed section, singing every word to every song at the top of our lungs. Topher—dear, sweet Topher, who never listens to anything but IDM and avant-jazz—bops along with us. He even sings along during the chorus to a new song, one with so much play you'd have to be from another planet not to know it.

Nick closes the encore with his best sappy ballad. The three of us lock arms and sway along as Nick croons. The whole place is filled with electric energy, and when the band finally leaves the stage, we all stand around yelling and screaming at the top of our lungs for a full five minutes.

It's a perfect end to a perfect show. We wind back down the stairwell, Chloe and me both gushing about the highlights and Topher beaming with his usual delight. I'm so glad I listened to Nana.

As we spill out into the near-empty streets of downtown Jacksonville, I feel that tug of nostalgia already. I don't want the night to end.

"Waffle House?" Topher asks.

"Abso-freaking-lutely!" Chloe replies. "You read my mind."

We're about a half block away when Chloe spots a classic sports car and gets all excited.

"Check it out," she says. "A Gran Torino!"

The car's green, and really old.

"Wait," she says, "can one of you take a picture of me and the car? I gotta send it to Carlos."

I'm left wondering what this old car has to do with Carlos, while Topher grabs Chloe's phone and starts shooting photos. She's leaning up against the car, with a silly grin and two thumbs up.

Chloe takes the phone back and points the camera toward us. "Smile!" she says. "It's amazing," she tells us, looking back at the car. "It's even the same color."

"As what?" Topher asks.

"The car in that old movie *Gran Torino*. Carlos is totally obsessed with Clint Eastwood. It's so freaking weird."

"Ugh, men," I huff.

"What do you mean?" Chloe asks, walking toward us.

"All Clint Eastwood movies are total testosterone fests," I reply.

She laughs. "Are you kidding me? Have you seen *Gran Torino*?"

"Wait, yeah. Is that the one where a kid tries to steal Clint Eastwood's car?" I'm pretty sure I watched that movie with my parents a few years ago.

"The kid is part of a Hmong family," she says. "They live next door to him, and he's an old bitter Polish guy. But they melt his heart, and everybody becomes friends. It's totally sappy—"

"I remember now," I say. "It was sweet."

"I liked it too, but a bunch of people hated it. They thought it was a white-savior movie."

I stare at her, confused.

"How so?"

"I mean, an old white dude swoops in and saves a Hmong family from their plight." She shrugs. "Anyway, Carlos bought the whole thing. He freaking wept during the funeral scene." She shakes her head. "Like a baby!"

I'm trying to figure out how to respond when Chloe looks down at her phone and laughs.

"I sent him the picture of you two, and he's completely baffled that the three of us are together."

She types again, smiling, and then looks up at me. "He says to tell Ruby hi. He wants to know what we're up to."

That's unexpected. Chloe sends a quick response. She watches as a text comes in immediately.

"That's weird," she tells us. "Carlos wants to come meet us. Poor kid hardly ever hangs out past nine-thirty. He gets up at five."

"Five in the morning even on a Sunday?" Topher asks. "That's obscene."

She nods. "Morning conditioning. Carlos works harder than anyone I've ever met."

She looks down at her phone again and then directly at me. "Is it cool if he comes to Waffle House?"

I'm tongue-tied. Carlos wants to hang out with us? With *me*? I have no idea how to respond. I look to Topher for help.

He studies my face for a moment, clearly seeing all the emotion I can't seem to hold in. His eyebrows arch, and then he says to Chloe, "Totally."

On the way to Waffle House, Topher grabs my arm and pulls me back until we're out of Chloe's earshot. She's texting someone, so she barely notices.

"Hey," he says. "I'm confused. Isn't this the same Carlos we were talking about the other day? Malena's cousin? Mr. Sporty Balls?"

"Yeah," I whisper back.

"Aren't we supposed to hate him?" he asks.

"Maybe not so much?" I say. "He's . . ." I let out a long sigh and Topher looks at me, puzzled.

"He's . . . ?" Topher draws out the question, urging me to finish my thought.

"I don't know, Topher. I just think he's really—"

"What? Sexy? You think he's sexy."

I stop in my tracks. For a moment, it becomes impossible to walk and think at the same time. "No, it's not that, really. He's kind of . . . surprising. It's hard to explain. He's genuinely kind. And he listens, you know?" I stare at Topher, confused. Am I making any sense at all? He nods, encouraging me to continue.

"It's like he doesn't think he already has all the answers. He's willing to change his mind. And he's sweet with Malena, so concerned about her."

"Well, that's interesting," Topher says, glancing ahead at Chloe to make sure she's still distracted.

"Yeah, it totally is."

I pause to gather my thoughts, still surprised by them, and

sick of tripping and stumbling across my words. What am I even trying to say?

"He's so—"

"Sexy. Admit it, Ruby. I'm not into guys, and even *I* think he's sexy!"

I feel a blush spread, bright red across my face. "Okay, yes. That too. But, honestly, I didn't find him even remotely attractive before. Not until I saw this other side of him."

"Really?" Topher asks, incredulous.

"Really! I thought he was a burly asshat with Popeye biceps and a cartoonishly chiseled chin."

Topher guffaws, and Chloe turns back to see us both dissolve into laughter.

"What's going on back there?" she asks.

"Just a stupid meme," Topher says, gesturing toward his phone. Then, through some deft magic that only Topher is capable of, he manages to pull up an actual stupid meme and show it to Chloe.

God, I love Topher. He always knows exactly what to do.

At Waffle House, we get a booth for four, and Topher sits down next to Chloe. We order three coffees and the triple hash browns, smothered and covered.

Chloe and Topher make small talk, and I'm trying to keep up with their banter, but my attention keeps drifting to the fact that Carlos is about to slide into a booth beside me. The whole thing is so baffling.

When the hash browns come, Topher and Chloe dive in, but I pick at them, my stomach suddenly flippy.

Carlos walks through the door, wearing Adidas track pants, a white T-shirt, and a baseball cap.

"Jo's gonna be so pissed she didn't come to the Nick Jonas

concert," Topher whispers as we watch Carlos stride across the restaurant toward us.

Topher has a point. Carlos is definitely looking like a baseball god tonight, all confidence and swagger.

I must admit, he looks *good*.

When he gets to the table, he takes off his cap and slides into the booth next to me. "Hey," he says. "I heard you like *Gran Torino* too." He's looking right at me, his dark hair falling over his eyes, searching my face for a response.

"Yeah," I say. "I watched it with my parents. We all loved it."

He smiles a big, wide-open grin. "Cool."

And just like that, Carlos Rosario, God of Baseball, turns into Just Plain Carlos. It's weird and surprising and maybe even a little thrilling, because—as it turns out—Just Plain Carlos is pretty great.

CHAPTER THIRTEEN

MALENA

On Sunday morning, I walk into Ruby's house with a big tumbler of Mami's heavy-duty Puerto Rican coffee. I got zero sleep and I'm feeling a little dazed.

Soraida and I rode with Carlos, even though Mami said she could drop us off. The whole thing was super weird. He texted us both at five a.m., before his morning workout, saying he wanted to give Mami a day to sleep in. Since when does Carlos care about Mami getting some rest? I mean, it was considerate of him, but still. Of course, he showed up late, which was incredibly annoying.

But not as annoying as his little antics when we arrived at Ruby's. He insisted on walking us to the door, like we're a pair of six-year-olds heading to a playdate. What's his deal?

So now I'm late, and Carlos is leaning against the doorway. He seems to be flirting with Ruby, which is totally creepy. Carlos always insists he doesn't have time for girls. But now here he is, loitering on Ruby's front porch, when she and I have important work to do. I thought he despised her, but the way he's standing so close, all moony-eyed and distracted, clearly his opinions have changed.

I watch them, trying to read Ruby's reaction. She's definitely not moony-eyed, but she's deep in conversation with him. What could Carlos possibly be telling her that she'd find interesting?

Maybe it's not his words that have pulled her in. Maybe Ruby's not immune to Carlos's charms after all. So disappointing.

Whatever. I need to focus.

"Is everyone here?" I ask Ruby.

"Yeah, they're all in the sunroom," she says. "I'll be right in."

I take a big swig of coffee and head inside.

I stayed up all night researching how to plan a protest, looking at ideas for T-shirts and banners, wondering how the school will react and what Calista Jameson will write about us next. I stressed about Mami, and whether she'll understand that I need to do this. I was going to talk to her when she got up this morning, but she looked so exhausted from all the extra shifts she's been working. So, instead, I told her Carlos was bringing me here and urged her to go back to bed.

After hours of research, I learned there's nothing straightforward about planning a high school dress-code rebellion. There's no manual, either—I actually searched.

I did find something unexpected, though. A whole article on storytelling in the context of social change, with interviews from a bunch of activists who are also documentary directors. They talked about their techniques for shooting and editing, which was pretty cool. It got me thinking about Ms. Baptiste's final project and that maybe I could do a video about us and our protest. Ms. Baptiste said we should pick a topic that's important to us. To me, this is more than important, it's meaningful.

Sure, I'm anxious and jittery, worried about how we are going to pull this off, but for the first time in weeks, practically an eternity, I also feel wholly alive. It's like someone jolted me awake from a deep slumber with a million kilowatts of high-voltage electricity—creating a feminist Frankenstein's monster from all the broken parts.

But now, as I take in our little tribe's "strategy session," I'm starting to stress again. This meeting is complete pandemonium. Everyone is talking over each other. Laptops and phones are scattered around the room. Social-media pages are displayed on half of the screens, news articles about student protests on the others. There's even a restaurant-size stew pot sitting awkwardly on the coffee table.

"Nadia has an idea involving pots," Ruby says, walking into the room. "I'm not really sure I get it."

Her face is flushed, like she just came in from a brisk jog. I decide to put her comments aside, since I'm still annoyed by the whole flirting-with-Carlos thing. Plus, I can't explain what a cacerolazo is without diving into a history lesson on Latin American politics.

Nadia and Xiomara are debating with Ruby's friends Jo and Nessa about what message to write on a poster board. Xiomara holds up a neon-yellow board with flowers drawn all over it and *I'm standing up for myself—I'm a nasty woman* written in big red letters.

"Why the flowers?" Jo asks.

"To match the shirts," Xiomara says. "There's a whole apparel line!" She opens her jacket to reveal a T-shirt with bright flowers and the words *Nasty Woman* written in cursive. "Nadia is a badass crafty chica! We made these last night. We used glitter fabric paint and iron-on stickers. Aren't they awesome?"

"And check out the stretchy fabric!" Nadia adds, tugging at her own flowery T-shirt. Then she pulls out some samples from a tote that's sitting on the floor and starts passing them around.

"Oh, these are soft," remarks Nessa, stroking her face with the fabric.

"We also have a Spanish line," Nadia says, showing off the *Chica Fuerte* graphic on her own tee.

Ruby's friend Topher is standing next to a flip chart, holding a huge marker and trying to keep up with the T-shirt debate. He's failing miserably.

I give him props for trying. It can't be easy being the only guy in the room.

On the couch, Soraida and Beatriz are basically ignoring him, deep in a rapid-Spanish argument over the design for T-shirts.

"We have to incorporate the pantyliners *and* the nipples," Soraida confidently declares. She turns to me for reinforcement. "Right, Malena? The nipple should be the symbol of the rebellion. The NippleRiot!"

"Ohhh, maybe we can wear neon-colored balaclavas like the Pussy Riot girls," Nessa adds, pulling a photo of a girl in a pink ski mask onto her screen.

I shrug, feeling both overwhelmed and empowered by the scene I've helped to create.

"Lucinda should be calling on Skype soon," Ruby says. "That should help get us organized. I feel like we're all over the place. We need some focus."

I pull out my notes from last night's research. One of the bullet points reads *Document your event and have fun.*

Maybe I should be recording all this. This is the kind of high-energy prep meeting I've seen in documentaries. I take out my phone and record a few clips around the room. I don't know what I'll do with them, but I'm enjoying playing with different angles and types of shots.

"What are you doing?" Soraida asks.

"Making a video," I say. "Just pretend I'm not here."

"If you're gonna film this, I need to put on some lipstick," she says, pulling out a tube of lip gloss from her bag.

"What about the petition?" Topher asks, still poised beside the flip chart. "We need to focus on getting people to sign the petition, fast."

"How hard could it be?" Soraida smacks her lips in front of a compact mirror. "How many signatures do we need, anyway?"

"Ten percent of the student body, at least," Topher says. "That's more than three hundred people."

Topher writes *PETITION* in bold letters on the page.

"How do we get three hundred people to sign a piece of paper?" Xiomara asks. "I don't know three hundred people."

"We have to hit the pavement—roam through the parking lots with clipboards and pens," Topher says.

"Sorry to break it to you, buddy, but I've never seen three hundred people hanging out in the parking lot at once," Xiomara adds.

Topher gives her a pointed look. He's about to respond, but Ruby cuts him off.

"We have to think big. We need to get Orange Grove to wake up!" she says.

"That's the whole point of the protest," Soraida declares. "We can set up tables and people can line up to sign. We'll get five hundred signatures! At least."

Abuela Joan enters the room, holding a snack tray and napkins. "Free the nipple!" she cheers.

Soraida moves a few magazines out of the way so Abuela Joan can place the platter of pastries, mini quiches, and fruit on the coffee table.

"This should hold you over until the pizza arrives," Abuela Joan says.

"Thank you," a chorus responds.

"Oh, hi, Malena," she chirps, wrapping me into one of her all-consuming hugs. "I didn't know you'd arrived."

I put away my phone and hug her back, taking in the smell of narcissus flowers on her collarbone.

It's not often that I find myself wanting an adult's approval—other than Mami's and Papi's—but Abuela Joan's exuberance is nothing short of contagious. It's what my former French teacher would call "joie de vivre."

"This looks like the start of good trouble. I'm so proud of you girls." She sighs, and I sense some nostalgia in the way she's gazing at everyone in the room. I wonder if she's ever planned a protest. I'm guessing she has. Maybe someday I'll get the chance to ask her.

But not today. There's way too much going on.

Ruby calls for the group's attention, and Abuela Joan leaves for the kitchen.

"Let's gather around the coffee table to get a call going with Lucinda," Ruby says, setting up her laptop.

"Who's Lucinda?" Xiomara asks.

"Some badass activist in Seattle," Soraida tells her. "Her mom is a lawyer, and she said she would help us if we run into any trouble."

"Like going to jail?" Xiomara asks tentatively. "Mami would kill me."

"I'm sure she'll bail us out," Soraida says. "In Seattle they're used to this kind of thing."

Oh, Soraida. I don't even know where she gets these wild ideas.

"No one's going to jail," I reassure Xiomara, right as Lucinda's face appears on the screen.

"Hi, everyone!" She waves at us with both hands from what

appears to be her bedroom. She's sitting at her desk. Behind her there's a couch covered in pink and white pillows and a framed canvas print of a llama's face. Not exactly what I expected. "This is so freaking awesome," she exclaims, her face beaming at a close angle.

We answer with claps, half laughs, and chuckles.

"Thanks for meeting with us at such short notice," Ruby says apologetically. "I know it's obscenely early in Seattle."

"No worries! I had to be up early anyway," Lucinda says with a dismissing wave. "We don't have much time, so let's get to it. My job here is to give you encouragement. It's up to you to find out what works in your area. I mean, let's face it—Ruby, you know this—Orange Grove is not Eastlake High."

Soraida edges forward so that Lucinda can see her as she asks, "That's great and all, but what should we be doing?"

For once, I'm glad she opened her mouth.

"Organizing!" Lucinda says, like the answer is obvious. "You need to craft a strategy to get the student body involved. Grassroots movements grow from the ground up. Start with the students, get teachers to buy in, then go all the way to the school board."

"Right," Ruby says. "But the problem is, we have to get support *fast*. We have one chance with the school board if we want to see change happen this year, and we need tons of signatures on a petition by a week from tomorrow."

Lucinda takes a breath and smiles, swaying her head as she says, "The word is *undaunted*."

"You don't know Orange Grove High School," Ruby exclaims. "People here aren't—"

"We don't really have a culture of protest," Nessa chimes in helpfully.

"That's why you need to be undaunted," Lucinda repeats, landing a clenched fist on her open palm. "You've got this!"

Undaunted, I recite to myself.

I pull out my phone and tap on the dictionary app. I type in the word to make sure I understand its full meaning:

> Courageously resolute, especially in the face of danger or difficulty; bold, brave, courageous.

Yes. Yes. Yes. That's exactly what I want to be. That's what I *need* to be.

"Think big," Lucinda says. "Do whatever it takes to get the signatures. If you can't get on the school-board agenda, then you might as well forget about it. Nothing's gonna happen." Lucinda leans forward in her chair. "If you get to the meeting, you'll probably only have two minutes to make your case."

Two minutes? The interview with Calista took an hour and there was so much more I wanted to say after it ended. How do you "make a case" in two minutes?

"You'll want to focus on promoting equity, not one-to-one equality," Lucinda says.

"Totally." Ruby nods. I want to ask what exactly does that mean, but everyone else is nodding, too, like they already know. I make a note to look it up later.

Then Lucinda points to Ruby.

"Ruby, I'm thinking you'll probably be the spokesperson, since you have some experience and you guys have, like, no time to prepare."

Ruby nods, her gaze searching my face. I shrug. Lucinda's right, I guess.

I mean, it's not like I'm completely inexperienced. I used to speak in front of students in my old school, but that was nothing compared to making an argument in front of a school board. Besides, I'll get super nervous, which means my accent will come through loud and clear. Which also means I may even forget a few words in English—like that god-awful day in Dr. Hardaway's office. The last thing I want is to embarrass myself, Ruby, or everyone else helping us—for the entire school to bear witness.

"We can figure it out later," Ruby says, her eyes holding mine. I nod.

"Okay, everybody. I gotta run," Lucinda tells us, waving.

"That's it?" Soraida blurts out.

"I had a last-minute thing come up," Lucinda says apologetically. "You can always ask Olive if you need help with the details."

"Who's Olive?" Soraida asks.

"Ruby's sister," Lucinda says, as if we all should know the answer. "She's like my personal hero. I totally wanted to be her when I was in middle school. She's super experienced and a killer organizer. Right, Ruby?"

Ruby nods, but her smile doesn't reach her eyes.

"You totally have this. Think in broad strokes. Fill in the details later."

And after those final words of wisdom, Lucinda's smile flashes off the screen.

For a while, we all stare at the dark square in front of us, as if expecting an encore. Then the room erupts into renewed chaos, everyone arguing over what to do next.

Ruby cups her hands around her mouth, shouting, "Hellllooooooo? Can we focus, please?" but no one seems to hear her.

"People!" Jo shrieks. "The World Series starts in exactly four hours and forty-three minutes, and I am *not* going to miss the pregame because we can't agree on a freaking T-shirt design!"

I'm wondering what a baseball game has to do with anything when Nadia pulls a giant slotted spoon from her backpack and bangs hard on the metal stew pot. Around the room, everyone's hands fly to cover their ears as the loud ringing bounces from every wall. Then, silence.

"See? It works," Nadia says triumphantly.

I'm beyond relieved when Abuela Joan walks in with news of the pizzas' arrival and everyone leaves the sunroom for the kitchen.

Ruby pulls me aside. "I thought Lucinda would be more . . . specific. This is total chaos. It's like a runaway train," she frets, rubbing the back of her neck with her open palm. "Where's this all going?"

Undaunted. I want to be undaunted. So I pull out my notes and grab a flip-chart marker. Then I say the most undaunted thing I can think of: "Full speed ahead."

CHAPTER FOURTEEN

RUBY

Way too early Monday morning, Topher and I are pounding the pavement of the senior parking lot, thrusting clipboards into the hands of anyone who pauses for even a millisecond to listen. We're both exhausted after the Waffle House all-nighter on Saturday and the marathon planning session yesterday. But I don't regret a moment of it, especially not Saturday night.

Carlos broke his high-protein, low-carb diet, scarfing down a double peanut butter waffle drenched in maple syrup. He ate as if the world was ending, and when Chloe tried to steal a piece from his plate, he slapped her hand away, glaring daggers at her.

He gave me a bite, though. It was delicious.

I know I need to focus. We have a gargantuan task ahead. But my mind keeps drifting to Carlos, and the few minutes we spent alone after we left Waffle House, walking and talking.

It's not like we talked about anything super important. We chatted about our favorite movies and restaurants, how weird it was for both of us to move to North Florida, and how much we still miss our hometowns. He told me about playing soccer at the Parque Central in San Juan and I described riding the ferry to Whidbey Island, my favorite day trip from Seattle.

It was so simple and nice. I wanted the walk to last longer. I'm pretty sure he did too.

After Carlos left, Chloe actually thanked us for being "totally normal" around Carlos.

"'Totally normal'?" Topher laughed. "That's not a descriptor typically attached to me or Ruby."

She explained that besides his family, no one really treats Carlos like a real person, a regular seventeen-year-old, and he needs that. She said he hates the way people, especially girls, "worship and fawn" over him—her words, not his. That made Topher laugh again.

"Believe me," he assured Chloe, "Carlos will get absolutely no worshiping or fawning from Ruby McAlister."

He's right, of course. I'm definitely not going to fawn all over Carlos, but—to my great surprise—I find myself wanting to maybe hang out with him more. I did see him yesterday morning for a few minutes, when he dropped Malena at my house, but that doesn't really count. Everyone was waiting for me to bring some order to the chaos inside—which proved an impossible mission.

I'm starting to wonder if I'm the right person for the job.

"Top o' the morning to you, Miss O'Sullivan." Topher practically ambushes Moira O'Sullivan as she's stepping out of her beat-up Honda. "You're looking a bit sleepy this morning. Wouldn't it be nice if you didn't have to waste those precious extra moments of sleep worrying about what you'll wear to school?"

"What the hell are you going on about, Pérez?" Moira is looking a little rough, like maybe she was out all night headbanging at some underground show. She probably was. Moira is mysterious and dark, the kind of person you wish you could follow around for a week, just to see what she's up to.

"The dress code!" Topher says brightly. "We need a gender-neutral dress code."

Moira shrugs. "Sounds cool. Good luck with that." She starts to push past him.

"Wait!" Topher says, shoving the petition in her face. "We need you to sign."

She takes the clipboard and looks down at the (still short) list of names. "What is this?"

"A petition. We have to collect *actual* signatures on a real piece of paper if we want to change the dress code."

"Not interested," she says, handing back the clipboard. "I'm an anarchist."

Topher looks to me, like I'm gonna need to step in and close the deal. *Might as well give it a try.* "An anarchist? Great! So, you must be all about getting rid of arcane structures, rules, and regulations, right?"

Moira looks at me like I'm a complete dumbass. "Anarchists don't sign petitions. We resist systems of authority. So if you wanna demolish the school board, come to me. Otherwise, not interested."

With that, she heads across the parking lot toward school.

"Wait!" I call out. "Here's something you might be interested in!" I chase her down and hand her a flyer for Friday's Nipple-Riot walkout.

Moira glances down at it with a bored expression and then keeps going.

At least she doesn't crumple it up and throw it away.

"This is harder than I thought it would be," I say, watching Moira disappear into the crowd.

"Who knows? Maybe everyone's forgotten how to write with a pen and paper," Topher responds, clearly trying to lighten my mood.

"Or maybe they just don't care," I sigh.

"That kind of thinking will get us nowhere, young lady," Topher exclaims, mimicking the annoying nasal intonation of Doris, the school secretary. "Back into the fray!"

By the end of yesterday's meeting, we finally decided on a two-pronged attack: a petition to get on the school board's agenda and a walkout to keep the momentum going and bring media attention to the school. We'll set up tables outside during the walkout, and Jo, Nessa, and Malena's friends will work them, encouraging protesters to sign our petition. With any luck, the strategy just might get us to the magic number before next Monday's deadline. Topher even found us an old megaphone at a yard sale, and Soraida and her friends are making a bunch of extra posters.

Olive assured me that abolishing the code wouldn't fly in Clay County, Florida. So we decided that once the school board is really feeling the heat, then we'll go in and make our case for a gender-neutral dress code. If we get enough signatures on the petition, that is.

"Okay," I tell Topher. "Let's divide and conquer." I'm trying hard to muster a bit of Topher's plucky optimism. "You head over to the junior lot, and I'll hit up some more seniors."

Topher grabs a stack of NippleRiot flyers and gives me a military-style salute. "Meet you at the lockers at oh-eight-hundred."

In the next several minutes, I learn a few surprising facts about my fellow seniors. The band kids want to replace the dress code with uniforms. In their assessment, uniforms keep students from being distracted by decisions about what to wear, and they also break down socioeconomic distinctions. The purity-ring crowd, while agreeing that it may not seem fair to target girls in the dress code, believes that modesty is a "virtue" all people should strive for, and so on and so forth.

They all refuse to sign.

When I see Marvin Wells across the parking lot, I'm sure I've found an ally. He's the president of the school's small but mighty Black Student Union—he's always saying super-smart stuff about discrimination and bias.

"Hey, Marvin!" I wave my clipboard over my head as I rush toward him and two other guys, all sitting on the hood of his car. "I need you to sign our petition."

Marvin stands up and waves me toward him. "Petition?" he asks. "I'm intrigued, Ruby."

"It's for the school board. We're going to the school board next month to demand a gender-neutral dress code."

He grabs the petition and stares down at it.

"*Gender*-neutral," his friend says, as if *gender* is some sort of bad word.

"You know, so girls don't get singled out. We want to take out references to bare midriffs, leggings, skirt lengths. That kind of thing," I explain, thrilled that someone's interested enough to ask probing questions.

"That's cool, but are you planning to have them take out all the crap about hoodies? Boxer shorts showing?"

"Oh, or what about dreadlocks and do-rags?" the other guy says. He jabs Marvin and they both start laughing.

"Do-rags?" I ask, confused. I think I remember seeing something about no undergarments showing, but I don't remember anything about do-rags in the dress code.

"How about weaves and hair extensions?" Marvin asks me, then turns to his friend and says, "Remember when Imani got in trouble for her braids last year?"

"I mean, I . . . we'll have to look into it, I guess." I sound utterly ignorant.

"Yeah, sorry, Ruby," Marvin says. "Do yourself a favor and research intersectionality. You may learn a thing or two."

"Uh, okay . . ." My voice trails off. I want to tell him that of course I know what intersectionality is, but the stern look on his face suggests that this is not the time.

He hands me back the clipboard. "We're not interested in your petition."

Oh my God, this is a disaster. Why isn't anyone getting on board?

I start to feel tears sting at the corners of my eyes. I grab the clipboard and walk away, looking around for somewhere to hide. I see Carlos across the parking lot, leaning against his big SUV. I feel a lightness in my chest, an urge to head toward him, but then I take in the scene and the lightness dissolves into dread.

He stands taller than most of the crowd, and he's clearly the center of their attention. It's like he's some sort of social magnet. It doesn't look like he's talking much or saying anything special. The group seems more like an entourage. It's disconcerting how different this larger-than-life Carlos seems from the one who slid in next to me in the Waffle House booth. I'm not sure I know how to approach this Carlos, or if I even should.

I feel almost relieved when three guys I've never met walk up.

"We heard you're doing a petition to end the dress code?" one of them asks. I hate to seem judgy, but they don't seem the petition-signing type.

"Yeah, um . . ." I'm about to tell them that, technically, we're not asking to abolish the dress code, just make it more fair. They grab the petition and start signing. "Does this mean I can wear my Second Amendment T-shirt to school again?" the first guy asks. "'Cause I really love that freakin' shirt."

Something about these clowns brings the fire back to my gut. I'm desperate to put more names on the page, so when I see Lacrosse Chad and his asshole buddies, I decide to be strategic. "Hey, Chad!" I call out. "I'm ready for you to help with that petition!"

He comes up and grabs the clipboard from my hand. "Dude, she's really doing this," he says to his friends. "Check it out— a petition to abolish the dress code."

Okay, whatever. If they think they're petitioning to abolish the dress code, who am I to tell them otherwise? It's signatures, and that's all that matters.

"I'm *so* in!" his friend says. "Where do I sign?"

Chad hands him the clipboard and he signs his name with a flourish, then hands it to another lacrosse kid. "This is gonna be awesome!"

Chad calls over a couple of other guys from his team. They're with Sarah and Lucy, two senior girls who are already pushing the boundaries of the dress code every day.

They all pass around the clipboard, laughing and signing. As the others start to lumber off, Chad looks directly at my tits and says, "Look at you go, Roobs. Freeing the boobs already, huh?"

One of his teammates, hearing his comment, turns to stare at my boobs.

"Niiiice," he says, nodding and grinning.

Ugh, gross.

I feel bile swell up in my throat as I clutch the clipboard tightly to my chest, flash in their direction what I hope is a vague and dismissive glare, and turn to walk away. Honestly, given my past experience, I didn't think anyone would notice that I chose to forgo a bra with this sundress. Chad and his buddy must have built-in tit radar.

I look up to see Carlos and his entourage heading straight toward me. "Hold up, guys," he says as they approach.

I freeze in place, still disoriented by Chad's stare.

"Stirring up trouble again, Ruby?"

"What can I say?" I respond, my heart pounding. "I *am* an instigator."

Carlos laughs and glances down at my chest, where I now hold tight to the clipboard. "I'm guessing that's the petition Soraida and Malena have been obsessing about."

"Uh, yeah," I say, suddenly nervous and bewildered. It must be the audience that's gathering around us. Or maybe it's that Chad and his asshole friend just ogled my nonexistent boobs.

"Those two wouldn't shut up about it on the way to school this morning." Carlos chuckles.

He bites his bottom lip and looks into my eyes. For a moment, his own uber-confident veneer is replaced by another expression. Concern? I think maybe he can tell that something's off with me.

"You okay?" he asks quietly, his brow furrowed.

"I'm fine," I lie.

"How many signatures have you gotten so far?" His voice is encouraging.

"We've gotten a solid response." I decide to try projecting success, not specifying that our most enthusiastic supporters have been the Second Amendment crusaders and the guys who want their girlfriends coming to school in lingerie.

"Can I take a look?" Before I have a chance to react, he pulls the clipboard out of my hands and glances down at the pathetically short list of signatures.

"How many do you need?" he leans in to whisper, still holding the clipboard.

"Way more than we've got," I reply.

"I'm on it." He smiles, his expression almost mischievous.

"All right, everybody," he says, turning toward the crowd gathered around him. "We need to sign this."

And that's all it takes. I don't even have to give my pitch. He doesn't even mention what the petition is for. Carlos just signs, and then he passes it into the eager crowd.

As the petition starts to make its rounds, Carlos pulls me aside. "Can we talk for a sec?"

"Aren't we talking already?"

"Like, somewhere not here," he clarifies.

I nod, and he places his hand gently on my back, guiding me around a corner, behind the field house.

When we're beyond the gaze of his entourage, Carlos drops his hand from my back and looks right at me, studying my face. "Seriously, Ruby. Are you okay?" he asks. "You look a little pale."

I try not to scowl, since this is, after all, coming from the guy who called me White Girl the first time we met.

"Yeah," I sigh. "Some gross lacrosse players just made stupid comments. I'm over it already."

"What kind of comments?" Carlos asks, anger swelling in his voice.

"You know, standard, run-of-the-mill body-shaming."

Carlos clenches his jaw and looks past me, scanning the parking lot. "You want me to—"

"What?" I let out a laugh. "Go beat them up? I can fight my own battles, thank you very much."

Taking a cue from my bright smile, Carlos drops the angry

grimace. He steps back and raises his hands above his head, as if in surrender.

"Didn't mean to offend, Ms. McAlister!" he says. "But just for the record, I've never been in a fight in my life." He gives me a playful shove on the elbow. "And I definitely won't be starting now. I've got a future to think about."

"Wise decision," I say, recalling what Chloe said about how hard Carlos works. I wonder what it would be like, to worry that any tiny misstep could erase years of hard work, jeopardize everything. "Nothing good ever comes of violence."

"Is that like a Gandhi quote or something?" he teases.

A girl rounds the corner of the field house, bringing the petition back to Carlos. Watching her approach, I find myself feeling wistful, wishing I had a few more moments alone with him.

"Thanks," he tells her.

"Let's go, Carlos," she whines. "Everybody's waiting for you."

I take the petition from Carlos and study it closely as we walk side by side to the gathering crowd. The pages have started to fill, and seeing all those signatures brings back the courage I so desperately need.

"Thank you," I whisper, gently nudging him.

He nods, but he doesn't respond. Instead, Carlos looks down at the place where our bodies touch.

"Hey, everybody," I call out, stepping away from his side. "If you wanna join in, we're planning a walkout during lunch period Friday." I dig into my backpack and grab a handful of flyers. Suddenly the flyers are making their way around the parking lot, and everyone's buzzing with conversation about the NippleRiot.

"Are you doing the walkout?" the girl who brought him the petition asks.

I watch as he smiles and shrugs. I'm left wondering: Is he or isn't he? And if not, why did he just help me?

Then he looks right past me and his smile falters.

I turn the direction he's facing. And then I see it: a Channel 2 Action News truck rolling into the parking lot of Orange Grove High.

"Oh shit," he says, directly to me. "I really hope they're not here for you and Malena."

CHAPTER FIFTEEN

MALENA

At a quarter to five, my family gathers around Tía Lorna's living-room TV to watch the five o'clock newscast. It's a chaotic ending to an otherwise exhilarating day.

"Everyone is watching," Soraida exclaims, nose in her phone as she plops down on the couch next to me. "I can't believe you're gonna be on TV. In English and español!"

"I can't believe I remembered how to speak," I say, looking out the front door for the hundredth time. Mami said she was leaving work early to watch with us, but she's still not here.

I get the feeling she's not too happy with me right now, especially since I waited until *after* I'd done the TV interviews to tell her about them. In my defense, everything happened so fast. One minute I was walking through the school parking lot; the next there was a guy shoving a camera in my face and a woman questioning me with a giant puffy microphone. There was barely any time to think, much less call Mami to debate what I should do.

Soraida's phone dings with a new string of text messages.

"The girls want to know how it went with Ms. Baptiste today," she says.

"Mission accomplished!" I high-five my cousin.

"That's my girl!" she responds, typing on her phone like a madwoman.

During lunch period, I called the school-board office to talk to someone about getting on the agenda for the next meeting and to check on how exactly they wanted us to turn in their precious signatures. Heaven forbid the whole petition be thrown out over a technicality. That was when the woman who answered the phone brusquely informed me that we needed a faculty sponsor to get on the speakers' list. The petition isn't enough.

I knew right away which teacher to ask. I walked—ran, really—to Ms. Baptiste's studio, praying she subscribed to the belief that we caribeñas should stick together.

At first Ms. Baptiste was reluctant to take on the job. Mostly because we only have three weeks to prepare. Then I pulled out my copy of *Sister Outsider* and started quoting from the essay she asked us to read. How remaining silent offers no protection. How we will never be a whole person as long as we remain silent, because there will always be a part of us—inside—that wants to be spoken. " 'If you don't speak it out, one day it will just up and punch you in the mouth from the inside,' " I quoted.

In the end, she couldn't say no.

She agreed to sponsor us under the condition that, to prepare for the meeting, we review the materials in a ginormous binder filled with all kinds of regulations. So far I've managed to slog my way through the student code of conduct, school board policies, and something called Robert's Rules.

It's all a little overwhelming. And, as if that's not enough, Ms. Baptiste also suggested we come up with a plan B. She was clearly pessimistic about the prospects of our plan A.

I wanted to make sure she knew we were serious, so I spent my entire study period in the library looking up things like *dress code student rights* and *changing the school dress code.* After multiple dead ends, I came across a potential plan B—something called a student-faculty liaison committee or student-faculty senate. Students and teachers get together to think through new school policies, get buy-in from the administration, and figure out how to implement them. I felt like a freaking genius just for finding the idea.

The more I learn about it, the more I'm convinced it could work. I cross-referenced the school district's rules, and because it's a committee, it doesn't require the approval of the school board.

Anyway, Poor María Malena accomplished something today— a few things, actually!

I just hope my family comes to see it this way. The sucky truth is that Soraida and I still aren't sure our moms are going to let us participate in the protest that we've been working so hard to plan. If we go ahead without their permission, both Soraida and I might never leave the house again.

"Did you put on lipstick for the interview like I told you to?" Soraida asks, applying a fresh coat of gloss to her own lips. "Xiomara said she could do Ruby's makeup for the school-board meeting. Give her a little color, you know? Xiomara thinks it will make her more approachable."

"I think she wears mascara sometimes," I say, trying to recall the details of Ruby's face.

"Every little bit helps," Soraida says. "Do you know how hard it is to keep the public's attention these days?" She pauses to apply a second coat. Her lips seem to have doubled in size. "You and Ruby are competing with like a million other stories. Calista Jameson is not gonna wait forever for an update. You need to keep the edge."

I'm about to ask if she really thinks wearing a darker shade of lipstick will be the thing to give us an "edge" when Carlos interrupts our conversation, squeezing in next to Soraida while cradling a giant bowl of popcorn.

"Popcorn? Really?" I ask. "It's news, not entertainment."

"Oh, I'm planning on being very entertained." He snorts, shoving a handful of popcorn in his mouth.

Soraida reaches for the bowl and passes it to me.

"No, thanks." My stomach is churning. The news anchors are already talking about the day's headlines. *Where's Mami?*

"Beatriz says the Telemundo interview airs at six," Soraida announces, reading a text on her screen. Beatriz's mother is friends with local anchorman Leonides Buenavides, and she got him to come out and do a special report after they found out about the interview on the English channel.

Tía Lorna and Abuela walk in from the kitchen carrying platters of cubed yellow cheese, Ritz crackers, and salchichón.

"Oh, I forgot the guava paste," Abuela says, rushing back to the kitchen, her chancletas going pit-a-pat as she hurries across the tile floor.

My family is acting like this is some kind of party, even though they have made it very clear—in two languages—that they think I am digging my own grave. I guess the excitement of having a family member on the news is too much to pass up.

We all stare at the TV as the words *local* and *late-breaking* fill the screen, animated to a score of urgent-sounding music.

Seconds later, Mami and Tío Wiliberto burst through the front door at the same time.

"Did we miss it?" Mami asks, out of breath. She kisses the top of my head and sits on the dining-room chair next to me.

I reach for her hand and hold it in mine. She squeezes it. "You should've called me before you agreed to do this."

I open my mouth to plead my case, but Tía Lorna shushes us. "It's about to start."

"Abuela!" Soraida calls, hands cupped around her mouth. "Hurry up! You're gonna miss it."

Abuela rushes back, her chancletas rattling even faster. She blocks the TV, arranging the guava paste on the coffee table.

"We can't see!" half of the room yells in chorus, waving frantically at Abuela to move.

She turns left and right, trying to decide where to go. She finally steps in Mami's direction and takes a seat in the armchair next to her.

Soraida aims the remote control at the screen and raises the volume.

I watch the little green bars move along the bottom of the screen, my pulse rising with each one.

A box with a photo of our school appears on the upper right corner of the screen. The words *Dress Code Debacle* are displayed underneath. The anchor, a middle-aged Black woman, looks straight at us and says, "And now we go to Orange Grove High School, where a group of students is demanding change to what they call a sexist dress code."

Suddenly, my face takes over the entire screen.

"I should not be punished for having breasts," I hear myself say. I don't have to look to know the gasp I just heard came from Tía Lorna.

Mami squeezes my hand a little harder. I squeeze it back, not wanting to take my eyes off the screen.

The reporter briefly explains how I was suspended for not wearing a bra. Then she talks to Ruby about the NippleRiot, the petition we have to submit if we want a chance to convince the school board, and the school-wide walkout we're planning for Friday.

"Any student who takes part in any demonstration faces the possibility of suspension," Dr. Hardaway tells the reporter.

Then the reporter cuts back to me and Ruby.

"We have a right to voice our concerns in a peaceful manner," Ruby says, looking directly at the camera.

"Just because we're students, they can't take away our constitutional rights," I add.

Now, though, I'm unable to recall saying that in the first place. *Constitutional rights* sounds so grown-up. How did I ever remember that line? I was so worried that my accent and bilingual brain would betray me that after Calista's interview, Soraida helped me come up with some "sound bites" I could memorize, just in case. I guess it paid off.

The final shot is our little band of rebels wearing the #NippleRiot T-shirts that Jo and Nessa hand-drew after our meeting—all white with two gold hearts over the nipples.

"NippleRiot was my idea!" Soraida bellows. But she quickly gets shushed by everyone, including me.

Jo used Soraida's concept, mostly to shut her up. But Jo and Nessa had the final word on the design, opting for a style they described as "Kinderwhore throwback." Whatever that means. I kinda liked Xiomara and Nadia's flower design better.

"I still think we should've gone with the pantyliners over the nipples," Soraida says in a huff, ignoring a new round of shushing. "I don't get the hearts. It's too artsy, if you ask me."

I roll my eyes. I've had enough talk of T-shirts to last me a lifetime.

After the piece ends, the reporter stands in front of the school

and reads a statement from the school board blaming us—
blaming me, really—for breaking the rules in the first place. They
say it's highly unlikely the issue will be taken up by the school
board in this academic year.

We'll see about that.

Then they go back to the anchor in the studio. She quickly
moves on to the next story.

"You killed it!" Soraida throws both arms around me, seizing
me in a hug that forces all the air out of my lungs. "I'm so proud
of you, primita."

"Thanks," I say, half smiling.

"And the T-shirts! Everyone is gonna want one!" Soraida is
texting furiously.

Mami, Tía Lorna, and Abuela are speaking over each other.
With the TV news still blaring in the background, it takes me a
moment to realize they're arguing in Spanish over our involve-
ment in the NippleRiot.

"If you ask me, nothing good will come from this," Tía says.
"And she's taking her cousins down with her."

"Uh, don't look at me," Carlos says, reaching for a piece of
salchichón and shoving it into his mouth. "I've been saying this is
a bad idea from the start."

Soraida elbows him in the ribs. "You're so full of shit!"

"Soraida!" Tía Lorna hisses.

"He signed the petition!" she shrieks at Tía Lorna. Then, to
Carlos: "I saw your name on Ruby's list." Carlos pinches one of
the chichos on Soraida's side. She swats him away and spits, "Get
your hands off my sexy love handles."

"How come you didn't sign it when *we* asked?" I give him a
pained look.

He looks away and shrugs. Soraida throws a handful of popcorn at him, singing for the whole family to hear, "Carlos has a crush on a skinny white girl."

Carlos pinches her again, his face going beet red. But this time Soraida just roars with laughter.

Tía Lorna throws Carlos a concerned look. "What skinny white girl?"

Carlos waves his hand dismissively, reaches for the snack tray, and pops a huge mouthful of cheese and salchichón. Big enough that he's too busy chewing to respond. Smart man.

"I don't know, Camila," Abuela tells Mami. "Do you want Malena to be known as a problemática?"

Mami kicks off her shoes and lets her hair down. Her manner is unperturbed, but the thin line of her lips is a dead giveaway. She's forcing herself to stay calm.

"How does speaking up make me a troublemaker?" I ask Abuela, trying to keep my tone respectful, but I'm too worked up to succeed.

"What are you going to do if she gets suspended?" Tía Lorna asks Mami, as if I'm no longer present in the room.

"I won't get suspended," I say confidently. "I called the ACLU office in Jacksonville. As long as we're not missing a class, we're not considered truant."

"You called the what?" Abuela asks.

"The American Civil Liberties Union. They said that if we hold the walkout during our lunch period, our school record won't be affected. At most, we'll get detention."

"Oh, so now detention is an acceptable alternative?" Tía Lorna argues, crossing her arms over her chest and leaning back in her chair.

"It doesn't look good, Malena, a young señorita like yourself wrapped up in all this nonsense. What are people going to say?"

Abuela inches her body forward, coming closer to me. "I don't want people saying my granddaughter is a buscona and a malcriada. Doña Lucrecia walked over this morning to ask if you had some kind of mental problem after María."

"What?" I ask, incredulous. "Is she serious?"

Abuela pulls a newspaper clipping out of the pocket of her apron and hands it to me. The headline reads AFTER HURRICANE, PUERTO RICANS GRAPPLE WITH MENTAL HEALTH CRISIS.

"She said maybe you have anxiety or depression. And God knows I normally don't agree with that vieja, but the newspaper says people are suffering from post-traumatic stress disorder. Maybe your mother should take you to one of the doctors at the hospital."

The black letters dance on the newsprint in front of me. Is this what they think? That I'm so upset after María that I can barely function?

A tide of anger surges from the darkest pit of my stomach and threatens to drown me.

I don't have a disorder. And I'm not anxious or depressed, either. Maybe I'm sad, but what am I supposed to feel when everyone seems hell-bent on treating me as a powerless victim and all I want to be is my own undaunted self?

I open my mouth to say something, but I'm still figuring out where to begin when a text comes in from Ruby.

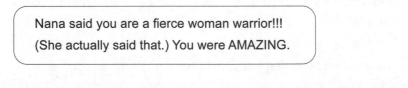

Nana said you are a fierce woman warrior!!!
(She actually said that.) You were AMAZING.

Thanks!

> And GREAT job getting Baptiste on our side!
> You're making it happen!

> She says we'll need a plan B. But no worries.
> I already found one!

My fingers hover over the phone, already typing a new message while simultaneously ignoring the chatter of my family around me.

> Plan B?????

> It's called a student-faculty senate. It's brilliant!

> It's all gonna work out. Don't worry. I promise, no need for a plan B.

I stare at the message on my phone. Not exactly what I thought Ruby was going to say. But maybe this is one of those times when I'm being what Soraida calls "island ignorant" and there's something about the workings of the local school district that I don't know, something not written in the pages of Ms. Baptiste's binder, which I read so carefully.

Then I think back to the agreement I made with Ms. Baptiste. If she is helping us, shouldn't we at least follow her advice?

> I really think we should have a backup plan. I watched a school board meeting video today where a teacher got arrested!!! A TEACHER. It was intense.

Ruby quickly responds.

> Okay sure we'll talk about it, but I promise nobody's gonna get arrested. And right now we have a Telemundo interview to watch!!!

I text her back a silly smile, but it doesn't feel right. Maybe I just need to relax. Eat some of Abuela's cheese and guava crackers.

> BTW what channel is Telemundo?

> It's 46. Give Abuela Joan a big hug for me.

Ruby sends back a string of emoji hearts.

Another text comes in. This one is from Calista Jameson. She's also copied Ruby.

> Keep me posted on how the petition is coming. I have a follow-up piece in the works if you get in front of the school board. First article got over 2 million views!

Ruby replies before I can even finish reading Calista's text.

> We will!

"Two *million?*" Soraida squeals next to my ear. Unbeknownst to me, she's been reading Calista's text over my shoulder. I set the phone on my lap, screen down.

"What's two million?" Carlos asks, reaching for a cracker sandwich that Tía Lorna made for him. Because heaven forbid he lift a finger to make his own!

"Let me get you something to wash that down, mijo," she offers, quickly moving toward the kitchen.

"Can you get me a beer?" Tío Wiliberto calls out to her. So far this has been his only contribution to the discussion.

"Her interview with Calista Jameson got over two million hits," Soraida announces, as if this is her bit of news to share. "Wow. Maybe you should have your own YouTube channel. I bet you could get sponsors."

"What would I talk about?" I say dismissively.

Soraida shrugs. "Books?"

Mami interjects. "Malena, mija . . ." She rests her warm palm on my skin. "I think you did a great job, on TV and in the article. You sounded so smart and well-spoken. And I want you to know how proud I am of you—we all are." She glances around the room, scanning everyone's faces. My eyes linger on the scowl on Soraida's face. Her arms are crossed over her chest and she's shaking her head in preemptive disapproval of whatever Mami is about to say next.

"But what your abuela and Lorna are trying to say is that we're a little worried about you. All this . . ." She nods toward the TV, where an ad for used cars is running, with a man dressed like a cowboy. "We've been talking. . . ." She pauses, gripping my arm a little tighter. "We've decided that maybe this has gone far enough. We think you made your point." Mami's calm and even voice only makes my anger rise again. "It's time to stop all of this, mija. Just focus on your studies."

"I want it stated for the record: I'm not part of this 'we,'" Soraida says firmly.

For once, I want someone in my family—aside from Soraida—to validate how I feel. I need to find a way to explain to my mother, to help her understand how important this is.

But now? Here? Not with Tía Lorna and all her talk of malcriadas and decent señoritas. I'll never convince Mami to see this our way if I have to go against the entire family (minus Soraida).

Tía Lorna returns. She hands Carlos a can of soda and Tío his beer. Then she takes the TV remote away from Soraida and changes the channel to Telemundo.

"I can't believe you met Leonides Buenavides," Tía Lorna says, enabling the recording function on the screen. "Is he as tall as he looks on TV?"

"Taller," Soraida says.

The Spanish newscast kicks off with a dizzying animation in red, white, and blue. Leonides Buenavides welcomes his audience from behind a huge glass desk.

Tía Lorna sighs the moment the camera zooms in on his face and his piercing blue eyes light up the screen.

I catch Tío Wiliberto shaking his head.

A banner on the bottom of the screen reads *María Evacuee Bra Dispute* in Spanish. Straight to the point, I guess.

They show various shots of me in the parking lot talking to Soraida and Ruby as Leonides's voice paints me as the tragic victim of a system ill prepared to handle an influx of Puerto Rican evacuees.

What is he even talking about? What does all this have to do with María? And why is *he* the only one talking? Ruby and I are just background images. He interviewed us. We had a lot to say. I said it in Spanish!

Then Dr. Hardaway comes onto the screen. Apparently, *she* gets to talk. When he shoves a microphone in her face and asks if my racial makeup and status as an evacuee played a role in this incident, Dr. Hardaway appears utterly perplexed.

She stumbles through the answer, trying to explain that Orange Grove doesn't discriminate, but Leonides is not having it. He keeps pressing her until the only things coming out of her mouth are one-word fragments. I actually feel sorry for her. When the newscast cuts back to the studio, Leonides launches into what can only be described as a diatribe.

"As a member of the Puerto Rican diaspora myself, I implore you, we must take care of our families and our neighbors . . . and innocent young girls. We must band together in this time of great need. After everything we have suffered . . . María . . . the devastation . . ." He pauses for dramatic effect. *This guy.*

"We must protect our children from discrimination and demand that the schools respond appropriately to these victims of a terrible tragedy. We, too, are Americans." He smiles, revealing a set of sparkling, ultra-white teeth. Another swirl of red, white, and blue flashes across the screen and the music swells. The image of the studio dissolves into an ad for international calling cards.

Tía Lorna mutes the TV and sets down the remote, edging forward in her chair. "Mija," she says in my direction. "Why didn't you tell us?"

I stare at her blankly. "Tell you what?"

"I didn't know they were treating you this way because you're a María evacuee. That's not right. I thought you were overreacting because you've been having such a hard time with the move to Florida. I thought it was about a bra."

For the life of me, I can't figure out how María, once again, has ripped away my voice. Why the hell won't she go away already?

It is *about a bra!* I want to shout it at the top of my lungs. *God, is anyone listening?*

Tía Lorna continues, her voice full of emotion. No one dares to speak as she says, "Leonides is right. It's not fair! You're a victim. I'm still not sure a protest is the best thing, but you shouldn't do it alone. Soraida and Carlos will help you. Don't worry, mija."

Soraida cries out a resounding "Yes!" raising both fists in triumph.

Yes? Does Soraida think I'm a victim? No way. She just called me freaking Juana de Arco!

Carlos groans, throwing his arms in the air for a completely different reason.

"I can't get suspended," he complains. "Or sent to detention."

"Don't worry, mijo," Tía Lorna tells him, "they won't send *you* to detention."

"We're *doing* this!" Soraida calls out to Carlos, repeatedly pumping her fist in the air. Carlos shakes his head, while Tía Lorna and Abuela nod in encouragement.

Soraida wants permission to join the protest, so she'll go along with anything that gets Tía Lorna on our side. Should I do the same?

I stare at the chaos, at my tía's smiling face, and I swallow a scream. If Tía Lorna thinks I'm a victim, then I'll just have to prove her wrong.

I can be a fierce woman warrior. All I need is a megaphone.

PART TWO

Sometimes a breakdown can be the beginning of a kind of breakthrough, a way of living in advance through a trauma that prepares you for a future of radical transformation.

—Cherríe Moraga

CHAPTER SIXTEEN

RUBY

Longest. Friday. Ever.

I can't believe we're finally doing this. Apparently, time slows to a crawl when you're waiting for a life-changing event.

The minute hand on this wall clock has been moving in slow motion today, while Coach Simpson drones on about healthy habits and the food pyramid.

I glance up, and there it is, finally—that long black second hand sweeping through 11:59. My hands start to shake, and I'm gripping my pencil so hard that I think it might break in two.

Noon. The moment has come. I drop my pencil and turn around to find Topher in the back row. I feel myself standing up, and by the time I'm out of my desk, I can't even find him because so many of us are on our feet.

Oh my God! This is working. The walkout is working.

I reach into my backpack and pull out the stack of small posters we made at my house. Small enough to stash in a backpack until the time came. They all have *NippleRiot* scrawled in bold print under a bunch of different slogans:

MY SHOULDERS ARE NOT A DISTRACTION!
STOP SEXUALIZING GIRLS' BODIES!
MY BODY, MY CHOICE!

"What's this all about?" Coach Simpson asks.

I start to pass the posters out. Xiomara grabs a few and turns back to face the class, all clumped around us.

"Let's do this!"

"Go! Go! Go!"

People are scrambling to grab the posters.

"Hell, yeah!"

I don't even know who's yelling, but that last one was definitely a guy's voice, and the walkout is starting to feel more like a race-out.

Only two people remain in their seats, both looking down at their feet.

Abby Suffolk and her boyfriend, Thad. Thad and Abby are Jesus people—full-on purity-ring-flaunting church kids. They're sweet, always holding hands and smiling mildly. Sure, they pray in the courtyard at lunch with the other Jesus kids, but they're not pushy or anything. They're pretty cool, and I like them well enough, but I can't figure out why they're still sitting there. Do they think Jesus would want a dress code? I mean, aren't we all created in the image of God?

Or Goddess. The jury is still out on that one.

"Where do you people think you're going?" I turn back to see Coach Simpson calling out, rushing toward the door.

It's too late. Thad, Abby, and Coach Simpson watch as the whole class presses forward through the door.

"This class period has not ended!" Coach Simpson says as the door flies open and we all launch out into the hallway, running, pushing, breaking free.

We're storming through the hall toward the school entrance. I feel a shoulder press against my side, and I look over to see Topher, grinning like the adorable doof that he is. I grab his hand as a huge smile spreads across my face. We join the chant that's come out of nowhere—or everywhere. Everywhere at once.

"My body, my choice!"

"Her body, her choice!"

The entire school seems to be pouring out into this hall. My heart is racing, beating to some collective rhythm that flows between us all.

"My body, my choice!"

"Her body, her choice!"

Sweatshirts and jackets start flying off; T-shirts are tossed overhead. I rip off my baggy black tee and, swept up in the moment, throw it into the air and keep moving, glancing down to make sure the pantyliners are still in place.

There they are, covering my nipples, attached with surgical tape to my so-not-dress-code-appropriate tank top.

No bra, of course.

Topher hands me his poster and unbuttons his cardigan. He pulls it off and wraps it loosely around his waist, revealing a white ribbed tank with a pantyliner stuck on over each nipple.

"Love it!" I call out.

"Had to buy them at the Raceway," he says. "These things are really damn expensive!"

I start to reply that the cost of period products is obscene and an absolute injustice to women, but then we hit a bottleneck. A sea of people. They're all pressed against each other, pushing toward the heavy metal doors that lead outside, straining to break out of here, to break away from it all. Chants move through the hallway; posters fill the air above us.

AM I COVERED UP ENOUGH?
DRESS CODES PERPETUATE RAPE CULTURE!

For as far as I can see, protesters are raising their phones, capturing this moment, furiously typing messages, sending their stories across countless networks, into countless feeds.

I can't believe this is all happening at Orange Grove High School. I mean, damn. I underestimated this place.

I'm looking around for Malena, but I can't find her. Maybe because I'm having to crane my neck around the huge sign I'm holding:

DOES MY BODY OFFEND YOU?

I can't lower it because of all the people crowding around us, so instead I lift it higher, in a feeble attempt to clear a path of vision. It's no use, though. Dozens of signs surround us, in every direction.

"Topher, do you see Malena?" He stretches onto his toes and looks around.

"No," he calls out. "You take a look." I feel myself go weightless as Topher hoists me onto his shoulders.

I clench my legs around his back and yell at the top of my lungs: "Not a distraction! Not a distraction!"

The chants swirl around us.

"Not a distraction! Not a distraction!"

The chaotic sounds of protest move in waves through the halls, and more girls climb onto shoulders, waving and yelling. I hear the raucous sound of banging pots and pans, and I know Nadia must be nearby. A few others also have pantyliners over their nipples, on top of T-shirts and tanks, but some have done their own thing, which is awesome. I see two baby-faced girls, probably freshmen, in matching handmade tees:

I'M NOT A DISTRACTION—I'M A CELLIST!

I'M NOT A DISTRACTION—I'M A CONTRA DANCER!

I catch the gaze of Lindsey, a quiet junior from my physics class. She's holding a black poster with FIGHT LIKE A GIRL written in gold glitter. Her face is contorted, red. The tendons strain along her neck; her lips curl back as she yells out in rage. I can't hear her words, but the words don't even matter. She's furious. That shy, sort-of-mousy girl is going off! Oh, and her pantyliners are affixed to a deep red bustier, out of which some serious boobs are spilling.

This is nuts.

Something is happening here. Something big.

Lindsey turns away from me, almost in slow motion, and glances behind her as another girl trips and falls into her side. She catches the girl and holds her up, and that fabulous glitter sign falls to the floor in front of me and Topher. Someone lunges against Topher and he almost loses his balance; I grab his head with both hands, watching my own sign tumble.

We all are at a standstill. I twist around to look at the entrance, watching people press against the door.

Then it dawns on me: we're locked in.

Oh my God, they've locked us in.

Signs wave, voices yell, and we press tighter and tighter against the door. I'm starting to worry that someone's gonna get really hurt—crushed by the crowd.

I lean into Topher. "Help me down," I say. "There's a problem."

"Down with the dress code! Down with the dress code!"

The voices are so loud, I can barely hear myself think.

"Topher, we're locked in. They locked us in!" I slide down into a narrow space behind Topher's back, landing on my now-trampled poster. "What are we going to do?"

Topher tries to move forward, but everyone is pushing against us, in all directions. We can't move. I feel my elbows press against my sides and my breath goes shallow.

I look to the floor for balance and see a hand—a guy's hand—wrapping around my waist. My head starts to swim. I exhale slowly and watch the fingers press into my flesh. Ragged cuticles, sprouts of blond hair between thick knuckles.

Everything slows down, the noise fades, and I watch the hand slip under my tank, across my stomach.

Is this really happening?

Rough, callused fingers reach up to push hard against my rib cage, kneading, prodding. A whisper in my ear. "Your body doesn't offend me, Ruby."

The hand starts to reach up toward my breasts, tugging against the elastic band on my tank top, shoving its way closer.

My stomach contracts and my eyes squeeze shut. I try to gasp in air, but my lungs won't expand. "No," I hear myself whisper.

The body thrusts against me from behind, pushing hard against my ass. His grip tightens. "I've got what you want right here," he says, shoving himself against my body again as his probing hand finds my nipple and squeezes hard.

"No!"

I hear my voice crying out and feel my own hand clench into a fist. I brace my feet, adrenaline coursing through my body. Using every ounce of energy I have to hurl my elbow back, I jab hard into his rib cage, forcing him away.

"Fucking tease!" he grunts into my neck, spit flying, landing in droplets across my bare collarbone.

His fluid on my skin.

Another contraction shoots through my gut. I turn my head to look toward his voice. But just then, space starts to open around me.

I'm going to be sick. I double over as the crowd shifts, voices calling out around me.

"This way!"

"We can get out through the gym!"

"The gym doors are open!"

A collective roar moves through the crowd as I crouch, watching bodies stream by, arms flailing, phones held high to take photos, signs waving. Topher's gone. Strangers flow past me like I'm a huge tree felled in the middle of a fast-flowing river.

I can't move. All I can do is clutch my gut and try to suck in air.

I'm not sure how much time passes. When I look up, everyone's gone and I'm alone in the empty hallway. I lift my hand to my neck and wipe the droplets of spit away. I wipe my fingers against my jeans and stare down at the floor.

My sign, facedown.

Topher's cardigan sweater.

I reach down to pick up the sweater and wrap it around me like a blanket, pulling it tight. I slide my arms through the sleeves and cover my body, taking in Topher's scent—patchouli and wood ash. I breathe in deep, try to get up and move toward the gym, but my feet won't carry me.

———

"Ruby, are you okay?"

Abby and Thad are standing above me, holding hands. Instead of the usual sweet smiles, though, their faces wear concern.

I press my palms to the cold floor, trying to regain my equilibrium. Why am I looking up at them? When did I sit down? I look slowly in both directions, through the wide hall, empty save for a few discarded shirts and trampled posters.

"Are you hurt?" Thad asks, reaching his hand out to help me stand.

I take his hand, grateful for the very act of chivalry that I would have mocked moments earlier. I even manage to squeak out a quiet "Thanks."

"Did you fall down?" Abby asks. "Did something happen to you?"

"I'm fine," I tell her. Because I am, or at least I will be, once I get back to the protest, find my people, get my bearings.

The hand on my breast flashes through my mind. The memory sears, hot and burning. I feel like I need to rush to the locker room and tear off every piece of clothing he touched, stand under a scalding-hot shower, and scrub away the skin his hand grazed, his spit.

Suddenly, my body is shivering, cold. I hug Topher's sweater more tightly around me. I try not to hear the words whispered in my ear. I try to forget the echo of that voice.

Fucking tease.

It was loud, chaotic. Maybe I imagined it. Maybe I misheard. I need to stop thinking about it.

"You're shaking," Abby says. "Are you sure you're not sick? Do you have a fever?" She reaches out to touch my forehead, but I instinctively push her hand away, my whole body cringing at the possibility of being touched.

"I think I fell down," I say. "I just need to catch my breath."

"We're headed outside to see what's happening," Thad says, nodding in the direction of the gym. "Wanna come with?"

I wrap my arms across my chest and take in another deep breath. My senses fill with Topher's scent. I want to sprint in the other direction, away from all the people and the noise, but I can't. They're all depending on me.

"Yeah," I say. "I guess I should. I'm sort of supposed to be running the show out there." I hear a pathetic laugh push through my lungs. "And I need to find Topher."

I *really* need to find Topher. And I need to forget. I need to let go of the image—that hand, those thick fingers, the feel of his spittle on my neck. I rub my hand across my throat, wishing I could peel off the skin.

Abby gently takes my elbow in her hand—the same way I have so many times with my nana. This time, I let her, and we begin to walk toward the gym. She's steadying me with her touch, and I'm grateful.

"Are you sure you're not hurt?" she asks once more as we walk through an empty gym toward the noise and the chaos outside.

Am I hurt?

I shrug. "Maybe I just got the wind knocked out of me. I'm all good."

It was nothing. A stray hand, a too-tight grip. A string of words.

It's time to move on.

The first thing I see when I step outside is Malena. She's standing on the football-field bleachers, surrounded by people holding up signs, yelling through a megaphone.

"'Too distracting for boys' gives us the impression that *we* should be guilty for what guys do!"

Cheers swell around her; posters sway above her head.

"This dress code tells us that if a guy harasses us, it's *our* fault. It's not our fault!"

Her eyebrows are knit together tight; her cheeks are flushed with energy. "If you agree," she calls out, "we need for every single one of you to sign the petition." She raises one arm in triumph. "We can do this! We can make real change, *now*!"

She looks incredible—powerful, bold, like a woman. A pissed-off woman. Malena Malavé Rosario, a fierce, pissed-off, strong woman.

"We will go in there and tell the school board: If you are sexualizing me, *you* are the problem!"

I tug Topher's cardigan tight around me, throw a feeble wave toward Abby and Thad, and head into the fray.

CHAPTER SEVENTEEN

MALENA

Every drop of anger, frustration, and sadness I've been carrying inside me swells out of my body like a wild river bursting over the bank—swells out of my very soul into the megaphone in my hands.

As if I'm watching myself from a distance, I hear my voice roaring, edgy and strained. It thunders rehearsed lines to a crowd of strangers who can't seem to get enough.

My voice shakes at times. My accent messes up the pronunciation of big words like *discrimination*, *disciplinary*, and *amendment*. But I keep going, stumbling my way through these new words. Refusing to let them faze me. Making them my own.

I'm the girl holding the megaphone. The rage in her voice is my rage. The polished arguments coming out of her mouth are my arguments. Loud enough for the whole school to hear, the whole damn world.

It's like I finally found my voice again, but something about it feels unfamiliar.

Is this Lucinda's version of undaunted? Or Abuela Joan's fierce woman warrior?

Which version exactly am I supposed to be?

I don't know.

All I know is that I'm angry. Angry enough to light the world on fire and watch it burn.

I grip the megaphone tighter, chanting along with the crowd under the scorching Florida sun. A rush of heat climbs up my neck, all the way to my cheeks. Sweat pools down my back, between my shoulder blades. My eyes scan the packed field, but I can't seem to focus on any one person in particular. Their faces look like charcoal smudges on drawing paper. Their voices sound like distorted echoes floating into a cloudless sky.

Ruby climbs up the bleachers, pushing her way through the unruly crowd gathered at my feet. She stands next to me, our bodies pressed shoulder to shoulder. She reaches for my hand and gives it a tight squeeze, nodding encouragingly.

I press the megaphone harder against my mouth and say, loud and clear, for the entire world to hear me this time, "I will not be your victim."

Nadia's cacerolazos clang somewhere nearby, reverberating through the assembly.

In the back, someone shouts, "Burn the bra! Burn the bra!" The chant spreads like wildfire through the crowd, making the bleachers vibrate with the frequency of their voices.

We did this. We created a real "safe space."

At this moment I feel the connection between me and Malala. Me and Joshua. And every other teen around the globe who has lifted a fist into the air to say, "Enough is enough. Our voices matter."

Panting, I hold out the megaphone to Ruby, who hesitates.

Her brow is covered with tiny droplets of sweat, and when she finally reaches for the megaphone, I see that her hands are shaking.

"Are you okay?" I ask, raising my voice so she can hear me.

She opens her mouth to answer but then seems to change her mind. She grips the megaphone and turns to address the crowd, but all that comes out is a shriek of static.

The crowd waits, impatient.

I pull out my phone to record—to document this incredible moment—but when I turn my camera on Ruby, she is standing perfectly still. Silent.

What is she waiting for?

She blinks a few times, then steps back and passes the megaphone to Jo. Stage fright? That doesn't seem like an issue Ruby would have.

Jo takes the megaphone instead, and within moments her voice is raging through space.

She kills it, sending her own words of anger and frustration across the crowd. "Down with the dress code! Down with the dress code!"

―――――

Later that night, I'm hoisted upside down in the middle of a very different chant.

"Chug! Chug! Chug!"

I can't believe I'm doing this. One of Soraida's friends is holding me up, my legs extended into the dark sky, my head upside down over a beer keg. Apparently, it *is* possible to swallow in this position.

"Chug, chug, chug!"

Before this moment, I had no idea what a "keg stand" was—or that I was capable of doing one. But after Soraida showed me a video of myself yelling out chants at the protest, I realized there's a lot about me I don't know. And if I can lead a few hundred people in a walkout, I can certainly do a keg stand. Why not? Tonight, I'm going for it.

I guzzle the bitter liquid until it's pouring out the sides of my mouth and spilling onto the cement floor.

My ears ring with cheers and whoops. A couple of guys call out my name, urging me to do it again. I search for a familiar face in the mass of bodies gathered around me. Where did Soraida go?

When she told me about the party, Soraida said it was just a few people from our school blowing off steam. Mostly the Latin contingent and nothing too crazy. "We need to celebrate!" she said, and I agreed. I thought it would be like the beach bonfires my friends and I had back home, laid-back and chill. Sitting around a firepit, drinking five-dollar bottles of sangría, talking and laughing. I haven't done an official count, but I'm sure there are more than a hundred people here—most I've never met before.

I wave one hand at the guy holding me up.

"Can you get me down?" I manage to ask over the clamor of cackles and sardonic boos at my refusal to keep chugging.

The guy's hands move behind my knees and onto my back, slowly flipping me around until my feet touch the floor. All the blood rushes from my head and I stumble, grabbing his shoulders for support. His hands catch me in a solid grip, pressing warm against my torso.

"Are you okay?" he asks, brushing a strand of beer-soaked hair off my face.

"Yeah," I giggle, a little dizzy. "It's hard coming down from that thing."

"I'm Javi," he says, grinning. "You're Soraida's cousin, right? Malena?"

"I am." He's easy on the eyes—dark, messy hair, long eye-lashes, full lips.

"I heard you had quite the day," he says.

"Epic," I answer, jutting my chin slightly.

Behind me, someone abruptly wraps both arms around my waist. "There you are, primita!" Soraida shrieks in my ear. I jerk forward, bumping my chest against Javi's. He doesn't move. He smiles, his eyes fixed on mine. There's something inviting about his face—a rush of energy in his gaze that's captivating. I take in the sharp lines of his jaw, my eyes traveling down to his collar-bones and broad shoulders. I like what I see. And maybe I'm the kind of girl who's not afraid to admit it.

Soraida contorts herself under my arm so that she's standing by my side in a half hug. Javi steps back, watching us, entertained.

"You met Javi," she says, pawing at him with her free hand. "He goes to some ritzy private school. His parents are out of town."

Javi flushes, sliding both hands inside the pockets of his jeans.

"They're in Argentina, visiting family. I thought I'd put the pool to good use," he explains with a shrug.

"It's nice." I take in the lush landscaping and the swanky in-finity pool that overlooks the river.

"So, Malena, where have you been hiding?" Javi asks. "I haven't seen you around."

"She just moved here," Soraida interjects. "María," she adds, as if that one word can explain everything he needs to know about me.

Javi nods. The smile on his lips momentarily falters.

Damn it to hell.

I will not be Pobrecita María Malena anymore.

Not tonight.

Not after today.

I am the girl holding the megaphone. I am the girl leading the chant.

I wave down a guy carrying a tray of shot glasses. A bottle of tequila dangles from his hand.

"Shots?" I ask, all swagger and confidence, even though I've never done anything like this before. I swiftly tamp down any self-doubt. *Fake it till you make it, right?*

"Now you're talking," Javi says, producing a saltshaker and lime wedges from behind the pool bar.

"You first," I say, trying to hide my lack of experience. For most of my life I've been the good girl, the reliable daughter, the exemplary student. But look where that's gotten me: in detention for refusing to bind my breasts. *Screw it.*

After Javi takes a shot, he fills the glass with gold liquor and hands it to me. I raise it to my mouth, but he stops me before I can drink. "First the salt," he says.

Javi takes hold of my free hand. Eyes set on mine, he lifts my hand to his mouth.

My cheeks flush. My whole body flushes as Javi's dark eyes bore into mine and his tongue, slippery wet, comes into contact with the soft skin between my thumb and my index finger.

"Eh-he, primita!" Soraida bumps her hips with mine, making me laugh hard. "Finally getting some action."

Javi laughs too, the entire time keeping his hold on my hand. He sprinkles salt where his mouth was and beckons me to lick it. I do as he says, my own thoughts lost in a haze.

Soraida clinks her shot glass against mine, giggling. "We did it, primita. ¡A tu salud!"

The shot glass brushes my lips and I tilt my head back. The

swig of tequila burns the back of my throat and warms every hidden cavity of my chest.

"The lime is the last part." Javi brings a lime wedge to his mouth and clenches the skin between his teeth, inviting me to take the lime directly from his lips.

I don't allow myself to hesitate. I thrust forward and my mouth connects with the sour pulp of the lime. My arms wrap around his broad shoulders. His hands land on my waist, pulling me in closer.

I'm a little surprised at how easy this all is. How good it feels.

No one seems eager to stop me. Not even myself. So I keep going.

The lime wedge falls. Javi leans his head next to mine, his raspy voice caressing my ear as he asks, "Can I kiss you?"

I nod.

Javi's hands travel to the small of my back, finding a sliver of exposed skin. His lips are tender and soft over mine. His tongue moves gently inside my mouth in a way that leaves me breathless. If his kiss were a song, it would be a bachata, all sultry waves and expert dips. I mean, this guy knows how to dance.

His open palm traces the ridges on my back, revving my heart up to a million beats per minute. My whole body goes into overdrive. A warmth, like I've never felt before, spreads across my skin. Even before we pull apart, I know I want more of this.

The moment is interrupted by the sound of someone calling my name. My eyes open but a camera flash, up close and dazzling, forces them shut again. Is someone taking pictures of us? I shut my eyes tighter, trying hard—and failing—to keep tabs on what's going on.

I push Javi back gently, unsure *exactly* how far I want this to go, but also needing to feel the intensity of that kiss again.

The guy with the drink tray returns, or did he ever leave? I find myself licking salt from Javi's neck and washing it down with a full shot glass. This time, the tequila barely stings. I barely feel anything at all.

My fingers bring a lime wedge to Javi's mouth, but before I can suck on it, and him, someone abruptly pulls me away by the arm.

"Burn the bra! Burn the bra!" a chorus chants in the background.

Soraida steers me through a crowd gathered around the firepit.

"Here she is!" she calls out to the group.

I glance around in a daze, trying to put names to this sea of faces. In the dancing light of the fire, their features appear warped and sinister, but also expectant. Do they want me to speak?

"Say something," Soraida whispers in my ear.

"Screw the dress code!" is the only thing I can think of. The tequila is starting to do weird things to my brain.

I catch Beatriz, Xiomara, and Nadia waving back at me from across the flames. I want to call out to them, but my voice is drowned out by a new chorus of "Burn the bra! Burn the bra!" Followed by "Take. It. Off! Take. It. Off!"

Soraida wriggles herself out of the bra she's wearing and pulls it through one of the armholes of her shirt. With a quick jerk of the wrist, she tosses it in the firepit. The pretty pink lace catches fire, burning red and black before turning to ashy gray.

"Take. It. Off!" The calls grow louder and louder until the words rattle inside my head the way Nadia's pots clashed and clanked through the hallways this afternoon.

All the girls are joining in, it seems, as the pile of bras in front of me transforms into a small mountain before my eyes.

Afraid the fabric will smother the flames, someone sprays lighter fluid over the pit, creating a sudden explosion that jolts everyone to step back. There's drunken laughter as a couple of new bras join the pyre.

I watch the flames lick the satin and lace, unable to trace this moment back to that day in Dr. Hardaway's office. Unable to determine the meaning of all this.

"Take it off, Malena," a guy's voice says behind me. I try to find the source, but the faces are a blur of laughter and dark shadows. My hands tentatively reach under my shirt until my fingers find the clasp in the middle of my back. They undo the metal fasteners and release my captive breasts. I exhale, lift my chest, and slide off the straps through my armholes. I pull out my bra from under my shirt and hold it limply by my side.

How can a few pieces of fabric and metal have so much power over our bodies?

No more.

My hand hurls my bra into the fire, where I watch it burn to a crisp.

Cheers rise around me, but my sedated brain wonders: Why doesn't this feel more satisfying? Why don't I feel free?

"To the pool!" a voice calls out behind me. The bodies gathered by the firepit all flock to the poolside. Guys strip off their shirts and pants and jump into the water in their underwear. The girls follow, wearing only T-shirts and panties.

Beatriz, Xiomara, and Nadia find me in the commotion. They pull me into a melee of hugs and kisses, congratulating me for my part in the NippleRiot.

Suddenly, the protest feels like a lifetime ago. My head is swimming.

"Everyone's talking about you," Nadia says. "I can't believe you got up there and spoke in front of all those people. You're, like, my hero."

"To Juana freaking de Arco!" Soraida calls out, holding a beer bottle in her outstretched hand and then merrily drinking in my honor.

"I couldn't find Ruby," I say, feeling confused, trying hard to remember why I grabbed that megaphone in the first place.

"Ruby?" Beatriz asks dismissively. "You stole the show. It was *all you* up there."

Xiomara momentarily disappears and then returns, balancing three Solo cups between her hands. A fourth one is clenched between her teeth.

We each grab one. I lower my nose to the drink and smell. It's not beer, but some hard liquor mix.

"Vodka and Coke," Xiomara says, as if reading the question on my face. "Mine's straight-up Coke. I'm the double D tonight."

"The what?" I ask, my voice growing strange, my words dragging. Full sentences seem to be slipping from my grip.

"Designated driver," Xiomara explains as the others raise their cups.

"To Malena!" Nadia sings, lifting hers in my direction.

"To Málena!" the rest call out, tapping each other's cups, then bringing them to their lips. I join the toast, barely aware of the effects the alcohol is having on my body.

Numb is good, I tell myself. *Numb is what I need.*

Xiomara nudges my arm and nods in the direction of the hot tub, where Javi is talking to a couple of his friends.

"You should go get some of that."

Javi steps out of the hot tub and starts walking in our direction. His torso is seriously cut. I look at him and smile, ready to find out just how far this new undaunted me is willing to go. I take a few mouthfuls of vodka and Coke, then peel off my shorts and flip my sandals aside. I'm glad I'm wearing my nice underwear, black with cream lace—very sophisticated. Very grown-up.

When Javi reaches us, I'm ready. I'm in control.

"Wanna go for a swim?" I ask, nodding toward the edge of the pool, where a bunch of couples are chicken-fighting. Every time someone loses, they have to take a shot.

"I bet we can take them down," I say.

A mischievous grin appears on his face. "I bet you can."

I take his hand and pull him as we both jump into the deep end.

CHAPTER EIGHTEEN

RUBY

I don't know how long I've been in this bath—long enough for the room to go dark, for the loud night song of cicadas to hum through the window. I've scrubbed at my belly and chest long enough for the skin to turn red, for the bath to go from scalding hot to cool. I'm not ready to get out.

I hold my breath and sink under again. Water surrounds me, blocking the loud echo of those chants ricocheting through the hallway, pushing out the memory of callused fingers, cold floor, that awful voice . . .

Fucking tease.

I feel my arms go weightless; my shoulders and my abs ache to release the tension that I didn't even know they were holding.

When my lungs burn, desperate for air, I sit up and suck in a deep breath. I reach forward to turn on the faucet, sending more searing-hot water into the tub. Maybe if I stay here a few minutes longer, I'll be able to climb into bed without the images swirling through my mind. I'll close my eyes and sleep deep. I'll wake up tomorrow and it will be a new day. I'll be refreshed, cleansed, purified. I'll be ready to focus on the other memories—the good ones. Maybe I'll wake up thinking of Malena, megaphone in hand, calling out, "I am not a victim!"

I am not a victim.

I mouth the words as I turn off the faucet. I grab a tube of green-tea mask and rub the grainy cream onto my cheeks, along my jawline and forehead, around my eyes.

The tingling sensation of the mask spreads across my face.

Purify. Detoxify. Cleanse.

And then my phone starts up.

God, I should have turned off the ringer.

I try to ignore the texts. Probably Calista Jameson wanting another interview. She said she was planning to cover the walk-out. But the thought of sharing my memories of the day with her? It makes me want to vomit.

Maybe it's Lucinda congratulating me again. She's been pushing images of the NippleRiot out on social all afternoon, and they're getting traction, or at least I guess they are. I turned off my notifications a couple of hours ago. Tonight, I just can't deal with any of it.

Another annoying ding.

It could be Topher telling me to sleep tight, or Nessa asking whether I want to go thrifting tomorrow. They can wait.

And another.

I guess they can't wait.

I dry my hands with a towel and reach for my phone to turn off the ringer. That's when I see the string of texts.

Are you with her?

????

> Ruby!!! Answer me!

It's a number I don't recognize. I type a reply.

> With who? Who is this?

> Carlos. Are you at the party?

Carlos? Okay, wow. Carlos is texting me.

> What party?

I haven't yet hit send on that one when the photo comes in. It's Malena in a pool, straddling a guy's shoulders, her arms held up in the air, like she's signaling victory. Beatriz and Nadia are on either side of the guy, all huge smiles and big poses. But it's hard to notice much of anything in the picture except this: Malena's wearing a very wet, very see-through T-shirt over bare breasts and hard nipples. She looks like she could be on the cover of a titty magazine, or on some pervy pedophile's website. And the random guy? His hands are gripping her upper thighs.

Oh sweet Mother of God. I start typing furiously.

> Where is she???? I have to go get her.

The phone rings. I pick up.

"Carlos? Oh my God! Did someone send you that picture? Who sent it to you? Do you know where she is? Are you with her? Who is that guy?" I stand up in the tub and start to wrap a towel around my dripping body as I struggle to hold the phone. "What is she thinking? Is she wasted? She must be wasted. I didn't even know Malena partied—"

"Christ, Ruby. Slow down."

"I'm not slowing down! We need to go get her."

I'm wrangling with my towel, so I put the phone on speaker and set it beside the sink, then furiously rub my body dry.

"Soraida won't answer my texts or calls. She told our mom they were going to a girls' sleepover. I thought she was with you."

"With me? No! I had no idea. I'm going to get her."

"No need," Carlos growls. "I'm on my way."

I drop the towel, grab my phone, and rush into my closet, all the while worrying about what might be happening to Malena, wondering if she's safe, hoping she's not making the kinds of decisions that can't be unmade.

"I'm coming too. Where's the party?"

"At this guy Javi's house. Over behind the Costco."

"What Costco? Listen, just text me the address. I'll meet you there."

A protective instinct I've never felt before takes over my body. Just looking at Malena makes *me* feel vulnerable, exposed. I have to find her. I need to see with my own eyes whether she's okay.

"I don't know the address. It's on that street behind the Costco, with the big-ass new houses on the river."

"I have no idea what street you're talking about."

Carlos lets out a long sigh. "I'm passing by your house in three minutes. Be ready."

And just like that, he's off the phone.

I throw on underwear and cutoffs, a sports bra, and a tank from the top of my clean laundry basket.

Oh crap. The green-tea mask.

I rush into the bathroom, turn on the hot water, and start

scrubbing my face clean. I'm still scrubbing when I see the headlights pull into the driveway. I drop the towel and head out the
front door.

"What's all that green stuff on your face?" he asks, the moment I slide into the passenger seat.

"Face mask. I wasn't exactly planning on going to a rager
tonight."

He shakes his head, peeling out of the driveway. "Sorry to
interrupt your beauty regimen."

He's pissed off, and I'm wondering if he's mad at me. I think he
deserves to be mad at me. I think I may be the one who launched
this whole thing into motion. I didn't mean for it to come to this.
I wish I could tell him, but I can't seem to form the words.

After a few minutes of driving in silence, he says, "I've been
to parties with those guys." He pauses. "A couple of them are,
uh . . ."

"What? What are they?"

"Let's just say they see any drunk girl who even looks their
way as fair game. If a girl dances with them, makes out with
them, they just go on and figure she wants it all. You know?"

Hell no, I don't know. "So you're telling me that—quote—a
couple of guys at this party think rape is okay? You know how
completely messed up that is, right?"

"Yeah, I know," he exclaims. "That's why we're hauling ass to
Javi's right now." He looks at me, his face etched with concern.
"Malena can't stay there—not in that condition. And she can't go
back to any of Soraida's friends' houses, either. Those moms . . .
they talk."

"So we'll just take her home," I say, matter-of-fact.

"Home? Are you shitting me? If her mom sees her like that,
she'll be on the next plane to Puerto Rico. Or, well—if there were

anything to go back to. But you know what I mean. She'd be on a tight leash. Forever."

"She can spend the night with me," I say.

"You wouldn't get in trouble or anything?"

"I don't really get in trouble," I say.

"And maybe Soraida, too?" he asks, his voice hesitant. "Would that be okay?" He grips the steering wheel tight, murmuring to himself, "If Mami sees her drunk, or hears about it from one of those chismosas—"

"They can both stay," I break in. "Not a big deal."

I flip the visor down, open the mirror, and inspect my face. He's right. There's still green gunk all around the edges. I pull up the bottom of my tank top, trying to use the inside to wipe my skin clean.

"Who sent you that picture?" I ask, scrubbing the mask off my chin.

"One of the guys from the team. I swear I'm gonna kick his ass if he sent it to anyone else."

A part of me is tempted to say I thought he never fought, but this doesn't seem like the right moment to tease.

"I'm sure he wasn't the only one taking pictures," I say. "You know the pictures will get out. They always do." As soon as I say it, I know it's a mistake.

He clenches his jaw and stares straight ahead.

My heart sinks as my chest drops. I wonder, after all that's happened in the past few hours, whether Carlos and I will ever make it back to our casual banter, our goofy exchanges and silly grins. It dawns on me, suddenly, that if—after all of this—Carlos finally decides he wants nothing more to do with me, I'll miss him.

I look back into the visor's mirror. Yes, remnants of the face mask still cling to the edges, but my attention isn't drawn to the green goop. Instead, I focus on my own eyes. They're unfamiliar, somehow. They look afraid and confused.

"You're so damn clueless sometimes," he says, staring at the road.

I force myself not to reply. Is this the first and last time I'll ride in a car with Carlos? This morning, I felt like everything was just beginning, like there was so much to look forward to. But now?

"If you were bouncing around in a pool wearing your stupid sports bra . . ." He glances over at my sports bra, which is basically in full view, since I'm still cleaning my face with my shirt. "If you were on some guy's shoulders, people would be all like, 'Oh, check it out! They look like a Vineyard Vines ad! Isn't Ruby so cute and fun!'"

"What are you trying to say?" I ask, my voice wobbly.

"I'm saying that Malena . . . people read her body differently."

I take in a deep breath. "Wow, okay. I know I'm flat-chested and all, but—"

We come to a red light and he turns to look right at me. "It's not about the size of your, uh, your . . . you know."

"My tits."

"Whatever, Ruby. What I'm trying to say is—it's the whole thing. You're a twiggy white girl. Malena's a curvy brown girl."

So now I've gone from just plain White Girl to Twiggy White Girl. I get what he's trying to say, but those groping hands at the walkout taught me that even this twiggy white girl isn't safe.

I'm fine. It wasn't a big deal. It's not like that troll with the gross hands hurt me or anything. He *didn't* hurt me.

Fucking tease.

I shove the words out of my mind, tuck my knees up to my chest, and wrap my arms around them. This isn't about me, or whatever did or didn't happen during the walkout. It's about Malena.

Suddenly it all feels so precarious and risky. My nerdy-sweet bookworm friend Malena in a wet T-shirt and undies at some party? A random guy gripping her bare thighs? Carlos wants what's best for Malena; he wants to keep her safe. Of course he does. He loves her. Wet T-shirt titty shots going viral? That's not exactly what's best for Malena right now.

Carlos eases into a space on the road behind a long line of cars. "We're here. Let's go."

He bursts through the door ahead of me and starts grabbing every person within his reach. "Where's Soraida? Where's Malena?" Most everybody he talks to is stumbling drunk, and nobody seems to have any idea where Malena and Soraida are—or even *who* they are.

I see Xiomara across the living room, sitting on the arm of a sofa. I grab Carlos's arm and drag him through the crowd.

"Xiomara!" I call out.

She looks up, sees me, and then spots Carlos behind me. I watch her mouth very clearly forming the words *Oh shit.* She leans over to nudge the person sitting on the couch beside her. I stand on my tiptoes to get a glimpse.

Soraida.

Carlos pushes past me and pulls Soraida off the couch.

"Where is she?" he spits.

"Who?" Soraida asks, and then she starts to giggle.

This is not going to be good.

"Who?" he yells. "*Who?* How about the girl you swore up and down to Mami you would take care of!"

"God, Carlos. Chill out," she says. "Malena's here. I'm taking great care of her." More giggling follows.

"Jesus, Soraida! Why did you even bring her here?"

"To have fun! Is it a crime to have a little fun?"

Carlos is fuming. He looks over to Xiomara, who appears straight-up terrified.

"Did you drive them?"

She nods vigorously.

"Have you been drinking?"

She shakes her head. "No."

"Not a single drop." He says it as a statement, but she knows he requires an answer.

"I promise," she says, lifting up her red plastic cup for him to inspect. "It's Coke."

He grabs it and takes a sniff, then shoves it back into her hands.

"Soraida, we're leaving." He takes Soraida's forearm.

"I wanna stay here," she whines, pulling her arm away. "With my friends."

Carlos ignores her and starts to glance around, over the heads of the partiers gathered in the living room. "Where the hell is she?"

"I'll check outside," I say, feeling anxious to find Malena, and also desperate to get out of Carlos and Soraida's family feud.

As soon as I get through the French doors, I see her. The girl is hard to miss. She's in the hot tub, her legs and arms draped around that guy, and they're making out. Hot and heavy.

"Oh my God," I sigh. Then panic sets in. If Carlos, in his current state, sees Malena wrapped around this random guy, he's gonna blow a gasket. I head toward Malena, calling out to get her attention. "Hey, Malena! Malena!"

I guess she can't hear me over the music and the drunk kids chicken-fighting in the pool, or maybe it's the tongue in her ear. Gross.

"Javi, you motherfucker!"

I turn to see Carlos striding toward the hot tub. Apparently, he knows the random guy.

He gets down on his knees and reaches into the hot tub, grabbing Malena around the waist from behind. He tugs her out and tries to stand her up.

"What the hell, Carlos?" Javi says. "Don't go all batshit crazy. We were just kissing."

"Yeah," Malena slurs. She's trying to stand up, but she can't. She's too freaking drunk. "I kiiiissed him. I'm a liiiiberated woman. I'm not wait—waiting around for ssssome guy to—"

"True that," Javi says, hopping out of the hot tub to stand beside us. "I was just following her lead." He grins a sloppy grin. It's pretty clear that both of them are wasted. "She kinda jumped me," he teases, giving Malena a playful shove to the side.

Malena tries to shove him back but ends up almost falling back into the hot tub. Carlos grabs her.

"I swear to God . . . ," he says, wrapping his arm around Malena's shoulder to prop her up.

He looks like he's about to launch himself at Javi, so I step between them.

"Let me give you a little tip," I say, finally finding my voice. "You know what you do when a wasted girl—quote—kinda jumps you?"

Carlos and Javi both look at me as if I've just materialized out of thin air.

"You go find her girlfriends, you make sure at least one of them's sober, and you ask them to take her home. It's simple, really."

"Drunk girls can't consent, you asshole," Carlos spits. "I don't care who starts it."

Javi shrugs. "No harm, no foul, man. We were kissing. Totally innocent."

"Tooootally," Malena slurs, grabbing a fistful of Carlos's shirt.

"She just moved here," Carlos says quietly, shaking his head. "She doesn't even—all this is—" He lets out an exasperated growl, apparently unable to complete his thought. "What the fuck, man?"

He scoops Malena into his arms and starts to carry her away from the pool. She doesn't protest. She slumps into his chest and rests her head against him.

"Thisss is nice," she mumbles into his shoulder.

Carlos carries Malena through the party and into what I assume is a guest room. This house is enormous. I could get lost here if Carlos weren't leading the way. I sit with Malena on the king-size bed while he opens and shuts dresser drawers, then disappears inside a walk-in closet.

"Heeeey, Mr. Sporty Balls, where ya goin'?" Malena slurs, and slumps back onto the bed. "You know Ruby caaaalls you that, right?" She starts giggling uncontrollably. "Miiister Sporty Balls?"

"Malena!" I scold gently. "Not now."

Carlos returns holding a white bathrobe. I'm really hoping he missed her last comment.

"Can you get this on her?" he asks. "I'll wait outside."

After I manage to wrap her securely in the bathrobe, I help Malena stumble out of the room.

"Malena, sweetheart," I whisper as calmly as I can manage. "Do you know where the rest of your clothes are? Your pants? Shoes? Bra?"

She starts to laugh. "Burrrrrned it!"

"You burned your bra?"

"Mm-hmm," she slurs. "It was awwwessssoome."

God, she's a mess. We need to get her out of here.

When I've wrangled Malena into the hallway, we see Carlos standing on top of the dining-room table. The music's turned off and he's calling out through cupped hands to get the attention of the entire room and everyone by the pool.

"Hey, people, listen up!" he yells. "You're all gonna take out your phones right now and you're gonna delete any evidence of these two girls right here"—he points to Soraida and Malena—"ever attending this party. I'm talking *any and all* evidence."

Remarkably, everyone starts to pull out their phones and scroll through pictures and social feeds.

"Believe me when I tell you," he calls out through his hands, "if I see even one single photo posted anywhere—anywhere!—I will personally come after whoever posted it!"

The room goes silent.

"No texts, no snaps, no DMs, no *nothing*. Understood?"

A few people respond, and the rest keep scrolling around on their phones.

"All right, people," he says when he glimpses us waiting in the hallway. "Carry on." He finds Soraida in the crowd. "Except you!" He points directly at her. "You're coming with me."

Carlos jumps down from the table and heads toward me and Malena. He scoops Malena up again and we make our way toward the door, the crowd parting in silence and Soraida following behind, still wearing her super-pouty face.

"Do me a favor and grab that trash can," Carlos says, gesturing toward a small wastebasket near the front door. I snag it and we head out.

When we get outside, I nudge him in the side.

"What are you," I ask, "like a mob boss or something?"

He shrugs. "Or something. I really hope that threat worked."

"I'm pretty sure it did," I reply, my tone lightening. "They were all very obedient."

He looks back at Soraida. "You're staying at Ruby's."

"Whatever," she mumbles. And then, under her breath, "Asshole."

To Carlos's credit, he doesn't respond. We cross the front lawn in silence. Carlos asks if I want to drive, so he can be on puke watch in the back seat. I find it strangely sweet that he wants to be in charge of holding the trash can, and that he's willing to let me drive his car.

He throws me the keys and we climb in. Soraida gets in the passenger side, leans the seat back, and closes her eyes. I'm not even to the Costco when I start to hear the sounds of puking in the back seat. Malena heaves three or four times and then falls back into Carlos's lap.

"Stroke of genius, swiping that trash can," I mutter.

Soraida lifts her head and turns to look at me. "He's such a machista!"

"A what?" I ask.

"A machista," she says. "Like, 'I'm the man and I'm in charge, and you're all gonna obey me.' He's always doing shit like that. And my mother lets him. Oh, but her little Carlitos can get away with anything."

"Would you please just shut up, Soraida," Carlos demands.

"See?" Soraida calls out. "He's doing it right now. Telling me what to do and say." She reaches into the back seat to swat Carlos on the shoulder. "You can't shut me up. I'm not your little servant girl. Maybe Mami and Abuela signed up for all that bullshit, but I never did!"

I don't say anything. This seems like a family squabble, and not really any of my business. I glance over to see Soraida's head rest against the window, and her eyes fall shut. I don't need to look at Carlos. I can feel him fuming in the back seat.

After a few moments of silence, when it's clear that Soraida has dozed off, Carlos says quietly, "I'm not a machista." I look into the rearview mirror and see him shaking his head. "I hate all that machista crap. I'm just looking out for them, you know? I don't want some asshole to take advantage of them when they can barely stay awake. I don't think that makes me a bad guy." His hand is resting on Malena's forehead, like he's a dad checking his kid's temperature.

I keep driving and keep my mouth shut, which—admittedly— is unusual for me. I guess it feels like he's trying to make sense of it all for himself, and he doesn't really need my opinion in this particular moment. But also, I have no idea what to say. I'm just as confused as he seems to be—probably more. After all, I'm the one who's supposed to have this stuff figured out.

"I know you're probably up there judging me, but I don't want them to get hurt, you know?" He sighs. "And it would be nice if they didn't make crap decisions."

Yes, yes, it would.

The next "crap decision" Malena makes is to start singing at the top of her lungs while Carlos and I are struggling to pull her out of the car and walk her up my driveway. I don't know what she's singing. Something in Spanish, something loud and out of tune.

Soraida, still following along behind us like a stray puppy, decides to join in.

"Shhhh!" I hiss back at her. "You're gonna wake up the neighbors!"

Malena stumbles and almost falls down.

"Malena," Carlos groans, picking her up to carry her to the house. "Just pass out again already, would you?"

Malena heaves.

"Do not puke on me," Carlos whisper-yells. And then, as if on cue, Malena starts to heave again.

"Shiiiit!" Carlos hisses. "She just puked on me."

I can't help letting out a yelp when I see the bile spread across his T-shirt.

"Oh my God, that's so disgusting," Soraida calls out. "Is she gonna be okay? She didn't even have that much to drink."

"Has she eaten anything all night?" I ask, trying to assess if I need to get Nana involved or call Malena's mom. Alcohol poisoning is no joke.

"Chips?" Soraida shrugs. "She stopped drinking a while ago."

"Empty stomach. Dehydration from the hot tub. It probably didn't take much," Carlos says. "I've never seen her drunk before. Malena doesn't usually party like this."

"I'm a parrrrr-tay girrrrl now," Malena roars before passing out again.

I unlock the side door and lead Carlos and Soraida through the kitchen and into the guest room.

"I'll keep checking on her," I tell Carlos. "She's gonna feel like crap in the morning."

"We need to make sure her puke doesn't go into her windpipe," Carlos says, setting Malena down gently on the edge of the bed.

"I'll prop her up on her side," I say, "so if she vomits again, she won't choke."

I arrange her head on a pillow and pull a wastebasket near her. Remarkably, she's come through the whole puke fest completely clean. Not even a drop of vomit in her hair. Carlos, though, is a different story.

"I'm gonna go outside and take care of"—he looks down at his shirt and sighs—"this. Be right back."

"Garbage bags are under the kitchen sink," I tell him as he turns to leave.

Soraida crawls into the bed beside Malena, turns her back to us both, and yanks the covers over her head. I'm rearranging pillows to be sure Malena's head stays propped up when Carlos arrives back in the doorway.

Oh sweet Mother of God, he's not wearing a shirt.

I feel my lower lip move between my teeth and I bite hard. I'm staring straight at the white elastic waistband of his boxers, peeking out above his low-slung jeans. He looks like a freaking anatomy lesson.

"I, uh, was hoping I had an extra shirt in the car, but . . ."

All I can do is bite down harder on my lip.

"Can I maybe borrow like a washcloth or something? I need to get rid of the stench."

I drag my gaze up to his eyes. "Mm-hmm." I point toward the guest bathroom, because apparently I'm no longer capable of forming words.

I'm sure he can feel me watching him. I need to turn away.

"Any chance you've got a large T-shirt lying around this place?" he asks as he walks into the bathroom.

Relieved to have a task that will keep me from gawking, I head upstairs to my room and find a faded old race shirt that used to be my dad's. It has *Thanksgiving Turkey Trot* written in orange letters and a huge cartoon turkey wearing running shoes and saying, "Gobble, gobble!"

I head back to the guest room and find Carlos sitting on the bed next to Malena. She's fast asleep. He's watching her, his expression soft. I try to focus my attention squarely on his face, rather than his bare chest, as I hand over the shirt.

"Thanks," he says, his head emerging through the neckhole. "It's soft."

"Yeah, I've been wearing it as a nightgown for, like, a decade." *Did I really just say that?* Definitely too much information.

He looks down at the shirt and then gets all pink-cheeked.

"I better go," he says, staring at his feet. "I have to be at training in four and a half hours."

I nod. I wish I could figure out a way to make him stay. I know I'm not supposed to rely on a man or whatever, but the whole situation somehow feels more manageable with Carlos here.

"You gonna be okay with them?" he asks. "I'm pretty sure Malena's done puking—there can't be anything left."

"Absolutely," I say, not wanting to admit to either of us that I sort of need him. "It's not a big deal. I'll stay with her and wake her up every once in a while. If she gets worse, we'll definitely be making a trip to the ER."

"Let's hope it doesn't come to that," he says. "But let me know, okay?"

"I'll keep you posted," I tell him, making an internal reminder to do a search for symptoms of alcohol poisoning.

He stands up and walks toward the door. "I'll be back for them after my workout, if that's okay—around ten."

"I'm sure they'll still be sound asleep."

"Sorry about my sister being such an ungrateful brat," he says. "You really saved us tonight."

I shrug, not sure how to respond.

I think what I want to say is that all of this is probably my fault, that he shouldn't be thanking me, that he has every right to hate me. None of this would be happening if I hadn't butted in where I didn't belong.

I really need to stop doing that.

I open the kitchen door to let him out. He pauses and looks down at the ground, then right into my eyes. My heart starts beating hard in my chest. He's studying my face, my cheeks, my jaw.

"You've still got some of that green stuff on your chin." He starts to reach toward me as my hand flies to my jaw. "Other side," he says, watching me rub my face. "You're gonna need water."

"Yeah," I say, a little embarrassed, as I run my finger across the gritty residue.

"So, I have to ask you one important question before I go," he says, his eyes probing and his tone serious.

"Okay," I say, suddenly feeling the most anxious I've been all night. "What is it?"

"Do you really call me Mr. Sporty Balls?" His face breaks into a goofy grin, and I can't help smiling too.

"Wouldn't you like to know?" I ask, shoving him playfully in the arm, feeling insanely relieved by the lightness spreading through my chest.

"You do!" he calls out in mock reproach. "Admit it!"

"I cannot tell a lie," I respond solemnly, trying to stifle a laugh. "I do."

"Figures," he replies, still smiling big. "Okay, now that *that's* settled, I really need to go." He looks down at his phone to check the time. "See you in a few hours."

I watch him cross the porch, go down the stairs, and walk

across the lawn toward his car. When I finally turn around, I see Nana standing by the kitchen table, an all-knowing look on her face.

"Care to explain why that handsome young man is leaving in your favorite nightshirt?" she asks, her eyebrows lifting dramatically. "Or would you rather begin with how Malena and Soraida came to be passed out drunk in my guest room?"

I think I'm about to test the claim that I never get in trouble.

CHAPTER NINETEEN

MALENA

My head feels ten times its actual size. Every tendril of my brain is pounding hard against my skull as if to complain of the damage I've done.

So this is a hangover? Why didn't anyone tell me I would feel like roadkill come morning? The pain was definitely not worth it. Maybe it's the good girl in me talking, but having a great time shouldn't feel this god-awful the next day.

I open my eyes and stare at the white ceiling fan spinning above my head, trying to make sense of the sounds and voices floating into the room. *Where am I?*

I toss the covers aside and try to stand up. The room spins, throwing everything off balance. I grip the side of the bed and tell myself to just focus on one small thing: a tiny glass sea turtle, sitting on top of the nightstand, suspended inside delicate branches of red coral.

I look away, not wishing to dwell on this beautiful reminder of island beach life. My mind has enough to process, and I haven't even gotten out of bed. God, I haven't even figured out where I am. What is wrong with me?

Last night's memories start flashing through my mind. Making out with Javi, throwing up in the back of Carlos's car, crashing at Ruby's house.

I'm at Ruby's.

My face burns hot with embarrassment and guilt, and I have to hold my head in my hands for support. This headache is otherworldly.

Did I make an ass of myself in front of Ruby and Abuela Joan? In front of people at the party? Is there anything to regret? I have no idea.

I sigh, long and hard, releasing the grip on my head.

Maybe I did. But I'm not gonna lie, it felt good to let loose—to let go of Poor María Malena for one night.

I press my feet against the cold hardwood floor and manage to stand, taking a quick inventory of myself. I'm wearing a bathrobe, a T-shirt, and underwear. That's it. I glance around, searching for my overnight bag—the one I packed to spend the night at Xiomara's—but it's not here. Instead, someone left a pair of sweatpants, a clean T-shirt, and a new toothbrush piled on top of the dresser.

I pull my hair up into a bun, wash my face, and change, then head out of the room.

"Well, good morning, sleepyhead," Abuela Joan sings from behind the kitchen island. She holds a platter with one hand, as the other slides a massive waffle onto Soraida's plate.

God, I hope she doesn't know anything. I don't want her to think I'm some floozy who can't keep track of where she's spending the night. Is that who I'm becoming?

"Are you hungry?" Abuela Joan asks, but it's more of a rhetorical question. Abuela Milagros does the same thing. Whether you're hungry or not is beside the point. They *will* feed you.

"I'm making you a latte," Ruby calls out from a far corner in the kitchen, apparently the coffee station, judging by the old-fashioned espresso maker. She presses a button on the machine, and the sound of grinding coffee beans takes over the lapse in conversation. The pulsing, grating noise lands like a jackhammer to my brain. When the coffee starts to drip, I inhale the aroma of fresh brewed grounds. The smell alone is enough to infuse a little life into me.

"These waffles are so good," Soraida says in Abuela Joan's direction. She's wolfing down the contents of her plate like she hasn't eaten in days. Then she turns to me and says, "She made bacon, too."

"A little grease is the best cure for a hangover," Abuela Joan says, winking at me. I'm mortified. Did she see me last night? I pray I didn't throw up in her bathroom. Oh, that would suck so bad.

Abuela Joan sets a plate in front of me, followed by a platter of bacon. The smell of fried pork fat sends my stomach into a downward spiral. I'm pretty sure grease is not what I need right now.

"Thank you," I say, grateful for her hospitality and hopeful that she hasn't called Mami. "Sorry we kinda dropped in unannounced. We were planning on staying with another friend. I guess that fell through."

I sit on the stool next to Soraida, trying to piece together exactly what happened.

A mug of steaming coffee appears, courtesy of Ruby. She's even topped it with foam in the shape of a heart.

"Pretty." My first sip tastes like pure heaven.

Ruby sets a glass of ice water next to my plate and deposits two ibuprofen tablets in my hand. "For the headache," she says, sitting next to me. "Did you sleep okay?"

"I did, thank you," I say before washing the tablets down with a gulp of water. "I'm just a little confused. I thought we were staying with Xiomara." I turn to Soraida for an explanation.

"Carlos showed up at the party and made a total ass of himself, threatening everyone like some kind of bichote." Soraida stabs a piece of waffle a little too hard. The metal silverware scratches the porcelain plate.

"What's a bee-cho-tay?" Ruby asks. Her terrible pronunciation makes Soraida and me snicker.

"It's a guy who thinks he's *all that*," I explain, omitting the more crass definition of the word out of respect for Abuela Joan.

"The biggest dick," Soraida blurts out. "That's what it means."

Abuela Joan smiles at us, amused.

"I'm sorry," I tell her. "My cousin has no filter, as you may already know."

"Oh, honey, I've known a bee-cho-tay or two in my lifetime," she says, sliding a waffle onto my plate. Then she hands me a dainty syrup jar, warm to the touch. "Have as much maple syrup as you want. Ruby and I already ate."

"Thanks," I say again, becoming more aware of every detail in Abuela Joan's kitchen. It's lovely, warm and homey. The plates have flower patterns in bright, bold colors. The silverware feels solid and heavy in my hand. And the white cabinets give the room an almost spiritual quality, like a holy sanctum.

Ruby clears her throat before saying, "Bee-cho-tay or not, he totally saved your butts last night." A text comes in as she's speaking. She glances at the screen and her cheeks go pink. She quickly types something back and sets the phone, screen down, on the countertop.

"Saved us?" Soraida scoffs. "From what?" Then she turns to Abuela Joan and says, "May I please have another one of those delicious waffles?"

"As many as you want, sweetheart," Abuela Joan says.

"Saved us from what, Ruby?" I ask, more evenly than my cousin and with genuine curiosity.

"Yourselves," Ruby says, trying to make her voice sound light. "And also probably some super-creepy drunk guys."

Slowly, it all comes back to me. The burning of the bras. The shots of tequila. The make-out session in the hot tub. And then Carlos. His deep voice roaring about I don't know what. *Why was he there, anyway?*

"I mean, in the state you two were in, who knows what could've happened? That guy Javi . . ." Her voice trails off as her eyes cut to Abuela Joan, busy making another batch of waffles. "And Carlos got this picture of you. . . . It was out of control."

"What picture?"

"Some stupid picture of you, Beatriz, and Nadia."

Her phone dings with another incoming text and she reaches for it.

"Let me see," I say.

Ruby looks at me tentatively and sighs. She unlocks the screen of her phone and types something I can't see. There's a swoosh of an outgoing text.

Then she swipes down her screen and passes me her phone. Beatriz, Nadia, and I are in the pool; I'm balanced on Javi's shoulders. My legs are wrapped around his neck and I notice that my nipples are visible under the wet white T-shirt. Last night, I didn't realize you could practically see everything.

But what does it matter, anyway? Why should I be ashamed? Isn't the whole point to own my body? To feel wholly comfortable in my own skin?

No more Pobrecita María Malena. No more playing the part of the victim.

Beatriz, Nadia, and I are laughing so hard you can almost hear it through the photo. Our faces are pure magnetic energy. Carefree, rebellious, and sexy. I barely recognize myself.

Undaunted. I am undaunted.

"I got worried," Ruby says.

"Why?" I ask, confused. "We were having fun."

Soraida peers over my shoulder. "Oh, that was a good one," she says, grabbing the phone from my hand. "Can you send this to me? Do you have any more?"

"Carlos made everyone destroy the evidence. Remember?" Ruby says with a half laugh, but I don't get what's so funny.

Ruby's phone dings again. Her hands jerk forward, reaching for her phone, but Soraida is quick to pull back.

"Why is my brother texting you?" Soraida asks, her tone hovering between surprise and annoyance.

We both stare at the text on Ruby's phone, then at her.

"He's coming over to pick you guys up," Ruby says, adjusting herself on the stool where she's been sitting. "Can I please have my phone back?"

She takes her phone before anyone else can make a play for it. "He's worried about you. We both are."

"Worried about what?" I ask, trying to make sense of this new version of Ruby. Her cheeks are flushed, and her voice sounds nervous and hesitant.

What happened to the ultra-feminist who was ready to liberate the nipples of women around the world?

"It's just that . . . you . . ." She wavers, staring at the dark screen of her phone. Her expression turns sallow and worn, like maybe she didn't get any sleep.

"Are you okay?" I ask.

"Can we go outside for a minute?"

I nod, then follow her to the back porch.

It's one of those unpredictable Florida mornings, where a sunny blue sky is set against heavy storm clouds in the distance. I have to cover my eyes with one hand to look at Ruby's face without squinting.

"What's going on, Ruby?"

"I . . . I just . . ." Her tone is agitated, and she is pacing the length of the porch with quick steps. Her movements are making me slightly nauseous. I wish she would stand still.

"I can't be okay with this," she finally blurts out. She bites her lower lip and crosses her arms across her chest, waiting for me to speak. My eyebrows gather into a confused stare. "You and Soraida getting drunk like that, with all those wasted guys. I mean, that wet T-shirt . . . baring your tits . . . I . . . I just . . ." She shakes her head and exhales, stumbling through more words that don't form a sentence.

"So, what? Now it's my fault if some asshole wants to take advantage of me because I had too much to drink?" The question turns my stomach inside out with disgust.

"Jesus, of course not," she says, unsettled. "I don't want anyone taking advantage of you. Period. That's what I'm trying to tell you. Last night . . . you weren't *thinking*." Her arms are flailing all over the place. "It wasn't safe, okay?"

"Wait." I hold up my hand, unable to make sense of what she's saying. "You're upset because I wasn't wearing a bra?"

"No, no. That's not what I'm saying at all." She's joggling here and there like a metal orb inside a pinball machine.

"Ruby, stop moving!" I snap. My head is whirling, and I can feel myself getting beyond angry with this conversation.

Ruby stands, pressing her back against the railing of the porch for support. Her arms are crossed over her chest again. We stare at each other in silence for what feels like a long time.

"Malena," she says quietly, "you have to understand. People judge you differently . . . because . . . because of your body type."

Suddenly, I'm back in Dr. Hardaway's office, smelling that minty-pine scent. Hearing the click-clack of Doris's heels hitting the tile floor of the school clinic. Feeling the walls of the bathroom stall closing around me as I open those wretched pantyliners.

Heat quickly rises from my stomach to my chest and up my neck and face. My insides churn with acid bile. I may be sick all over again.

"How can you say that?" I ask, spitting the words, unable to hide my anger and hurt. "You of all people! I mean, you sound just like—like Dr. Hardaway! What is wrong with you?"

Blotches of red crawl up Ruby's neck and cheeks. Her arms fall to her side and she balls her hands into fists. But I'm the one who feels like punching something.

"All I'm saying is that you need to be more careful," she says, visibly struggling to control her voice, her expression, her movements. "Some guys are assholes and predators, and you shouldn't give them a reason to think your body exists for them. They act like they're entitled to a girl, just because she's right there half-naked in front of them."

"I can't believe this crap." I can feel the words burning my tongue as they flow out. "I hate to break it to you, Ruby, but this is your own internalized misogyny. You're no different from the rest of them."

Ruby steps back and brings her hands to her stomach. I know I've landed a punch.

Internalized misogyny. I didn't know exactly what that meant until a week ago. It still feels new and foreign in my mouth. But right now, I have to speak in a language I know she'll respect and understand. She has to know that I'm no longer that pathetic girl crying in that bathroom stall.

"Okay," she says. "Now you're just pissing me off." She lets out a huff and then launches in. "Are you freaking kidding me right now?" Her composure is gone. Her arms are flailing. "My internalized misogyny? *My* internalized misogyny? What the living hell, Malena? You have no idea—"

"No idea of what?"

"Forget it. . . ." Ruby looks up to the sky and blinks a few times. After a long pause she says, "It's nothing," mostly to herself.

"You don't get it," I say, my voice softer.

"What? I don't get why you took your bra off and basically entered a wet T-shirt contest? No, I don't. Please explain."

"Because I wanted to."

"Yeah, okay. And I bet every guy at that party also wanted you to! Don't go lecturing me about internalized misogyny, Malena. Don't you dare."

"God, get off of your high horse. It doesn't matter how we're dressed. It's never been about the clothes. I thought you knew that."

Ruby's arms drop to her side, her hands opening and closing in a mechanical gesture. She closes her eyes and takes a deep, long breath. When she speaks again, her voice is forced, as if she's putting all of her energy into keeping her tone even.

"Malena, I'm sorry. I'm just trying to be honest with you. I don't want you to get hurt."

"I've already been hurt," I cry out. "I thought the whole point of the NippleRiot was to empower us. To make us stronger. To give *me* back control over my own damn body."

Ruby takes a step toward me, but I instinctively step back.

"Seriously? Control?" she says, her voice going high. "Last night, I sat beside you for hours, making sure you didn't have alcohol poisoning—hoping I wouldn't have to rush you to the hospital to get your stomach pumped. You weren't in control, Malena. You were wasted."

Hot tears are pushing hard against my eyelids, but I force them back. *Damn it, I will not cry.* Undaunted girls don't cry.

"This is it, Ruby," I say, gesturing at the pair of breasts I've inherited from the Rosario women. "This is my body, whether you think it's appropriate or not. If anyone has a problem with it, it's *their* problem, not mine."

I swallow hard and try to keep my voice flat as I say, "*My* body. And I don't care what you or anyone else thinks. It's mine to do with as I please. And if that means getting wasted and playing chicken in a hot guy's pool, then that's my decision."

I turn and walk away, toward the riverbank, trying to put as much space as possible between Ruby and me. Behind me, I hear her calling my name, but I don't stop. Who died and appointed her feminist queen? Flat-chested white girls get to be liberated, but Latinas with D cups have to play it "safe"?

When I reach the end of the dock, I sit on the worn wood and hang my feet over the water. The minutes stretch in silence.

My head is pounding even harder than before. I need to find some calm. I can't go home like this. Mami will see how upset I am and start asking all kinds of questions. And I don't want to lie to her—not more than I have to, anyway.

I hear boards creaking behind me and turn to see Abuela Joan walking toward me.

"Are you all right, Malena?" She sits beside me, dangling her feet next to mine.

I shrug and breathe in hard. If I open my mouth to speak, I may cry.

We sit quietly for a while, listening to the chirping of a flock of white-feathered birds roaming the riverbank.

Behind us, I hear the crunch of gravel on the driveway. Carlos's SUV is pulling up in front of the house. We should walk back, but I'm not ready. I want to be here with Abuela Joan.

"Abuela Joan?" I ask, my voice soft. "Do you think women can be empowered by our . . . our . . ." I gesture to my body, a little self-conscious, unsure of the right word for what I mean to say.

"Your sexuality?"

I nod. "Yeah, sexual freedom. Like, as a way to empower ourselves."

I don't know why I'm asking Ruby's grandmother these things, but there's an openness to Abuela Joan that invites difficult questions: life philosophy–type stuff.

"Wow, that's a doozy of a question," she says, laughing to herself. Then she turns her body to face mine. I feel her full attention on me as she says, "When I was in college, women were told, by other women, that we had to either dumb ourselves down to get a husband or become more like men—be all about dominance, money, and sex. Forget about being a mother and wife. That just made us look weak."

I listen intently, trying to understand.

"Some of us—myself included—were using sex to feel powerful. But hating ourselves after. We thought we were behaving like men, but we were never really in control, you see. Later—much later—I realized sex shouldn't be about power. It should be about respect and trust. And love, when it's with a special person."

I nod, but I'm not sure I understand. What if it's about respecting and trusting myself? Isn't that enough? What if I just want to feel good with someone I like? Do I have to wait until I'm in love with someone?

A bright bluebird flutters between us and stops to rest on the dock. For a moment, we stare at its delicate wings in silence, admiring the burst of orange on its chest, its tiny black beak and round dark eyes. I reach for it, hoping it will climb onto my hand, but it jumps off and flies away toward the tall grass.

"As I get older, I'm beginning to think we were all duped. I mean, who exactly are these *men* we were supposed to use as role models? Maybe it's because I'm an old lady, but I think young women are being taken for a ride, thinking hookups are liberating." She huffs. "We women have our own powers, our own strengths. Our own ideas of freedom."

We both watch as the bluebird hops from one branch to the next, gliding over yellow leaves. My eyes linger on the stems swaying in the wind as dense, gray clouds roll over us. The sun, shining only seconds ago, is now hidden from view. Rain is coming.

"Sometimes it feels like I don't have power over anything, even my own body," I say quietly. "Everyone expects something from me. My family. My teachers. My friends. And now even Ruby. What about what I want?"

"Do you know what you want, dear?"

The question gives me pause. What *do* I want?

I strain to come up with an answer. I must have some idea, right?

Why did I start the NippleRiot? Was that what *I* wanted? Or did I just go along with Ruby's plans? And what about last night? Why did I take off my bra? Because I wanted to, or because everyone was cheering me on? And why did I make out with a guy I'd just met? Is it wrong that I liked kissing Javi? That I liked how it made me feel?

My head spins. What I really want right now is to climb back into bed and cover my pounding head with a pillow.

Abuela Joan studies my face. After a moment of silence, she pats my thigh with one hand. "Try to be patient with yourself, Malena. You don't need to have all the answers."

Well, that's a relief. Because, clearly, I have no answers.

CHAPTER TWENTY

RUBY

"Christ, Soraida. You smell like a brewery."

Carlos just came through the kitchen door—hair still wet from a shower, damp T-shirt clinging to his broad shoulders. It's strange, but I feel a wave of relief wash over me. Just seeing him in my kitchen helps me to breathe a little deeper after that disaster of a conversation with Malena.

He's standing over Soraida, who is sopping up one last puddle of syrup with her fourth or fifth waffle. I've lost count.

"Back off," Soraida hisses, pushing her chair out and standing up to take her plate to the sink. "I'm warning you."

Honestly, I get why she's pissed. I know she was drunk trash-talking last night when she said all of that about him being a macho or whatever, but she's got a point. He did storm into that party to protect his sister and cousin. And Soraida, she would have been fine. Sure, she was tipsy, but she wasn't blackout drunk. Malena, though . . .

How did that conversation go so far off the rails? When I try to remember the actual words we exchanged, my mind draws a blank. All I remember is the way Malena was looking at me. I've never seen that much anger in her face. I didn't even recognize her—or myself. Did I really tell her that her body was more dangerous than mine? That she needed to be more careful? To cover up? Or was that just what she chose to hear?

"Where's Malena?" Carlos asks.

"How should I know?" Soraida spits. "I'm not her keeper. You are."

I jump in, desperate to smooth things over. "I'll take your plate, Soraida. Why don't you hop in the shower?" I gingerly motion toward the bag of clean clothes that Carlos managed to smuggle out of his house this morning. She swipes the bag up (without saying thanks to her brother), storms into the guest room, and slams the door shut behind her.

As soon as the door closes, I feel the energy change in the kitchen. Carlos and me, alone together.

"Wanna wait out on the porch?" I ask. "I need some fresh air."

He nods and gestures for me to lead the way.

The French doors open with a gust of wind. I can smell the damp chill in the air, the mist from the river. A nor'easter must be coming. I lean against the porch rail, looking out to the river, feeling the wind move between us, watching it kick up whitecaps on the water.

Malena and my nana are sitting across from each other on the dock, deep in conversation. Malena is probably telling her what I said, or—more accurately—screamed. She's mad at me. I know I should have handled the whole thing better. But ever since yesterday, I've felt like the world is tilting, off balance. I've been trying so hard not to fall flat on my face.

"Looks like we've both managed to piss off a Rosario girl this morning," I say. "I think Malena hates me."

"Nah," Carlos says. "She practically worships you."

I shake my head. "I tried to make her see that what she did last night was dangerous, that she needed to be more careful, to not get out of control. I totally botched it."

We watch in silence as Malena and Nana make their way across the back lawn toward the house. Nana smiles and waves; Malena pretends we don't exist.

I open my mouth to call out to her, but then change my mind. Maybe she needs some space. What would I say, anyway?

"Storm's coming!" Nana says before heading through the back door. Malena disappears behind her.

"We'll be right in," I call back. But I don't want to go back inside to all those complications. I don't think Carlos does either.

"I was thinking on the way here how wrong this all is," Carlos says, leaning forward on the rail.

"You mean what we did last night? Going to get them?"

"No," he says firmly. "Even if they both hate me, I don't regret that." He shrugs. "Plus, I'm used to being despised by my sister."

"Soraida tends to have strong opinions." I smile.

"I dunno. I guess she's got a point, though. If I got wasted last night, or hooked up with some girl, my mom and my tía and abuela would be all like, 'Cosa de hombres.' You know, 'Boys will be boys.' But Soraida and Malena—it's like the whole world's gonna come crumbling down if they get a reputation."

"But *do* you go out, get wasted, and hook up with random girls?" I ask, not sure I want to know the answer.

"I don't get wasted. Gotta take care of my body. It's my ticket into the majors."

His body. The memories flood in: him standing shirtless in the doorway, brushing past me as he walked toward the bathroom, crouched on the edge of the bed. I start to push them aside, but then I realize how relieved I am—finally—to have this exhilarating rush overcome the image of that rough hand groping me during the walkout.

"And the random girls?" I ask.

"Despite what you may think—or hear—I'm not a player."

"You mean you're not the kind of guy who walks into a party and makes everyone's head turn," I say, knowing that I'm messing with him and it's making him crazy.

"Shut up," he says. "You think I'm a machista, don't you?"

I shrug. "I'm still not even sure what that word means."

"Oh God. You do. You think I'm some asshole machista jock. I can tell."

He steps back from the porch railing and crosses his arms over his chest.

"I don't, actually. I used to, but not anymore." I take in a slow breath and then make myself look right at him. "All I really know is that you love your cousin. And you want what's best for her. I guess that's what matters."

"Yeah," he says, all serious. "I do—*and* my stupid-ass sister."

Am I letting him off the hook too easily? Carlos is the kind of guy who threatens people if they touch his little cousin; he's the one everybody listens to, a little afraid, when he tells them to erase the pictures from their phones. He's not exactly a model of feminism, that's for sure. I guess I'm realizing that when it comes to Carlos, things aren't so clear-cut. He has a lot to learn, yes. But he is also good. He's kind. He's trying really hard to do the right thing.

And I trust him.

"Can you do me a weird favor?" I ask, stepping in front of

him. I'm standing between him and the porch rail, with both of us facing the water. I'm surprised to hear the question come out of my mouth.

"Depends. How weird?"

"Can I borrow your hand for, like, a second?" I can't believe I'm doing this, but I need to. "I'm going to put it right here," I say, lifting my shirt to expose the red patch of skin on my stomach, the place that has been burning with heat and shame since yesterday in the hallway, when I collapsed to the floor. The place I scrubbed raw with a loofah, and then—when that wasn't enough—a pumice stone meant for the tough skin of my feet.

I don't know why I want his hand there. It's not because I need some guy to help me feel better. I know that much. But I'm so confused right now. So angry and torn.

A stray hand, a few words—it all lasted for less than a minute! Why am I letting that moment have so much control over me? Why do I feel so vulnerable, so . . . violated? Will I always feel that way about another person's touch? Even a person I trust?

I need to know.

I take his hand in mine, not looking back to see how his face registers my action, or whether he notices the red scratches on my skin. Instead, I study his fingers, the dark hair, smooth cuticles, and clipped nails. Nothing like that other hand—the one that makes my skin crawl and fills me with panic and disgust. I place his hand over my wounded skin.

Carlos's soft touch is nothing like that prodding grasp I want so desperately to remove from my memory. He is standing behind me, both of us looking out across the water, his hand gently resting on my stomach. I feel his fingers cool against the raw skin.

He steps a bit closer to me and whispers softly in my ear, "Is this okay?"

I nod. "Yes, good."

Our bodies are close, but not touching, except where his hand rests. I can feel him looking past me, over my shoulder, across the water. I can hear his breath, smooth and deep.

"Do you think we're doing the right thing? All this? Do you think it's gonna help?" I ask.

"With the dress code?"

"I guess, or with girls feeling less . . . like objects."

"I dunno, Ruby. I hope so."

We stand together, quiet. He keeps his hand perfectly still against me. I interlace my fingers with his and lean back into him. I feel the gentle pressure of his chest against my shoulders and the wind from the river brush across us both.

My gut isn't contracting. I don't feel revulsed, or like I need to step away. He's not pressing or prodding; he's not trying to take anything away from me. Our bodies, pressed gently together, send waves of grounding energy between us.

Carlos and me, standing here, touching each other—this is two people deciding together to be physically close, deciding together how to touch and be touched. It's about connection, not control. And, yes, I think we both feel desire, but not a desire to *have* or consume each other, instead the desire to get even closer, in every way.

I want that very much—to be closer to Carlos. But not now. Not yet. I'm a mess.

The wind kicks up, blowing a gust from an entirely different direction. My hair flies into my mouth as the sky starts spitting drops of rain.

I turn away from the rain, and suddenly I'm face to face with Carlos, with the wind and rain at my back. Carlos reaches out and moves the clumps of hair from my face. The wind gusts again, and he holds his hand firmly against my cheek, keeping my hair from flying wild.

"I think I want to kiss you," he says. He has to raise his voice over the suddenly gusting wind and the trees and the waves. "Would that be okay?"

I think I want to kiss him, too, but I need time. "I'm sorry, I'm just not . . ." My voice trails off as I lean my forehead against his chest and take in a deep, long breath. "I'm not ready," I whisper, my voice so quiet that I'm not sure he even hears.

He tries to tuck the hair behind my ears, but the wind is too strong. He brings his other hand to my head and threads his fingers through my hair—he's holding it down, his grip strong. I feel his chin firm on the top of my head. The gesture is unexpected, but also sweet and reassuring.

"Is it something you want to talk about?" he asks.

I shake my head and step back, wishing I could but knowing I'm not ready for that, either. "Maybe later," I say.

I lift my hand to my hair as his hand drops. I tug the loose strands into one fist as the wind keeps blowing around my face.

The porch door swings open and Malena peers out. "Carlos, we should go. It's gonna storm."

Carlos glances out to the river, where the whitecaps have whipped up to a frenzy, and then he looks back at me.

"Yeah, we better get out of here," he says.

"We'll meet you at the truck." With that, Malena whips around and walks back inside.

I go after her. "Malena—" I reach out and touch her arm, trying to think of what to say, how to start over, but she doesn't give me a chance.

"What?" she snaps.

I stare at her face, trying to find the sweet girl who belted out reggaeton in my passenger seat, who split a Sundae Scream with me. But all I see is a girl who wants nothing to do with me. Malena shakes her head and turns to leave.

My heart aches in a way I've never known before. I want her not to hurt the way I'm hurting. All because some asshole decides to touch her against her will.

I never want her to be in a situation that makes her vulnerable to *that* kind of touch.

I never want her to go home and scrub her skin raw, to sit for hours in a scalding-hot tub.

I never want her to feel the way I felt last night.

If wanting to keep Malena safe makes her hate me, then I guess that's just how it will have to be. At least until I can figure out how to explain all of this to her. To myself.

"Come *on*, Carlos!" Soraida calls from the front door.

I walk Carlos to the front door, watching as Malena and Soraida take off across the lawn toward his truck.

"I'm sure she'll call to thank you after that hangover passes," Carlos says, attempting some levity.

We stare at each other for a moment, trying to figure out how to say goodbye.

"Just tell me when, Ruby," he says. "I'm ready when you are."

CHAPTER TWENTY-ONE

MALENA

On Sunday, my ass is taking up space in a front-row pew at Inmaculada Concepción Catholic Church.

The church thing was Tía Lorna's idea. In her practiced pious tone, she guilted Mami into attending Mass by telling her that "maybe if you had more faith, God would smile down on you more."

I wanted to ask her if this God of hers gets a sick satisfaction from unleashing the forces of nature onto the world, but for Mami's sake, I kept my mouth shut.

The last time my parents and I set foot in a church was for my confirmation two years ago. I wore a brand-new soft blue dress with delicate white ribbons on the sleeves. Mami even took me to the salon to get a fancy updo. After the confirmation Mass, and the archbishop's special blessing—an open-palm touch on the cheek—we went out for a seafood mofongo en pilón dinner at our favorite restaurant. Honestly, the dinner was the best part.

Now, listening to a sermon about the virtues of Mary as a role model of obedience to the Father and a portrait of virginal purity, I want to gouge my eyes out.

How is it possible that Mary was married to Joseph her entire life and not once did they have sex? What kind of marriage is that?

And why do we have to blindly oblige the patriarchy? What good did that ever do anyone?

It's a reminder of why religion class was so confounding back at Sagrado Corazón—common sense and logic need not apply.

Sitting next to me in the pew, Mami clutches her rosary beads and nods along, not once flinching. Is she buying this crap?

I try to relax into the rigid oak pew and follow her example, resolving to listen without judgment.

I know she's probably ignoring it. She's probably praying to La Virgencita for Papi to come back to us safely.

The priest continues his rant about obedience, and I decide I've had it. My cranium will literally explode in a bloody mess if I sit in this pew for a second longer. I don't even care if I get in trouble with Tía Lorna. I excuse myself, turning to slide out of the pew.

"Where do you think you're going?" Tía Lorna whisper-yells.

"Bathroom," I whisper back, giving her the only answer that will get me a pass.

"Can't you hold it? It's disrespectful."

I press my legs together and grimace. "I can't. I think I got my period."

I lie because, as every girl knows, having your period makes you an untouchable.

Tía Lorna purses her lips into an ugly scowl and moves her legs aside so I can edge past her.

Soraida slides forward as if to follow me out, but Tía Lorna grabs her arms and drags her back. "You stay right here," she demands between clenched teeth. Carlos, who is watching the whole scene unfold from the end of the pew, tries and fails to suppress a snicker with a cough. He also gets one of Tía Lorna's death stares.

I mouth a *Sorry* to Soraida and double my stride toward the back of the nave. I have no idea where I'm going, so I take the first door I see.

A long corridor leads me to a small chapel, tucked away from the hubbub of the congregation. The room has beautiful stained-glass windows and only a handful of pews. An open shrine displays a statue of Mother Mary, heart ablaze and arms wide open. Her face wears a soft expression of kindness that touches my heart.

A moment of recognition passes between us. This Mary is my Virgencita—all compassion, love, and acceptance. None of this guilt-trip, judgmental, ever-virgin nonsense.

I reach for a votive candle from a box of freebies and place it on the massive candleholder in front of the shrine. I strike a match and move it toward the wick, then watch the flame come to life.

This tiny light is my prayer. This solitary room is my church.

I rub the medal on my necklace and ask La Virgencita to protect my dad wherever he is. Across the ocean that stands between us, I send him so much love it makes my heart ache.

Last we heard, he was delivering blue tarps to cover damaged roofs in the most remote towns, high up in the central mountain range. Some areas are completely cut off, and the only way to access the homes is by helicopter. Papi hates to fly. He gets heart palpitations, his stomach gets queasy, and his hands start sweating buckets. Mami usually holds his hand during takeoff and landing, but now he's all alone.

I think about Papi and everyone I left behind on my Island. I think of the loss and heartache, the despair so many are still living through.

And I think of my own life, everything muddled and confusing. I wonder if I have the right to complain about anything when—at the very least—I have a roof over my head, one not covered with a blue tarp.

My eyes linger on Mary's open arms, and I interpret them as a silent promise to be the keeper of my secrets.

"I don't know how to be me," I confess quietly. It feels like a stupid thing to say. But everyone has a different Malena in mind.

I don't know which is the real one.

———

After Mass, I'm desperate to go home, but Tía Lorna ropes Mami into staying for a lunch potluck hosted by the women in her rosary group.

"Thanks for leaving me behind," Soraida sneers.

"Every woman and child for themselves," I tease.

"Whatever. I had to sit there and listen to Padre Francisco drone on for another half hour. I'm starving."

We grab some disposable plates and join the food line. I glance ahead and see that someone made pernil and arroz con gandules. Even a flan sits on a platter, floating in a pool of caramel sauce. My stomach growls with anticipation.

My phone dings in my pocket and I have to maneuver my plate and cutlery and a cup of soda to read the screen.

Hope that hangover wasn't too bad

It's Javi BTW

"How did Javi get my number?" I stare at my screen, running through what little I can remember from the party.

"He asked me for it. Did he text you?" Soraida reaches for my phone, but I pull away with ninja-fast reflexes. My drink spills all over my hands.

"Watch it, Soraida!"

"Let me read it," she whines.

"Nope."

"Damn, you're so lucky. That guy is so sexy . . . and filthy rich. I'm sure he's great in bed, too. I wouldn't mind losing it to someone like him."

"He *is* a really good kisser," I offer, quirking an eyebrow.

"No more virgencita Malena," she guffaws. Then her tone turns serious. "Don't put out until after a few dates. That way no one can accuse you of being easy."

I cut her a sideways glance. As if she's ever been any further with a guy than getting felt up by a neighbor in the seventh grade, in an especially intense game of spin the bottle. She likes to talk a big game, but in truth she probably gets all her info from those smutty novels she reads.

Tía Lorna doesn't even allow her to date. Carlos, of course, can do whatever he wants—though dating privileges are wasted on him, given that he's only into baseball. I guess that will change with Ruby. Who knew that a flaca con pecho de plancha was gonna be his grand slam.

He's been standing in the corner texting, with a stupid grin on his face. Probably Ruby. How could I have been so wrong about her?

Soraida glances at a life-size crucifix in the garden and makes the sign of the cross. "Be careful, prima," she jokes. "Loose girls don't go to heaven."

I scoff. I had a boyfriend last year, when I was fourteen. We walked home together after school and hid behind trees in the park to kiss—but it wasn't like Javi. It was a quick and clumsy cha-cha-cha to Javi's sultry and experienced bachata. We broke up after he got too clingy.

In truth, I don't know if I want a boyfriend right now.

But then I think of Javi. The way his hands felt around my waist. My legs, sliding around his hips in the pool. My breasts, barely covered, pressing hard against his bare chest. There was a look in his eyes, his entire face, that I'd never noticed in a guy before.

Wanting.

Javi wanted me. I could see it in his face, the glimmer in his eyes. The way his features softened as he reached for me with both hands. For the first time in forever, I felt in control. He wanted me and it was up to me to decide what to do with that wanting. I had the power.

I may not care for the complications that come with a boyfriend—dealing with my family asking a million questions, in particular. But after what I've been through in the last few weeks, I wouldn't mind feeling that way again. I wouldn't mind being the one in control.

Carlos suddenly appears by our side and squeezes himself between Soraida and me.

"The line starts back there, buddy." Soraida gives him a playful shove.

"You may want to grab your plates and head outside," he says, leaning in closer. He then nods in the direction of Tía Lorna, who is deep in conversation with one of the rosary ladies. Tía's arms are tightly wrapped over her chest, and her jaw is shut so tight, her teeth may crack.

"What's going on?" I ask, watching Tía wave Mami into her gossip corner.

"I heard both your names mentioned in passing. And not in a *those girls are such saints* tone. Whatever it is, it's not good."

"Did you say something about the party?" Soraida snaps.

Carlos holds both hands up in the air as he says, "I'm no snitch."

Soraida grunts.

"Do you think they know?" I ask, racking my brain for an explanation.

"No way!" Soraida says confidently. "Let's just eat. I'm gonna start chewing on my arm, I'm so hungry."

Carlos grabs the plate I'm holding and walks away with it as his own. He winks, with an impish "Gracias." I don't protest, but Soraida hisses some obscenity under her breath.

"I'm sure it's nothing," Soraida says, passing me a new plate. This time the confidence in her tone falters.

Mami turns her head here and there, searching for me amid the potluck gathering. When our eyes meet, I know. It's not nothing.

We don't even get to enjoy lunch. The moment we sit down to eat at one of the picnic tables in the garden, Tía Lorna is by our side with Mami standing next to her. They look equally pissed.

"You two," Tía spits. "Inside. Now."

I glance at my untouched plate, then at Mami, searching for reassurance. But there is none.

Soraida and I groan about how hungry we are.

"Can we eat first?" Soraida whines.

"Now," Tía repeats, her voice edgy.

Leaving our plates on the table, we follow Tía Lorna to the sacristy.

Once the four of us are inside, she shuts the door behind her. I look around, trying to decide where to prop myself. The floor-to-ceiling cabinets in high-gloss wood make the room appear smaller than it is. There's a padded kneeler in front of a table where the Blessed Sacrament is exposed. And a wardrobe that I guess is meant to store the priest's robes.

"Where were you Friday night?" Tía Lorna asks. Judging by the crazed look in her eyes, she already knows. "And don't you dare lie to me. Not in front of the Body of Christ. Remember, mija, the Holy Father is always watching." She points a finger toward the very ornate monstrance holding the Eucharist.

I look straight ahead, afraid Soraida's lack of control over her facial expressions will betray us.

"Malena?" Mami steps closer to me and I inch back. Why don't they have any chairs in this place? "You told me you were going to your friend Xiomara's house," Mami says, studying my face. "What happened?"

My brain goes into high gear, trying to come up with a cred-ible story fast. I'd rather burn in hell—*sorry, Holy Father*—than tell the truth and risk never leaving our apartment again.

"Xiomara's cousin was throwing a small party," I say. "We went for, like, an hour. What were we supposed to do? Stay at her house all alone? We had to go."

Until this precise moment, I have never lied to my mother. But this one lie came so easily that I begin to wonder if this is also part of being undaunted. Maybe lying is more of a necessity than a choice.

"People saw you kissing a boy," Tía Lorna says, turning her accusatory finger toward me. "In one of those hot tubs, of all places. Like some cualquiera who has no self-respect. This is what this bra thing is all about? You parading your tetas around?"

My face burns red hot with anger. Who died and appointed Tía Lorna chief of the morality police? And what power does she think she has over me?

"Wait, I think whoever told you this got confused. That was Beatriz in the hot tub with her boyfriend, not Malena," Soraida says, so calmly and innocently that she catches me off guard. *Thank you, primita.* "They both look the same from behind. It's the long hair. People have mistaken them before."

I force myself to stare Tía Lorna in the eyes.

"No more parties," she says curtly. "And no more sleepovers."

Soraida moans, pressing her luck. "But we didn't do anything wrong."

Mami finally chimes in. "You should've told us where you were going and asked for permission first."

"You would've said no," I dare say.

"Don't be a contestona, señorita." Tía Lorna chastises me for talking back.

I open my mouth so she can really see what a contestona I am, but Soraida gently presses her hand against my shoulder, holding me back.

"Can we finish lunch now?" Soraida asks. "Please?"

Two worry lines cut across Mami's forehead. I can see the unease in her eyes. I can also see that she's not buying our story.

But they won't understand the truth. And, frankly, deep down I think they prefer the lie. Because the lie is not at odds with whatever image of Soraida and me they have created in their own minds.

"I'll send in Carlos with your plates," Tía says. "You can eat here, and then you can clean this room and then the altar."

"But that will take all afternoon," Soraida complains.

"Call me when you're done. I'll come pick you up," Tía says, turning to leave.

"I don't understand," I say. "We have to clean the church?"

"Think of it as your atonement, young lady," Tía says. "And maybe next Sunday you won't get your period in the middle of Padre Francisco's sermon."

Next Sunday? I have to come back next Sunday?

And with that, Tía Lorna leaves and Mami follows. For what feels like an eternity, I stare at the closed door, refusing to let the feeling of entombment crush my soul.

My phone buzzes in my pocket and I pull it out.

> Any plans tonight?

Another text from Javi.
This time I respond.

> Pick me up in an hour?

I include the address for Inmaculada Concepción.

> At a church?

> Haven't you heard? Catholic girls really know how to party.

"I'm gonna need you to cover for me," I tell Soraida.

"Finally," Soraida exclaims.

"What do you mean?"

"Prima, don't take this the wrong way, but it's about damn time you got out there and lived a little."

"I *have,*" I retort, but I think I know what she's trying to say.

"I've been waiting for you to start making a life *here,* that's what I mean. Not just the protest. Parties, dating. Honestly, prima, I've been worried about you. You've seemed so different after María, like you didn't know how to laugh—how to have fun anymore. But now it's like you're coming back."

I don't know if that old Malena is ever coming back. Do I even want her to? What I do know: *This* Malena is ready to break some rules. If I'm getting punished, I'm gonna give them a damn good reason.

Javi pulls up in a bright red Jeep and I climb in. The moment our eyes meet, that feeling I've been chasing bolts through me, like lightning during a sea storm.

"I didn't think you'd text," he says, driving out of the now-empty church parking lot.

"You were wrong, I guess." The words come out bold and flirtatious—*so* not me. Or maybe this *is* me, the me I'm becoming.

"I was about to watch a movie when you texted back. Do you want to go somewhere or just hang?" He grabs his phone, keeping his eyes on the road, and taps at the screen. The cabin fills with the sounds of soft Spanish rock.

"We can hang," I say, unsure if I've just agreed to go back to his house. God, I suck at this. But now is not the time to be a coward. Now is the time to be undaunted Malena.

Javi gives me a sideways glance, and a half smile tugs at his lips.

My palms are sweating like crazy, but Javi wouldn't know it by looking at my face. I return the smile with coqueta eyes, but my damp hands are clutching my purse like we're about to skid off the road and hit oncoming traffic.

We drive the rest of the way mostly in silence, me trying to decide how far this fearless new me is willing to go. I'm sure Javi is wondering the same thing.

———

Before I have time to make up my mind, we are parked in his driveway and walking to the front door. The ultramodern house looks different in the daylight, hard and uninviting. The combination of concrete, thick windows, and sharp angles makes for an unnatural-looking home.

I follow Javi through the glass front door and we head into the large open kitchen.

"You hungry?" He opens the fridge and peers in.

"I'm good," I say, looking around. White walls. White cabinets. White furniture. "I'll have some water."

He takes out a bottle and hands it to me.

"Thanks." The water tastes cold and crisp, a perfect complement to the room we're in.

"What kind of movie are you in the mood for?" Javi leans on the white stone countertop, catching my eyes. "We have a theater downstairs."

I grip the water bottle harder, plotting how to push every boundary I've ever known. How to take control. How to be that girl who makes her own decisions.

"I want to see your room," I say flatly. This clearly takes Javi by surprise.

Yo soy dueña de mi vida, a mí nadie me manda. The lyrics of "Ahora Me Llama" by Karol G and Bad Bunny scroll through my mind. Am I ready to prove that I own my life? That no one calls the shots but me?

He crosses his arms over his chest and cocks an eyebrow in amusement. "Are you sure?"

"It won't be anything we haven't already done," I say, suddenly uncertain of exactly *what* we did in the hot tub before Carlos arrived.

Javi's cheeks go red, and for a moment he looks away. Is he embarrassed?

Our hands may have traveled a little farther than I thought.

"Yeah, but you know," he says with a shrug, "we were both kinda wasted."

"I'm not wasted now." My heart is drumming so fast, I can hear it behind my ears.

"Carlos is gonna lose it," he mutters to himself, rubbing the back of his neck with his open hand.

"Carlos doesn't get a say over what I do." I step forward, my tone edgy and defensive. "I decide."

Javi takes me in, his hands falling to his waist. Something in his expression changes from amusement to consideration. I hold his gaze. Why does it feel like I have to convince him to take me to his bed?

"Are you sure?" he asks.

My heart is still pounding like a drum line inside my chest, and I don't know what I'm ready to do, but I say, "I'm sure."

I must be getting good at lying, because it even sounds like the truth.

"It's this way," he finally says.

I trail him up the stairs to the second floor. His room is at the end of a long hallway, and it's massive—larger than our living room and kitchen combined.

A king-size bed with hotel-style bedding serves as the main focal point. It makes the twin in my own bedroom feel like a bad joke.

It strikes me how clean everything is, for a guy's room.

Javi stands by the door with an awkward smile on his face. "This is it."

I walk in, making a conscious decision to sit at the edge of the bed.

How far are you willing to go, Malena?

Now, sensing the softness of the comforter under the bare skin of my thighs, I'm starting to panic a little. I tug at my skirt, briefly bringing down the hem.

Javi hesitates by the door. His face wears the expression of someone unable to believe his luck. I watch his eyes until I find what I came here looking for. The wanting. It's there. Suddenly I feel like I've swum out too far and I'm treading in dark water, a sea current threatening to pull me under.

How far are you willing to go?

I'm undaunted Malena, I tell myself. *It's my body and I get to decide.*

I nod and Javi takes it as a cue to close the space between us. He sits next to me on the bed, gently sliding his hand behind my neck, caressing my hairline.

"God, you're so . . . exquisite."

How do I even respond to that? I'm so overwhelmed that I can barely process his other hand landing on my bare thigh, tentatively moving under my skirt.

I gently push Javi onto the pillow and climb on top of him.

We kiss hard, almost hungrily. Pressing against each other until our lips are swollen. It's like I'm melting into Javi. I don't want it to stop.

Our hands travel under clothes, exploring, wandering, caressing. I pull Javi's shirt over his head, and he does the same with mine.

How far?

He pauses to take in the blue bra cupping my chest. His touch is knowing but gentle, not pushy or hurried. Unlike me, I'm sure Javi has the benefit of experience to guide him.

He slowly kisses the skin on my neckline, gliding his fingers over my breasts. I close my eyes and let myself feel the sensation.

My body can't get enough of his touch. It feels like we are the only two people in the universe. But my mind is waging a war against itself. A voice that refuses to go quiet reminds me that I don't even know him. Do I even know his last name?

What does it matter? Why should this so-called purity have so much power over me? I'm pretty sure guys don't think about all this stuff. They just do it. No strings attached.

I shut my eyes tighter, willing these thoughts to go away—to leave me alone so I can enjoy myself and focus solely on the mind-blowing sensation of his touch.

Javi slips his hands under my skirt and, in one expert motion, pulls me under him. I can feel his full weight over me. The soft skin of his chest touching mine. He snaps off my bra, and something shifts inside me.

My heart has never felt so vulnerable and exposed. There are so many conflicting feelings floating to the surface that I think I might cry.

No strings attached? I was so wrong.

There's nothing casual about this moment. There are a million strings tugging at every cell in my body. And they're all telling me to stop.

I can't do this. Suddenly it's so clear to me. This is not what I want.

I don't even give Javi an explanation as I slide out from underneath him, pull myself back together, grab my clothes, and quickly get dressed.

I rush out of his house like it's on fire.

CHAPTER TWENTY-TWO

RUBY

It's finally Friday, the end of a long and painful week of avoiding memories of the walkout and being ignored by Malena, even though I busted my butt to make sure we had enough signatures to turn in our petition on time—three hundred and twenty-three, to be precise.

We did it. We earned our two minutes.

In just ten days, we're going to the school-board meeting to make our case.

Malena's still massively pissed at me, though. I was hoping that if I focused on getting the petition done, I'd prove to her that I still care about all this—that I care about *her*. But she refuses to talk to me, and instead sends short bursts of texts about planning meetings, or the ins and outs of school-board protocol. A few days ago, she left an enormous binder on my car with a note that read, simply, *Read it.*

Truth is, I didn't realize how much I would miss her. She was sort of starting to feel like the sister I had lost somewhere along the way—the one who listened instead of always bossing me around, who cared about my ideas and opinions. A sister who actually saw me.

Meanwhile, my parents have been sending moment-by-moment color commentary on their extended visit with Olive—the afternoon they spent with her adorable students, how effusively her school principal gushed about her talents, all the great restaurants and coffee shops in Atlanta, even how cool her apartment is, in some edgy neighborhood near this place they call the BeltLine.

It's all so exhausting.

Maybe a piping hot bowl of pho is just what I need.

This morning, Topher showed up at my car, begging me to take him downtown for pho and dumplings after school. It's his comfort food, and Topher needs some soothing right about now.

Topher found out last week that he's a finalist for some fancy scholarship to the University of Virginia. I'm driving him to Orlando tomorrow morning for a two-hour interview with a panel of alumni. It sounds terrifying to me, like an interrogation, but he's super excited about it.

Anyway, it didn't take much begging. I love pho, and today, rainy and dreary, with all of us feeling stressy and overwhelmed, is the perfect day for it. Plus, Topher has a rare Friday off work at the Raceway. That in itself is cause for celebration.

We're loitering by the auditorium, waiting to meet up with the girls. Nessa and Jo head toward us, both wearing black lace-up boots, high-waisted stonewashed jeans, and oversize cardigans.

"Really," Topher calls, "do you set out your outfits every night before bed and text photos to each other?"

It truly is uncanny how often they show up dressed alike.

They stop across from us, and Nessa wraps her arm around Jo's waist.

"Nope," Jo says, "don't need to."

"Our connection is spiritual," Nessa adds, leaning in to kiss Jo on the lips. "Modern technology plays no role."

"Ugh," Topher groans sarcastically. "You two are too much."

Seeing how perfect they are for each other makes me wonder, again, if I'll ever find a relationship like that.

"Let's get out of here," Jo says. "I'm dying for dumplings."

Jo pulls away from Nessa fast, her eyes going wide.

"Don't look now," Nessa loud-whispers, "but Mr. Sporty Balls is heading our way."

Since I possess exactly zero cool, my entire body swings in the direction she's looking, while an enormous grin makes its way across my face and my heart lurches into my gut.

As he nears us, Carlos slings his backpack off one shoulder, unzips it, and pulls out my Thanksgiving Turkey Trot T-shirt. He continues toward us, his gaze locked on mine.

I glance toward Topher, whose eyebrows are raised so high that they're nearing his hairline, and Jo, whose jaw has dropped to the point that it's practically dragging on the linoleum floor. At least Nessa seems to be keeping it together.

"Your nightshirt," Carlos says, now standing directly across from me. "Washed and folded. Thanks for letting me borrow it."

I feel my cheeks burn red as I reach out my hand to take the shirt from him. He doesn't seem embarrassed at all. He just keeps looking at me with a sweet, crooked grin, as if we're the only two people in the building.

"I've been wanting to bring it by your Nana's all week," he says, "but practice keeps running late." He lets his hand rest on mine for a few seconds.

The image of my nightshirt slipping over his shoulders comes crashing into my memory.

"Thanks," I say, my voice sounding weird and croaky.

"You borrowed her nightgown? Well, that's kinky," Nessa says. "You go, Roobs!" It sounds more like something Jo would say, and I can see that Nessa's proud of her bravado.

Oh sweet Jesus. Since I'm unable to form a word, Topher jumps in. "Ruby somehow forgot to tell us about your slumber party," he says, staring hard at me.

Carlos releases a deep laugh. "It's way more innocent than it sounds." He rests his fingers lightly on my forearm. "Right, Ruby?"

He looks over toward the others. "You're Jo and Nessa, right? Ruby and Topher told me a lot about you."

"Glowing reports," Topher says.

"I'm Nessa, and this is my girlfriend, Jo. You'll have to excuse her."

"She's really into baseball," Topher says. "I think she's been overtaken with emotion."

"Maybe you could, like, sign a ball for her or something?" Nessa laughs, wrapping her arm around Jo's waist and pulling her in close.

Carlos cuts a glance at me that clearly signals, *Are they joking?* The adorable thing is that if Jo wanted a ball, he'd probably sign it for her, even though it would massively embarrass him.

"Hey," Topher says, "wanna come get pho with us?"

I bite my lip and my heart drops into my gut. Did Topher really ask Carlos to come along with our little group? To join the sacred ritual of the pho? I *know* Topher. If he invited Carlos, it's because he thinks it's what I want. And maybe it is, but I'm not sure it's what I need—what any of us needs. I don't think I'm ready for this.

"I'm sorry," Carlos says, confused, " 'pho'?"

"Vietnamese soup?" Topher tells him. "The kind you put the raw meat in. You know?"

Carlos looks over at me, watching for a reaction. Is he waiting for me to invite him? I bite down harder on my lip.

"Wish I could"—Carlos shrugs—"but I've got this thing tomorrow. My coach is making me practice and then get some rest. I've got to get up insanely early to go down to Orlando."

"Wait!" Jo blurts out.

Well, look at that . . . the girl has remembered how to speak.

"Do you mean the showcase? Are you in the national showcase?" He doesn't have a chance to answer before she continues. "Oh my God! You totally are! That's so amazing."

She looks to the three of us for confirmation, but of course we have absolutely no idea what she's freaking out about.

"Uh, care to fill us in?" Topher asks, looking back and forth between the two of them.

"It's like, all the best players in the country come and all the MLB scouts and college coaches are there, and I mean—oh my God!" Jo stops to take a breath, giving Carlos a chance to speak.

"Something like that, I guess." He digs into his backpack again. "Hey, you guys can come if you want. I know Ruby's not into baseball, but if any of you want to make the trip, I have some extra passes."

He pulls an envelope from his bag. "It's probably kinda boring to watch, but . . ."

Jo lets out a little squeal as Nessa grabs the envelope from his hand and peers in. "Oh, we are *so* there!" she says.

"What about you, Ruby?" he asks, his gaze searching my face again. "Any chance you can make it?"

If he's looking for clues about how I feel about all of this, he'll be looking for a while. I have no idea. I'm utterly bewildered by the enormous range of emotions rushing through me. All I know for sure is this: before I can dive into anything with Carlos, I've got some stuff to work out.

"Will Malena be there?" I ask.

"Yeah, probably," he replies. "Mami usually forces the whole family to come along to these things."

I guess it can't hurt to give it a try. I know Malena has no interest in baseball either, so maybe the two of us can hang out in the bleachers—try to reconnect. Plus, I'm finding it exceedingly difficult to say no when Carlos is looking at me with those pleading brown eyes.

"Sure," I say. "I don't have much going on tomorrow."

"Sweet," he says. He glances down at his watch or fitness tracker or whatever. "I gotta go to practice. Sorry again that I can't join you for the—uh, the raw-meat thing. Maybe we can do something after the showcase tomorrow."

And with that, he turns to walk away.

"Really, Ruby?" Topher asks, his voice accusing. "You don't have much going on tomorrow?"

It takes approximately a nanosecond for me to identify the source of Topher's accusation.

"Oh shit—I mean, donkey doo—I can't believe I forgot."

Topher slouches against the wall and crosses his arms tight. Then he continues, his voice thick with sarcasm. "It's nothing, really. Just my entire freaking future! Just my only way out of the hellhole that some people might call my home! But hey, if you wanna go play with Carlos and his balls, then fine. No biggie."

"She wants his balls *and* his bat," Jo says, sending herself and Nessa into fits of spasmodic laughter.

"Can you three even begin to wrap your heads around it? You three have any idea at all?" Topher pleads, ignoring Jo's crude remark. "Don't you get how absolutely critical this is?"

"Of course we do, honey," Nessa coos.

Jo forces herself to stop laughing and joins in with her most soothing voice. "That's right, sweetheart. We didn't mean to—"

"No," Topher announces, hugging his arms more tightly around his chest. "You don't. You have no idea. Nessa, didn't your *mom* schedule your SAT-prep class, and pay for it? Without you even having to ask? And, Jo, your aunt the college professor— correct me if I'm wrong, but is she not, in fact, proofreading all of your essays?"

Nessa's face drops into deep concern, or maybe guilt. Jo reaches out to grab Topher's hand.

"And, Ruby. Don't even get me started on Ruby," Topher exclaims, pulling his hand away from Jo's. "The world is this girl's oyster!" He flings his arm toward me. I flinch. Maybe he's right, but that's not how it feels to me. If the world is my oyster, I definitely haven't found my way to the pearl.

"Meanwhile," Topher continues, his voice still high and angry, "I am working my ass off over here! No help. No advice or encouragement. If it weren't for the freaking Raceway, I couldn't even afford to put sheets on my dorm-room bed." He pauses. Crosses his arms across his chest again. "That is, if I actually manage to go away for college."

We all watch, silent, as Topher slumps back against the wall. "Okay, I'm done."

None of us seem able to produce a word in response. I'm sure Nessa and Jo are just as shocked as me by Topher's outburst. He is, after all, the most giddily optimistic person I know. All this senior-year stress must finally be taking its toll.

"Topher." I step forward to wrap my arms around him. "You have support. *We're* your support. You *know* that." He sinks into my arms, releasing at least some of what must be a crushing weight. "I totally won't go to the stupid baseball thing. I'm taking you to the interview," I whisper into his ear. "Of *course* I am."

Nessa and Jo join us, and we wrap our precious Topher into a big group hug.

"Awww," Topher croons. "Y'all love me!"

"So much!" Jo responds, pulling away to break up the group hug. "Now let's go get you a ginormous steaming pot of pho. Extra sprouts, just the way you like it."

"And some bubble tea?" he adds, his voice mockingly childish and pleading.

We all nod vigorously as Topher threads his arm through mine and leads us out into the drizzly day.

"Wait, isn't the interview at some big law firm *in Orlando*?" Nessa asks, sliding into the back seat of my car.

"Yeah, but—"

"What time?"

"Ten," Topher says, climbing into the passenger seat and brushing stray raindrops from his sweater vest. "But I *must* get there early. If I show up late, it's all over."

"We can all go," Nessa exclaims. "We'll be your cheering squad, Topher! And then we can make Jo's baseball dreams come true!"

Jo, cuddled into the back seat beside Nessa, grabs the tickets from her and then types something into her phone. "Give me a second," she says. "Checking the schedule."

Topher turns to watch them.

"Yup, no problem," Jo says. "Carlos's exhibition game doesn't start until one p.m. We'll miss the sprints, but that's not a big deal."

"Perfect," Nessa calls out, clapping her hands vigorously. "It's a road trip!"

———

At exactly noon the next day, Nessa, Jo, and I pull up to the circular drive in front of a sleek high-rise in downtown Orlando to wait for Topher. It's not until 12:23 that he emerges from the interview, wandering out into the light in his only suit. It's adorable—a vintage gray pinstripe with a broad collar. One of my best finds ever at Fans & Stoves, if I do say so myself.

Topher throws his hand over his eyes and pretends to almost faint. He stumbles slowly toward the car, prompting Jo to roll down the passenger window and yell, "Hurry the hell up, Topher. We've got three hundred astonishingly good baseball players waiting for us to ogle them!"

For someone who's not into guys, Jo is remarkably pumped to go watch a bunch of boys run around in tight pants.

"Shhh!" Nessa demands. "We're here to be Topher's cheer squad. Remember?"

Topher climbs through the back door and collapses onto Nessa's lap.

"Setting the GPS, and . . . we're off!" Jo says, fumbling with her phone. "Forty-five minutes. We're gonna be late."

"There shouldn't be traffic on a Saturday," I say, easing onto the highway. "Topher, sweetie! How'd it—"

"It's Orlando, Ruby," Jo breaks in. "Saturday is the big traffic day—remember? Disney? Universal?"

"And we're headed right toward it all," Nessa says, reaching down to stroke Topher's head. "What took you so long?"

Topher burrows deeper into Nessa's lap. "Is no one even going to ask me how it went?" he exclaims. "Are you all so focused on Mr. Sporty Balls that you can't even pause to give me support in my time of need?"

I wish he could be a little less grumpy. After all, we woke up at an obscene hour to get him to his interview on time, *and* I picked out the perfect tie for him while he was being stressy and wishy-washy this morning. Jo brought him a mocha (extra whipped cream!) from the super-fancy coffeehouse in her neighborhood, and Nessa fed him an entire bag of powdered-sugar doughnuts.

Come to think of it, maybe he's having a sugar crash.

The GPS breaks in. "Construction ahead on I-4. Estimated time in traffic: twenty minutes."

Jo and I let out simultaneous groans as my car slows to a crawl on the highway.

"Damn tourists," Jo hisses.

"Dag-blam construction," I add. I'm still working on the whole not-cussing thing. It may be a lifelong endeavor.

"Since you asked," Topher cuts in, "it was horrifying." He launches his body into a sitting position. "Me, two old white men, and a completely vicious twentysomething woman in a red power dress and stiletto heels." He starts to shrug off his suit jacket. "Two hours of constant interrogation. They asked me what my tombstone would say. *My tombstone!*"

"Isn't that a little morbid?" Jo asks absently, still staring at the GPS map, as if watching it will somehow make the traffic go away.

"Exactly!" Topher says. "That's exactly what I said. But, no, my friends. No, indeed. It's supposed to capture the essence of who I am." He launches himself back into Nessa's lap. "And do you know what I said? Do you *know*?"

"Tell us, honey," Nessa coos, stroking his head again.

"'Looked dapper in fedoras'! I described my lasting legacy as being able to wear a freaking hat!" He sighs again. "I'm doomed."

We all burst out laughing. I mean, what other response can there be?

"I'm never going to college. I'm going to follow in my mother's footsteps and spend all my years in suburban Jacksonville as a bitter, overworked, constantly sleep-deprived nurse's aide."

"Don't be such a drama queen," Jo says.

"You're smarter than the three of us put together, and your test scores are beyond amazing. You're going to college," Nessa adds. "And you do look damn good in a fedora."

The GPS lady interrupts. "Recalculating. Alternate route found. Saves ten minutes."

Jo, Nessa, and I let out a spontaneous cheer as I ease off the highway and begin speeding down a side road.

"There it is," Jo calls out. "Champion Stadium!"

At 1:12, we pull into an enormous, almost-empty parking lot. We all tumble out of the car and run toward the nearest stadium entrance. It strikes me that we're not hearing any cheering crowds, music, none of the noises I expect from a big-time baseball game.

But what would I know? This is my first baseball game ever.

"Why is it so quiet?" I ask as we burst through the gates.

"This is serious stuff, Ruby," Jo scolds. "Only the best high school players are invited, and they don't come for the cheering fans—they're here to get the attention of college coaches and MLB scouts." Jo takes Nessa's hand and yanks her into a jog. "Every high school player drafted in the first round of MLB comes through this showcase."

"I bet *they* won't get asked about their tombstone inscriptions," Topher mumbles bitterly as we chase Jo and Nessa through the corridor. "What's this MLB anyway? Something else I don't know."

I can't resist rolling my eyes at his self-pity.

"Oh. My. God. You people are hopeless," Jo exclaims. "MLB—Major League Baseball."

"You mean, people go straight from high school to playing professional baseball?" I ask. "Is Carlos gonna do that?"

"He committed to the University of Florida a couple of years ago, but he could get drafted and skip college ball altogether—depends in part on how he does today." Jo leads us past a hot-dog vendor that makes my stomach growl.

"Wait," Topher says. "He got into college when he was a sophomore?"

"Probably got into a bunch of colleges, with a full ride." Jo shrugs.

"Lucky bastard," Topher groans. "I should have learned how to throw a ball."

We step out into the bright sunlight, the baseball diamond stretching out emerald green in front of us.

"He's on the mound," Jo whispers, excited.

I rush down the stairs, past the empty bleachers. Without thinking, I cup my hands around my mouth and yell, "Woo-hoo! Go, Carlos! Throw that ball!"

My voice echoes through the stadium, and a few scattered spectators turn to glare at me. *Oops.* I'm not sure what it was, but clearly I've done something wrong.

Carlos, standing perfectly still and staring down the guy with the bat, appears not to have heard me at all.

"Shut up, Ruby!" Jo snarls. "He's trying to concentrate."

We slide into empty seats about ten rows back. Really, the turnout is pathetic. With the exception of a few families and a bunch of old guys with clipboards, nobody showed up for this game. I scan the bleachers, and it looks like maybe his family didn't make it after all. I kinda feel bad for Carlos.

Jo doesn't have to worry about Carlos's concentration, though. I can feel his laser-sharp focus from fifty yards away. I watch, awed, as he lifts his left leg so high that it almost touches his shoulder, pulls back his arm, and then launches his whole body forward, hurling the ball at light speed.

It's like a weird, super-athletic dance move. I'm completely entranced.

The batter stands there and watches the ball whiz by, and then everyone starts cheering like crazy.

"Now can we cheer?" Nessa asks.

"Hell, yeah!" Jo screams, rising back onto her feet. "Carlos just touched ninety-six miles per hour!"

I jump to my feet and start yelling, until Jo pushes me back into my seat. We watch and cheer (only when instructed by Jo) as Carlos throws a bunch of super-fast balls at two more dazed batters. Some of them try to hit his balls, but it seems like the poor kids haven't got a chance.

Jo loud-whispers a bunch of incomprehensible things as we watch:

"Look at that windup!"

"Oh my God, you guys, that was a nasty curveball!"

"His slider is perfection!"

I have no idea what a slider is, but it's becoming abundantly clear to me that Carlos is, indeed, nearly perfect. He's unflappable, and strangely beautiful when he winds up to pitch. He keeps doing this adorable thing where he touches the brim of his baseball cap, maybe for good luck or something.

When the third batter walks off the field, the crowd erupts into the loudest cheers yet. I'm cheering too, but I'm mostly gawking as Carlos takes off his cap, runs his hand through his hair, looks down at the ground, and then starts to jog to the dugout (another baseball term Jo had to teach me). He looks so sweet and humble, even though he clearly just dominated the game.

For the first time, I allow myself to admit it. "I'm falling hard for Carlos Rosario," I whisper under my breath.

"You're what?" Topher nudges me, still watching the players run off the field. "I can't hear you over the noise."

I didn't even realize I said it out loud. "Never mind," I mutter.

"Noise?" Jo shrieks. "Those were wild cheers! Carlos just pitched off a perfect inning. That second guy was one of the strongest batters in the country." Jo collapses into her seat. "Carlos is officially a baseball god."

A couple of innings later, I think I've learned an important baseball fact: when a "baseball god" is pitching, the game is super boring. There's not much to watch on the field, except Carlos's perfect pitches, which produce massively disconcerting butterflies in my gut.

Every. Single. Time.

After a while, I have to look away. I stare down at my phone, scrolling through my feeds but not paying any attention. My mind is racing in a million directions, all of them anxious. What does it even mean to admit that I like Carlos? He says he's not a player, but he definitely fits the mold. What if he just wants to hook up? My hand instinctively finds the skin on my belly, the place I can't stop rubbing raw. Am I even capable of hooking up? And, maybe even more disconcerting, what if he actually wants a relationship? Could I really date a baseball player? A jock whose sister and cousin are my close friends?

At least, I think they're still my friends.

I wish Malena were here. I wish we could go back to how things were. She'd be sitting next to me, whispering snarky things in my ear, and we'd both be struggling to hold back our laughter. I bet there's an ice cream stand in this stadium. We could even wander off together and find some fudge ripple to share.

Maybe, scarfing down ice cream, we'd find a way to apologize to each other—get a fresh start.

When the game ends, Jo says we need to give Carlos time, so we find a concession stand and order hot dogs. I eat about half of mine, but my stomach is all wobbly, so Nessa finishes it for me. After what feels like forever, Jo leads us to wait outside the locker room. Carlos comes out, showered and wearing jeans and a T-shirt, surrounded by other players, who appear to be congratulating him. I can't help myself. I rush toward him, pushing people out of the way, and I fling my arms around him.

Carlos laughs and pulls back. "'Go, Carlos'? 'Throw that ball'?" he asks, incredulous. "That's definitely the most *literal* cheer I've heard at a baseball game."

He keeps his hands on my shoulders, and I love the way they feel there.

"You heard me?" I ask. "It didn't seem like you noticed."

"I noticed," he says, smiling at me. "And then I threw my fastest pitch all day, so maybe you should keep up the weird cheers."

I launch back in for another hug, wanting nothing more than to stay wrapped in his arms. But then I hear a crowd of people behind me, all calling his name.

I pull away fast and turn to see what appears to be his entire extended family rushing toward him. How did we not see them in the stands?

I reluctantly step back to make way for his mom, who is actually bouncing up and down as she approaches him.

"Carlos! You were so wonderful out there!" She hugs him and squeals. "You hit your targets, just like I knew you would!" She turns to Carlos's dad. "Didn't he, amor? Just like I told him!"

Carlos's dad steps up to enfold him in a hug, which is super cute, since Carlos is about a head taller than him.

As the family chatters on excitedly, Malena and Soraida step over to talk with me, Topher, Nessa, and Jo.

I'm feeling optimistic, suddenly. Maybe it's a good sign that Malena decided not to ignore me. Then she opens her mouth to speak. "What are you guys doing here?" She hurls the question directly at me.

"What do you mean?" I snap back, immediately sensing the need to defend myself. "The same thing you're doing here. We're supporting Carlos."

Oy, this is not going as I hoped it would.

Nessa, clearly feeling the tension, breaks in. "Jo's a total baseball fanatic." She throws her arm across Jo's shoulder. "When Carlos offered us passes, we couldn't turn them down."

"He was so amazing!" Jo says, clasping her hand against her chest.

Soraida shrugs. "He does this all the time." She's trying hard to be blasé about it, but I notice a hint of pride as her chin inches up.

Nessa elbows me playfully on the side. "I have a feeling Ruby is not gonna miss another game."

"Huh?" Malena shoots me a quizzical glance. "I never really thought you were the baseball-wife type." She stares me down hard, and I feel my gut fill with rage. "I guess I was wrong."

What the hell? *Baseball wife?*

Suddenly, apologies don't seem the right approach. I'm so close to unleashing on her, struggling to push down the anger that's rising in my chest, using every ounce of my will to keep from going off. But then I see Carlos across the crowd, his head rising above his family. He looks right into my eyes and mouths a question: *Come with me?*

Yes, I'll go with him.

At this particular moment, there's nothing I want more. My entire body lightens at the prospect, and the anger melts away. Plus, the whole world already seems to think Carlos and I are a thing. Who am I to disappoint them?

I nod at him, ever so slightly, and he starts to walk away. From the corner of my eye, I catch Malena glaring at me.

Oh, pluck it. I'll work things out with Malena later.

"Meet you at the car in a few," I say to Jo, Nessa, and Topher, trying to avoid the daggers Malena is still hurling at me with her eyes.

Once Carlos and I are out of view of my friends and his entire extended family, he grabs my hand and we begin to speed-walk past clusters of people and through the back hallways of the baseball stadium.

We turn a corner and find ourselves in a short corridor leading to an empty concession stand.

Alone, finally.

"Where are you taking me?" I ask.

"Here, I guess," he says, turning to face me. "I was hoping maybe . . ." He pulls me closer, taking my other hand in his. "If we could be alone, you'd tell me . . ."

"I'm ready."

Before the words even finish leaving my mouth, we are both stumbling toward the wall. I press him against it as our hands fumble to grasp each other. He pulls me toward him and my lips crash into his. My body lights up and my hands search for his bare skin. We're kissing hard, my fingers grasping his forearm, his neck, while his slide under my shirt and onto my lower back.

My mind feels like it's about to explode from the sensation coursing through my body. My hand, apparently with a will of its own, finds its way under his shirt. Feeling the curve of his abs, I let my eyes close and my lips seek his again.

"Wait," he whispers in my ear.

I open my eyes to see him staring straight at me, his gaze intense and maybe a little anguished. He touches my cheek and gives me a soft kiss on the lips.

"Shouldn't we go on a date or something?"

I laugh, throwing my head back with glee, a burst of pure Florida sunshine filling my entire chest.

"I guess maybe we should," I say. "How's tonight?"

"You're asking me out on a date tonight?" he asks.

"Why, yes," I reply, trying to make my voice sound formal and silly, but still breathing hard from the intensity of our make-out session. "Yes, I am."

"Perfect," he replies. "It would be my pleasure."

"Wonderful," I say through a wide-open smile. "I'll pick you up at seven."

He leans in to kiss me softly on the lips. "Your face is flushed," he whispers.

"Mm-hmm," I murmur.

His lips trail down. "Your neck, too."

"I'm pretty sure my whole body is flushed," I admit, the thrill of his kisses washing over me.

He lets out a soft groan. "Thanks for coming today," he says, his forehead pressing against mine. "It meant a lot to me, having you here."

"It was my first baseball game ever," I whisper.

We're both looking down at the ground, foreheads touching, ragged breath evening out.

"Really?" he asks, surprised. "Ever? In your life?"

"I'm pretty sure it won't be my last." I tip my chin up to look him in the eyes.

He laughs and kisses me again, wrapping his arms tight around my waist—which is a very good thing. Because this boy is making me quite literally weak in the knees.

CHAPTER TWENTY-THREE

MALENA

A text from Ruby comes in just as Ms. Baptiste informs me she has to leave in fifteen minutes.

> On my way.

My irritation only grows as I grip the phone harder and start typing Don't bother coming. My thumb hovers over the tiny blue send arrow but I can't bring myself to press down on the screen. She needs to be here.

As much as I hate to admit it, I need her.

I delete my response and turn to Ms. Baptiste, who is adjusting one of the pleats of her skirt. The fabric has a print of big amapola flowers. It's beautiful.

"That's Ruby," I say apologetically. "She's coming."

Ms. Baptiste glances at the clock hanging on the wall behind me.

"Sorry," I mumble, annoyed at having to apologize for her. Where is she, anyway?

This was supposed to be our last strategy meeting before we present our case to the school board on Monday. I imagined a gathering of three women on a mission, empowered and self-assured. I even let myself hope that Ruby and I could talk after, clear the air. Maybe even go back to the Puerto Rican restaurant and share some guava pastelillos.

Obviously, this was a fantasy. The reality? Bitter disappointment.

"I'm sure she has a good reason for being so late," I say with little conviction. My fingers are balancing a pen, tapping repeatedly against the stack of notes in front of me—my research on examples of student-faculty committees and equitable dress codes. Lucinda was right. There's a big difference between equality and equity. Equality means everyone gets the same thing; equity means everyone gets what they need to succeed.

"Have you read through her presentation?" Ms. Baptiste asks.

I shake my head. It dawns on me that it's already Thursday and I have no idea what Ruby is saying at the meeting on Monday. Has she even looked at the binder of school-board policies Ms. Baptiste gave us?

After a long silence, Ms. Baptiste asks, "How is your final project coming along?"

"I've been playing around with the video I shot during the protest," I tell her. "I thought it would be cool to do a retrospective on the whole thing?"

"Great idea," she says.

I'm editing a timeline of the events I've filmed on my phone, but something about it doesn't feel quite right. All the documentaries I've seen—the really good ones—are anchored in something bigger than the story itself. They have some important message that stays with you long after you've finished watching.

"Have you done any interviews yet?" she asks.

"Not yet." We have to interview at least three people for the project. I had Ruby on my list, but now I'm not so sure.

"I've been meaning to ask after your dad. Is he still in Puerto Rico?"

I sigh, trying to remember the last time I heard Papi's voice. A knot forms in the back of my throat. Thanksgiving is only two weeks away and my mind goes blank every time I try to imagine dinner without him. He slices the bird with the gusto of a world-class chef—using a special serrated knife, pleasing everyone with their favorite cut of meat, taking a whole leg for himself. Thanksgiving is Papi's favorite holiday, and by extension mine. It's the one day of the year when it's appropriate—expected, even—to pile our plates tower-high and eat ourselves into a coma.

Mami and I have been dutifully avoiding the subject. There has been no mention of Thanksgiving or even Christmas, New Year's, or Día de Reyes. The only latent reminder is Abuela's pasteladas. There's no avoiding those.

Ms. Baptiste's face goes soft with kindness. But it's the compassion in her eyes that compels me to look away so as not to tear up.

"He's been working in areas with no cell reception. He tried calling from a satellite phone a few days ago, but there was too much static on the line."

"Your father is a saint for the work he's doing. How are *you* handling it?"

I shrug, and take a minute to form an answer. No one has asked me that before.

"It's hard," I say, choking on the words. "I've been trying those meditations you have us do in class, at home. They help a little."

"I'm so glad to hear that, Malena. If you ever need to talk—"

"I'm soooooooo sorry!" Ruby bursts in the door twenty minutes after our appointment time. "I had to deal with an emergency. What did I miss?"

"Where were you? We've been waiting forever." I try not to sound as disheartened as I feel.

"Carlos's SUV wouldn't start. I had to give him a ride to practice and it's all the way across the bridge," Ruby says, as if this is news to me. When did she become an all-things-Carlos expert?

"So, what? You've gone from being his baseball wife to his chauffeur?" I scoff, unable to hide my annoyance. "Couldn't he get a rideshare or something? He has a phone, you know."

"Well, y-yeah, I guess," she stutters. "But he's got all that equipment."

I stare at her hard as she sits down across from me, suddenly realizing what's changed. Ruby has lost herself—to my cousin. I don't know who I'm angrier with, Ruby or Carlos.

"All right, ladies. We don't have much time left, so let's get to it," Ms. Baptiste says. "I want us to discuss your plan B—how you'll proceed if we get a negative outcome at the school-board meeting. Malena told me about the idea of a student-faculty liaison committee, which could be very effective."

I open my mouth, ready to share all the ideas I've been researching, but Ruby speaks first.

"Dr. Hardaway won't go for that," Ruby asserts dismissively.

"How do you know? We haven't even asked her," I counter, my tone high-pitched and upset. I hate when I sound like this—frenzied and emotional—the out-of-control Loud Latina.

"I already met with her, remember?" Ruby's voice is the total opposite of mine: calm and collected. It hits me that this is the way Carlos usually responds—a cool, even tone. I guess he's rubbed off on her. "She told me, point-blank, that there's nothing we can do about it. Not anytime soon, at least."

I feel my cheeks flush with anger. "What is your suggestion, then?" I ask, my voice accusing. "What if the school board doesn't listen? What then? We've done all of this . . . all of it for nothing? We just give up?" My heart sinks at the possibility. "I just think we need to be prepared for the next step," I say, composing myself.

"The next step? I guess we could sue. I'm sure the ACLU would love to get involved," Ruby responds, her voice still chilly and dismissive. "Have you two seen the open letter they posted on their website? About gendered dress codes being illegal? It's so good. I'm telling you, our work is right up their alley."

Ms. Baptiste reaches toward us with her palms spread out, her gold bracelets jangling around her wrist. "Let's not get ahead of ourselves, ladies. No one is going to sue anyone." She lets out an audible exhale as she adds, "At least, we hope not."

She stands and walks around her desk, pulling up a chair to sit directly in front of us. For a few seconds, she studies us both, her relaxed expression unchanged.

"Ruby, did you bring a draft of your presentation for the school-board meeting?" Ms. Baptiste asks.

"I've been working on an outline," Ruby says, leaning back in her chair. "It's hard to focus during the week with tests and homework, you know?"

No, I don't know, I want to say, because this is too important, more important than stupid homework. Plus, I know for a fact she's been spending most of her waking hours with Carlos, at least when he's not in practice.

"When will you have it ready?" I ask, unsure how Ms. Baptiste feels about the homework excuse. She is a teacher, after all.

"This weekend," she says, shifting her eyes between Ms. Baptiste and me. "I've already started it. I just need time to fill in a few things." She sits up straight in her chair, clearly trying to project competence.

I'm not buying it.

"Do you need help?" Ms. Baptiste asks. "Maybe if you're overwhelmed with school, Malena could work with you to fill in the outline. She's done extensive research."

I stare at Ms. Baptiste, surprised at her suggestion. Does she really think I can write the presentation? Do a decent job at it? Why don't *I* feel the same way? I mean, I could give it a shot.

"Or I'd be happy to spend some time brainstorming with you," Ms. Baptiste says. "Perhaps tomorrow before school?"

I turn to Ruby, wait for her response.

"I appreciate the offer," Ruby says, pulling in a breath, then breaking into a strained smile. "But there's no need for you to rearrange your schedule. I said I would get it done and I will. Trust me, I've got this." She nods, shifting in her seat. "Easy-peasy, as my nana says."

My shoulders tense. I so badly want to believe the words coming out of her mouth. But right now, I don't even know this girl. Her expression is poised and confident, but it's nothing more than an empty veneer. Something about her is off. She's distracted and withdrawn, so unlike the no-holds-barred Ruby of only two weeks ago. And her face looks different—even paler than usual. Maybe it's Carlos. Maybe it's nerves about the meeting on Monday. Whatever it is, I wish she would pull it together. And I wish she'd stop putting this off to the last minute. Too much is at stake—for us both.

"I think you should let us help, Ruby," I say forcefully. "This is important."

"I know that," she says, her tone defensive, and momentarily dropping the smile she's been holding. "But I have this under control. I'll get it done, Malena." She pauses, shrugs. "Plus, Olive said she'd read through it. Make some edits." Ruby turns to Ms. Baptiste. "My sister has tons of experience with this kind of thing."

I'm sure Olive will try her best to help, but it annoys me to no end that Ruby is refusing Ms. Baptiste's guidance. She is the only person in this room with any actual knowledge of how to best approach the administration. And as a Black woman, she can bring a different perspective to our crusade—issues we haven't thought about. I hate that Ruby doesn't see that.

Ms. Baptiste nods quietly, her lips forming a small smile. My mother uses that same smile sometimes. It's forced and polite. I wouldn't want to be on the receiving end of it.

"If you are feeling good about your plan, Ruby, there's not much else I can offer. Why don't you send your presentation to Malena over the weekend so that she can make suggestions. Or you two can meet here in the studio Monday morning."

"Sure," Ruby says. "I can totally do that. Malena and I will work out the details."

"All right, then," Ms. Baptiste announces. "I think we're done."

We're not done, I want to blurt out. *Not even close!*

Before I can object, Ms. Baptiste stands. "And now, I really need to get going," she says, walking behind her desk and reaching for her purse.

Ruby stands and heads toward the door. "Thanks for being our sponsor," she says to Ms. Baptiste, and then she's gone.

Ms. Baptiste and I watch in silence as Ruby walks away, suddenly absorbed by her phone. It's probably Carlos, making plans to meet up. Looks like we won't be going out for guava pastelillos after all.

I shove my notes into my bag, pissed that we didn't even get to talk about my plan B. Pissed that Ruby blew off our meeting because of some guy. And maybe also pissed at myself. Why didn't I step up—way back when Lucinda was giving that not-at-all-helpful advice? Why didn't I say I'd be the one talking at the school-board meeting, when I was the one with a story to tell? What kind of undaunted girl am I, anyway?

"Will you walk with me to my car?" Ms. Baptiste asks, swinging the strap of her purse over her shoulder.

I nod and follow her out of the classroom to the faculty parking lot, weighed down by my backpack, my frustration with Ruby, and my own pathetic self.

"Your faculty-student senate idea is promising," she says as we reach her car—a bright yellow Volkswagen Beetle with daisies bursting out of a tiny flower vase next to the steering wheel. They make me smile. "I think Ruby has misjudged Dr. Hardaway. I've known Penny for quite some time, and she wants solutions. Between you, me, and the sidewalk, I think the whole business with the pantyliners was misguided. But trust me on this: Penny doesn't have a cruel bone in her body. Tough, yes. But not cruel. There's room for dialogue, for finding common ground." She opens the door and drops her bag inside.

I stand quietly, wondering: How in the world does a person go about finding common ground with someone who's hurt them—the way she hurt me?

"No offense," I say, "but she seems so clueless. She doesn't know what we have to deal with every day."

I can't believe I'm admitting this to a teacher. But it's not just any teacher; it's Ms. Baptiste. I know I can be honest with her.

Ms. Baptiste seems to consider me for a moment. After a long pause she asks, "Have you ever heard of a book called *This Is What I Was Wearing?*"

I shake my head, then quickly pull up the title on my phone. The book's description says it's a collection of photographs and first-person narratives depicting victims of sexual violence.

"It's a hard book to read. When I first saw it, I realized I had more in common with Dr. Hardaway than I imagined." Ms. Baptiste slides into the driver's seat, holding the door open. "You should check it out. It may help you to see that too."

"I'm not sure I get what this has to do with me?" I ask, confused.

Her hand lingers on the door handle. She looks away, across the highway, and sighs. I stand in place, waiting for her to explain.

"Sexual violence is a spectrum, Malena," she says, turning to look at me. There's an intensity in her eyes that wasn't there before. "We talk a lot about rape, but it can also be revenge porn or a crude text. Name-calling or an unwanted touch. Any sexual activity we don't consent to."

I nod, leaning into her words. I read some of these things online, but they sound different coming from Ms. Baptiste—more real somehow.

"And women like us—women of color—have a higher risk," she says. "Gender, racism, and sexism intersect in a very ugly way. Half of transgender people and bisexual women experience sexual violence at some point in their life. Half," she repeats, hitting the steering wheel with her open palm.

"I understand," I say, letting this information sink in. My heart aches at the thought of anyone having to go through something much, much worse than what happened to me.

"You are doing such important work, Malena," she says. "But

from what I know, this sort of thing takes a lifetime to fully understand."

The driver's door shuts and I watch, repeating the book's name in my mind, as the yellow Bug pulls out in reverse, then turns and exits the faculty parking lot.

This is what I was wearing.

———

Later that afternoon, I'm alone at the Orange Park Public Library looking for the book. It doesn't take long to find it. I pull the heavy volume from a high shelf and sit at a reference table in a far back corner. The strangers circulating around me dissolve into the periphery as I sink into the images and stories.

I've never seen anything like it. It's one of those large photography compilations printed on glossy paper. The photos capture the faces and bodies of rape victims in the eighties, holding the clothes they were wearing at the time of the attack. Did Ms. Baptiste want me to look at it because it's like a documentary in book form—victims of sexual violence telling their own stories?

I pause on every page, engrossed. I'm in awe of the courage of these women—awed by the power of their collective voice.

I'm about halfway through the book when I see her. I blink multiple times, waiting for something on the page to shift. Or for the synapses in my brain to catch up, to tell me that I'm mistaken. That the woman holding a white dress, staring directly at the camera, cannot be who I think she is.

Her face is soft and youthful, with no wrinkles around the eyes, none of the age spots that now mark her skin. A wild mane of red hair flows freely over her shoulders without any of the grays that have seized it almost thirty-seven years after this photo was taken.

Her body is encased in a nude leotard, a wafer-thin protective layer between her and the world. I wish she were wearing chain mail instead.

But what captures my full attention is the expression in her eyes. They possess a determination that could knock down a wall with just one glare if she wanted it to.

The dress hangs from a wire hanger, like the ones they hand out at the dry cleaner's. It is stained with dirt and blood, and one of the shoulder straps is ripped, hanging limply over the front bodice.

The quote on the side of the page reads:

My favorite white dress. It was a first date, and I was very excited. He was handsome, from a good family—a medical student. I felt lucky to be seen by him. But when I said stop, he didn't. And when I cried out, no one heard me. I never told anyone, until now.

I read her name out loud: "'Penny Hardaway.'" I repeat, even slower, "Penny Hardaway." My eyes fill with tears for this girl, now a woman. My attention dancing from the quote to her face to the dress and back around, in an infinite circle of pain.

A pitiful voice in the hollow of my chest repeats, *I know her, I know her.*

Dr. Hardaway.

High school assistant principal.

Penny Hardaway.

Rape survivor.

They are all one.

They are all the same.

Studying Penny Hardaway's photo, I'm overwhelmed by the fearlessness it must have taken her to speak and to expose herself for the world to see. It's as if she's trying to tell the world, *I am more than the flesh hanging from my bones. I am not a sexual object. And I am not afraid.*

Ms. Baptiste's words come back to me: *I realized I had more in common with Dr. Hardaway than I imagined.* Is Ms. Baptiste also a rape survivor? Why didn't she tell me?

Then I catch myself. Ms. Baptiste gets to decide whether and how she'll share her story. Ms. Baptiste and no one else.

My hands gently close the book. I take it into my arms and carry it to the checkout desk in the same way I'd carry a fragile glass vase.

I owe it to Penny Hardaway and all the other women in this book to treat their stories with care and respect. This is how they chose to tell their stories.

How will I choose to tell mine?

CHAPTER TWENTY-FOUR

RUBY

"Hey, Ruby . . ." I look up from my blank computer screen, relieved to have a distraction from the incessantly flashing cursor. "Do you think your nana would mind if I go heat up some leftover lasagna?"

Carlos is sitting in my window seat, legs stretched out along the very cushion where I once read all those Baby-Sitters Club books. I mean, Logan and Mary Anne were entertaining, but watching Carlos—even watching him sit and do nothing—is perfection.

"You ate half a tray of it," I tease. "An hour ago!"

Carlos shrugs. "What can I say? Her lasagna is really damn good. I mean, my mom makes lasagna, but it's got, like, Velveeta or something."

"Orange cheese in lasagna?"

"Yup," Carlos replies, smiling in a way that makes me feel as gooey as Nana's melted mozzarella. "Soraida calls it Lasagna La Llorona."

I don't know what that means, but I let it slide. It's embarrassing, always asking Carlos to translate. He must see the confusion on my face because he adds, "Because every bite makes you wanna cry?" He chuckles to himself, but I still don't get the joke.

"Be my guest," I say. "But last I checked, lasagna isn't high-protein or low-carb."

"What are you now? My nutritionist?" He laughs. "No need to worry, Ruby. My mom and abuela have that job covered."

He gets up, takes off his headphones, and sets his laptop, screen open, on the window seat. I glance at the screen and can't help teasing him.

"Is that *you*? Are you hanging out over there watching yourself play baseball?"

He nods. "Yeah, why?"

"I mean, I knew you had a big head, but isn't that a little . . . self-indulgent?"

"I'm watching film, Ruby." He shakes his head slowly from side to side. "I *have* to do it."

Another thing about Carlos's world I don't understand.

"Is it weird?" I ask. "All the special attention?"

"What do you mean?"

"Malena told me your whole family moved here because of you, when you were barely even a teenager, and everybody's world revolves around baseball."

Carlos shrugs. "Yeah, I guess she's got a point, but I didn't ex-actly ask for it, you know? I just wanna play ball. I always have—since I could first hold up a bat, way back in my Vaquerito days."

I quirk an eyebrow, hoping for a translation.

"The Little Cowboys." He grins. "My T-ball team."

I smile, thinking about how adorable Carlos must have been, a toddler wielding a bat almost as big as him.

"But even though you didn't ask for it," I press gently, "you get the royal treatment—at school, at home. You know that, right?"

"I guess?" he says. "Honestly, I don't really think about it."

"Ah, the beauty of male privilege! It shapes every single aspect of your life, but of course you don't *think* about it," I announce, my tone light. "You're like a perfect specimen."

"Is this your way of saying I have a great body?" Carlos teases. "'Cause I know that's what you're thinking."

All the time. I feel my face flush, and I know he can see it too. Time to change course.

"Seriously, though. I bet it can be overwhelming, all that pressure. Everyone expecting you to be great, to excel all the time."

"Nope," he says, matter-of-fact. "I love playing baseball, Ruby. Yeah, it's hard work, but it's fun. If I weren't having fun, I'd stop."

I find that hard to believe, after his family sacrificed so much to bring him to this point. But who am I to know anything about having a purpose? A passion? Any sense of direction at all.

"I'm not stressed out by the attention. I just stay focused," he continues. "Train hard, practice, and play ball the best I can. I try not to worry too much about what's going on around me." He nods, resolute. "I'm looking ahead, to my future."

"Yeah, okay," I scoff. "But in your present, an army of women is busy ensuring that you don't have to worry about a thing."

"They like it," he replies, his voice light and teasing.

"Soraida?" I exclaim. "She most definitely doesn't like it."

"True, that." He smiles.

"You know it's not fair, right? How she's expected to help out all the time, and you're not."

He pauses, clearly thinking carefully about what to say next.

"Right?" I prod.

"Life's not fair, Ruby. But, yeah, I get what you're saying."

He makes his way over to my bed, where I've been holed up with my computer since dinner, struggling to make headway on tomorrow's school-board presentation. Malena keeps texting me, asking when she can see it. I know I should have accepted her help, and probably Ms. Baptiste's, too. I think I was just embarrassed— that I'd put everything off to the last minute. Now I'm drowning, totally overwhelmed.

I promised Malena we'd meet tomorrow morning, early. I promised we'd look over the presentation together. The only problem is, I'm down to the wire, and staring at the same pathetically skeletal outline I had when we met. Why couldn't I just admit that to them? What is wrong with me?

Carlos glances at my computer and then leans in to kiss me on the lips.

"Your house is so quiet," he says.

"Is that good or bad?" I ask, not sure what he's getting at.

He shrugs. "Just different, I guess. Want anything?"

I tug him in for another kiss. "Are you asking me what I want?" I whisper, somewhat awed that I'm already comfortable enough with Carlos to be so suggestive.

"From the kitchen," he announces, pulling away from me. He gestures toward my blank computer screen. "You have work to do."

It's only been eight days since Carlos and I went on our official first date. But already it feels like he belongs here. Nana insisted that I invite him for dinner last Sunday, after I burst into her room that morning to recount every last detail of the prior twenty-four hours.

Well, not *every* detail. I told her about how we split a meat-lover's pizza but skimmed over the part when I attacked him in the back of his SUV.

Over the past week, he's come over every day after practice to hang out, and most nights he has stuck around for dinner. He and Nana get along great. She asks him all about being a pitcher, and he peppers her with questions about the sea-turtle patrol.

After Carlos goes downstairs, I hear a soft tapping on the door, and then my nana comes into view.

"Can I interrupt?" Nana asks. Holding the screen of her phone out for me to see. "Your parents want to wish you good luck." Mom and Dad are wrapping up their extended visit to Atlanta, still basking in the afterglow of Olive's successes.

Before I can even say hi, Dad has already launched into a signature Dan McAlister pep talk: "Give 'em hell, Ruby. Tear down the patriarchy."

I close my eyes and let out a sigh, hoping he doesn't notice. His enthusiasm is stressing me out.

"Olive's here too," Mom exclaims.

Nana sits down beside me on the bed as Mom passes the phone to Olive.

"You didn't send me a draft of your presentation," Olive says, her voice accusing. "I told you I'd read through it and offer suggestions."

Another person I've let down. I stare up at the ceiling, trying to keep my breathing steady. "It's not quite ready," I say.

Nana wraps her arm around my shoulder. "She's been hard at work up here."

Hard at work staring at a blank page.

"Be bold," my mom urges.

"Abolish that dress code!" Dad adds.

Carlos is back. He's leaning against the doorway, casually taking a bite from his huge slab of lasagna. He catches my gaze and nods encouragingly.

"Yeah, okay," I say. "But we can't really do that, so—"

Nana takes the phone from my hands. "It's past my bedtime," she announces, "and Ruby needs to get back to work. We'll talk again tomorrow."

"Tell Ruby we can't wait to read about it all in the papers," I hear my dad call out.

Nana hangs up the phone and shakes her head slowly.

"Wow," Carlos says, walking into the room. "They're really, uh . . . supportive."

"Yeah," I say, my voice defeated. "There's no limit to what the McAlister girls can accomplish."

Carlos cocks his eyebrow but stays silent.

"I'm off to bed," Nana says. "I'll let you get back to work, Ruby. Don't you worry about them." She gestures toward her phone. "It will all turn out as it should. I promise." She kisses me on the cheek and stands up to leave the room. "And, Carlos," she says, looking over at his plate, "please take the rest of the leftovers for lunch tomorrow. You're a growing boy."

"Oh, thanks," he says, sheepish.

When she's gone, Carlos sits down on the edge of the bed. "I thought your parents were in Indonesia or Cambodia or somewhere?"

"They came back early," I explain. "My sister was getting a big award up in Atlanta and they didn't want to miss it."

"That's cool," he says, shoveling another huge bite of lasagna into his mouth. "What for?"

"She just started teaching at this school in a really poor part of the city. All the kids are Black and Latin. I think she's one of two white teachers."

"*All* the kids are Black and Latin?" he asks, his fork pausing in midair.

316

"That's what Olive told us. And she got upset because she showed up in her classroom and the kids didn't have basic school supplies, so she started a drive. I think they collected like ten thousand crayons or something."

"That's pretty awesome," he says, cutting off another bite of lasagna, "that she could pull the community together to do something that big."

"What community?" I scoff. "It's all Olive."

"Seriously?" he asks, sounding genuinely curious. "She didn't have any help? From anyone?"

It's a legitimate question.

"Nope," I say. "Just Olive, the great crusader for crayon justice. I think she got a bunch of big companies to donate."

"Huh," he says under his breath. He stares down at his half-empty plate. It feels like all the air in my bedroom has just been sucked out, and I'm sitting here wondering what I said wrong.

"What?" I ask. "I know you want to say something. Spit it out."

"I guess it's just weird that this rich white teacher shows up and immediately starts trying to fix things, without getting the families involved, or the kids. Like, you know? The 'helpful white lady.'"

"She *was* trying to help," I blurt out. "And we're not rich."

Carlos looks around the room and then lets out a laugh. "Uh, yeah, Ruby. You are. Your parents just retired early and went off on a world tour. Now they're hanging out in Atlanta for fun. That's what rich people do." He scoops yet another enormous bite of lasagna onto his fork. "Meanwhile," he says, fork poised in front of his mouth, "my dad's gonna be replacing carburetors and changing oil until the day he dies."

He's got a point. I could explain how long they saved money

for the trip, or how their early retirement was partly out of necessity, but I don't.

I guess Carlos is right. Life's not fair.

"Mmmm, this is so good," he exclaims, licking his fork.

It's kinda cute how much joy he finds in eating carbs.

"Anyway, Olive sounds like a serious overachiever," he says, casually inspecting the fork for any remaining cheese. "Is it hard, being her sister?"

My chest fills, and I feel a strange sense of relief wash over me. No one has ever asked me that question. I didn't realize how much I needed to hear it.

"Honestly," I say, "it's suffocating—trying to live up to Olive McAlister's legacy."

"Yeah, it's not easy being a Great White Savior." He chuckles and takes one last bite of lasagna. "I'm just sayin'"—he shakes his head—"sometimes people do shit like that to make themselves feel good, but they're not really solving anyone's problems."

How can I respond to that? Should I be mad? Defensive? Should I agree with him? Even though I feel like I have to stand up for my sister, and I know she does good work, a big part of me is relieved that Olive hasn't earned her place as someone else's hero.

I sit in silence beside him, feeling five different emotions at once. Talking about all this stuff with Carlos feels complicated and confusing. I think we both want to be truthful, but we also don't want to offend each other. It's like walking a tightrope.

"That was kinda harsh," he says quietly, clearly struggling to read my silence. Maybe he's just as confused as I am. "I didn't mean to stress you out."

I lift my hand to my forehead, rubbing out the creases. "You didn't say anything wrong," I tell him. "Really."

I think I'm being honest with him, but I'm still not sure. My hand drops to my lap and I clench my fist hard.

"Ugh," I exclaim. "*Everything* stresses me out right now. Especially this stupid school-board presentation!"

He glances down at my computer. "Maybe I should go," he says. "We can hang out later. I know you have a ton of work."

"Don't go," I say, releasing my fist and putting my hand over his. "Let's watch a dumb Clint Eastwood movie or something."

"But do you need—"

"What I need is to take my mind off of all this for a while," I interrupt, ceremoniously shutting my laptop. "I can finish in the morning."

Carlos sets his empty plate on my nightstand.

"Are you telling me you need to be distracted?" he asks, smiling in that way that makes me gooey. "Because I think I can help with that."

He climbs up onto my bed and we tumble back against the pillows, laughing.

———

Carlos and I are pulling into the parking lot of the county offices. He texted this morning and offered to take me so that I could do some last-minute prep on the way to the school-board meeting. I think he felt a little guilty about how excellent a distraction he turned out to be.

I woke up early to finish my outline before school, which meant I didn't have time to meet with Malena. She's pissed, and for a good reason. I spent the whole day studiously avoiding her and her string of frantic texts, trying to steal moments between classes, needing desperately to turn this outline into an actual presentation. I'm staring hard at the page now, wishing it were more fleshed out, wishing I had written out a full draft of my presentation, even wishing I had sent it to my sister for revisions.

I rest my forehead against the warm window and close my eyes, trying to find some calm. My palms are sweating profusely, and my breath is flowing in uneven and agitated bursts.

"Damn." Carlos lets out the word under his breath. "Look at all these people."

I open my eyes and take in the dozens of students who turned out to support us. Everyone's gathered in the parking lot, signs held high, chanting.

"My body, my choice!"

"Her body, her choice!"

Lindsey, the quiet junior, is wearing her red bustier again, and holding her sign high and proud: *FIGHT LIKE A GIRL.*

My mind flashes to that day. Is he here? Is he blending into the crowd, pretending to care?

Fucking tease.

I hear the words in my mind and feel the urge to vomit. The entire world starts to tilt again, and I'm struggling to stay upright. Carlos looks at me, concerned. "Wait there," he says.

I watch as he comes around to my side of the car. He opens my door and I step out, feeling wobbly.

Carlos studies my face, puts his hands on my shoulders. Then he leans in to whisper, "You got this."

I turn to see the protesters heading toward us, posters and signs held high.

"Ruby! Ruby!"

They gather around us and chant as I take Carlos's hand in mine and lead him past the crowd and toward the boardroom's glass entrance. Malena is standing in the doorway, her arms crossed over her chest.

"You're late!" she loud-whispers. "They're about to start. We saved you a seat up front."

Then she throws a fierce glare at Carlos. "Not you," she says. "You can sit in the back with Mami and Abuela Joan."

I squeeze in next to Malena, trying to block out the judgment and anger rising off her like steam.

God, I'm doing my best. I wish I could find a way to make Malena see that.

I glance around the room, trying not to hyperventilate about the fact that every chair is full. I see several Orange Grove teachers—Ms. Markowitz, Mr. Cruz, and of course Dr. Hard-away. Even the principal is here. I think it's the third or fourth time I've actually seen the man outside all-school assemblies. I can barely even remember his name.

Davis? Davies?

Hoping for some distraction from my jangly nerves, I clandestinely text Topher about the principal's cameo appearance, but he doesn't reply. I'm guessing his phone is silenced.

Twenty long minutes later, after a series of riveting conversations about such important topics as altering bus schedules by two minutes and cafeteria water-fountain-use policies, I'm called forward to the microphone. Though the debates were inane, I frankly felt nothing but gratitude for the time they gave me to pull myself—and my scattered thoughts—together.

Carlos is right. I've got this.

As I'm standing up, Malena whispers, "Where are your notes? Don't forget them."

I dig into the pocket of my pants and pull out a single folded sheet of paper. Malena stares at the page as I slide past Ms. Baptiste. Clearly, she's not impressed.

At the podium, I grasp the microphone with both hands and look over at the panel of school-board members: Seven old white men with white hair and potbellies. One oldish white woman with dyed-blond hair. She appears to be the note taker.

Go figure.

"Good evening," I start, my voice shaky. "My name is Ruby McAlister. I am a senior at Orange Grove High School. I am here to represent a group of students calling for immediate and sweeping change to the Clay County Schools dress code."

I look around quickly, taking in the mood: quiet, still. No signs. No cheers. No nothing. Pure silence, except for one soft cough from the back left corner—the sort of muffled cough I associate with pauses between movements at the symphony.

I glance at the school board. Two of the old guys shift back in their seats and cross their arms defensively, and the blond woman's eyebrows arch.

Okay, good. I got their attention.

I pull in a deep breath and launch in.

"As written, the dress code converts young women into sexual objects, and it sexualizes perfectly mundane body parts. Collarbones, upper arms, knees become areas of arousal." I look at one of the school-board members, a white guy in a red polo shirt. He's watching closely, his eyes encouraging me to continue. "Dress codes discriminate against girls, especially girls with certain body types. They distract girls from learning—make us on edge, uncomfortable, worried about whether we will get called out. When we do get called out for dress-code infractions, we feel embarrassed, ashamed, violated."

I try to make eye contact with the other school-board members, but they avert their eyes, clearly uncomfortable. I glance at my outline to help me remember what to say next.

Educational access. Okay, I can talk about that.

"We have unequal access to education, because when girls are called out, we miss valuable class time."

I look down again, hoping for more information to jog my memory. But there's nothing under those words except for a couple of empty bullet points. I guess I forgot to fill them in.

On to the next topic, apparently.

"Not to mention"—I plow ahead—"the exact same clothing on a boy or a girl gets different treatment."

One of the old guys at the table, who appears to be the school-board chair, lifts his hand and leans forward. "I'm going to stop you right there, Miss McAlister."

"But I'm allowed two minutes," I retort, wishing I had taken the time to learn his name.

"You'll get your thirty remaining seconds, young lady," he says, "but we'll need some clarification first. Are you referring to section 4.6.8 of the code of student conduct? Or section 4.9.12? You need to state this for the record."

I look down nervously at my pathetic outline, knowing that the information isn't there but praying that it might somehow magically materialize.

Olive would have made sure to include this detail in the notes.

I glance up and look around the room, my heart pounding. Malena catches my eye from the front row. She's mouthing something, but I can't read her lips. Of course Malena knows. She did so much research, so much work.

But not me. I have no idea.

I clear my throat nervously. "I'm sorry, sir. I just moved here last year, from Seattle—"

"From Seattle?" Another school-board member jumps in. He chuckles. "Well, that explains things."

"Here in Clay County, Florida," the board chair says, each word coming out slow, "we may do things a little differently than over in Seattle, Miss McAlister. And we'll expect you to abide by Robert's Rules if you want to continue to address this body."

"Whose rules?" I think back to the enormous binder Malena gave me, the one I couldn't manage to get through.

"Robert's Rules of Order," he replies, a sneer slowly making its way across his ruddy face. "Standard parliamentary procedure."

"Okay, sure," I say. "I'm really sorry about that."

My heart beats so loud that the noise is starting to drown out the room. I grip the podium and stare back down at my useless outline.

"What do I have to do, exactly?"

"Well, for starters, Miss McAlister, you'll need to reference the code."

"You can call me Ruby," I say. That elicits a laugh from a couple of students in the back of the room, which appears to piss off the school-board chair.

Why didn't I learn his name? How hard would that have been?

He stands up. "And I'll expect order in this chamber!" he calls out. He sits down with a thud. "Miss McAlister, you may offer your concluding remarks."

"Okay, where was I?" I look back at my outline, scanning the page to see what bullet points I've written under *Conclusion*. The blood is pumping so hard through my veins that I feel it thrumming in my eardrums.

The sentences swim in front of my vision, and I have to use my finger to trace down the page. When it finally lands next to the word *Conclusion*, I see that I've only put two bullet points under it:

- Summarize arguments already made
- Wrap up with confidence

Oh, I am so screwed.

I grip the podium and watch the blood drain from my fingertips. "And, uh, the dress code really isn't doing anything to help us learn. And, well, uh, I guess that's it."

I hear uncomfortable shuffling, a few nervous coughs. I quickly look back down at my notes, unable to muster the courage to look out over the disappointed crowd.

"We'll open for questions from the board," the school-board chair announces.

I straighten up and try to focus. Questions I can do. Coming up with the right answers on the fly is my specialty. I can still salvage this.

The white guy in the red polo shirt jumps in. "We're trying to teach our students how to dress for success—to be ready for college and career. Wouldn't you agree that a dress code is valuable in that regard? Might there be a way to revise the dress code with a focus on career readiness?"

I'm grateful for the softball opening question, but my mind draws a complete blank. "Like wear suits to school?" I ask, knowing I sound clueless. "I guess all I can say is that when I went to visit my sister at college, half the students went to class in their pajamas, and she went to a really prestigious school, so . . ."

I watch as the blond woman whispers something to her neighbor, making him grin as if they're sharing some sort of inside joke at my expense.

"Miss McAlister." Another old school-board guy breaks in. "It's our responsibility as adults to create conditions where students are not going to be subject to harassment—sexual harassment based on what girls are wearing. I've seen this happen too many times. And boys at this age, their hormones are out of control."

He grins a creepy grin, and a couple of the other school-board guys chuckle under their breath.

Which has the effect of shifting my mood immediately.

Heat rises to my face and a coarse energy rushes through my body. I'm no longer sheepish and embarrassed. Suddenly I'm really pissed off.

"Okay, here's the thing," I say, my cheeks burning and my voice abrasive. "That's sending the message that guys are perverts and that it's girls' responsibility to control guys' behavior." I glare at the creepy board member. "With all due respect, creating conditions that don't allow for sexual harassment is a much bigger project than banning off-the-shoulder tops or yoga pants."

"Well, it's a start," the blond woman says.

Oh, fabulous. Now the woman is jumping in to bolster the patriarchy.

"Yes, it's a start," I say. My hands are starting to flail. I feel them, but I can't seem to quit. "It's a start to teaching boys that they're predators, and that it's not their fault. Is that really where we want to start?"

The school-board chair reaches out his hand as if he's stopping oncoming traffic. "Let's dial it back a bit, Miss McAlister."

"Ruby," I spit. "You can call me Ruby." I need to hold it together. I need to calm down.

"Okay, Ruby," the man in the red polo says, bringing a calm, measured tone back to the conversation. "You offer important observations. But per section 8.3.16, we must have a dress code, so what are you suggesting exactly?"

"Clearly, she's uninformed," the blond note-taker lady breaks in. "She hasn't done her research, and she's wasting our time."

"Okay," I say. "How about San Francisco? Last year their county school system implemented a 'no-shame dress code,' and it's working really well, so—"

"San Francisco, huh?" another school-board member says under his breath, his tone filled with sarcasm.

"Which county?" the woman asks, poised to add this to her notes.

Again, my mind draws a blank. "I don't remember the name of the county—I mean, it's whatever county San Francisco is in."

"And are you providing us with a document outlining the specifics of said dress code?" Mr. School-Board Chair asks.

I shake my head once, trying to gather my courage. I know the answer to this one.

"No need. Its beauty is in its simplicity, really—genitals, buttocks, and nipples must be covered with opaque material; anything else is okay."

"Anything?" the blond woman exclaims. "By that standard, you could wear your lingerie to school! Is that what you're proposing, Miss McAlister?"

From the back of the room, a male voice calls out, "Do it, Ruby. NippleRiot, baby!"

The room seizes up with gasps and titters, but it's all fading away. The entire scene is fading as I sink into a realization: I'll never forget that voice.

Fucking tease.

He's here, watching me. I shudder, feeling the heaviness of his gaze on my body. I clutch my gut, scan the room quickly. I feel the room blur and begin to tilt sideways. I think I might faint.

"We will have order!" the board chair calls out, bashing his gavel against the table. With each thud of the gavel, I feel weaker. My head spins and my stomach contracts. I need to sit down.

"Miss McAlister!" the blond woman barks at me. "Are you, in fact, proposing to wear lingerie to school?"

Fucking tease.

I can't sit down. I can't give in to this—to him. I have to keep talking. I clench my jaw hard and lean into the podium for support.

"Let's give this young woman a chance to respond," the nice man in the red shirt says calmly. "She has come here to share with us—"

"I guess I could wear lingerie," I interrupt, hearing the harsh anger in my raised voice. "But I don't even own any."

"We cannot subject our young people to this kind of anything-goes attitude toward their bodies!" the man sitting next to Red-Polo Guy exclaims. "It's bad enough out there with the kids groping each other in public, no shame. . . ."

I'm trying hard to focus on what he's saying, but my mind rushes back to the hallway, to the groping I didn't ask for.

Fucking tease.

I remember his touch, the growl of his voice, the cold droplets of spit as they landed on my collarbone. For one moment, I feel vulnerable and scared, but only for a moment. Then my body stands tall and I launch in.

"Oh my God! This conversation is going nowhere," I shout, arms flailing. "Clay County just needs to abolish the stupid freaking dress code, effective immediately."

I pause, expecting the gallery to burst into cheers, hoping the cheers will drown out that one terrible voice—make it go away. Instead, the room expands with a cavernous silence.

And suddenly my mouth is unleashing a massive string of profanities. I don't even know what I'm saying anymore. All I know is that it must be bad, because the old school-board guys are up on their feet and I hear a gavel banging, banging, banging against the table.

I can't stop. I can't even think about stopping. I'm going off, raging, fuming. Suddenly I hear myself screaming about tampons—tampons!

"And another thing!" I slam my hand down on the podium. "It's completely absurd that schools don't provide tampons. They're a basic hygiene product—equivalent to toilet paper! Don't you see how completely screwed up it all is? Our school made a girl cover her nipples with pantyliners, but won't even put a few free period products in the bathrooms?" I hear my hand slam against the wood, again and again, but I can't even feel it. I can't feel anything except white-hot rage. "And don't even get me started on gendered bathrooms—they're dehumanizing!"

And then I feel a hand on my forearm. I fling myself around to see a security guard.

"Miss, you're going to need to come with me."

The security guard, his hand light against my forearm, is pulling me away from the microphone, toward the row of doors at the back of the room. I don't resist. Instead, my gaze searches the crowd, and I find Malena. It's the look on Malena's face that brings me to the crushing realization of what I've just done.

Her expression is stony; her lips are slightly pursed. It takes no time at all for me to recognize one emotion: disappointment. Deep and profound disappointment. All the rage flows out of me, and what's left is a void opening right into the center of my being. And into that void rushes a string of devastating realizations.

This was our chance—the two minutes we worked our asses off to earn. Malena trusted me to do this well, and I let her down. Spectacularly.

I ignored Ms. Baptiste's advice.

I didn't accept Malena's help. Or Olive's.

I didn't prepare anything but a flimsy, useless outline.

I didn't take the time to read the actual code.

I didn't learn the names of the school-board members.

I didn't offer any alternative policies for them to consider.

I didn't even learn how to use Robert's freaking Rules of Order.

And the worst part? The most shameful and humiliating thing about this whole scene? The reason I didn't do those things is that I was too busy hanging out with Carlos. I was too busy obsessing *over a boy.*

Who am I to think that I can be a social-change maker? An activist? A model of feminism? I'm just a pathetic little girl who crushed too hard on a baseball god and then broke down because some asshole groped me and tossed a slur my way.

I feel the tears sting at the corners of my eyes. The security guard leads me through the heavy double doors, and I turn back, hoping to make eye contact with Malena. She won't look at me.

She's staring down at the floor, but Soraida is glaring right at me, and so I mouth, *I'm sorry.*

When we get into the hallway, the security guard begins to speak to me, his voice firm but gentle. "Do you understand why I've removed you from the proceedings, miss?" I lean against the wall, feeling like I might collapse. I hear the door swing open and look up, hoping against hope that it will be Malena.

It's not. It's Dr. Hardaway.

I slump back to the wall and let my eyes fall shut, certain that I'm about to get an earful. But when I open my eyes, she and the security guard have stepped away from me, and she's speaking to him in hushed whispers. He nods, glances over at me, and says, "You're free to go, miss."

The security guard heads back into the school-board meeting, but I can't seem to move.

And then, to my enormous shock, Dr. Hardaway walks over to me, leans in, and folds her arms around me. I bury my head in her shoulder and release against her. She holds me tight, bearing the weight of my entire body, while I let out a deep and defeated sob.

PART THREE

There are always more opportunities to get it right, to fashion our lives in the ways we deserve to have them. Don't waste your time hating a failure. Failure is a greater teacher than success. Listen, learn, go on.

—Clarissa Pinkola Estés,
Women Who Run with the Wolves

PART THREE

CHAPTER TWENTY-FIVE

MALENA

The week following the school-board fiasco drew out, long and strange. The whole mess brought out the worst in everyone involved, including me.

It's finally Saturday, and I'm relieved to have two days away from Orange Grove High—and everyone in it.

This morning, it takes every ounce of energy to open my eyes, even though sunshine is bursting bright through my window, and the buttery smell of Mami's pancakes wafts in the air.

How did things get so off track?

Monday night was catastrophic, a fact that remains undisputed, but I expected the incident to be forgotten by midweek. Instead, the next day, someone thought it would be hilarious to draw a pair of breasts behind bars on Ruby's locker. The words *Roob's Big House Boobs* were scrawled on top with black permanent marker. They didn't even bother to put the apostrophe in the right place.

Ruby went MIA after school on Tuesday, which only served to fan the most absurd "Where's Ruby?" rumors.

On Wednesday, Nadia told me that someone told her Ruby had moved back to Seattle.

By Thursday, Beatriz said a girl in the bathroom had heard from a girl on the volleyball team that Ruby quit school to join a hippie commune in California.

"It's a West Coast thing. She'll fit right in," I heard someone say.

Even Topher was clueless as to her whereabouts. He approached me yesterday during lunch period while I was trying in vain to come up with a film treatment for Ms. Baptiste's final project. My nonexistent class project seems to be another victim of this horrible week.

"Has Ruby called?" he asked.

"Why would she?"

He looked taken aback. "Because you're friends?" he said in an awkward tone that implied confusion and disbelief. "Because you're in this together?"

"I don't know, Topher. Are we?" I got up from the table, walked past him, and tossed the untouched slice of pizza into the garbage, followed by all my stupid faculty-student committee notes and all the research I did for the school-board meeting. No point in keeping any of it. Those pages and pages of work are just a sad reminder of what could have been.

Carlos also seemed to have a case of the malhumores, or maybe I should say *mal amores*. No one knows what went on between him and Ruby. All we know is that Carlos has been in the foulest of moods, lashing out at Soraida even more than normal and complaining about pretty much everything under the sun.

Yesterday, his car wouldn't start—as usual. He went off on a temper tantrum for the ages. Pacing back and forth between the open hood and the trunk. Muttering something about turkeys and T-shirts. All very bizarre. I thought his head was going to explode in a gory blast of brains and blood. Even Soraida went uncharacteristically quiet. Carlos's angry mumblings somehow managed to shut her up.

God, how did we manage to turn our *big plans* so spectacularly on their head? I bet Calista Jameson didn't see this one coming. What would the headline be? BRA WARRIORS PULL OUT ALL THE STRAPS, LAND FLAT-CHESTED.

She emailed Ruby and me midweek to let us know that she watched a livestream of the school-board meeting, and would hold off writing a new story until there was another "significant development." *Don't hold your breath, lady.*

"Are you awake, nena?" Mami opens the door and peers into my room. I squeak out a "Barely" from under the covers.

Mami walks in, sits on the bed next to me, and begins running her fingers through my hair.

"I made us breakfast," she says. "I thought we could catch up."

Ay, Mami, I want to say, *I wouldn't even know where to begin.*

I reposition my head so that it's resting on her lap. Her fingers gently rub my eyebrows, then my forehead, and travel down my hairline, all the way to my neck. It's been so long since I lay like this that I forgot the power of Mami's healing touch. Her patients must love her for it.

"Have you spoken to Ruby?" she asks in Spanish.

"No."

She sighs, winding strands of my hair between her fingers and scratching my scalp in one soothing motion. I could stay here forever.

"Are you going to call her?"

"I don't know."

"Sweetie, I'm sure she feels terrible about everything. Joan told me she's barely left her room in days."

"You spoke to Abuela Joan?"

"She called to check in on you. She's worried. I'm worried." Her face goes soft.

I wish I could tell her there's nothing to worry about, but I'm sick of lying to her. Sick of feeling like a mentirosa.

"Did you make pancakes?" I manage to peel my body off the bed and push myself to a sitting position. I wrap both arms tight around my bent legs and lean my head against her warm shoulder.

"I did. I even got that maple syrup that you like." Mami kisses the top of my head, tenderly stroking my cheek with her palm. "I know things have been rough these last few weeks . . . but I hope you know I'm very proud of you, mija."

I scoff. "Proud of what? We didn't get anything done. We just embarrassed ourselves in front of the whole school—the whole county! Trust me, that's nothing to be proud of. You were right. I should've kept my mouth shut."

"I'm not so sure about that," she says, caressing my hair the way she used to do when I was a little girl. "Joan filled me in on everything you had to accomplish to get to that meeting. Watching you girls sit up front on Monday night, I realized what a big deal this was and how much effort you made. I know you understand how busy I am with work, but I felt a little guilty that I missed out on so much." Mami sighs, wrapping one arm around me. "This is all just so new. I wish I could've done more to help you."

The sadness in Mami's voice breaks my heart. I kiss her on the cheek and scoot closer to her. "It's okay, Mami."

"Monday night was a roadblock. You'll find a way around it," she says. "Mija, I know you will."

Mami holds my gaze. The kindness in her eyes hits me like a bullet to the heart. I want to crawl back inside her and shut out the world. I want her to make it stop hurting. To make everything return to the way it was Before María, when I knew exactly who I was and what my life was about. Back to when I didn't have to fight against the injustices of the world.

I can't keep in the tears any longer.

"It's okay, mi nena," Mami coos. "Go ahead and have a good cry."

"It all feels so stupid now," I say between snot-filled sobs. "What did we think we would achieve? Not wearing bras to school? Big freaking deal. What about all those other people who left Puerto Rico because of María? Some don't have jobs or a place to live. Some are living in hotel rooms or worse! In their cars. Maybe I should be trying to help them. Like Papi. He's doing something worthwhile. What am I doing? Nothing. I'm helping no one. I can't even help myself."

Mami envelops me in her arms, smooths my hair with both hands. She cradles me like a child, reminding me to breathe as I weep into her chest. I'm crying so hard that my body is shaking with anger, sadness, and frustration.

"You listen to me, mija." Mami gently carves some space between us so that our eyes can meet. "You are comparing two very different things. Alberto had to stay behind because it's his job. ¿Me entiendes? He is helping those poor souls, but that is his job. If he could be here with us, trust me, he would. You and Ruby stood up for yourselves. It wasn't a job or an obligation. You did it because you knew it was right. You both took responsibility and made yourselves heard." I hold her gaze, even though it makes me want to cry harder. "That is something to be very proud of. Not everyone has the guts to speak up, Malena."

Did I speak up? No. I just sat there, petrified, as Ruby flailed around, trying and failing to present our case at the school-board meeting. All the while thinking, *I'd be doing better up there. Why am I not the one speaking?*

I was prepared. I had notes, with references to regulations, studies, and news stories. I could have memorized talking points, like I did for the interviews and the protest.

Why didn't I present our case?

Because I was scared.

I thought no one would listen to a brown girl talking about bras. An island girl. A Spanish speaker with an accent. I thought they would see me as Pobrecita María Malena.

I was afraid I might relive that moment in Dr. Hardaway's office—and later in the school clinic—when I saw so clearly that there will never be justice for girls like me.

Mami kisses my forehead and cleans the last tears off my face.

"Now wash that pretty face and let's eat before the pancakes get cold. No one wants cold pancakes."

My arms wrap her in a tight hug. She hugs me back and I kiss her cheek, my heart sick, but also overflowing with love and gratitude.

"Thank you, Mami." I kiss her other cheek. "For everything."

She tears up a little but doesn't say anything. She doesn't have to.

———

After breakfast, I decide to share *This Is What I Was Wearing* with Mami. Her first reaction is similar to mine, a stunned silence.

After a few minutes of studying the photos in the book, she asks, "What are you going to do with this?"

I'm about to answer that I don't know when we're interrupted by the ringing of her phone. We both glance at the screen, where Papi's face smiles back at us.

"Pick up, pick up!" I yell, fumbling for the phone and spilling a half-empty glass of OJ in the process. I run to the kitchen for a towel.

"Alberto? Is that you?" Mami asks in Spanish.

"Speaker!" I whisper-yell, soaking up the juice on the table.

Mami's hands are trembling, so I take the phone from her and set it on the table, hastily pressing the speaker button on the screen. And then I hear Papi's voice on the other side of the line, clear as day.

"How are my two girls?" Papi's cheerful voice roars through the line.

Mami squeaks a "Bien," too overcome with emotion to form a sentence. My heart swells with compassion for her. For weeks she's been holding it together, being the strong, independent superwoman Papi and I love and admire. But now I realize how much she relies on Papi for support. They need each other, as much as I need them.

"We're doing well, Papi," I say, smiling at the screen even though he can't see me. "We miss you."

He swallows hard and takes a beat to answer. "I miss you, too." He sighs, his voice turning worn and tired. "I can't wait to be home with you."

Mami clears her throat, wiping her tears and pulling herself together. "How are things on the Island? How's the recovery?"

Papi exhales into the phone. "Slow. Very slow. But people are resilient. La vida continúa, you know?"

Yes. We know. Life goes on.

"Is there some way we can help?" I ask.

"It's tough right now, Malena. We're trying to get basic infrastructure up and running again."

"Should we come back?" I add. Mami glares at me, shaking her head silently.

"Not right now, nena. Right now I need you to focus on school and helping your mother. Okay?"

"Okay," I respond, disheartened. I don't know what I expected him to say.

"Alberto, has there been any progress at all? Any good news?"

"Here and there," he says. "I met with this nonprofit group working with kids in the barrios. All the schools are closed, so the kids don't have anything to do. This group—mostly young artists—brings in brushes and paint. Then they pick a spot around town and teach the kids how to paint a mural. It's nice to see them smile again. There's hope there."

Mami and I look at each other and share a smile.

Hope.

The Spanish word is *esperanza*. But I realize: no matter the language, the feeling is the same. A belief that the future will be better. And faith that we can create what we want that future to be.

After we've talked for a while, I blow Papi a kiss and leave, carrying *This Is What I Was Wearing* to my bedroom, the seed of an idea slowly sprouting in my mind.

What if I could also use art to heal? What would that look like?

I glance at my computer and see the unfinished timeline of the protest video I've been working on.

I think of the clothes that landed us in detention. The discriminatory clothes. The gender-biased clothes. How do we push our story forward? What about the clothes that we wear when we're feeling empowered? Our undaunted clothes. The clothes that show the world who we are. Or who we want to be. The clothes that we're wearing when we feel hopeful and courageous.

My mind is suddenly feverish with ideas and images of people standing in front of a camera telling their story. They're stronger. More confident. Simply fearless. Just like Penny Hardaway.

I send a frenzy of texts to Soraida, Xiomara, Beatriz, and Nadia explaining the idea and asking them to meet me in Ms. Baptiste's studio on Monday to go over the plan. If I can get everyone on board, we'll be filming my video Tuesday after school.

> Tell anyone you know that's gotten in trouble.
> Bring your dress-coded outfit and whatever clothes you wear when you're most yourself, when you're feeling strong and confident.
> When you're empowered!

Xiomara replies.

> Does makeup count?

> Yes.

I'm thinking of the Uncensored red lipstick Soraida once daubed onto my lips as she was getting me "interview ready." Red lips have a weird way of making a person look braver than they feel.

And then I do something only undaunted Malena would do. I write an email to Calista Jameson, telling her about my project. Hitting send never felt so good.

Two hours later, I've already drafted a treatment for the project, and I'm working on the rough beginnings of a script.

I'm starting to feel optimistic, like this project might really work, when a new text from Soraida comes in.

> Has he come by yet?

> Who?

> Javi. Duh.

> He doesn't know where I live.

Javi texted me a few times during the week, but I couldn't deal with one more ounce of drama, so I just ignored the messages.

> I may've told him.

"Soraida! Seriously?" I yell at the phone in my hand, hoping she will telepathically sense my annoyance.

And I guess she does, because another message quickly comes in.

> Don't be mad! I was trying to help. He's been nagging me all week.

> This is NOT helping.

Our doorbell rings and I can only guess that Javi and his million-watt smile are standing outside our apartment.

"I got it," I cry out, grateful that Mami is taking a shower. I can't handle the kind of interrogation that would follow a guy showing up unannounced—a cute guy, at that.

As I'm rushing to the door, my phone dings with a new email alert.

Sender: Calista Jameson

The doorbell rings again.

"Ugh!" *Soraida, you're so dead.*

I open the door and there he stands. Sexy, experienced Javi. The last time I saw him, I was desperately pulling my clothes back on while running out of his room. Awkward. In retrospect, I realize I never actually told him why I just got up and left in the middle of our make-out session.

All I knew was that whatever answers I needed, I wasn't going to find them hooking up with him. I didn't know how to explain this to him. Still don't.

"Hey. What are you doing here?" I ask, genuinely curious but also dying to get back to Calista's response.

"Wow, nice to see you too." He titters nervously, stuffing his hands in the pockets of his jeans.

"S-sorry," I stammer, staring down at my bare feet.

Javi shifts his weight from one foot to another. He glances down at my legs and I register, too late, that I'm still wearing pajamas. They have a unicorn print that suddenly feels very childish. I also realize that I'm not wearing a bra.

For a moment I have to fight the urge to cover myself with my folded arms. But then I remind myself that my breasts shouldn't be a distraction. And if they are, it's on Javi to deal with it.

"Are those My Little Pony?" He points at the fabric of my pajamas with one finger.

"Please, I'm not five," I say sarcastically. "These are proper unicorns, I'll have you know. A gift from my abuela."

"I totally get it." He chuckles. "I used to be obsessed with Legos when I was a kid. My abuela still sends me a kit from Argentina every Christmas."

"It's the universal Latin abuela experience," I say, smiling.

We watch each other in silence for a while. Javi seems to have something on his mind, but he can't quite say it. He unpockets his hands and they fall to his side limply.

I decide it's time to woman up. I really need to get back to Calista's email.

"Listen, Javi," I start, but it feels like I'm stumbling my way through whatever it is I want to say. I take a deep breath, clear my throat, and start again. "About the other day . . ."

"Did I do something wrong? Did I hurt you or something? 'Cause if I did, I'm sorry, Malena. I didn't mean to . . ." He knits his eyebrows, and two worry lines appear on his forehead. It's sweet. It never occurred to me that he might think he did something wrong.

"It wasn't like that," I say, shaking my head. "It just wasn't right. I was at your house for all the wrong reasons. And I think we both deserve better than that. I'm sorry I left without an explanation."

"Maybe . . ." He hesitates. "Things were moving too fast?"

I look away, my cheeks burning at the memory of my bare chest against his skin.

"I wish you would've said something." He shrugs, hiding his hands back inside his pockets. "I'm okay taking it slow."

Is that why I left? Because we were moving too fast?

Sure, when I have sex for the first time, I want it to be with someone I know and care about. But I realize now that something else made me rush away—something more important. I didn't want to be the girl using sex to prove a point. Or as a way to rebel against the world.

That's not who I am. And it's not who I want to be.

"I know," I say. "I should've said something."

I watch him for a moment. The charming, self-assured smile he usually wears has momentarily come down. It's been replaced by an expression that I can only guess is vulnerability. But it's only a guess. Javi and I have never had an actual conversation. It's all been physical.

"I'm sorry if I messed up in any way—I like you, a lot." In an instant he transforms into charming Javi again, with a smile a hundred times hotter than the sun. "Can we give this another try?"

I'm dumbfounded. Javi the player was never supposed to turn into Javi the boyfriend.

He is charming and sweet, and it was probably wrong for me to assume he was going into this without any feelings. But as much as I hate to say it, he's not what I want or need right now.

What I want is to get back to my project.

What I need is to tell my story in a way that matters to me, and others like me.

Right now, I don't see where Javi fits in.

I think of Ruby and how she went off the rails. After the protest she became a whole different person—distant and withdrawn.

I guess when she fell for Carlos, she lost interest in us and our mission.

I don't need that kind of distraction.

"What are you doing tonight? Can we hang out?" he asks.

I sigh. I know what I need to say.

"I like you too, Javi, but I have this thing I'm working on right now," I say, pulling myself to full height. I glance at my phone. My screen is full of texts from the girls. "This new project I'm super excited about. I just . . . I don't have time for dating and stuff right now."

His smile falters. "Oh. Okay." He pulls his phone out of his pocket. "Well, you have my number. Call or text if you change your mind. Again, we can just go grab a bite or something chill."

I lean in and kiss him on the cheek.

"Goodbye, Javi. I'm glad you came by."

I'm not changing my mind.

Before he's even to the bottom of the stairs, I rush back inside, desperate to read Calista's email. I can't wait to find out what she has to say.

CHAPTER TWENTY-SIX

RUBY

"You're a McAlister, Ruby! McAlisters don't give up, just because of one little setback."

None of this feels *little* to me, but I have no idea how to explain it all to my dad.

Yes, Mom, Dad, and Olive have all come home, with Zoë the yellow Lab in tow, just in time to witness my utter and complete meltdown. At least I had enough presence of mind to hide my good shoes from Zoë.

On the upside, my parents' return after so many weeks of travel has provided a great excuse to skip school for a couple of days. I haven't had the energy to share much with them, but they know enough to confirm what I think they've always known: I am not my sister. I am not a go-getting, world-changing, ass-kicking activist.

I'm Ruby, and I suck.

Not only do I suck at being a change maker, but I—perhaps more importantly—suck at being a friend, as evidenced by my inability to apologize to Malena. Every time I try to pick up the phone to call her, I lose my nerve. I'm not sure I can bear the crushing weight of her disappointment.

Nana always tells me that putting old-fashioned pencil to paper can work wonders. So I tried writing her a letter. But after a few crumpled attempts, I found myself staring at a blank page. How do I even begin to make sense of what happened behind that podium? How can I unravel all the ways that everything went so wrong?

I've also ignored every single one of the texts and calls pouring in from Topher, Nessa, and Jo. At least they finally quit trying. And don't even get me started on being a girlfriend. I've come to realize, with painful clarity, that "baseball wife" obviously is not my calling.

I made it pretty clear to Carlos, too, when I refused to let him drive me home after the school-board hearing, avoided him all day Tuesday, and then declared when he showed up at my house with a meat-lover's pizza that "I'm perfectly capable of buying my own goddamned pizza, thank you very much." I basically tore into him, blaming him for distracting me from the important things in my life. And just before I slammed the kitchen door in his face, I huffed out something along the lines of "I'm so totally over being your stupid baseball wife."

Mom and Dad came through that same kitchen door on Tuesday afternoon, shortly after I fled school and the disgusting image Sharpied onto my locker. Last night, I told Mom and Dad that I can't go back to Orange Grove. I insisted on moving back to Seattle for my senior year, and I threatened that if they won't go with me, I'll just move in with Lucinda and her family.

Unfortunately, Mom and Dad don't exactly see eye to eye with me on this one. Which is why I'm sitting on the back porch after our Sunday dinner, staring out across the placid river and enduring another one of Dad's colossal pep talks.

"When your sister first started seeking supplies for her under-served school in Atlanta, all she got was no—from her supervisor, the principal, the superintendent."

He turns to look at Olive, who's sitting in a rocker with her laptop. "Right, honey?"

Olive looks up from her screen. "Mm-hmm."

"She had to go all the way to the Department of Education. And when they turned her away, she didn't stop."

"I know, Dad," I say, impatient.

"She went out on her own to start a supply drive, reached out directly to companies—"

"Dad! I know!"

He turns to look at me, surprised by my little outburst. Nana, who's been sitting in a rocker beside me, quietly listening to the conversation unfold, finally breaks her silence.

"In my experience," Nana says, "a setback—especially a big setback—offers a chance to step back."

"Cute play on words," I say, leaning back in my rocker, "but I'm not sure what you're driving at."

I'm grateful that she interrupted Dad, but I'm also a little confused.

"There's a difference between stepping back and giving up, Ruby. Maybe it's time to pause, to reflect, to seek advice from people you trust."

"Right," my dad says, his voice perky and enthusiastic. "And then dive back in there and do the work!"

I roll my eyes, unable to help myself.

Olive closes her laptop and places it gently beside her chair. "Dad," she says, "we love you, but this isn't helping."

"Why don't we head inside," Nana suggests to Dad, "give Olive and Ruby some time to talk."

"Sister time!" he announces cheerfully. "That's a *great* idea. Just the ticket!"

I'm not sure I can handle sister time, but it doesn't appear that I have a choice.

Once Dad and Nana are inside, Olive plops herself next to me, into Nana's rocker. "I'm so sick of talking about that damn award ceremony." Her voice is quiet. She's looking out across the river, avoiding eye contact with me.

"Wait, why?" I ask, feeling concern well up inside me. I thought she was thrilled about the award. My parents sure were. "Did something happen?"

Olive puts her thumb to her mouth and starts gnawing on the fingernail—a telltale sign, for as long as I can remember, that she is super stressed. "Everyone at that school hates me," she says, still gnawing away.

"Don't be so dramatic, Olive," I say. "That's my role in the family."

This is so unlike Olive that it's freaking me out a little.

"Oh, but they do! Another fourth-grade teacher on my team told me—and I quote—I parachuted in and bulldozed my way through problems they had been battling for years."

"Wow," I say. "That's harsh."

Olive nods. "I thought she was just jealous at first, but honestly, I think maybe she's right. I'm a bulldozer with a parachute."

I unintentionally laugh at the image.

"It's not funny," Olive says.

"I know. I'm sorry," I say, clearing my throat. I remember that conversation with Carlos in my bedroom. My shoulders tense as the moment floods back. How squirmy I felt listening to him, how awkward and uncomfortable the whole thing was. I guess this is what he was trying to tell me.

"Carlos calls it a Great White Savior," I say. *God, I hate it when he's right.*

Olive's whole body sags into the rocker. I've never seen her look so defeated. "I think he's got a point," she says, shaking her head and starting again to chew on her fingernail. "Can I tell you something?" she asks. "In confidence?"

"Of course."

"I want so much to leave that school, to run away from that place. I applied for jobs in other cities. When I get back to Atlanta, I think I'm gonna give my two weeks' notice."

"Olive," I say, trying to hold back my shock. "Since when do you run away from your problems?" My mind searches desperately for the right thing to say. "Plus, the kids love you."

"I love them too, Ruby," she says, her voice wistful. "So much." She inhales a big gulp of air and lets it all out slowly. Her head falls back as she says, "I probably just need to go back to my classroom, put my head down, and do my damn job!"

"Exactly," I say. "Step back, like Nana said. Just be a great fourth-grade teacher. That's really important work."

"You're right," she says, eyes set on the dark sky above us. "But it's so hard sometimes. I'm not sure I can muster the courage."

We sit for a while, rocking back and forth in silence. It's so strange that Olive is confiding in me. It makes me feel like an adult.

"Your turn," Olive says, breaking the silence.

"For what?" I ask, skeptical.

"Secrets—things you're afraid to even say because you can't bear the thought of disappointing Mom and Dad."

"Oh, that's easy." And it is. I know right away. "I get that you and Mom and Dad are really into the idea, but I have exactly zero desire to take a gap year. I don't want to go out and save the world." I feel a huge rush of relief, saying it out loud. So relieved, in fact, that now I can't seem to stop myself. "I just want to find a tiny college with a lovely tree-filled campus and an awesome library. I want to go there, bury my head in nineteenth-century English literature, and nerd out on feminist theory."

I look at her, hopeful. I want Olive to be okay with this, but also, hearing myself say it, I'm absolutely sure it's the right thing for me. "Do you think that's a terrible decision?"

"Of course not," she says, her voice high with excitement. "It sounds absolutely perfect—so good that I wish I had suggested it myself."

We both laugh. It feels nice—and so unexpected—to have this moment with Olive. It's been way too long since we have talked as friends.

"I hate to break it to you, but first you need to graduate from high school. Which means you have to actually show up," she says, her tone playful.

I sigh. Suddenly recalling all the reasons I don't want to go back. But I know I have to.

"Maybe we should make a pact," I say. "You know, to not run away."

She looks up at me and smiles. "I love it," she says. "A pact!"

"Should we shake on it or something?" I ask.

"Absolutely."

And then, through some strange telepathy, both of us jump up, remembering the silly handshake we choreographed together when I was five and Olive was twelve. We slap high fives, twirl around twice, and bump hips. When our hands finally clasp, we're both laughing our asses off.

Oh sweet Jesus! What was I *thinking?*

It's Monday morning, and I'm sitting in my car, in an empty parking lot down the road from school, cursing that stupid pact. It's like my body steered me here—clearly in survival mode, knowing how crucial it is that I avoid close proximity to Orange Grove High School and all the mistakes I've made there.

Running away now seems like the only option.

I sit in my car beside the road and watch a line of buses backed up, waiting to turn into the senior parking lot. I roll down the window and lean out, staring at an algae-clogged retention pond, trying to figure out what I'm going to do. I can't face any of it.

I'll get a GED. Go to online school. Ask Topher to home-school me. *If he ever talks to me again.*

I lean my head back and close my eyes.

Regret, shame, guilt, humiliation. They all wash over me at once. I grip my steering wheel hard, as if it might somehow keep me from drowning in all these feelings.

Eyes still closed, I hear Carlos's SUV before I see it. The loud rumble causes me to glance into my rearview mirror, just in time to watch him pull up beside me. He's not alone. Soraida is glaring at me from the passenger seat.

She jumps out of the car and slams the door behind her. Carlos sits stony-faced in the driver's seat, staring straight ahead. It hurts to watch him, so I turn away.

Soraida knocks loudly on the passenger window, and I mash the button to roll it down.

"Let me in," she says when the window opens. "We need to talk."

I lean across to open the passenger door. I know Soraida. She won't leave until she says whatever is on her mind. It comes as no surprise to me that while the rest of us hide from pain, she's the one with the gumption to rip off the Band-Aid.

She plops down into the seat beside me, lips bright red and loose hair whipping around her shoulders. "Carlos is pissed that I made him stop when we saw you sitting over here—all pathetic and alone. What? Are you trying to work up the nerve to go to school?"

I chew on my lip and stare down at my lap.

"I knew it," she says, her voice accusing. "Anyway, we've gotta make this quick."

"Soraida," I say, my voice pleading. "I'm so sorry—"

"I'm not here to listen to you grovel," she cuts me off. "I'm here to tell you that—for once in your life!—you need to shut up and listen."

I can feel it pulsing through my tiny car—Soraida's anger. She's about to let loose, and it's gonna hurt like hell.

"First of all, you invited your stupid friend Lucinda to help us, and she didn't do jack shit. Then you and your artist buddies decided my T-shirt design wasn't edgy enough, when it was a *damn* good idea." Her arms are waving violently around the car, knocking into the gearshift and bumping up against the steering wheel. "But we *all* listened to you because we thought you knew what the hell you were doing. Obviously, we were wrong! Why did we let you be in charge after you froze at the protest? I have no idea. We should've known that you were going to totally botch the school-board hearing."

"Soraida—" I try to break in, wanting so much to apologize, or maybe explain. But how can I explain this away?

"I *said*," Soraida interrupts, "shut up and listen. You might actually learn something."

I wrap my fingers tighter around the steering wheel and press my lips together. I have the feeling we might be about to drive off a cliff together, but I also know she's right. I need to keep my mouth shut. I need to listen.

"I can't believe what a mierda job you did up there. We could've grabbed a stranger from the street and they would've pulled it off better than you. You embarrassed us in front of the whole school. And you ruined our chances with Calista Jameson. When are we ever gonna get a chance like that again? We could have made a real difference! But here we are. All that work for absolutely nothing."

"Nothing?" I ask, incredulous. "It wasn't all for nothing, Soraida. What about all of us? Our friendship?"

"Okay," Soraida says. "Great point." Her voice is dripping with sarcasm. "Please do tell me: How's your friendship with Malena these days, or with your bestie, Topher?" She strikes the pose of a probing psychiatrist, hand resting against her chin. "Oh, or how about my brother? How do you feel about your"—she lifts her fingers to make air quotes—"'special friend-ship'?"

I don't respond. Instead, I sink deeper into my seat, my heart aching. I lean my head out the window, badly needing some fresh air. Desperate to get away from this place, to escape Soraida's bitter accusations and all the truths behind them. But there is nowhere left to go. I guess I need to woman up.

"Okay, you can talk now," Soraida says, crossing her arms.

"Let's say I agree with everything you've told me," I tell her.

"Because I'm right," Soraida deadpans.

"I just don't know how to fix it," I admit. "I don't even know where to start."

"I'm not here to tell you how to fix your problems," Soraida says. "Put on your big-girl panties and figure it out." She grabs the handle, ready to open the door and jump out of the car. "But I'll tell you this: you can begin by cleaning up that mess right there." She points to her brother. "He's been a royal pain in the ass since you dumped him. And his moping is really starting to get on everyone's nerves—especially mine."

And with that she steps out of the car and yells at Carlos through his closed window. "You two need to work out your shit. I'm walking to school."

I steal a glance at Carlos, slouching in the driver's seat, eyes trained on Soraida as she sets off across the street toward the senior lot. My heart skips a beat, and then another. I recall the day I was collecting signatures in that parking lot, when he pulled me aside to ask how I was doing. I remember all the times I sat next to him in his truck, felt his hand casually reach out for mine. I remember the night I drove while he cradled Malena in his lap, worrying for his little cousin, practically begging me not to dismiss him as a machista. And I didn't.

Carlos is far from perfect. He's constantly getting special treatment, surrounded by people who worship him. He's the center of his own universe, and while everyone orbits around him, he doesn't even see it. He's blinded by his own brilliance.

But he's also decent and kind. And he's living in a screwed-up world, trying to do the right thing. Sure, he's making plenty of mistakes along the way. But aren't we all?

God knows I am.

I take in a slow breath, reach down to unbuckle my seat belt.

I'm not sure I can repair the damage I've done, but I think I need to try.

When I step out of the car, he glances toward me and then quickly away. I approach his window but he doesn't turn to look at me. I tap gently on the glass. "Can we talk?"

He keeps looking forward, his face betraying no emotion. His head leans against the headrest. He looks up at the roof and then over at me. I stand, silent. Waiting. Hoping he'll say yes.

Carlos doesn't say a word as he gets out, shuts the door, and faces me, so close that I can feel the waves of energy radiating from him, so near that I can smell his scent: Ivory soap and worn leather.

"Okay," he says. "I'm here."

I try to look him in the eye, but he looks away. "Soraida told me I need to do more shutting up and listening," I say, "so . . ."

"Wow," he replies. "Soraida actually said something wise. Who would have thought?"

"So," I say quietly, "I'm listening."

He shifts on his feet, rocks back on his heels, looks past me. I know the words are forming in his mind. I just need to wait, be patient, give him time and space.

"I never wanted a baseball wife!" he finally blurts out. "What you said to me wasn't fair, Ruby. I wasn't trying to distract you; I was trying to support you!"

I can tell he feels sad and confused. So do I. But I resist saying anything. I know he's not finished.

"I've been going crazy trying to figure it all out. When did things get so messed up with us?" His hands gesture to the space between us. "Was it that night before the school-board hearing? Maybe I was out of line, what I said about your sister. But I've been thinking about that, and about what you said about *my* family. It was okay for you to call me out, for my male privilege or whatever. But then I tried to talk to you about this thing with your sister, and you went all quiet." He leans back against his car. "Still, though, I stayed. Why? Because I cared about you."

We stand in silence for a while, and my heart aches. I wonder if he meant to put it in the past tense. Yes, he cared about me, but does he still?

"Jesus, Ruby," he finally exclaims. "I think this is the longest you've ever gone without talking. It's freaking me out."

I let out a heavy exhale. My head is suddenly spinning, trying to sort out where to begin. I need to apologize to him, but I also need for him to get it—why I couldn't move past the whole "baseball wife" thing.

Why I still can't.

Or maybe it's not even about being a "baseball wife." At least, not totally. Maybe I needed more time than I gave myself—needed to deal with what happened in that hallway, and how much it hurt me.

Fucking tease.

I rub my forehead, try to pull myself back into the present. I'm not ready for all of this at once, but I know where to begin. "Okay, to start," I respond, my voice tentative, "you were right about my sister. I get what you were saying. Believe it or not, I think Olive finally gets it too."

His eyebrows shoot up in surprise. "That's a start."

"And I went quiet that night because I had no idea what to say. I guess I'm realizing that sometimes it's hard to accept the truth about the people you love, about yourself. . . ."

"Listen, Ruby," Carlos says. "I get it. Talking honestly about the special treatment you get because you're white and rich, that's hard. But you gotta face it, you know? And when people who care about you try to point it out, you need to try hearing them."

I take in the challenge in his words, willing my defenses not to come up. And they don't, but I also realize that Carlos and I both have a lot to learn.

"Yeah." I nod. "You're right. I could do a lot better with that. But it's complicated, Carlos," I say, trying to keep my tone even, to share what's in my heart—even though it takes all my courage to do it. "You also get tons of special treatment. Just because you're a guy who knows how to throw a ball really fast."

His muscles tense in a line that runs all the way from his jaw to his forearms. He tucks both hands into the pockets of his jeans and looks away, as if distracted by the cars driving by.

"You get that. Right?" I urge.

I can tell by the crease in his forehead that he's thinking about what I just said.

"What am I supposed to do, Ruby?" he asks in a guarded tone. "I can't control how other people treat me."

"You have a say." My voice pitches high. "You told me you hate all that machista stuff, but you sure enjoy the benefits."

"It's not like I'm telling my family they have to do all that shit for me," he replies, shoving his hands deeper into his pockets. "They just do it."

"Okay, I see that. But if you want things to change, *you* have to find a way to start changing them yourself."

His jaw clenches and releases. He squeezes his eyes shut tight. I watch as he processes the words that have passed between us. The hard truths we both need to hear.

Carlos sighs, shifting both hands to his back pockets.

"I guess I could start by getting off my ass and serving my own food," he admits with a shrug. "Maybe even learn to do laundry?"

"Someone else washes all those sweaty uniforms?" I quip, trying to shift the onerous energy between us.

The tips of his ears go pink with embarrassment. He *should* be embarrassed.

"I can't believe you don't know how to use a washer and dryer." I roll my eyes in an exaggerated way. "You're such a mama's boy."

"Soon-to-be-reformed mama's boy?" he asks, tentative.

We smile at each other. It feels so good to fall back into our easy banter. But then an awkward silence follows. He crosses his arms over his chest, while I fiddle with my earring. I think we're both overwhelmed by that lingering question of where to even start if we want things to change.

"Malena is a complete wreck," Carlos bursts out, his voice anxious. "It kills me to see her this way. What you did up there . . . it crushed her."

"I know," I say. "I can't believe I botched it all so completely, after all the work she did."

"Yeah," he says. "When I came over and brought you pizza that night—"

"When I slammed the door in your face?" I interrupt.

"Yup. When you left me stranded with an extra-large meat-lover's." He grins. "I was hoping to get you to go to Malena's with me. I thought maybe you'd apologize."

"That's what I should have done. I was a disaster. I couldn't even leave the house for days. Have you talked to her since then?" I ask, concern rising in my chest. "Has she said anything . . . about me?"

"She doesn't have to say anything," he responds. "Our Friday-night family dinner was brutal. She sat there, barely speaking, while Soraida and my mom went off, mostly asking why she ever got mixed up with the skinny white girl in the first place. Gotta say, she took it like a champ."

"Did they go off on you, too?" I ask, curious. "For getting mixed up with me?"

"Soraida did her best to drag me into it," he says. "But I refused to take the bait."

"They're right about one thing—Soraida and your mom," I admit. "It was my fault. I should've never butted in. I'm sure you're all more than ready to get me out of your lives forever."

"Honestly, I think Malena is. She's really hurt about the whole thing."

I wince, wishing it weren't true. I turn my face toward the road, not wanting him to see how much it pains me.

"But I'm not," he says. "I don't want you out of my life."

My head spins back to meet his steady gaze. Everything else falls away and finally it's just us—as we used to be when no one else was around. Carlos steps toward me, his expression vulnerable and open.

"I need you to understand, Ruby. At first, I thought I had you all figured out."

"You mean when you called me White Girl and told me I didn't know anything about consequences?" I ask, my tone defeated. "You were right."

"Yeah, maybe. But then you surprised me. You were *different*. I loved how fearless you were, how committed."

I flinch at his words. I was fearless, but am I still? I want so much to recover that part of myself.

"And I saw how all the baseball stuff didn't matter to you—

I *liked* that. I love that you don't care about how fast I can throw a ball, or whether I'll play in the majors."

I smile at the memory of being in the stadium that day. "I have to admit it was really fun watching you play that day. Even before I attacked you in the stadium."

His shoulders relax and he cocks an eyebrow, almost playful.

"I was glad you came," he says. "I mean, not because I wanted you to cheer for me. It wasn't like that. I just wanted to *be* with you." He pauses, moving closer to me.

"Well, that's a relief." I lean in toward him, feeling the mood finally change around us. "Because—since we're being honest here—I think baseball is pretty boring."

"No future as a baseball wife, then?" he asks.

"Not a chance," I say, breaking into the biggest smile.

He lifts his hand and rests it gently on my cheek. His touch is tentative, questioning. But to me it's the same firm touch I felt after that terrible moment. It's a touch of connection, of care. It's just the sort of touch I know we both need.

I look into his deep brown eyes, study his thick lashes, notice dark circles ringing them.

"You look tired," I say. "Your eyes, they're—"

"I haven't been sleeping much," he breaks in, dropping his hand to his side. Then he looks at me with a sideways grin. "My girlfriend was trying to break up with me. She even slammed the door in my face the other day when I tried to bring her favorite pizza." His eyes sparkle mischievously and he shrugs. "I'm pretty heartbroken."

"God, she sounds like a total nightmare," I say, struggling through my emotion to match his teasing tone. "You should just get it over with and dump her."

"Yeah." He sighs dramatically. "I wish I could, but—just between you and me—I might be falling in love with her, so that complicates things."

Lightness spreads through my chest as our hands intertwine.

"You're falling in love with me?"

"Yeah," he says. "I think I am."

"And you can accept my apology? I've been so awful."

"Everyone makes mistakes."

"So you can forgive me, really?"

"Yeah," he says. "I'm pretty sure I can."

I throw my arms around him. "Oh my God, that's the best news ever." I lean back to look at him. "Because I think maybe I'm falling in love with you, too."

"I know." He flashes me his signature uber-confident smile.

Strangely, his cocky tone gives me a sense of relief. He's still Carlos Rosario, God of Baseball, and—amazingly—he's still mine.

I search his eyes. "Hey," I say. "Do you think I might have a chance with Malena?"

"There's only one way to find out," he replies.

I nod and plant a kiss on his lips. "You're right," I say, pulling back. "I have to go—"

"Whaaat?" he whines, wrapping his hands around my hips and pulling me close. "You're leaving me already?"

"Yup," I say, wriggling out of his grip. "I have to go get my friend back."

CHAPTER TWENTY-SEVEN

MALENA

On Monday, I get to school earlier than usual. I have so much to do before my big filming day tomorrow. After last period, I'll be using Ms. Baptiste's studio to record the interviews for my project. I hope a few people show up. I've spent all weekend fleshing out my outline, writing down questions, and making a list of all the equipment I'll need. In her email, Calista offered to provide feedback on my treatment and the rough cut, which was beyond amazing. If I'm able to pull it off—if it's good enough—maybe she'll even boost it on her social media. A girl can dream.

But first, there's someone I need to talk to.

I approach Dr. Hardaway's office carrying the library copy of *This Is What I Was Wearing*.

I knock softly on her door, clutching the book against my chest. "Dr. Hardaway?" I ask, peering into her office.

"Oh. Hi, Malena. Come in." She stands, then walks to the other side of her desk to greet me. "I was just reading Ms. Baptiste's email about your project. She said you'll be working late tomorrow, after school?"

"Yes, is that okay?" I ask, stepping into her office.

"Of course. It sounds exciting."

"It is," I say, trying not to feel intimidated by the mere fact that I'm standing in the disciplinary AP's office, where this all began. "I was inspired by you, actually."

She tilts her head and furrows her brow in what seems like a mix of surprise, confusion, and apprehension. "God, I'm afraid to ask." She stifles a laugh.

I need to choose my next words carefully. Mostly because I want to convey my utter respect for her decision to take part in *This Is What I Was Wearing*. I can't seem to come up with the right thing to say, so I let the book speak for me.

I slowly turn the cover outward. At first, her face falls in bewilderment. Then a flash of recognition passes across her eyes. She sighs, reaching for the book in my hands. Her body slowly sinks into one of the armchairs in front of her desk. I do the same, so that we are sitting side by side.

I watch her open the book and flip through the pages. When she finds her younger self, her hand caresses the image printed on the high-gloss paper. The same way I did when I first saw it.

"Where did you find this?" she asks, eyes scanning the page. "My copy got destroyed in a basement flood years ago."

"At the library," I say quietly. I don't want to disturb the solemnity of the moment.

A long time passes in silence. Or it feels like a long time to me.

"It's like I'm looking at a different person," Dr. Hardaway says, then lifts her eyes to meet mine. "She had all this raw courage. Pure unbridled emotion. A little like you and Ruby, I guess."

I smile, aware that it's a sad smile. I want so badly just to feel nothing but respect and adoration for this woman, but life is not that simple, is it? It's hard to trust someone when they have betrayed you.

Dr. Hardaway takes a deep breath, then lets the air out slowly. Her whole body seems to collapse against the armchair.

"I'm sorry I failed you, Malena. I was just trying to help." She turns to look at me, her face soft, her expression caring. "I guess the pantyliners weren't a great idea after all."

I nod. It's going to take some time for the mental pain of that ordeal to wear off. For now, though, I want to turn it into something meaningful for both of us.

"Would you be in my video?" I ask, realizing now how much having her in my video means to me. A quiet victory I didn't know I needed.

She considers my request, glancing from me to the book and back again. I can see the hesitation, so I try to make it easier for her to agree.

"You can wear anything that you wear when you're feeling strong and fearless."

Dr. Hardaway closes *This Is What I Was Wearing.* There's a finality to the way the pages come together. It's time for all of us to move on.

"I'll come by Nia's studio tomorrow afternoon." Then her face lights up like a rainbow. Whatever she has in mind, it's going to be spectacular.

During study hall, Ms. Markowitz gives me permission to work in the library. I told her about my project and she was happy to let me come here so I could focus, spread out my documentary books, and finalize the details of tomorrow's shoot. I'm deep in camera angles when someone pulls up a chair beside me.

Ruby.

What is she doing here?

Again.

Before she's even opened her mouth, I glance over at Mr. Ringelstein, who is still behind his desk, perpetually sorting catalog cards. It's like he never left.

"We can't talk here. I'm not getting in trouble again," I say, throwing a stony glare in her direction. "Because of you."

"Please," Ruby says, her voice pleading. "Just give me two minutes."

I sigh, taking in the small piles of books in front of me. Part of me is relieved to see her. Another part of me—a big one—wants nothing to do with her.

"Malena?" Ruby insists. "Please? Can we talk?"

To my enormous surprise, Ruby's face registers only one emotion: remorse.

Against my better judgment, I push my chair back, stand, and walk toward the stacks at the opposite end of the library. Ruby follows me.

When we get as far from Mr. Ringelstein as possible, a memory flashes through my mind—me lifting my shirt, Ruby taking a picture. Why did I trust her? How could I have been so naive?

I know better now.

Ruby stands across from me, clasping her hands in front of her chest. She gulps in a breath of air. "I completely botched everything," she spits out. "I owe you—God, I owe *everyone*—a massive apology."

I glance down at her hands. She's squeezing them together so tightly that the tips of her fingers go red. I don't respond. I don't know how. *Sorry* seems like such a small thing to say, considering everything that's happened. Considering everything she's done.

"Malena?" she asks, her eyes searching mine. I hold her gaze.

"I can't undo things. I just spent a whole week wishing I could. I should've prepared. I should've listened to you and Ms. Baptiste. I don't know. I just couldn't—"

"I trusted you," I lash out, my temper rising.

"I'm so freaking sorry."

I close my eyes, anger coursing through every pore of my body. "You lied to me. You lied to Ms. Baptiste." The words burn my lips. "You said I could trust you and I did. I *believed* in you. I thought we were friends." The pain I've been holding suddenly gushes out of me like a wild river, flowing through my strained voice. "I thought you had my back. I thought we were a team. And in the end, you just gave up. You gave up on us—on me."

She winces, taking a step back and gripping the side panel of a bookshelf for support. "I . . . I didn't."

"Yes, you did," I spit back, heat consuming my face.

My words land like a slap on the cheek. Ruby looks away, silent.

"You just threw away those two precious minutes we busted our asses trying to get, like they were nothing!" I throw my hands in the air in frustration. "Maybe all that work didn't mean anything to you, but it meant everything to me. And to Soraida and even Topher, and everyone else you forgot about when you were busy not caring."

Ruby shakes her head. "That's not true, Malena. I *did* care. I mean, I *do* care, still. Very much." She wraps her arms tight around herself, looking off into the small courtyard behind the library. "When I was behind that podium, totally going off the rails, I saw you in the front row, trying to mouth the answers. I realized—way too late—that you should've been up there. *You* did all the work. *You* had all the answers. You should've been the one talking, not me."

"You're right," I say, releasing my fists, which have been clenched by my side. "I should've been the one up there. I *did* do all the work. I *did* know the answers to *every single question* they asked. I even memorized freaking Robert's Rules of Order." Ruby opens her mouth as if to speak, but I hold my hand up to stop her. I'm so not done.

I'm just getting started.

"I had all these notes. Pulled together a ton of research. I was ready to help and you blew me off. Did you even think to ask for my opinion? No. You did not. Why, Ruby? Have you ever stopped to consider why?"

I take a deep breath, letting my words sink in. Her face is stunned. Her arms drop to her side and her shoulders droop forward. She looks as tired as I feel right now.

"I'm still trying to figure that out," Ruby says quietly. "And also wondering why you didn't offer to do it. You were totally prepared and I obviously wasn't."

"You just took over," I cry out, louder than I intend to.

"Because no one else volunteered!" Ruby lets out her own frustrated cry. "Including you. Even though we both know that it should've been *you* up there." Her voice is hoarse and her arms are flailing in that way of hers. "But you could have told me that you wanted to do it. You never told me. Why?"

"Because I thought no one would listen to me, okay?" I spit. I hate hearing the words come from my lips, but they're true. "I knew they would listen to you. I trusted you to tell my story. I trusted *you*."

"That doesn't make any sense." She shakes her head. "Why did you think they'd listen to me and not you, when it was *your* story, and when you did so much work to get ready?"

"Look at me, Ruby." My arms thrash in exasperation. I step

forward, inches from her, as if being closer will make her really hear me. "I'm a brown island girl who talks with an accent when she gets nervous. I'm talking with an accent now! It doesn't matter if I have all the answers. They're always gonna believe the white girl over me. Even *I* believed you over me."

To me, this is so clear now. Ruby needs to see it too. Otherwise, how can she even understand what it's been like for me? How can we even be friends?

A long pause stretches between us. Ruby seems to be wrestling with what I've just said, her brow furrowed in deep concentration.

"You're the most badass fifteen-year-old I've ever met," she says, choking on her words. "How can you even——"

"Because it's true!" I cut her off, wanting to shake her into reality. "If my last two months in this place have taught me anything, it's that I have to try twice as hard, work twice as much, to get half the recognition that *you* get without doing a damn thing."

Ruby nods, tension lines taking over her jawline. "That's so wrong. It's not *fair*."

"It's a fucking nightmare." I don't want to cry but I can't help it. Tears pour out of me uncontrollably. I try wiping them away with the sleeve of my sweater, but I can't keep up. There's all this raw emotion inside me, boiling over, spilling around me.

As painful as it is, if Ruby hadn't set us off on this unpredictable journey, I'd still be wondering if I'd ever be good enough for this place.

I am good enough.

I know that now.

"I'm sorry, Malena," Ruby says softly. "I know I've said that like a million times already, but I really am. I thought I understood what you were going through, but I didn't. I had no idea."

"Let's face it, Ruby," I say, drying my cheeks with both hands. "You and I are not the same. Your experience will never be my experience." I bring my palm to my chest, feeling the need to ground myself. Needing her to see me—to fully see me. "At that school-board meeting, when I watched you getting escorted out by a security guard, I saw the shock and confusion on your face, the complete disbelief that this could be happening to *you*, and it dawned on me."

"What?" Ruby asks. "What dawned on you?"

"You wander around this world with absolutely no freaking clue how lucky you are. If I had gotten up in front of the school board and started cussing them out, or if Soraida had, we'd probably be kicked out of school. *We* don't get the benefit of the doubt. And Carlos, if he pulled a stunt like that, he'd probably be handcuffed and taken to jail! Charged as an adult. His baseball future? Gone."

Ruby scoffs. "Carlos? He totally gets the benefit of the doubt. All the time. No one at Orange Grove even expects him to carry a hall pass."

"Outside of this place, Carlos is just another brown kid, having to watch his back," I say, shaking my head. "Another thing you just don't understand."

"Jesus, Malena. Can't you see that I'm trying? I'm trying to get it!" Her voice shakes and her arms start to move erratically. But then she seems to stop herself mid-thought. She steps back and leans against the bookshelf. I watch, wondering whether she's gearing up to launch into another one of her all-consuming rants.

She doesn't. Instead, she looks down at her feet in silence, lets her arms fall to her side, and quietly says, "I'm not sure what you're trying to tell me. I know I probably don't deserve it, but can you please explain? I really want to understand."

I pause, wondering whether it's even worth it. Whether I'd just be wasting my breath trying to make her see what it's like. I'm tempted to spit out, *Go read a book*. But then I look at her face, filled with concern and maybe even shame, and the memories flood back—of riding in her car and singing at the top of our lungs, of swapping our favorite novels and drowning our worries in ice cream, of our surprise trip to El Faro. I sigh. Why is everything so complicated?

I glance at Ruby. The pain in her eyes makes my heart ache a little. It reminds me that we were—and maybe still can be—friends. I think she may be worth it.

"I've been talking to people at school about their experiences with the dress code—students of color, mostly. People who don't live inside your privileged bubble." I know my words sound harsh, but she needs to hear this—and I need to be the one to tell her.

Her eyebrows arch, but she remains silent.

"Two guys from the baseball team, Eduardo and Otis, both of them have been sent to detention three times for wearing hoodies. You know who else wears hoodies, like, every day? The entire lacrosse team."

"Yeah, I hate those guys," Ruby growls, glancing away for a moment.

"Those guys are white, Ruby. Eduardo's Latino. Otis is Black. Latino and Black boys are going to detention for wearing a hoodie or even baggy pants, while the white boys get a pass. A Black kid on the wrestling team told me he had to cut off his dreadlocks to compete." I pause to take in a breath. "And don't even get me started on the outright homophobic crap. Rae, a queer kid in my precalc class, got suspension for wearing nail polish. Freaking nail polish!"

Ruby shakes her head. "That's so messed up. I didn't know—"

"You didn't think to ask," I say. "And do you know what really makes my blood boil? If the school board had listened to your little tirade and abolished the dress code, it would be open season for all kinds of asshats. White supremacists would be walking around wearing their Nazi shit to school. I bet you didn't think about that when you decided to throw away all we had planned and go rogue, did you?"

Ruby rubs the back of her neck and squeezes her eyes shut. "I've been so freaking arrogant," she says, her voice heavy with emotion. She looks up at me. "I hear what you're saying and—it's just—" she stammers. "It's really hard for me to admit how incredibly stupid I've been. I thought I was some kind of social-justice crusader!" She laughs at herself. "What a fucking joke."

I nod, a small acknowledgment that she is only beginning to see the truth of how differently we're treated—because of the way we look, because of the bodies we live in.

"Case in point," I tell her. "You were supposed to be making our case for a gender-neutral dress code. And remember what Lucinda said? Way back when we first met to plan the walkout? She said we should focus on equity, not one-to-one equality, and you nodded like you totally agreed. It was so simple. But then you were up there screaming about abolishing the dress code. Not worrying for even a second about the impact that might have on the rest of us. What were you thinking?" I ask, trying to hold back the bitterness from my tone. I need to know.

"I wasn't thinking," Ruby says quietly, grief showing in her eyes. She shakes her head slowly, running her fingers through her hair. "Here I've been lecturing Carlos about how blind he is," she says almost to herself, "and I didn't even notice—I wish I had seen it." Ruby meets my eyes. "I should have seen how hard it was for you. I should have listened to you. I made a lot of mistakes up there, but I hope you understand that I never meant to hurt you."

"But you did," I murmur. "The whole thing really hurt. It still does."

She steps forward, like she's trying to hug me, but I pull away. The pain is all too fresh. I'm not ready for her hugs and tears. I lean back against the bookshelves, trying to create some space between us, needing to catch my breath. I browse the spines of the books on a nearby shelf. History tomes no one reads anymore.

"I'm sorry for all the pain I've caused," she says. "I don't expect you to forgive me right now. Honestly, if you never forgive me, I'll understand. I'll totally get it. But I need you to know that I miss you—I miss *us*—and even though I haven't earned it, I would really like the chance to try and rebuild our friendship." She looks right at me, her expression contrite and expectant.

For a while I don't say anything. I just stand there, staring at the oak tree in the courtyard through the window, trying hard to make sense of this mess we're in. I'm still angry at her, at how she stomped over everything we worked for, at how naive she can still be. But I'm also tired. I just want to let it go, at least for now. Take a breath. Figure out where we go from here. I also miss my friend. I miss all the moments when we made each other laugh and held each other up. I miss the good stuff. I can't just let go of that.

"Maybe we can go back to El Faro after school. We can just talk?" I ask, a little hopeful. "We could share a tres leches."

An optimistic smile breaks across her face. "That sounds perfect."

And it does. It sounds just right.

A loud jostling sound comes from the end of the stacks. Mr.

Ringelstein, trundling along with an overflowing cart of books to be shelved.

I glance at him, then out to the courtyard, and back at him.

"Let's hit the benches out there," I say. "I think we both could use some fresh air."

"Are we allowed?" Ruby asks.

"I got this," I tell her, my voice confident.

I head over to Mr. Ringelstein. "It's such a nice day out," I say, gesturing toward the double glass doors. "Can Ruby and I go sit in the courtyard? We've got a project to work on and we don't want to disturb anyone."

Mr. Ringelstein looks at me down the bridge of his nose, his thick glasses slipping slightly. "Oh, I've heard about your projects," he says, his expression impossible to read.

Okay, I guess our reputation precedes us. Behind me, Ruby stifles a laugh.

"Door's unlocked," he says, nodding toward the courtyard. "Listen for the bell. If you're late, you won't be getting a hall pass from me."

I turn around and grab Ruby's arm, half walking, half running outside before he changes his mind.

"Nice work!" Ruby loud-whispers.

We both stop, look up at the blue sky, and feel the humid air against our skin.

"You were right," Ruby says. She takes in a deep breath through her nose, then releases it slowly. "This is nice."

We head across the empty courtyard and find two benches in the shade of the giant oak tree. We stretch out on two side-by-side benches and watch the dappled light through the leaves.

I turn to look at her, feeling the warm air blow softly against my skin. Sensing that something's not right.

She sits up and presses her knees against her chest, wraps herself into a tight ball. All the blood drains from her cheeks and her face goes pale.

"Ruby, are you okay?" I ask, sitting up to look at her. Her skin is suddenly covered in a sheen of sweat, like she's about to be sick.

"Honestly, no."

"I've been wondering what's going on with you," I say quietly. "Since the protest, you've kinda been checked out."

"I tried so hard to hide it," she sighs. "I should have known that you'd be the one to notice."

"It's weird that way, between us," I say. "I think it always has been, since the day we met."

"Yeah." Ruby smiles, pulling her knees in tighter. "Mr. Cruz would probably tell us it's a karmic connection from another life, or something."

We both watch as two squirrels loudly scamper across the oak tree's broad trunk.

"Listen, Malena, I don't want to take away from all that we just talked about, I don't really know how to do this. I just . . ." Her face twists into anguish.

I nod, silently giving her space to continue.

"I haven't told anyone," she says. "Not even Nana. I know I shouldn't expect anything from you, from our friendship. But . . ." Her voice trails off.

"It's okay, Ruby," I urge. "You can trust me."

"I know," Ruby says. "It was . . . this asshole at the protest." She inhales a gulp of air and tosses her head back, looks up at the rustling leaves. "When we were all trapped in the hallway, he forced his hand up my shirt and grabbed my . . ." I'm holding my breath, unable to comprehend what she is saying. "He grabbed my tits and pressed himself against me from the back. He told me I was a fucking tease." She bites her lip hard, clearly struggling to hold back tears. "After, I just sort of collapsed in the hallway."

Oh my God. How could that have happened? Right there in the hallway—the same hallway where I felt that huge rush of energy and excitement. When I was clutching the megaphone and finding my voice, Ruby was crumpled on the hallway floor. Was she alone?

I don't know what to do, or say. I had no idea. Why didn't she tell me?

I get up from my bench, walk over to sit next to her, and place my hand on her knee. Ruby is startled by the touch, so I move away. She gives me a tentative smile and I wait, knowing there's more but afraid to ask.

"He was at the school-board hearing, too. He was the one who blurted out—about the NippleRiot. I didn't see him, but I'll never forget that voice."

"Oh God, Ruby," I say. "I'm so sorry."

"I was already flailing, but I just couldn't hold it together after that," she says.

It all makes sense now.

We both look down at the ground, studying the dense roots intricately intertwined below us.

"What happened after the walkout, all the ways I checked out . . ." She leans down to pick up an acorn and absently rolls it between her fingers. "I wanted to push it aside and forget it ever happened. Believe me! I wanted to blame it all on Carlos. I think you did too."

"Yeah, I kinda did."

"I wanted to dismiss my super-flaky behavior as me going boy-crazy, or whatever." She looks down at the acorn, balanced on her palm. "Baseball wife, right?"

I wince, remembering the ugly things I said to her at Carlos's exhibition game. If I had known what she was dealing with, I never would have said those things. I wish I had known.

"It was . . ." She stops to wipe a tear from her eye. "I can't believe I'm about to cry. I *refuse* to cry." She hurls the acorn against the wall. We both watch as it bounces to the ground. "It was horrible, and it made me feel so gross."

She presses her palms against the skin below her eyes, trying to keep the tears from falling. "I need you to know, I want to be clear—I'm not saying all this as an excuse."

"I wish you would have told me," I say softly. Ruby lets her hand fall open beside her, and I reach out to take it. "We could've gone after him. Exposed him."

"He said my name when he assaulted me," Ruby says quietly. "It's someone I know. Or who knows me." Her shoulders hunch forward and she looks down at our intertwined hands. "I was embarrassed. I thought maybe it was my fault. You know, the whole 'she asked for it' thing."

"No!" I cry out. "How could you think it was your fault? That's bullshit, Ruby."

It's so hard to believe that Ruby, of all people, would ever let herself feel that way. I'm still trying to process it all when I hear her murmur, "I know." She breathes in and out a few times, trying to calm herself. "Believe me, I know."

I stroke the top of her hand with my thumb, the way Mami does with me, and we both sit in silence. This is a lot to take in. He's still out there, roaming our halls. Maybe doing the same thing to another girl. I shudder at the thought.

"Remember that night, after the protest?" she asks, still staring down at our intertwined hands. "When you and Soraida were partying at Javi's?"

"Most of it," I say, trying to bring some much-needed levity. "As you may remember, I was wasted."

She lets out a laugh. "True, that." Then, her voice serious, she continues. "When Carlos sent me the picture—the one of you in the pool—I was in the tub. I'd been there for hours, trying to scrub myself clean. I think that's also why I got so upset when I saw you with Javi at that party. I didn't want you to get hurt," she says.

"That makes sense," I tell her, trying hard to understand what she must have been feeling. "But we were just having fun."

"I get that." She nods. "But I was scared. I wanted to cover myself with metal armor that night. And when I saw that picture of you, I had this overwhelming urge to cover you up too." Ruby squeezes my hand harder and I do the same. She sits up taller and looks me straight in the eye. "I messed up a hundred times in a hundred ways that I didn't even see, the first one being right in there"—she gestures toward the library—"when I stuck my stupid, overeager nose in your business. I shouldn't have swooped in to try and save you. I should have left you alone."

"Yeah, you probably should have," I say. But I'm not so sure about that. Do I wish none of this had happened? Do I want to go back to being Pobrecita María Malena?

No. Never.

"And the stupid things I said the morning after the party, about your body and how it's different for you . . . God! I can't believe I said all that."

"Yeah." I tsk. "I definitely wanted to revoke your feminist card. Or burn it!"

"I was so wrong, Malena. It doesn't even matter what we wear, what we do. It doesn't matter what our bodies look like. It can happen in a freaking hallway at school—to a girl whose boobs are so small they don't even make bras that fit me!"

I lean in and wrap my arm around her. "My abuela would call you a flaca con pecho de plancha."

She looks at me, puzzled.

"A skinny girl with a chest like an ironing board," I explain.

"So true." Then, mercifully, we both burst into laughter.

Once we've stopped laughing, I reach for her hand and tuck it into mine.

"You have to know, Ruby. It's not exactly true that it doesn't matter what we look like," I say. "It does matter." Ruby looks at me, her eyes full of questions, but she waits for me to continue. "The other day, Ms. Baptiste said something that made me think. I started looking into sexual violence, and who it happens to. It's way more likely that women of color and LGBTQ people get assaulted." I squeeze her hand gently.

"Malena," she says, squeezing my hand back. "If you ever don't feel safe, I'm here for you. Okay?"

"Okay," I repeat, like we are sealing a pact. And maybe we are.

"I promise I'll never stop you from chicken-fighting in a wet T-shirt or burning your bra. But no matter what you do or don't do, please just make sure you have backup. I know you have Soraida, but I'm always here to be your 'wing-woman' if you end up in a scary situation."

"I love her to pieces," I say, "but Soraida makes a terrible wing-woman, now that I think of it."

"Carlos and I shouldn't have made a big scene that night at the party, but you were so drunk. Probably too drunk to consent, you know?" Her voice breaks, and she looks away, closing her eyes for a breath. "If someone had . . . done something you didn't want? I don't even want to think about it."

I nod. I know she's right. I need to be able to take care of myself. Even when I'm out having a good time.

"You can ask me to come along next time, you know," she says. "I swear I'm not usually so uptight."

"And I can be your wing-woman too, if you ever need one."

She holds on to my arm with one hand. "I just love you so much, Malena," she says. "I don't want anyone to have to feel the way I've felt—especially not you."

We lean against each other, close enough for our heads to touch.

"I'm so sorry you had to go through that," I whisper. "I really wish I could have been there for you."

"Me too," she whispers back. "I should have told you."

"We're gonna find that asshole and make sure he gets what he deserves," I say. "We should start asking around—talking to people who were at the hearing." I squeeze her shoulder. "And you should tell Dr. Hardaway. You judged her too harshly. She would understand."

It hurts to think of that photo in the book. That dress. Why do so many girls—women—have to go through this kind of thing?

"Yeah," she groans. "Another person I was wrong about, I guess. I'll talk to her. I promise. I don't want that creep to hurt anyone else." She sighs, her shoulders falling in exhaustion. "Thank you for not giving up on me."

"I hope you realize that I think you're amazing. I believed in you for a reason."

She pulls back, still holding tightly to my hands.

"But I'm *not* amazing," she says, again struggling to speak.

"Everyone keeps saying that. My parents think I'm some kind of feminist warrior, but I'm all over the place. I'd probably get lost on the way to the battlefield." We're both laughing and crying at the same time. "I just screw everything up. I just wish I could go back and get a do-over."

"Ruby," I say, pulling back enough so we can look each other in the eye, "it was never yours to do." I exhale, long and hard. "I know you were trying to help. But I need you to know, from now on I can fight my own battles."

"I know." She sighs. "It's taken a while, and I've made some massive mistakes along the way, but I really do see you. I hear you. Yeah, you'll fight your own battles, and you're also gonna kick some serious butt."

"I will," I laugh. "Soraida's right. I'm Juana freaking de Arco."

She smiles, and we lean into each other, sitting in silence for a while, enjoying our last few moments of fresh air before the bell sends us back inside.

"I've missed you so much," she says.

I pull her into a hug. I've missed her too.

———

The following day, after school, we're all gathered in Ms. Baptiste's studio in the biggest video production Orange Grove High has ever seen—at least that's what Soraida says, and we all know she's not prone to embellish.

My finger presses the record button on the camera and a red dot starts blinking in the corner of the viewfinder.

"Ready?" I ask, adjusting the focus wheel around the lens to sharpen Chloe's facial features.

Chloe, the baseball team's manager, is standing in front of the camera. The glow on her face says she's excited to be here, even though she had to stand in line for over an hour for her turn to speak.

Soraida, Xiomara, Beatriz, and Nadia did a great job spreading the news about my project. And, to my complete shock, the result was a line of students a mile long. I've heard from students who got pulled out of class for wearing shorts when it was a hundred degrees out. A group of five freshmen showed up together to tell me how, on the first day of school, some teacher lined them up by the entrance. She made them check to see if the rips in their jeans were above their fingertips. They were all written up. A transgender girl got suspended for wearing a dress to school. She was also told that she was too "distracting." Equally distracting, it turns out, were a Black girl's hair extensions. She couldn't go to prom until she took them out.

Ruby was right, way back then. This is so much bigger than us—in ways we weren't even thinking about.

Chloe nods, clears her throat, and looks straight at the lens. Her dark brown eyes pierce the screen with an intensity that makes it impossible to turn away. Her hair is styled in a gorgeous parted Afro. She's wearing a cropped T-shirt and low-rise jeans—her detention outfit.

Chloe takes in a deep breath and settles her face into an even countenance. It's the no-nonsense look I've seen her use when she's addressing the guys on the baseball team, including Carlos.

"I would like to apologize to everyone who was too distracted by my crop top to focus on their classes. I'm sorry if my midriff prevented you from graduating. May your failures turn into every girl's success."

There's not even the slightest hint of sarcasm in her voice. Unlike some of the other students, who stammered their way through their recordings, Chloe nails her message in one take. It makes me wonder how long, aside from standing in line today, she has been waiting to say these words.

"Was that good?" Her eyes shift away from the camera to find mine. "I can do it again if you need me to."

"No need," I assure her. "It was perfect."

And, by La Virgencita's blessings, I hope it was. For some bizarre reason, everyone who steps in front of this camera has been treating me like I'm a Hollywood film director. Sure, this is my project, but in truth I'm super jittery about all the technical things that could go wrong. Like messing up the white balance and ending up with blue-hued video. Or fuzzy video because I forgot to adjust the focus. Or audio that crackles. Or, worse, no video (or audio) at all!

"Should I change now?" Chloe asks. Something about the way she straightens her spine tells me she's chosen exactly the right outfit.

"You can change behind that curtain." I gesture toward the back of the room, where Beatriz is overseeing the changing area. She even bought a metal garment rail and extra hangers to keep everyone's outfits organized. Next to her, Xiomara and Nadia set up a hair-and-makeup table, with a big mirror framed in bright lights. Nadia, it turns out, is a hair savant. And Xiomara's cosmetology skills have been honed on the beauty-pageant circuit. These girls are miracle workers. They've already gotten a few requests for prom makeovers.

Seeing how much they've put into my project, I can understand why everyone else thinks this little production is serious business.

Ruby volunteered to be the official gopher—or, more accurately, Soraida volunteered her. After our talk yesterday, we got the gang back together again so Ruby could apologize to everyone and make amends. Of course, Soraida told her an apology "isn't enough" and that she actually had to "do something," such as drive all over town after school to pick up the truckload of pizzas and ice cream that the crew ordered. Ruby happily obliged. She's been on her feet for hours, passing out water and snacks to everyone waiting in line.

At the mention of food, Topher, Jo, and Nessa also jumped in to help. It's awesome to see them all reunited. I guess Ruby found a way to patch things up with them, too. Topher is *way* more animated than usual, which is saying something. Today he's wearing some college sweatshirt—instead of his usual vintage vest—and Ruby keeps telling everyone who will listen about the fancy scholarship he managed to get.

"I'm getting the hell out of Florida exactly five minutes after graduation," he keeps announcing. Watching him float on cloud nine, and seeing how excited Ruby, Nessa, and Jo are for him—all of it makes me so glad I have them as friends.

Nadia disappears into the changing area to help Chloe prepare her next outfit. When they reemerge, Chloe is dramatically transformed. She's stunning, in a white pantsuit and pointy heels in a pale shade of pink. Nadia has side-swept her Afro and added a jeweled hair comb.

"Wow," I exclaim. I've lost count of how many students I've recorded today. But this feeling—witnessing someone become their own person—fills my heart with equal parts triumph and hope.

"It's my power suit." Her chin inches up slightly as she says it.

In this suit, it's not hard to see Chloe as the CEO of some Fortune 500 company. Or the GM of her own baseball franchise. The clothes only serve to highlight Chloe's natural poise.

I make sure the camera is recording before asking the one question I've asked dozens before her.

"How do you feel now?"

I've explained to each of them that it's not about putting on clothes to make you feel a certain way. It's about calling attention to what's already inside—bringing out your inner confidence. I want them to choose outfits that express their most natural, confident selves. True empowerment, I now realize, has to come from within.

Chloe pauses for a second, considering her response. When she seems to have an answer, a smile spreads across her glossy lips.

"Like I can rule the world."

Two hours later, I have more video interviews than I know what to do with.

Even Mr. Cruz stopped by at one point. He thought it was "very mature" that we "found a way to protest peacefully."

I bit my tongue and gave him my most polite smile. *We were always peaceful!* I wanted to call out. But this was not the time to get into a debate of how society chastises strong, assertive women as being too aggressive.

"I see a great college essay emerging from all of this," he told me.

I guess those little rebellious acorns may turn into majestic oaks after all.

After such an extraordinary day, I go about the room congratulating everyone for a job well done. I especially thank Ms. Baptiste for being so flexible with her studio space and her time.

Soraida tries to get class credit for helping me, but Ms. Baptiste informs her she still has to turn in her own project.

"What about a profile on overbearing Puerto Rican mothers?" Soraida asks.

Ms. Baptiste laughs, but I know better. Soraida is dead serious.

Just then Dr. Hardaway enters the studio. I was starting to think she wouldn't show up. I guess she was waiting for the students to be done.

She's dressed in a yoga tank top and leggings printed with green leaves and butterflies. They're the coolest yoga pants I've ever seen. In these clothes, she's no longer the assistant principal, but only a woman offering her most authentic self.

"We're ready for you," I say.

Dr. Hardaway steps in front of the camera and I signal for her to start.

"Hello," she says, then pauses to clear her throat. "Let me start again."

She presses her bare feet to the floor and lifts her spine. Her hair is pulled back in a bun at the nape of her neck.

"Hello," she says again, staring intently at the camera. "I'm Penny Hardaway, and this is what I'm wearing when I feel empowered."

I'm readying myself to ask a follow-up question, but then Dr. Hardaway bends over and lays both palms flat on the floor, in front of her feet.

I scramble to catch up, zooming out so I can see her entire body on the screen.

We all watch in silent fascination as Dr. Hardaway finds balance on her palms and lifts both legs straight up toward the ceiling. I'm in awe the whole time, wondering how a body can do that.

The greenery on her legs reminds me of the palm trees back home. In photos, I saw them still standing after the storm. They bent but never broke.

After a few beats, she bends her left leg down and lifts her left hand to catch the bottom of her foot in midair. The pose defies all laws of gravity. Dr. Hardaway is practically floating on one hand, while the rest of her body is towering above her. She looks strong and graceful.

I don't regain my ability to breathe until she unbends her body and her feet touch the floor.

"Was that okay?" she asks, standing upright.

Mad clapping bursts from the back of the room.

"That was unreal," I say. "Where did you learn to do that?"

"I started doing yoga after I was assaulted," she says only to me. "It was a way to take back control over my body."

"Did it work?"

She nods. "It took a while, but yes."

Suddenly we are surrounded by the others, and the conversation erupts into a riot of admiration and cheers.

There is so much creative energy in the room that I'm inspired to tell Dr. Hardaway about our idea for the student-faculty liaison committee. "We would love to meet with you to discuss it in more detail," I say after I've explained the concept.

"And because it's a committee, it wouldn't have to be approved by the school board," Ruby adds. "Malena already checked."

"I'll be happy to oversee the committee, if you think it's a good idea," Ms. Baptiste tells Dr. Hardaway.

Dr. Hardaway nods. She's standing straight and tall, still looking like a palmera.

"I like this idea," she says. "Let's look at my calendar and find a good time to meet."

I smile, letting the excitement shine through every pore. Even though this is a small victory, it feels colossal in every possible way.

I reach for Ruby and lock my arm in hers.

"We'll be there," I say.

Ruby tugs at my arm and we step aside while the others continue talking excitedly.

"Did you tell her?" I whisper into Ruby's ear.

"Yeah," she whispers back, "and you were right. She was super supportive. She said I need to file a formal complaint so she can open an investigation."

I step back and look at her, the question in my eyes.

"We're meeting again after Thanksgiving break," she says. "I need to talk to Nana and my parents first. And she asked that I write down everything I can remember, including names of students who were in the hallway. She said these kinds of things . . ." Ruby's voice trails off, and she looks away, her eyes glassy. "She said assault is usually between people who know each other." Her voice lands hard on the word *assault*. I nod, sensing how much she's working to process what happened. "And that I may remember more details, with time."

"Maybe someone else saw him," I offer. "Maybe there were witnesses."

"I don't know," she says, leaning her head on my shoulder as we watch the others from the sidelines. Ms. Baptiste says something funny and everyone laughs.

"But even if it's a losing battle, it's a battle I'm willing to fight," Ruby says.

"I'm gonna be by your side, no matter what. Okay?" I wrap her in a side hug and kiss the side of her head, like a sister would.

Suddenly, everyone is calling my name.

"Malena, when do we get to see this video?" Dr. Hardaway asks.

"First I have to edit the whole thing."

"What about *your* story, Malena?" Ms. Baptiste asks, pulling me back into the fold.

"Yeah, I guess I was saving myself for last."

I ask Ruby to take over filming so I can concentrate on what I want to say. I don't have to think about it much. The words have been captive in my heart for a long time.

CHAPTER TWENTY-EIGHT

RUBY

Nana and I stand side by side at the kitchen island, crumbling fresh-baked cornbread into an enormous stainless-steel bowl.

It's always been our Thanksgiving ritual to wake up at dawn and make the stuffing. I usually go to bed early the night before, in anticipation of our early morning. But last night I stayed up late starting the college essays I had put off for so many months. It felt awesome to get my future under way, even though I was a little bleary-eyed when the alarm went off at six. Once my sister and my dad come downstairs, I know I'll be relegated to sous-chef duty: rolling dough into balls, separating pomegranate seeds, basically doing whatever they instruct—whatever they don't feel like doing. But until they wake up, I get my time with Nana. Nana always makes an extra chess pie for us to share—our decadent Thanksgiving breakfast treat.

"Time for breakfast," Nana announces. "Let's take a break while we wait for the broth to heat." She wipes the crumbs from her hands and then pulls a pie knife from the drawer. "Make mine a big piece," she says, her voice buoyant, as she hands me the knife.

My phone dings, and a text comes in from Topher.

> Happy Turkey Day.

> Hey sweetie! You're up early.

It's amazing how ridiculously relieved I feel to be back on the receiving end of Topher's constant communication.

> Couldn't sleep. Did I happen to mention I'm going to my dream college?!?!?!?!

I respond with an elaborate fireworks GIF.

> I'm already planning your farewell party!

> It better be fabulous.

> Oh, you know it will.

Topher already told us that he'll be the first in our crowd to leave for college. He's been invited to a special pre-orientation for first-generation college students. We're all beyond thrilled for him. Even his mom and grandma finally seem to grasp how enormously significant the scholarship is.

> You and Nana making stuffing?

> Of course. Come over for breakfast
> tomorrow? Leftovers

> If I'm not still in a food coma.

> Bring pears and red hots?

It's his grandmother's signature dish. Must be a Southern thing.

> If you save me some of that chess pie you
> and Nana are about to scarf down

Ah, Topher. He knows me so well. It won't be easy to save some of this fabulous pie for Topher, that's for sure. But it's the least I can do, after all the shitty-friend moments he has put up with and—miraculously—forgiven. He's one hundred percent worth the sacrifice.

I send him a thumbs-up and a string of kiss emojis and then cut Nana and me two huge slices of chess pie. Nana pours us coffee, and we sit down at the kitchen bar, side by side. Since Mom, Dad, and Olive got back, we haven't had a quiet moment, which makes this time together especially sweet. I've missed having Nana all to myself. As we savor the sugary goodness of the pie, I catch Nana up on every detail of Monday's conversation with Malena. It feels so right to tell her. It's almost like the big things that happen in my life aren't quite real until I've had a chance to share them with Nana.

And the terrible ones, too—the ones that make me feel

ashamed and humiliated. I've been so busy trying to convince myself what happened to me was nothing, and I knew that as soon as I told anyone—especially Nana—it would become all too real.

But it's time.

"There's something else," I say, my voice hesitant. "Something happened, and I need to tell you about it. It wasn't a big deal but . . ."

She puts down her coffee mug. "What happened?" she asks, placing her hand on my shoulder.

"It's nothing, really—I mean, I don't know why I'm so fixated on it. During the walkout, we were all pushing and shoving to get outside, and some guy pushed himself against me and put his hand under my shirt." I put the bowl on the counter and stare down at it. I'm afraid that if I look at Nana, I'll cry, and I don't want to cry. "He started to feel me up, and when I shoved him away, he called me a 'fucking tease.'"

"That's not nothing, Ruby," Nana says, her voice firm. "That's very much something. That's something terrible." She pulls me into her arms and folds me into a hug. I put my head on her shoulder, breathing in the soothing scent of narcissus and talcum powder, and I let myself release a long, deep sigh.

"It was," I say. "It was so terrible. I can't shake it. I'm trying really hard, but I can't."

She leans back, holding firm to both my shoulders, and looks me directly in the eyes. "It's not something we 'shake,' sweetheart. It doesn't leave us."

I nod. She's so right. I'm not going to shake this one off, no matter how hard I try.

"And I keep running it all through my mind, thinking about

what I should have done differently, how I could have avoided it—avoided *him*."

She squeezes my shoulders gently. "You have every right to feel violated by what that boy did, but you have to resist the urge to say any of it was your fault—resist it with every ounce of your being."

"I know. I'm trying," I say. Because in my mind I know she's right. But my heart is still so confused. I can't blame myself for what he did, but I also can't blame him for what I did—for all the ways I botched things after the protest. How can I explain this to Nana?

"But I also know I made a thousand mistakes," I tell her. "I was so self-absorbed and blind to other people, especially to Malena. I really hurt her, Nana."

"Yes," Nana says, "that's true. You did. And you apologized, from your heart. So now you work to make amends."

Nana pulls the last pan of fresh cornbread from the oven and prepares to assemble the dressing.

"I'm not sure anything I do will make it right," I say, taking a bowl of chopped celery from the fridge. "I've been thinking that what I probably ought to do, what would be best for everyone, is to just step away from it all." I pause to dump the celery into a steel bowl. "Malena wants me to be on the student-faculty liaison committee, but I feel like I'd just get in the way. No one needs to hear from me—I've said enough already. I've done more than enough damage."

Nana begins to chop the onions, swiftly and deliberately. We both work in silence for a few minutes, my mind racing with questions that I have no idea how to answer.

"I can see how you might feel that way," Nana says, finally.

I think about Malena and Soraida, Beatriz, Xiomara, Nadia. I remember Chloe and how boldly she faced Malena's camera, all the people with mad skills as organizers, and with their own powerful stories to tell. Wouldn't the best thing be for me to just disappear? Shouldn't I just shut up and go home?

"I think I need to find a hobby or something," I say, trying to lighten the mood. "Something super benign, like maybe crochet." We both laugh at the idea. "It might keep me busy, keep me from sticking my nose where it doesn't belong, from trying to fight other people's battles."

"Well," Nana says, coming to stand beside me, "crochet is nice, I suppose. It could be relaxing. But I've been thinking as I listen to you, Ruby." She tips the cutting board against the mixing bowl. "Have you ever heard of Joan Trumpauer Mulholland?"

I shake my head and plunge my hands into the bowl, then stir together the cornbread and celery as Nana adds chopped onions.

"Let's look her up," Nana says, gesturing toward my computer.

I rinse my hands in the sink and then go over to the laptop, already open on the counter with a recipe for yeast rolls that Olive was using last night. Nana begins pouring hot broth into the cornbread while I look up the name. Several articles come up immediately, and I click on the first photo I see.

"There she is," Nana says, pointing toward the screen.

It's a black-and-white photo, and it only takes a second for me to realize the image is from the 1960s civil-rights era—a lunch-counter sit-in. Nana puts down the saucepan and walks over to stand beside me. Her finger guides me to a thin white woman, not much older than I am, with a dark black bun at the nape of her neck. Her face is turned away from the camera, her elbow on the counter. She's looking over at a young Black woman, who must be her friend. Both of them sit surrounded by young white men—teenagers, boys, really. They're all standing over the women, heckling them, harassing them. That's clear. Joan and her friend are covered in food—maybe ketchup, sugar, syrup. It's hard to tell. One asshole guy is pouring sugar over Joan's head. You can't see Joan's face because she's looking over at her friend, but the other woman's face appears both anguished and resigned.

"Jackson, Mississippi. 1963," Nana says, her voice almost reverent. "Joan's great-grandparents were slave owners in Georgia. Her parents sent her off to school at Duke, expecting her to become like them. She didn't, though. She left Duke to be a freedom rider, a friend of Stokely Carmichael, a nonviolent activist." Nana returns to the bowl of cornbread and stirs in the remaining broth. "She went to jail, submitted herself to all manner of humiliation, including physical assault."

"Wow," I say, studying the image of her slight frame. "She sounds like a total badass."

"Yes," Nana says, nodding. "She was a badass, but she never held the megaphone, never took the mic. She stood beside her Black friends and colleagues, but she never sought the spotlight. She worked hard. She did so much—the kind of behind-the-scenes stuff that doesn't win people awards." She stops stirring and sends me a pointed glance. "She didn't want to be a hero. She didn't need any of that. She wanted to see change, and she'd do whatever it took to help make that change happen."

"I get that," I say.

"I know you do," she replies, reaching over to touch my hand gently. "I want to make sure you hear it from me, Ruby. You have so much to offer, so much passion to give to any cause that matters to you." She pinches salt into the mixing bowl and passes it to me to stir. "You have gifts and talents that your sister and your parents can't even imagine. One of the most important is that you've learned how to listen. You should be grateful to Malena. I think she taught you that."

I nod, thinking back to the conversation in the library. Malena could have just walked away from me, but she didn't. She stuck around and helped me see all the ways I messed up, hear all the things I needed to hear. I'm thankful for that, even though it hurt like hell.

Nana hands me the pepper grinder and gestures toward the bowl. "If you want to work with others to make change, you don't have to be the one with the megaphone. In fact, quite often, you shouldn't be."

I nod, feeling my chest swell with emotion—maybe relief. I don't have to be extraordinary. I don't have to be magnificent. I don't have to win any awards. I just have to be committed, willing to do the work. And I have to keep listening.

I grind in the pepper while she stirs. Watching our fluid movements, the way we create this dish together without even needing to exchange a word, I feel so grateful that I had the courage to move past my shame and humiliation and tell Nana everything. Sharing my burdens with her, I feel like a thousand-pound weight has lifted off my shoulders.

I dip the spoon into the dressing and offer her a taste.

"Good?" I ask. "Enough salt?"

"It's just right," she says, triumphant. "Well done, us."

Yes, I think. *Well done, us.*

CHAPTER TWENTY-NINE

MALENA

"Turkey coming through!" Soraida calls out, raising a knife and carving fork into the air. "Get out of the way!" The girl finally gets her own Juana de Arco moment.

I follow behind Soraida, holding Abuela Joan's silver gravy boat with both hands as Soraida directs "the Great Turkey Conquest"—her words.

Everyone steps aside as Carlos and Ruby's dad balance an enormous platter between them containing the largest turkey I have ever laid eyes on. "The Great Turkey" must weigh at least thirty pounds. Abuela Joan had to extend her dining table as far as it would go to make room for the bird and our two families.

After our big talk, Ruby and I convinced Mami and Abuela Joan to ditch our families' individual Thanksgiving plans in favor of a shared Thanksgiving dinner. It was totally last minute, but after everything that's happened, Mami was more than happy to bring "las familias" together. Plus, Ruby and Abuela Joan insisted that we needed a big blowout celebration for the premiere of my short film—or, as I keep reminding them, a very rough cut of my short film.

Being at Abuela Joan's house for Thanksgiving, surrounded by so many people, seemed like it might lessen the glaring pain of Papi's absence. Plus, Abuela Joan promised she would make her famous chess pie, which Ruby said was "life-changing." I mean, she's got stiff competition. Abuela's flan currently holds the title for "most life-changing dessert."

In all fairness, Mami and Abuela Joan were the ones who did all the work to make this celebration happen, but everything is exactly as I imagined it. Various pieces of my life—old and new—have been rearranged to form a life I never expected, but one I'm grateful for.

It's far from perfect, but every day I find a surprising moment that brings me joy.

Like right now. I'm watching Mami and Abuela Joan standing by a record player, laughing over an ancient Madonna album and swaying their hips while trying to hang on to the glasses of sangría in their hands. I guess Abuela Joan has discovered Mami's undying love for eighties pop music.

Next to me, Tía Lorna fusses over a tray of pasteles piled so high that a few topple into the cranberry sauce. I stifle a laugh.

"Ay, bendito!" Abuela throws her hands up in the air, clearly not happy. She is furiously cleaning her pasteles and scolding Tía Lorna in Spanish.

Cranberry sauce, it must be noted, is a new addition to our family's Thanksgiving. Along with the pumpkin pies, green beans, and mashed potatoes prepared by Ruby's family—"comidas de Americanos," according to Tía Lorna.

These new dishes are squeezed on the sideboard, mixed in with the Puerto Rican specialties my family brought: an appetizer tray of surullitos, empanadillas, and bacalaitos, a huge pan of arroz con gandules and another of mofongo, and Abuela's pasteles, of course.

We are almost ready to eat when Ruby's sister, Olive, strides into the room unveiling a tray of steaming-hot, perfectly browned and buttered homemade yeast rolls.

She tries to navigate around Tío Wiliberto's cooler, which holds bottles of coquito and Medalla beers. Ruby's mom seemed confused as to why we had a cooler in the dining room, but I mean, where else are we supposed to keep the coquito? The kitchen fridge is full of food.

Just as Abuela is a pastel craftswoman, Tío Wiliberto is the family's authority on coquito. He's planning to introduce Abuela Joan and Ruby's parents to his legendary Puerto Rican eggnog—a family recipe. Ruby's dad seemed especially excited after he learned that it's made with island rum.

Olive throws a hard glare at the cooler, just before she trips over the handle. She shrieks, and suddenly her rolls are in midair. Carlos catches two of them in his left hand and one in his right. There's no doubt my cousin is getting into the majors.

Olive is left with an empty silver tray and looking like she's about to self-combust. "Don't just stand there," she barks at Ruby and me. "Help me!"

I've only hung out with Olive once this week, but it's funny how quickly she fell into the big-sister role around me. I can see why she annoys Ruby a little, but I think she's cool, regardless.

Ruby and I both drop to our knees and crawl under the table, searching for a few runaway buns, while Olive firmly insists, "Can someone please move this cooler into the kitchen?" Tío Wiliberto is not gonna be happy.

We scramble to pick up the rolls before the five-second rule kicks in. Tío Wiliberto is also scrambling but for a different reason. He is reaching into the cooler to grab two Medallas before Carlos drags away his precious cooler. Tío passes a beer to Ruby's dad, who seems more than happy to take it.

"I think Tío has a new drinking buddy." I laugh, scooping up a roll from under the table. "I can't believe we made this happen."

"Total pandemonium." Ruby giggles. "You may be getting a Christmas Eve invite. This is so much more fun than last year."

"Oh, Christmas is even louder. More food, more drinks, more music," I say. "You would love it. This reminds me of home." A larger, extended home, I think—surrounded by people who really know me and care about me.

"That makes me so happy." Ruby smiles. "We never celebrate like this. Last year, Olive and Dad spent the whole meal debating whether it was really possible to ethically source turkey. Olive tried to convince us to switch to Tofurkey this year." She guffaws at the memory and I laugh with her. Now that I've met her family, I can see them politely debating around the table.

"Yeah, Tofurkey wouldn't fly in my family. I'm pretty sure Tía Lorna would've taken Abuela's pasteles and marched right out."

"Thank God for Nana's powers of persuasion."

"I wasn't looking forward to today," I admit with a sigh. "You know, with Papi not being here."

Ruby drops the buns she's holding on the tray and scoots closer. Around us, people are starting to take their seats, but we remain concealed by the long tablecloth.

"It must suck that you can't go home," she says quietly.

"Yeah," I say. "It does. But you know, on a day like this"—I gesture toward the beautiful chaos unfolding around us, the loud voices, the delicious smells, the joy and laughter—"I think maybe one day I could call this place home too."

She climbs to her knees to give me an awkward under-the-table hug.

"That's so fucking sweet!" she says, squeezing me tighter.

I laugh and hug her back. "What happened to your no-cursing pledge?"

"I'm over it," she says, resting back on her heels. "I've grown comfortable with being a girl who swears like a South Seas sailor." Ruby shrugs and grins, making her eyes crinkle. "It's freeing in a small way, you know? To just be me."

"That's great, but don't cuss around Tía Lorna, okay? Trust me, the punishment is not worth the crime."

We both laugh, leaning into each other, until Soraida peers her head under the table.

"Can you two get a move on? We are starving here," she says.

Ruby hands her a roll, wise to the fact that the way to Soraida's heart is through her stomach.

We crawl out from under the table and find our seats. Abuela offers a blessing in Spanish thanking God, La Virgen María, Joseph, Baby Jesus, and a litany of saints—even though we asked her to keep the prayer nondenominational for the sake of Ruby's family. The woman can't help herself. Poor Carlos has to translate the whole thing, while everyone sits, impatient, ready to attack their plates. Needless to say, no one is thrilled that Soraida keeps interrupting him to remind him of a saint that he's left out.

Finally, we dive in. The next hour or so entails a blur of smiles and laughter, a mix of languages, an occasional clinking of glasses, and several second helpings—and third and fourth for Carlos.

After we've all had a taste of Tío Wiliberto's coquito—he even made a nonalcoholic version "for the jóvenes"—and we've settled deep into a post-feast stupor, Ruby stands up and clinks her glass for attention.

"Ladies and gentlemen, damas y caballeros! We now have a short intermission. Please make your way to the family room, where we will be serving dessert and coffee. And get ready for the amazing world premiere of Malena Malavé Rosario's award-winning documentary film."

"Award-winning?" Soraida calls out.

"Soon-to-be-award-winning!" Ruby declares.

"It's already won my vote," Abuela Joan chimes in.

Abuela Joan put Ruby and me in charge of coffee and desserts, so we head to the kitchen while Tía and Olive wrangle over containers for leftovers. Ruby gets the coffeemaker going, while I prepare each person a dessert sampler plate with Abuela's vanilla flan and her little cups of tembleque, Abuela Joan's chess pie, and Ruby's mom's pumpkin pie.

It's nice to have a moment of stillness after our noisy dinner. In the calm of Abuela Joan's kitchen, I start looking back on the last months, my life in Florida after María. It feels like years have passed since I got here.

Ruby is organizing cups and saucers on a big tray, arranging a sugar caddy, and pouring creamer into a vessel shaped like a cow. We work beside each other in comfortable silence.

"Do you wonder sometimes," I ask softly, "what would've happened if you hadn't gotten your period that day?" For some stupid reason, the thought gives us the giggles. "Or if I had never gotten a sunburn, and had just worn a bra that day?"

"Or if I had actually remembered to bring a tampon to school?"

"Or if the school actually had a tampon machine in the bathroom!"

"Not a machine!" Ruby exclaims. "Free tampons for all!"

"In all bathrooms! For all people!" I add. "Hmm . . . Should that be an agenda item for the student-faculty committee?"

"Sounds good to me," Ruby says.

We slip back into silence, our focus on arranging the desserts. I methodically organize the plates in front of me, adding a napkin under each one, and a small spoon.

"What if we had never met?" Ruby says, "If we were wandering around school, passing each other in the halls. Strangers."

For a moment, I allow myself to go down the rabbit hole of infinite what-ifs, just to see where it leads me.

"That moment, when we met," I say, "it's like every decision we ever made was guiding us to that exact time and place. Isn't that wild?"

"Like if I had stayed in Seattle," she says, pulling up a chair by the kitchen island, where I'm cutting desserts.

"And I in Puerto Rico . . ." I shrug, trying to focus on the flan I'm slicing through. My heart is not fully healed from the grief of losing my home, but it hurts a little less every day. I look forward to the day I can go back and reclaim some part of that old self—of the life I loved.

I place a big slice of flan on a plate and pass it to Ruby. "You have to try this," I tell her.

"Oh, I'm ready," she says, tearing into it and moaning with pleasure at the first bite. "Best. Flan. Ever." She instantly goes in for a second, larger bite. "I love your abuela."

"She's amazing," I say.

Ruby turns pensive as she eats the rest of her flan, while I finish arranging the dessert plates on an extra-large tray. I have no idea how we are going to carry this thing to the living room.

"You know, back in my old school, I had this art teacher—Mr. Nguyen. He made us do all kinds of cool stuff," she says, helping herself to a second slice. "One time, he took us to a big junk store on Market Street to scavenge around for old broken clocks. We had no freaking idea what we were doing. We thought maybe he was going to make us fix them. But he didn't. Instead, he told us to tear the clocks apart. We spent the next month rearranging the pieces into art. Some kids made all kinds of fantastical creatures—dragons and serpents, centaurs, and even a phoenix. But I stuck with the real world and made a dragonfly. I pieced it together with shards of glass, bent gears, and broken cogs."

She stops to lick the caramel from her spoon. "It was so weird in a completely awesome way. I still can't believe I lost it in the move. As you were talking, I started thinking about that dragonfly. I realized that to make something like that, a bunch of things have to get broken first." Ruby's own voice breaks a little, and she has to clear her throat. Her eyes go misty, and seeing her get emotional has the same effect on me. "We took all these torn-apart, messed-up pieces to make something gorgeous and strange—something entirely unique."

That's us, I realize. Ruby is talking about us, and about what we've made—a beautiful new creation made from endless broken parts. Unusual? Yes. A little flawed at close range? Totally. But also magnificent.

"Yup, definitely unique," I say, glancing out at our families, crammed together on sofas and chairs in Abuela Joan's living room. Soraida waves with both arms to catch our attention.

"What's taking you two so long?" she calls out. "The flan's already made. All you have to do is slice it!"

Ruby and I smile at each other, knowing our quiet moment has passed.

Carlos saunters into the kitchen and helps himself to a cup of tembleque, pulling it from one of the plates I've so carefully arranged.

I slap his hand. "Hey!" I yelp. "Don't mess up my presentation."

"Are these ready to go out?" he asks, and takes a big mouthful of tembleque.

"Almost," I say, sliding the last slice of pie onto a plate. "Done!"

To my astonishment, my cousin rinses out the now-empty dessert cup, puts it in the dishwasher, and turns to pick up the serving tray where I've stacked the dessert plates.

"You want me to take these out for you?" he asks. I almost choke on my own surprise.

"Sure," I croak out.

He grabs the tray and balances it on his shoulder, like some kind of professional waiter. Then he leans in to give Ruby a kiss on his way out. She looks like she's about to faint from emotion.

The coffeemaker beeps and it's our cue to return to the living room. Ruby and I make our way around the room, passing out fresh cups of coffee, while Carlos distributes plates of dessert to a very eager crowd.

Eventually, everyone settles around the TV. Ruby nestles under Carlos's shoulder, her legs draped between his. She kisses Carlos on the cheek, and I catch Tía Lorna glaring at her. I laugh to myself, thinking Tía is probably upset she is no longer the number one woman in Carlos's life.

I cue up the film on the TV, and am confused when Ruby's

dad starts fiddling with his desktop monitor. Suddenly, Tía lets out a happy squeal.

"Malena," Ruby says. "Look!"

I turn around to find Papi's face on the screen. His smile is broad and warm; his eyes are dancing with joy. I'm so overwhelmed by his image that I walk to the computer and touch the screen, just to make sure it's really him.

"Papi?" I ask, my eyes flooding with tears.

"We're all here!" Mami calls out from the back. Everyone in the room waves to welcome him, and I step aside so that he can see them.

"I don't understand," I say to him. "I thought you didn't have an internet connection."

"I'm back in San Juan," he says. "Mami told me all about the video. I couldn't miss it!"

"I'm so glad you're here, Papi," I say, crying-laughing. Mami walks behind me and extends her arms over my shoulder, pulling me into a side hug. "He's always with us, mija."

Mami and I take our seats as the title slate flashes onto the screen:

This Is What I'm Wearing
by Malena Malavé Rosario

The room erupts with cheers and clapping.

My opening montage fills the screen. My voice narrates over the video I shot during our initial planning meeting at Ruby's. "Our first meeting was a disaster. If we had known how hard it would be to work together, we probably would have quit then and there."

"I'm so glad I had on makeup that day," Soraida blurts out

behind me. "You should've told me you were filming this for posterity. I would've worn a different shirt."

Carlos shushes her. "We're trying to listen."

The sequence moves to quick shots of Calista's first story, news clips from before the protests, and social-media messages of support. Then the film cuts to the protest.

"I shot that!" Soraida yelps, unable to help herself.

My voice booms through the TV speakers, filling Abuela Joan's living room. I watch myself on this big-screen TV, megaphone in hand.

I think of Malala from Pakistan and Joshua from Hong Kong. I remember their courage—how awed I was the first time I watched their stories unfold. I may not be taking down an oppressive regime, but I'm speaking up. Just like them, I'm making my voice heard.

The film shifts to the best part. My chest fills with satisfaction and anticipation as we are transported to Ms. Baptiste's studio. It's a side shot of me behind the camera.

"That's my shot!" I overhear Ruby whisper excitedly. "I filmed that with my phone."

A parade of faces and voices makes its way across the screen. Chloe stands proud in her power suit. Ms. Baptiste flaunts her favorite flowery skirt. Xiomara carefully fills her lips with bright red lipstick. Ruby makes a quick cameo appearance, jumping in front of the camera to demonstrate her lack of boobs. And Dr. Hardaway balances herself firmly on one hand. They're all wearing different clothes, striking different poses, telling their own stories. And even though I've seen these clips a million times, stayed up all night to piece them together, it dawns on me for the first time: this is what *undaunted* looks like.

I think of all the times I fumbled around, trying so hard to be undaunted. Getting wasted at that party. Burning a perfectly good bra. God, jumping into Javi's bed. Even lying to Mami. Did I ever become the person I wanted to be?

My own face finally fills the screen. Seeing myself standing there, I'm struck by how much I've changed. Even though I'm wearing the same tunic I wore on the day my back was sunburned, I'm a different person. I know that much, at least.

I grasp Mami's hand to stop the trembling of my own, and muster the courage to watch.

> *"Mi cuerpo es un regalo de mis padres.*
> *El templo de mi alma, mi mente, mi corazón.*
> *Mi cuerpo es orgullo,*
> *un retrato de mi tierra,*
> *una canción de amor.*
> *Mi cuerpo no es tuyo para juzgar.*
> *No es tuyo para decidir.*
> *Ni tuyo para criticar.*
> *Es mío, solo mío, y de nadie más."*

Mami gently squeezes my hand. I keep my eyes trained on the screen, anxious about the way my voice will sound speaking those words in English, but also knowing that as much as I own my body, I own my voice—no matter the language.

> *"My body is a gift from my parents.*
> *It's a temple for my soul, my mind, my heart.*
> *My body is pride,*
> *a picture of my homeland,*
> *a song of love.*

My body is not yours to judge.
Not yours to decide.
Not yours to criticize.
It's mine, only mine, and no one else's."

In the silence after my last words have been spoken, it hits me. Maybe I *am* undaunted. Maybe having the courage to keep going after being humiliated and shamed, after making big mistakes but also owning up to them, after speaking my truth, even after all that—maybe that's exactly what it means to be undaunted.

We all watch as the film rolls to credits. I hear a gentle sniffle in the background, and I know Mami is crying.

Hearing her tears and turning back to see Papi's proud face on the screen, I think of everything we've had to give up to get here, all the pain we've had to move through. It's impossible to be undaunted without first facing hardship. I know that now. It's impossible to have a new life without losing the old one.

After every storm, we rebuild.

I am undaunted.

La vida continúa.

AUTHORS' NOTE

It's been our great joy to work on this project as co-writers, friends, and sisters—not by blood, but by choice.

Does My Body Offend You? was inspired by voices of protest all across the world. Girls everywhere are speaking up for women's rights and the rights of historically marginalized communities.

Their stories prompted us to explore themes of feminism, intersectionality, allyship, and student protest from the point of view of two girls—one brown, from a humble, conservative Puerto Rican family, and one white, from a liberal, privileged background. As we watched real-life protests unfold throughout the United States, we wanted to explore the tough questions of what happens after the protest, when media attention has moved on and energy has ebbed. What then? And how can girls build strong movements for change inside systems of power that amplify some girls' voices over others?

The story takes place in the fall of 2017, after Hurricane María barreled through Puerto Rico and most of the Caribbean, causing unprecedented devastation. As a result, more than 135,000 Puerto Ricans left the island and relocated to the mainland United States. Over 24,000 of them were students (K–12).

Most of them relocated to Florida. (Source: Center for Puerto Rican Studies.)

We are so proud of the story we have accomplished together and hope this book will inspire girls and young women everywhere. We also hope that Ruby and Malena's story will serve as a bridge, leading to many positive, constructive, and compassionate conversations.

RESOURCES FOR STUDENT ACTIVISTS

American Civil Liberties Union: A nonprofit organization dedicated to defending and preserving the individual rights and liberties guaranteed under the Constitution and laws of the United States. There is a section on its website devoted to students' rights, and you can also visit the website of your local ACLU chapter to find a student handbook specific to your state. aclu.org/know-your-rights/student-rights

Girls Inc.: A nonprofit organization that encourages all girls to be "strong, smart, and bold" through direct service and advocacy. The organization equips girls with the skills to navigate through economic, gender, and social barriers.
girlsinc.org/

Girl Up: "A movement to advance girls' skills, rights, and opportunities to be leaders," founded by the United Nations.
girlup.org/

Global Changemakers: An international youth organization that empowers young people to catalyze positive social change in

their communities through skills development and capacity building, creating access to opportunities, networking, and providing grant funding to youth-led community projects.
global-changemakers.net/

Youth Activism Project: An international nonpartisan organization designed to encourage young people to speak up and find solutions to problems they care about.
youthactivismproject.org/

ACKNOWLEDGMENTS

This book is the product of dozens of minds and hearts that worked tirelessly to see it through publication, and a group of badass women who supported us every step of the way.

First, we wish to thank all the young women who have spoken out against racial and gender disparities in their schools and communities. We were inspired by your voices and your stories.

We owe the completion of this book to our publishing madrinas, extraordinary women all: Knopf Young Readers publisher Melanie Nolan, executive editor Michelle Frey, editorial assistant Arely Guzmán, copy editor Karen Sherman, and agents Saritza Hernandez and Erin Harris.

Our cover was designed by the amazing Camila Rosa, a Brazilian activist whose work reminds us that art is one of the most powerful forms of activism.

At home, we are humbled by the constant love and care of our first sisterhood—Abuela Cuqui; our mothers, Zulma and Elizabeth; our sisters, Lourdes, Lee, and Carroll Ann; and our daughters, Mary Elizabeth, Pixley, and Annie. We love you, far more than words could ever express.

Our sisterhood also extends to our various communities.

A big thank-you to the beautiful women of our Atlanta writing community who read early drafts of our book and encouraged us to keep going: Kimberly Jones, Gilly Segal, Maryann Dabkowski, Rachael Stewart Allen, Jessi Esparza, and Elizabeth Henry. We love y'all!

We are equally grateful to our family, friends, and neighbors in Atlanta, Decatur, and Norcross, Georgia, in Florida, and in Puerto Rico; and to the spiritual communities of Kadampa Meditation Center Georgia, St. Thomas More Church, and El Refugio Ministry. A special thanks to our neighbor Dana Borda, who helped us with all things baseball.

And to the men in our lives, we offer our hearts full of love. To our husbands, the two Chrises, thank you for making life (and home) as sweet as can be. And to our son and stepsons, Nate, Alex, and Caleb, thank you for giving us the joy of loving you.